Praise for *Quieter Than Killing*:

'Hilary is my drop-everything writer; always original, always bang-on psychologically, always gripping. I am a huge fan' **Alex Marwood**

'It's dark, it's brilliant, and it tightens like a noose. Sarah Hilary is downright dangerous' **Mick Herron**

'A compelling read, emotionally intense and intelligent. I love her fierce, flawed characters' **Cath Staincliffe**

'As tense, twisty, tremendous as ever, Sarah Hilary's *Quieter Than Killing* nails it' **Angela Clarke**

'Hilary's writing is as precise and deadly as a fine blade . . . by turns terrifying and tender, with a twisty, gripping plot . . . a fine addition to a superb series' **Jane Casey**

Praise for *Tastes Like Fear:*

'Contemporary, yet elegant and with a heart, it underlines the author's place as one of Britain's best new crime writers' ***Daily Mail***

'A tense, terrifying tale of obsession and possession . . . a writer at the top of her game' ***Radio Times***

'A truly chilling exploration of control, submission and the desire to step out of a normal life' **Eva Dolan**

'Marnie goes from strength to strength . . . this one drips with the gritty, dirty danger of the urban wastelands around the river' **Julia Crouch**

'Truly mesmerising from its opening page to its thunderous denouement. A haunting, potent novel from a bleakly sublime new voice' **David Mark**

'Heart-breaking . . . I can't recommend this highly enough' **SJI Holliday**

'Hilary's attention to detail is scrupulous, and she is at her absolute best when it comes to marshalling a cast of characters' *Crime Review*

'Marnie Rome is back and Sarah Hilary has knocked it out of the park for us yet again' *Grab This Book*

'Sarah Hilary explores her characters with forensic insight and serious skill' *Live and Deadly*

'A genius at sending the reader in one direction, while pointing clues in another . . . Totally and utterly recommended' *Northern Crime*

'A masterclass in developing crime fiction series characters' *Crime Reader Blog*

Praise for *Someone Else's Skin*:

'An exceptional new talent. Hilary writes with a beguiling immediacy that pulls you straight into her world on the first page and leaves you bereft when you finish' **Alex Marwood**

'I absolutely loved it' **Martyn Waites**

'An intelligent, assured and very promising debut' *Guardian*

SARAH HILARY

QUIETER THAN

KILLING

HEADLINE

First published in 2017 by
HEADLINE PUBLISHING GROUP

1

Cataloguing in Publication Data is available from the British Library

Hardback ISBN 978 1 4722 4110 8
Trade Paperback ISBN 978 1 4722 2644 0

Typeset by Palimpsest Book Production Ltd, Falkirk, Stirlingshire

Printed and bound in Great Britain by
CPI Group (UK) Ltd, Croydon, CR0 4YY

MIX
Paper from
responsible sources
FSC www.fsc.org FSC® C104740

Headline's policy is to use papers that are natural, renewable and recyclable
products and made from wood grown in well-managed forests and other
controlled sources. The logging and manufacturing processes are expected to
conform to the environmental regulations of the country of origin.

HEADLINE PUBLISHING GROUP
An Hachette UK Company
Carmelite House
50 Victoria Embankment
London EC4Y 0DZ

www.headline.co.uk
www.hachette.co.uk

For my sister, Penny

Six years ago

He's washing the car – slapping water, sloppy. She's in the kitchen, cutting. Not meat and not bread, something that chunks under the knife. Carrots, or onions. The sounds soak up through the house to where Stephen is sitting in the room with the red wall.

Her room. The shelf over the bed is full of her things. Books and pictures, and the dark blue box with its snarl of bracelets. His favourite is the horseshoe charm, silver, curved like a half-finished heart. He wears it under the sleeve of his pyjamas, in bed. They said they'd put her things away into the attic if he wanted but he said no, he didn't mind. He likes looking at her things; it makes him feel safe. He sleeps with her books weighted around him like stones.

She painted the red wall herself. He can see the places she had to stop and stand on a chair to finish, stretching her arm to reach the ceiling's right angles. She was angry when she did it; the paint's too thick and too thin and where it's too thick it's full of tiny holes where air bubbles burst.

1

She's not been here in years, but it's her room.

Marnie Rome's room.

He finds the shape of her in the bed at night and it's his shape, narrow. He wriggles down into it, imagining a trench dug in the mattress, a place to lie low. Her eyes tracked these same shadows across the ceiling, and watched the sun crouch outside the cracked window.

The crack's at the top corner, in the shape of a hand. He measures it most weeks, to see if it's grown. Stands on a chair and reaches until he's touching the tips of his fingers to it. The last time, it drew blood. He climbed down and stood looking at his red fingers, like hers after she'd painted the wall. The fingers tasted rusty, old. He shut them up in a fist and set its side to the window, thinking about punching, thinking of the noise it would make and the feet that would come running, arms open, mouths lopsided, words worrying at him. Just thinking it makes him tired.

He's lonely. If it wasn't for her here with him, he'd have gone crazy by now.

'Marnie Rome.'

He says her name when he's held down by her books, the horseshoe charm biting at the inside of his wrist. They have the same wrists, thin and square. They're the same shape, lying together in the narrow bed, counting the holes in the red wall, all the places pricked by her anger. Not just anger. Sadness, too. She was lonely here, like him. Hurting, the way he hurts.

A slop of water from outside.

He's making the car shine.

From the kitchen, the smell of onions frying in butter.

She's making a casserole.

Stephen had never eaten a casserole until he came here, when he was eight years old. Now he's fourteen, 'a growing boy'. In the other place it was all scraps and mouldy sandwiches made with whatever was left in the fridge. Here, they won't stop feeding him. Proper food, she calls it. 'Let's get a proper meal inside you,' as if she can see his emptiness. He's so empty it hurts.

Food doesn't help, stretching his stomach until he has to get rid of it to make more room for her, for Marnie. Food just gets in the way.

He's whistling as he washes the car.

Stephen can hear water running onto the drive. He used to help when he first came here, when he was scared and wanting to please. He's not scared now. Not of them, not of anything, thanks to her.

'Marnie Rome.'

He counts the holes in the red wall, starting over.

From the kitchen—

The yellow smell of onions frying, and the slow chunking of the knife.

1

Now

'Upgrades . . . Another circle of hell successfully breached.' Tim Welland gave up the struggle with his phone and set it aside. 'DS Jake, take a seat.'

Noah did as he was told, puzzling over what had prompted this meeting. First thing in the morning wasn't Welland's style any more than it was his, but here he was in the OCU Commander's office at 7.55 a.m. without a cup of coffee in sight and Welland looking like a double espresso wouldn't even scratch the surface of his mood.

'You and DI Rome make a good team.' He treated Noah to his heaviest stare. 'That's the station gossip. But the trouble with station gossip is I wouldn't stuff my wet shoes with most of it. I want to hear it from you.'

'We make a good team, sir.'

An easy answer because it was the truth, but where was Welland going with this? Christ, he wasn't about to hand out a secondment, was he? It was too early in the morning for dodging bullets and Noah liked his job, wanted to keep working with Marnie Rome and the major incident team. Ambition dictated that he took any leg-up on offer, but Welland's face wasn't saying leg-up.

On his desk was a sheet of paper, an incident report. Noah wasn't equal to the task of reading it upside down while maintaining eye contact.

'She's got your back, and you've got hers.' Deep lines were scored either side of Welland's nose, as if he'd paid to have censure tattooed in place. 'You've found out things about her you didn't know a year ago. Is that a fair statement?'

'I . . . Yes, sir.'

'From the station's self-appointed agony aunt.' Touching the taut skin under his eye. 'DC Tanner.'

This was a disciplinary? Debbie Tanner had pushed her luck, one piece of well-meaning gossip too many. 'Not just from her.'

'Remind me to dig out my thermal underwear.'

'Sir?'

'If DI Rome's sharing secrets then hell must be icing over.'

'Not . . . secrets. But we did speak a little, about what happened six years ago. Not much, but—'

'Enough for you to know why I don't want her anywhere near a case involving this address.' Welland put his thumb on the incident report and pushed it across the desk. 'Yes?'

At last. They were getting somewhere. Okay, maybe nowhere *good*, but—

Noah read the report, his throat tightening. Definitely nowhere good. 'Yes, sir.'

'Our victims are in the hospital, not the morgue. Robbery gone wrong. Not a major incident, and not homicide. So. We let Trident take this one.'

'That makes sense.' Noah kept his eyes on the paperwork.

Six years ago, Welland had been the first officer on the scene. At Marnie's old address, her family home. This new crime—

Robbery and assault, two victims in hospital. Alan and Louise Kettridge. Her tenants, Noah guessed. The assault had taken place while he was sleeping with Dan curled at his back, around 1.30 a.m. It'd happened in the house where her parents were killed by her foster brother, Stephen Keele.

'Trident have their eye on a local gang, kids. This has their thumbprints all over it, apparently.' Welland sat back, rubbing at his face. 'If we're lucky, *literally* their thumb-prints. But even without the kick-and-run gods smiling on us, we leave this to Trident. They've got the contacts, plus some private mediation outfit falling over itself to get the local community onside.' When he dropped his hands, his face held the shadow of their shape. 'DS Kennedy's heading up the Trident team. He'll keep me posted. And I'll keep DI Rome posted, on a need-to-know basis.'

How would he quantify that?

This house, what had happened there six years ago . . .

Marnie's need to know wasn't going to fit Trident's boxes, or not neatly.

Welland reached across the desk for the report. 'You've got her back.'

He nodded a dismissal at Noah. 'I'm glad of it.'

2

Marnie was in the incident room when Noah returned. 'Good,' she smiled at him, 'you can drink one of these.' Two flat whites from their favourite coffee shop. 'You heard, then.'

'About—?'

'The latest assault.' She moved in the direction of her office, unwinding a green scarf from her throat. 'No robbery. Just plenty of violence.'

Noah had thought for a second that she knew the secrets Welland was keeping; she could be uncanny like that. But she was talking about another assault. 'Where?' he asked.

'Pimlico.' She hung her coat and scarf on the back of the door, tidying her red curls away from her face. 'Page Street.'

'Our vigilante's going up in the world. Who's got the crime scene?'

'DS Carling. We'll go over there, but I wanted to check in here first. See what Forensics has for us, whether there's a link yet.'

For weeks they'd been seeing a pattern in the assaults, but what they needed was hard evidence. As it stood the attacks were random, the victims unknown to one another. No matching DNA at the scenes, no clear motive and no obvious *modus operandi* other than a savage beating.

'Kyle Stratton,' Marnie said, anticipating Noah's next question. 'Our new victim. Twenty-six years old. A management consultant. Works in Westminster, lives in Reigate. Right now he's in St Thomas's with multiple fractures.'

'Weapon?' Noah asked.

'Blunt, heavy. A baseball bat, or similar.' She was checking her emails. 'Defensive wounds in the shape of two broken wrists and a broken elbow. A shattered eye socket too.'

Noah winced. 'Facial injuries again. Like Stuart Rawling.'

'Not like Carole Linton, but yes. All the injuries are front-facing. Our assailant wants you to see what's coming, and isn't afraid of you fighting back.'

'And yet neither of them could give us a clear description.'

This reluctance to ID the assailant had prompted them to look more closely at the victims. Wondering about their lifestyles, whether they were making bad choices, courting chaos.

In the incident room, Noah and Marnie stood shoulder to shoulder, studying the whiteboard.

Two victims, each with two faces: before and after the assaults.

Stuart Rawling wasn't smiling in the first photograph. In the second, his mouth was forced into the mockery of a grin, thanks to a badly dislocated jaw. Carole Linton's was the more disturbing face, despite all of her injuries being below the waist: knife wounds and bruises stamped by feet which had ruptured an ovary and her spleen. Burns too, where her skirt had been set alight. She'd aged twenty years after the attack, shoulders hunched, bleak terror in her stare.

And now Kyle Stratton, with a shattered eye socket.

Marnie pinned the location of this latest attack to the map.

'Has he been in prison?' Noah asked.

It was the one thing connecting the two earlier assaults; Stuart and Carole had both served time for crimes involving violence, and worse. This fact, and the savage silence they were keeping, had sounded alarm bells. Marnie and Noah had been on high alert for a third assault, fearing a vigilante.

'Yes, he has,' Marnie said.

'What did he do?' Noah studied Kyle's face.

'A spell in a juvenile detention centre for racially aggravated assault, eleven years ago. He and a school friend thought it would be fun to set fire to a younger boy's blazer. They pleaded guilty, said they hadn't intended anyone to be hurt.'

'What part of "setting fire to" didn't they understand?'

'The judge decided they'd shown remorse,' Marnie said. 'Kyle was let out after three months.'

'How badly was he burnt? Their victim.'

'Badly enough.' She put her hand on the new map pin. 'Let's see what DS Carling's found at the scene. And whether Kyle's well enough to give us a statement.'

Page Street was lined with apartments built like a toddler's first attempt at stacking bricks, in alternating blocks of grey and white. Security gates gave the place a penitentiary air not helped by the trio of kids kicking a bald tennis ball around the paved courtyard. Not the nice spot Noah had imagined; hard to believe they were a short walk from the Houses of Parliament.

Ron Carling was waiting inside the police cordon, fielding the kids' antics with a glare. 'Little bastards won't move off. No parents around to make them.'

Marnie ducked under the tape, holding it for Noah who said, 'Is that CCTV doing its job?'

'Three guesses.'

In other words, no. Marnie had lost count of the number of cameras in London that existed purely for show. A deterrent supposedly, like the life-size cardboard police officers propped inside pound shops. 'Forensics have finished?'

'A while back.' Ron stamped his feet, trying to keep warm.

Most of the day's cold had congregated in the right angle where the assault took place, as if the crime scene had sucked a breath six hours ago and was still holding it. Noah measured the short space with his stare, hands deep in the pockets of his coat. It was always useful to see the crime scene, even one as carefully picked clean as this. Blood spatter on the paving slabs, but unless their assailant had got sloppy, it was Kyle's and it would be the only DNA found here.

'He's getting his confidence up,' Noah said. 'Or he knew that camera wasn't working.'

'We're assuming it's him,' Ron said. 'Because of the broken face?'

The kids kicked the tennis ball towards them, dancing away when Marnie looked up.

'Because Kyle has a criminal record,' she said, 'like our other two.'

'Vigilantism.' Ron stamped his feet. 'As if we don't have enough arseholes on our hands without the arsehole-hating arseholes pitching in.'

Eloquently put.

11

'We're going to St Thomas's,' Marnie told him. 'Keep us posted on the door-to-door.'

'We won't find him.' Ron sniffed. 'Not from this. He's too bloody crafty.'

'He can't stop. That's how we'll catch him.' Noah took a last look at the crime scene, the street light, the blind CCTV camera. 'He can't stop, and he's getting louder.'

The route to the hospital took them past Kyle's offices, close to St James's Park tube station. Marnie pulled up and parked, to consider the layout. A pub on the corner – where Kyle had been drinking? Ten minutes on foot to Page Street.

'He wasn't going home,' Noah said, 'or he'd have headed for Victoria, taken a mainline train to Reigate. Page Street was out of his way.'

'He wasn't going home,' Marnie agreed.

CCTV right around them, a steel circuit of surveillance. Had their vigilante known where the gaps were, or didn't he care? The earlier assaults had taken place in dead ends, dark corners. Last night was hardly broad daylight, but it was a lot riskier. Louder, just as Noah had said.

'I want names.' She considered the tinted windows of the office block. 'Who was he drinking with, what time did he leave, was he on his own. DC Tanner can lead on that.'

'Eleven years,' Noah said. 'Since he set fire to that boy. Over a decade since he was paroled. Our vigilante's playing a long game.'

'Or it doesn't matter to him who he attacks.' Three faces indiscriminately damaged, wiped out. Even Carole's untouched face – wiped out. 'He's happy to attack anyone guilty of a violent crime, regardless of circumstances, or gender, or age.'

'So he's . . . sticking pins in parole records? Using DBS checks?'

'It's possible. You know what Welland would say. We're clutching at straws, seeing connections that don't exist.' Marnie pulled away from the kerb, pointing the car towards the hospital. 'What did he want, by the way? You were in his office when I got to work.'

'Pep talk.' A muscle played in Noah's cheek. 'About our teamwork.'

Welland was heavy work first thing in the morning. And more than usually dour of late, making Marnie worry about his health. For nearly five years he'd been in remission but cancer, like their vigilante, didn't care. Indiscriminately destructive.

'Our teamwork's great,' she told Noah. 'There's no one I'd rather be clutching at straws with.'

'Maybe we're about to catch a break.' He kept his eyes on the other side of the river. 'New victim, new evidence. This could be our first decent ID.'

Below them, the Thames shuddered with the same cold breath trapped in the right angle where Kyle Stratton's bones had been broken.

Marnie took the turning for St Thomas's.

'Let's find out.'

3

St Thomas's was becoming a second home. How many hours of hospital CCTV footage had Noah and Marnie starred in? Walking through the main entrance, waiting to interview patients, not all of whom were victims. That smell, though—

Hot and cold and sweet and sour all at once. Noah would never get used to it.

Marnie went ahead of him, stripping off her gloves. Should he have said something in the car, about what was unravelling at her house? Alan and Louise Kettridge might be here in St Thomas's. Noah hated secrets. He hoped DS Kennedy and the Trident team would clear it up quickly.

'Kyle Stratton?' Marnie was speaking with the woman at the desk. 'He was brought in around two a.m. following an assault.'

Noah hung back, turning to watch the people on the plastic chairs. A red-eyed mother and her baby, two drunks propping each other upright, a man in stained overalls holding his towel-wrapped hand in his lap. What would tourists make of scenes like this? London showing the other side of its postcard-gloss. A tourist could've stumbled on Kyle in the early hours, lying in the gutter not far from Westminster Abbey. Instead, a cabbie found him, calling for an ambulance that took eleven minutes to respond. Fortunately the cabbie knew enough first aid to keep Kyle's airways clear until the paramedics reached them. Door-to-door was yet to find anyone in Page Street who'd heard or seen anything. If the attack had been head-on, like the others, then Kyle had chosen not to shout when he saw his attacker approaching. Or it happened too fast for him to realise the danger, or he was too drunk to make sense of what was happening until it was too late. Apartments all around him, packed with people. Surely someone had seen or heard something.

'He's in surgery,' Marnie said. 'We need to wait to speak with a doctor.'

Noah moved with her, away from the crowded A&E. 'Surgery for the orbital fracture?'

'They wouldn't say.' She frowned, dark-eyed. 'But it didn't sound good. Emergency surgery.'

Their vigilante was keeping a lot of surgeons very busy.

'We should speak with the cabbie who found him,' Noah said. 'I'll get Colin to send us a name and address.'

Kyle's surgeon was a young Iranian woman with beautiful eyes. She'd washed the blood from her hands, but spots of it clung stubbornly to her scrubs.

She beckoned Marnie and Noah to a quiet part of the corridor.

'Traumatic subarachnoid haemorrhage,' she told them. 'He was bleeding into his brain.'

'Was?' Marnie repeated.

'He died,' her eyes were sorrowful, 'twelve minutes ago. I'm very sorry.'

4

The fly wouldn't die. He'd sprayed it with enough polish to turn it white – it was wearing a fur coat of furniture polish – but it kept moving. Walking along the window-sill leaving little gobs of foam like footprints. Fly prints. It kept trying to get off the ground but its wings were too heavy so it was walking towards the corner where the light was brightest, where it could see the sky.

'Idiot.' Finn aimed the can of polish. 'Just die.'

He pressed his thumb on the nozzle. More spray hit the fly, knocking it back down, legs kicking stickily. It rolled sideways, found its feet, started walking.

'Will you not just *die*—? There's no way out. The window doesn't open. It's painted shut. You're finished, you silly fucker. Just – give up already.'

The spray made Finn's eyes sting. He coughed, hiding his mouth in the crook of his elbow. He was meant to be cleaning. He had the kitchen to do, and supper to cook. He should've finished in here half an hour ago. Would have if it wasn't for this idiot fly who thought just because it could see sky it could get out, who didn't know a window when it saw one and who wouldn't just *die*.

'You'll freeze out there, you mad fucker, it's fierce cold.'

Buzzing – he could hear it buzzing under the white fur left by the spray. There shouldn't even *be* flies in winter. It should be hibernating not crawling, dragging one of its legs like it was broken. It wouldn't give up, thought it could escape, fly home. How stupid could you get?

Finn was only ten but he'd stopped thinking he could escape after two days.

The house was locked down, tight.

He had cleaning to do, and washing, and cooking. He didn't have time for this fly's fantasy escapism shit. He lifted the can of furniture polish and set it down on the windowsill.

Not hard, but not gently either. The can had a hollow in its base that stopped it being flat. When he leaned in, he could hear the fly buzzing inside.

He pressed his cheek to the cold of the can, listening, wondering how long it'd take to suffocate, or even if it *could* suffocate. Air was getting in underneath, the windowsill wasn't flat. He could be here a long time waiting for the fly to die. When he'd first seen it, he'd wanted it dead. He hated insects, especially flying ones. Didn't mind spiders so much, liked beetles. But flies were all up in your face, walking with their shitty feet on your food. Butter, sugar—

Finn was meant to keep this place spotless. Fucking Brady would flip his lid if he saw a fly in here. For one thing, he'd think it meant an open window somewhere, a way out.

The can grew warm under his cheek, the fly throbbing on the windowsill.

He straightened slowly, raising the can.

The fly struggled to its feet and straightaway started dragging itself towards the bright corner where the windows met. Until Finn put the can on its back, rolling it until it crunched.

It was red and yellow inside, like pus from a bloody knee. He wiped the mess with a sheet of kitchen roll, carrying it to the metal bin. He pressed the pedal, dropped the ball of paper inside and let the lid come down on it slowly, bringing with it the reflection of his face.

He looked scared. Specks of white spray on his lips, sticky.

He licked his lips and tasted polish.

Dead fly taste.

He ran to the sink and spat then puked, spattering toast and tea so he'd have to clean twice as hard now, enough to see his face in the sink, like the bin where the rubbish went, the rubbish and his face and he'd better not cry, Brady *hated* that, he'd better not—

He turned the taps on full blast and let his knees give way.

Sat on the floor with the drops splashing back on his head like rain.

Water thundering in the sink above, draining down into the pipes behind, finding something he couldn't find—

A way out.

5

'Kyle Stratton died at ten minutes past nine this morning. He was alive when he was found in Page Street seven hours earlier, and alive when he arrived at St Thomas's. But he suffered a massive haemorrhagic stroke caused by the blow to his head. So. This is now a murder investigation.'

Marnie looked around the room, waiting for questions.

'He's killing them now?' Debbie Tanner shook her head.

'Or it's not the same guy,' Ron said.

Of everyone on the team, he was the most sceptical about the connection between the attacks. London had criminals stretching to every dark corner and back. Why look for just one of them?

'Frontal attack. Broken bones. Blunt instrument.' Noah stepped up to the whiteboard. 'Nothing stolen. Kyle had a wallet full of cash and cards, plus a brand new iPhone. If this was a robbery then someone missed a trick.'

No robbery at the earlier crime scenes either, as if the attacker hadn't wanted the police wasting time identifying his victims. Nothing taken, and nothing left behind.

'So what'd *this* poor bastard done to deserve it?' Ron asked. 'If it's our mystery vigilante?'

'Kyle spent three months in juvenile detention for racially aggravated assault.'

'When he was fifteen.' Debbie frowned. 'That's a long time for anyone to bear a grudge. Why wait all that time?'

'Why wait seven years to smash Stuart Rawling's jaw? Or twelve years to set fire to Carole Linton's skirt?' Ron glared at the whiteboard. 'And why haven't we got a hundred more GBH cases pinned up here? What makes this little lot so special?'

'That's easy. The criminal records. All three served time for violent crimes. Look what Stuart and Carole did, and now Kyle.' Debbie smoothed the front of her blouse. 'I can understand *why* someone might want to punish them, but I don't understand why it took them so long to get around to it. All the paroles happened years ago. Why's our vigilante only getting to work now?'

'Two theories,' Colin Pitcher reminded them. 'Our attacker was a kid at the time of the parole. That fits with Carole's victim.' He winced when he said her name. They all did. 'And now it fits for Kyle. Second theory: this is a recent parolee. Someone who's only just out of jail themselves.'

'Different prisons, different timescales,' Ron objected. 'No link between our victims. So what link's *he* seeing that we can't? Or has he got a random list he's sticking pins in?'

Marnie was glad of his scepticism. It helped her to field Welland's objections, and it was always good to have a voice of cold reason when they were testing the strength of a spider's web of evidence. 'Let's find out as much as we can about Kyle. From his family, friends, workmates. Get his records from the detention centre. Look at his conviction and his parole. If our killer's finding his victims from prison records, I want to see what he's seeing.'

'Do you think he meant to kill Kyle?' Debbie asked.

'Is the violence escalating? We'll find out from the post-mortem. According to the surgeon who tried to save his life, the blow to his face was brutal but it was a single blow. If someone set out to kill Kyle then I'd have expected them to keep hitting until the job was done.'

'None of these three,' Debbie said, 'were high-profile cases. In terms of public record, I mean. The press and so on. Well, except for Carole.' She shuddered when she said the woman's name.

'Third theory.' Colin polished his glasses. 'Our killer's working in the legal system, or the justice system.' He put the glasses back on, registering the silence in the room. 'I didn't say it was a popular theory. About as popular as Jar Jar Binks being a Sith Lord, but I'm putting it out there.'

'It means there could be victims we've missed,' Debbie said. '*Murders* we've missed.'

'Jar Jar. Sith Lord.' Colin spread his hands in apology. 'I said it was unpopular.'

'Fanboy conjecture aside,' Marnie said, 'let's ask awkward questions of Kyle's workmates. He was drinking late last night, and he wasn't headed home when he was attacked. I want to know who was with him when he left the pub, and where he was going.'

'I've put a call in for CCTV footage,' Colin said. 'I'll move it up the line now this is a murder.'

'Good. DS Jake?'

In the corridor, Marnie said, 'Welland wants to see me. I'll bring him up to speed. Can you check in with Fran on the forensics and post-mortem? And speak with the parents as soon as you can, find out whether Kyle was in any trouble lately. Take DS Carling with you.'

'Will do.' Noah nodded. 'I'm here when you need me.'

She smiled thanks, walking in the direction of Welland's office.

Noah tried not to think about the news Welland was about to break to her. He needed to focus on finding their vigilante before they had a fourth face to pin to the board. Broken and bloody like Stuart, or terrorised like Carole.

Was it sheer luck neither of them had died?

Or was there something special about Kyle? Some reason why the vigilante had gone further, stamping indelible damage, tipping over the edge from rage to full-blown murder.

Had he enjoyed it?

Gone home with the taste of Kyle's blood in his mouth, still wet on his clothes.

Washed away everything but the itch, lodged under his skin, to do it again.

6

'Detective Inspector Rome, this is Detective Sergeant Kennedy.'

'Trident?' Marnie shook the man's hand. 'Yes, we've met.'

'Of course you have.' Welland nodded at them to be seated. 'I was forgetting how often gang tension resolves itself into homicide.'

'Always happy to have DI Rome's help.' Kennedy took the chair next to Marnie, facing Welland across the desk. He was her age, dark hair and blue eyes, a swimmer's build. Dressed neutrally in a grey suit over a white shirt, no tie. If he knew he looked good he gave no sign of knowing it, didn't cross his legs or fuss with the hang of his jacket. One of Trident's rising stars.

Welland rested his gaze on Marnie's face. 'DS Kennedy is heading up an investigation into an aggravated burglary that took place in the early hours of this morning.' A beat. 'At your house on Lancaster Road.' His left eye was shadowed by a red bruise. 'Your tenants are in hospital.' He nodded at Kennedy. 'Trident think a local gang, kids.'

'Were they badly hurt?' She fought to numb her first

reaction. Terror, at the thought of blood on those floors all over again. 'The tenants. I'm sorry, I can't remember their names, it's handled through an agency . . .'

'Alan and Louise Kettridge,' Kennedy said. 'They took a beating, but they'll be okay.'

'May I see the report?'

Welland started to shake his head but Kennedy said, 'I don't have a problem, sir. I'd want to see the report, in DI Rome's place.'

How much had Welland told him? Did he know how Marnie had knelt on the pavement in Lancaster Road with Welland's hand heavy on her neck while Forensics walked blood to the mobile unit with their poly bags and boxes? She took the incident report from his hand.

'We made the house secure.' Kennedy kept his distance, didn't try to lean in while she read. 'Hopefully the agency can sort out the rest. If you're able to give me a name and number, I'll make the calls. It'd be useful to know who else has access to the house during the tenancy.'

'They broke in at the back.' She kept her eyes on the report. She was thirsty, and knew it was shock. 'Through the kitchen.'

'Crowbarred the door. A neat job, considering the mess they made inside—' Kennedy stopped.

'What was taken?'

'Very little, as far as we can tell at this stage.'

She nodded, glad that he hadn't apologised; she'd had her fill of sympathy six years ago. And whatever mess these kids had made, it couldn't compare with the chaos left behind by Stephen. From the way he'd bitten his tongue, Kennedy knew that.

'It's early days,' he said, 'but we think it's most likely an initiation rite. Very young kids hoping to get into an established gang by showing off their muscle. We've had a number of break-ins along those lines, but this one got out of hand. It's possible the Kettridges pushed back.' He paused, watching Marnie. 'Have you met them? Are they the type to do that?'

'I haven't met them.' She handed back the report. 'Like I said, it's all done through the agency.'

She would meet them now. Visit the hospital, take flowers. Was that appropriate? What did you take to your tenants after a fresh act of barbarity carried out in your former home?

'DS Kennedy will keep me informed of progress with the investigation,' Welland said. 'I'll keep you in the loop but you're busy, I know that.'

He didn't want her anywhere near this. Protecting her, the way he'd tried to six years ago. He'd told Noah, she realised. That early morning meeting then the awkwardness in the car; Noah knew about the break-in. Had Welland warned him to watch out for her?

'Pep talk,' Noah had said, 'about our teamwork.'

Now Welland was saying he knew how busy she was. Wanting her at arm's length from what had happened in Lancaster Road. Her ears popped, as if the pressure in the room had changed.

'I appreciate it.' She kept her tone neutral. 'I'm sure DS Kennedy runs a tight ship. I'll text the number for the agency. If you need anything else from me at any stage, just ask.'

She met Kennedy's eyes finally, relieved to find no pity there.

'Thanks. And if you have questions, do the same.' He matched her tone, hitting it dead centre. Professional courtesy, mutual respect. A nod for Welland. 'If that's all, sir?'

Welland waited until he was gone before saying, 'He's a good detective. He'll steer this right.'

25

'I don't doubt it.' Marnie watched him get to his feet and walk to the table by the window. He came back with two bottles of mineral water, handing one to her. 'Thanks.'

She broke the seal, drank. Held the bottle in her lap. 'I'm okay.'

He gave a slow nod, pinching the bridge of his nose with his fingers.

'Bad memories,' Marnie said. 'For you as well as me. But it's okay. I'm not about to go to pieces, or demand a role in the investigation. Believe me, I don't want to be back inside that house.'

She'd made a promise to herself six years ago that she would never again set foot in there; a rare act of self-compassion at a time when she was flaying herself with guilt and remorse.

'I'm sorry for Alan and Louise.' She followed the water bottle's moulded shape with her thumb. 'I always wondered how they got on in there—'

How anyone was able to live in that house.

Welland moved his hand. 'There's more.' He paused. 'I'm stepping out for a while. DCS Ferguson's stepping in.'

Her mouth dried again at the look on his face.

'Lorna Ferguson. I doubt you've met her. She was in Manchester until recently.'

The bruise under his eye spread its red shadow down his cheek.

Marnie's heart thumped. 'You're not . . .'

He gave a slow nod. 'The cancer's back. I need an op and chemo, you know the drill.' He didn't smile, wouldn't make a joke of it coming after the news about Lancaster Road. 'DCS Ferguson's a tough cookie, to put it in the vernacular. She'll keep DC Tanner and DS Carling in check. You think Kennedy runs a tight ship? She favours a frigate, type twenty-three.'

Marnie wanted to reach across the desk and hold his hands. 'How bad is it?'

'Oh, you know. Nothing a good surgeon can't sort out. Providing they keep the kale and chia seed smoothies away, I'll be fine.'

She returned his smile, but felt a cold rush of dismay. 'How long will you be gone?'

'Four months. Long enough for DCS Ferguson to convert you to her tactics. Up north they call her *H.M.S. Dauntless.*'

'*Dauntless* is a destroyer, not a frigate.'

Welland pointed a finger at her. 'I'm going to miss you. And you're going to be all right. Leave Kennedy to do his thing. He's got a big brain so don't let the boyish good looks fool you.'

'Not a mistake I'm likely to make.'

She wished he'd stand up from behind his desk; she needed to hold him. How many times had she reached for this man six years ago? Her rock, her rescuer. So tightly tied to her recovery, the distance she'd managed to put between herself and that period of self-flagellation, self-destruction. She struggled to set her pain aside; this wasn't about her. Other people, better people, were going through worse. 'You'll stay in touch? Or I can, via Sean.' His son.

'I'm counting on you to smuggle me a decent single malt.' He got to his feet. 'And you can stick a pin in any "Get Well" balloons they send me. Damn, I hate hospitals . . .'

He opened his arms. 'Are we doing this?'

He'd held her after the verdict, as Stephen was being led away to start his sentence. Eight weeks later, he'd told her about the cancer. It'd been coming on for a while but the diagnosis was new. She couldn't remember hugging him after he beat it that first time but she must've done, weak with relief, with not having lost him too.

'You'll catch your vigilante.' Gruffly, across the top of her head.

She kept her face pressed to his shoulder. He smelt of bacon, and aspirin. 'I thought you didn't believe in my vigilante.'

'I've been known to get it wrong.' He set her at arm's length, raising an eyebrow. 'Don't tell DCS Ferguson I said that.'

Marnie fought to keep the fear from her face, skin tightening in resistance to the idea of Ferguson – or anyone – taking this man's place. 'It doesn't sound as if she'll believe our theory any more than you do.'

'Catch her half a dozen vigilantes and do the paperwork in record time. She'll be happy.'

'I'll settle for one arrest. And an end to these assaults.' Marnie knotted her hair at the nape of her neck. 'Kyle Stratton died. Whether or not he's a vigilante, we're looking for a killer now.'

7

From the outside, Kyle's house matched all the others in the street. Grotesquely gabled, faux leaded windows winking, mock Tudor with a heavy emphasis on the mock. A suburban CEO's wet dream of a home, right down to the rake tracks in the frozen gravel drive.

'Shit,' Ron said. 'How'd he afford this? Twenty-six, I was living in a cruddy bedsit in Peckham with other people's toenail clippings for company.'

'The house belongs to his parents.' Noah checked his phone before pocketing it. 'They know what's happened. His dad was at St Thomas's earlier.'

Brenda Stratton answered the door. Briskly, unsmiling. In an orange cashmere tunic and black leggings, strappy sandals on bare, bony feet. 'You're the police. Gerry!' Calling up the stairs. 'The police are here. Come on, come through.'

She marched them to a sitting room shiny with furniture polish, the light crazing off glass cabinets and framed photographs, central heating at full blast to combat the cold outside. She knocked the cushions into shape before offering Noah and Ron a seat on the sofa. 'Gerry!'

'I'm here.' A short, round man in a red roll-neck and grey slacks, the same savage suntan as his wife, incongruous given the weather.

All four of them sat before Brenda jumped back up. 'You'll want coffee. I've made coffee.' She headed towards the back of the house.

Gerry shook his head, but didn't try and stop her. 'We're knocked for six by this.'

Noah nodded. 'We want to find the person who attacked Kyle as quickly as possible. We have a few questions, and we'd like to see his room.'

'I knew you'd ask that.' Gerry's face was tanned so deeply its creases were black. 'They want to see his room, Bren!'

His wife returned with a tray of cups, her sandals slapping at her heels. Brittle bronzed hair, brown eyes under plucked brows. Expensive body lotion, lilies and jasmine. She seated herself next to her husband, twisting a gold cuff at her wrist. Above their heads, photographs showcased the Strattons holidaying in world-cruise-brochure locations. Gerry was a foot and a half shorter than his wife, her bare arm resting across his shoulders with a hint of bingo-wing, but only a hint. She kept herself bikini-ready. Gerry was balding but his face was boyish, blue eyes fringed by blond lashes.

'He should've been on a train coming home,' Brenda said. 'Have you spoken to his work?'

'We'll be doing that next,' Ron told her. 'We wanted to see you first. When was the last time you heard from Kyle?'

'Saturday lunch,' Gerry said without hesitation. 'He honoured us with his presence. Of course it was breakfast, for him. He'd only just got out of bed.'

'He keeps late hours.' Brenda blinked but no tears came; it was too soon. 'Kept late hours.'

'He was running late,' Noah said, 'last night. He didn't call to let you know he'd be late?'

'Not a chance.' Gerry laughed. 'We'd have been in bed in any case.'

'He often stayed out late? Didn't keep in touch?'

'That was Kyle.' Gerry's tone was nine parts resignation, one part pride. Or possibly envy.

'As far as you know—' Ron started.

'No enemies,' Gerry interrupted. 'No. Absolutely not. No funny business there. He knew better than that.' He drank a mouthful of coffee. 'Credit where it's due. He did know better than that.'

At his side, Kyle's mother beat time with her sandal against her heel. Her toenails were painted the same electric orange as her tunic.

'Do you know the names of the workmates he was drinking with?' Ron asked. 'It'd save us a bit of time down the line.'

'Oh he was mates with the lot of them. Made friends like that,' Gerry snapped his fingers, 'easy-going.' He polished his bald patch with the palm of his hand. 'Very easy-going was Kyle.'

Noah had been in a lot of rooms like this one, breaking terrible news to bereaved parents. Always the atmosphere was empty, as if the loss had taken a chunk from the house and the people in it. Often they held onto their grief until he'd gone. One woman had smiled and nodded and thanked him until the door clicked shut and she howled on the other side, her grief unwinding, filling the house. Here, it was different. The Strattons were different. It didn't feel as if anything was missing. More as if something had been added – a wall of resistance around Brenda and Gerry, their sun-beaten faces blank beneath the holiday snaps.

'If we could see his room . . .'

Gerry nodded at his wife with a hint of triumph. 'I told you they'd want to do that.'

'I'll do the washing-up.' She scooped the coffee tray from the table, power-walking away. 'And put the bins out.'

Kyle's room was at the back, overlooking a garden as trimly spacious as the house. Half an acre of lawn tortured into icy stripes, frozen shrubs like sentries on all sides. Central heating was cooking the bedroom. Double bed with a blue duvet pulled neat to its pillows, double-fronted wardrobe with mirrored doors, desk and chair, iPod dock, expensive speakers. Two suitcases at the side of the ward-robe with luggage tags on their handles. A trouser press hung with a pink silk tie. Everything clean and tidy. Stripes hoovered into the carpet to match the lawn outside.

'How long's he lived here?' Ron asked.

'Never moved out.' Gerry rubbed his thumb at a smear on the mirrored wardrobe. 'Property prices in London, can you blame him? We've got the space, as you can see.'

'You didn't see a lot of him, though.' Ron sent a look of sympathy across his shoulder. 'Treated it like a hotel, did he?'

Gerry gave a stiff nod. 'Put a bit of money our way for food and fuel. That was the trade.'

A business arrangement? It didn't sound like a family.

'He liked to go drinking with his mates.' Ron opened drawers in the desk. 'That was a regular thing? Making friends, going out, coming back late?'

Gerry nodded again and folded his arms, staying beside the wardrobe. He was sucking in his gut, either from force of habit or because he was on edge. Detectives in his dead son's room; that would put anyone on edge.

'Had he ever run into trouble before?' Noah asked.

'Drinking late in London, travelling back on the last train. That can be . . . lively.'

'Never any trouble. Not like this. No.'

Nothing in the room suggested that Kyle had known his attacker. No drugs stashed in the desk or wardrobe, both suitcases empty. His passport was in the desk, together with a recent bank statement. No unusual transactions. He'd earned a good salary, and known how to spend it.

'When was the last time he left the country?' Noah asked.

'Oh he was always flying off here and there. Stockholm before Christmas, with friends. He got the travel bug from us, but hated hot countries. We like the sun. He liked the clubs.'

'Did he have a partner?'

'Nothing steady. Work and play, that was Kyle. Work and play.'

Noah returned the passport to the drawer, sliding it shut. 'He was in a juvenile detention centre when he was fifteen. That's right, isn't it?'

Gerry clenched his jaw. 'What's that got to do with anything?'

'We're looking at all the angles,' Ron said appeasingly. 'We have to.'

Kyle's dad ignored him, focusing on Noah. 'He did three months for being a bloody idiot, falling in with the wrong crowd, with a thug. Jack Goodrich.' He spoke the name with a ripe contempt. 'Kyle thought the sun shone out of him. He was fifteen. A bloody idiot, but it was nearly twelve years ago. Ancient history. I can see why you'd bring it up.' Slight emphasis on *you*. Because Noah was black? 'I can see that. Makes me ashamed to this day. Kyle was ashamed too once he'd woken up to what a fool he'd been.' Pride in his voice, and a certain grim satisfaction that he'd helped his son towards his epiphany. 'Never fell for any of that tomfoolery again, never followed anyone else's lead. *He* was doing the leading. Not wild. Just working hard, and having fun. Good and clean, nothing you'd need to look into. Nothing like that.' He walked into the centre of the room, eyeing the bed. 'He'd moved on. Nearly twelve years. I told him at the time, "This'll dog you. It'll dog you." And I was right.' His voice sharpened. 'I saw him at the hospital. Thank God his mother didn't. His eye must've been hanging out of his head—!' He tapped with his thumb at his right cheek. 'Nothing here, smashed to bits he was.' He blinked. 'That's the lunatic you need to be looking for, the one who did that. Not digging up old dirt, raking it up. He did his time when he was fifteen, learnt his lesson the hard way. Never forgot it. You want to be finding this maniac.'

'We will,' Ron said. 'We'll find him.'

Gerry nodded, stepping back a pace, out of breath. He looked around the room again. 'I knew you'd want to see in here. And I knew you'd bring up that nonsense from years ago. First thing I said to his mum when I got home from the hospital.' He glared at the bed. 'Oh, I knew.'

'Thanks for letting us look round,' Ron said. 'We'll keep in touch.'

'I know how this works.' His neck was flushed with anger. 'You'll keep in touch, yes.'

Ron walked to the door, and Gerry followed.

Noah crouched to collect a scrap of black plastic from under the desk, the room's sole trace of untidiness. Pocketing it, he went down the stairs to where Brenda was waiting in the hall.

'They'll be in touch,' Gerry told her. 'Everything's just like I said it'd be.'

His wife held the front door open. She'd washed her

34

hands, taken off her rings, fingers pinched white at the tips. Cold crawled in from outside, making her toes curl inside their sandals.

'Thanks for the coffee,' Ron said. 'And sorry, again.'

'Shit. Well, that was fun.' Ron started the car, rubbing an elbow at the inside of the windscreen. 'Awkward, when you brought up the detention centre.'

'You heard him. He was expecting the question.' Noah fastened his seat belt. 'Drive round the block, would you? I want to check something.'

'What?'

'Whether it's bin day.' He took out the scrap he'd pocketed. 'This's from a bin liner, right?'

Ron peered at it. 'Brenda was putting them out, that's what she said, doing the washing-up and putting the bins out.'

'Gerry knew we'd want to see Kyle's room. He'd tidied in there.'

Ron whistled under his breath.

'It might not be relevant.'

'Yeah. Could just be ditching his porn. But still . . .'

The bins were out in the road behind the Strattons' house. Wheelie bins with house numbers painted on them. If all the bins in the neighbourhood followed the same pattern it wouldn't be hard to identify the one into which Brenda had put the black plastic bag from Kyle's room.

Noah took a photo on his phone, texting it to their contact at the local police station with a request to monitor the waste collection from outside the Strattons' house.

'You reckon they're dodgy?' Ron rested his forearms on the steering wheel. 'They weren't too cut up about Kyle. Busy planning their next cruise, probably.'

'I think they were upset. I'm just not sure what was upsetting them.'

Ron pulled away from the kerb, joining the traffic back into town. 'He hated being asked about the detention centre. She'd been told to keep quiet, I reckon.'

'I don't know. I didn't get the impression Gerry was in charge in there. Or Brenda, especially.'

'A house that clean and tight? Like a bloody drum.' Ron shook his head. 'Someone's locking it all down. I reckon it's him. Napoleon complex.'

'Napoleon was five foot six. Two inches taller than Nelson.'

'Taller than Gerry, too. Wonder if she hates having to wear flats all the time . . . If he's not making the rules in that house, who is?'

'Maybe no one. Or maybe Kyle. Out late, using the place like a hotel, not letting them forget the trouble he was in once before. You're right, Gerry hated me bringing that up, but I didn't have to bring it far. He hadn't forgotten what his son did. Racially aggravated assault.' Noah watched the houses going by, each with the same Tudor pretension. 'What did their neighbours think of that? It must've made their lives tricky. And if Kyle didn't grow out of it, whatever his dad says, if he was making trouble for someone the night he died . . .?'

'Or being made to pay for it, by someone who's not forgotten what he did any more than his dad has. You reckon they'd cover for him, if they knew something? If he'd been threatened?'

'Possibly. It'll be interesting to see what's inside that bin—'

Noah's phone buzzed. 'DS Jake.'

'Your post-mortem results await.' It was Fran Lennox. 'You'll want to bring DI Rome. This gets interesting.'

8

Finn emptied the bins, going from room to room with a plastic liner, checking for dust balls and scraps of tissue, anything that might make trouble for him. Dirt was his enemy, he'd learned that lesson the hard way. He hated bin day, hated hearing the lorries in the street, the one that rattled with glass and the big one with the crusher at the back that dripped all the way up the road.

He watched from the window upstairs for the bin man with the tartan beanie. His lorry had a purple Teletubby jammed in the grill at the front. He'd seen Finn standing in the window. Weeks ago, right after Brady took him. He'd pushed the beanie to the back of his head and looked up and *seen* Finn. Their eyes had met.

Finn had waved his arms and thumped on the window. 'Help me—!' He'd hated doing it, like some shithead Disney princess, but it was the first time anyone had seen him and he'd been starting to feel invisible. He'd thumped on the window, 'Call the police!' and okay so the windows were soundproofed maybe, the whole place was sealed up tight, but that pig in the beanie had *seen* him. Their eyes had met. And he'd – *waved*. Put his hand up and wriggled his fingers like Finn was a fish in a tank he was teasing. Not even a proper wave, like – like a fucking *finger-tickle*.

Finn had thumped the window with both fists, kept thumping until the lorry drove off and the road was empty again. He'd watched for them after that. Made a sign, writing on the inside of a cereal box, holding it pressed to the glass: *Call the police! I'm Finn Duffy! I've been kidnapped!*

The man hadn't looked up again. Not once in ten weeks.

Finn had destroyed the sign, scared Brady would find it. He'd wiped away the marks he'd made on the window because he still had the bruises from the last time Brady found him out, on both legs under his jeans which were proper Gucci, bought with money his dad sent home. Wrecked now, bleached from all the cleaning Brady made him do, and that time he had to kneel in his own piss to learn a lesson. If Dad could see him now . . . He'd make someone pay. No one messed with Finn's dad. He'd be ashamed, though, of Finn for getting himself in this state. For not getting himself out.

'Shit happens,' Dad had taught him when Finn was five. 'It's how you deal with it that counts.'

Finn hated the bin lorries crawling up the road like tanks, a pretend rescue party. That pig in the beanie waving at him. If he ever got out of here he'd tell the police to find that man and arrest him for failing to report a crime, assisting a kidnapper. Dad would've sorted that pig in no time, but Dad wasn't here. It was up to Finn to deal with this shit.

He wrenched a knot in the neck of the bin bag, setting it by the kitchen door. And then, because he couldn't help himself, he reached out and put his little finger in the lock.

He'd done this with every lock in the house.

In case he ever got hold of Brady's keys. So he'd know right away which ones fitted the important locks, the ones that'd let him out of here.

He put his little finger in the back door lock and turned it, sucking down a sob.

Imagining his finger was a key and he could leave, any time he liked.

9

Marnie stood with Noah at her shoulder, looking down at the remains of the vigilante's third victim. Five hours ago, they'd hoped for answers from Kyle, perhaps even their first description of the attacker they were hunting. Now their hope rested in Fran Lennox, whose clever hands and eyes extracted secrets from the long dead or those, like Kyle, more recently killed.

'No DNA from your vigilante, or not yet. But here . . . in the orbital socket.'

Kyle's right eye had been laid to one side, allowing them to see inside the fractured socket to where Fran was pointing with a fine-tipped swab, at a black patch in the red and white wreckage. 'That's a burn mark. They cleaned him up at St Thomas's which made it tricky but I found traces of aliphatic solvent naphtha. Lighter fluid.' She straightened. 'Whoever did this?' Indicating the rest of Kyle's broken body. 'Thought it would be fun to set fire to the inside of his eye.'

They stood in silence for a moment, studying the vivid patch of damage.

'No other burn marks?' Marnie asked.

'None. Fractured wrists. Broken femur, broken elbow. All done with the same blunt instrument, most likely a baseball bat – radius of impact's too wide for a hammer, too narrow for a cricket bat.'

The injuries were mapped starkly across Kyle's body, all the places he'd been struck, all the ways in which he'd tried to save himself.

'His wrists and elbows,' Noah said. 'Defensive wounds?'

Fran nodded. 'He saw the attack coming, and tried to protect his face and head.'

Marnie could see it: Kyle cornered on Page Street, surrounded by CCTV and street lights, disbelieving the audacity of the attacker. Putting out his hands, getting them smashed aside. Then falling back, trying to make a tent with his arms, hoping to protect his head from whatever weapon was being used to break his wrists, his face. She couldn't look at the mess of his eye, kept seeing Welland's surgeon wielding his scalpel, her own flesh retreating in panic. Fear had been at the surface of her blood since he'd broken the news that his cancer had returned. If she wasn't careful she was going to start jumping at shadows, losing her focus. She concentrated her attention on Kyle, the marks around his mouth where they'd unpeeled the tape used to hold tubes in place, a puncture wound on his left arm where a cannula had been inserted. The evidence of how they'd tried to save him was almost more distressing than the injuries inflicted by his killer. The tape had left a furred outline around his mouth, smudged by blood. He looked younger than twenty-six. Blond hair waxed into a fringe, a recent manicure, body hair clipped short. He'd cared about his appearance.

'Do you think he was conscious after the blow to his head?'

'It's possible,' Fran said.

41

'So he was conscious when they burned his eye?' Noah sounded nauseated.

'I'm afraid that's possible, yes. The damage is very precise. If they'd been trying to set fire to him, they'd have started with his clothes. The human body doesn't ignite easily, too much water content. When I see these sorts of burns?' Fran tipped her head. 'I think torture.'

Beaten, bones broken, then burnt. Deliberately.

'Our other victims,' Marnie said. 'Carole had burn marks, but Stuart?'

'I knew you'd ask.' Fran stepped back. 'Let's reconvene in my office where there's tea. I'm out of biscuits, but I have Easter eggs.' She cocked an eyebrow. 'Of the kind they hide in DVDs.'

'Let's talk about Stuart Rawling.' Fran pulled on an over-sized grey jumper, drawing its sleeves over her hands as she cradled a mug of tea. 'His jaw was broken with a golf club. Bruises and contusions, but it looked like a mugging. Stop me if I'm getting any of this wrong.'

'You're right,' Noah said. 'If it hadn't happened so close to where Carole was attacked, we might not have made any connection. We don't usually ask victims for details of crimes *they've* committed, not those dating back any length of time. Stuart was paroled nearly seven years ago.'

'He'd served thirteen months of a two-year sentence.' Fran sipped at her tea. 'For beating his wife over the course of their twenty-year marriage.'

'He pleaded not guilty,' Marnie said, 'but yes. What did you find?'

'I looked over the hospital reports after discovering that burn, and knowing you're after evidence to link the assaults. Your vigilante theory.' Fran pinched at the high part of her right ear. 'Rawling's ear was pierced through the cartilage. Under the hairline, out of sight.'

'Helix piercing. It's a look,' Noah said uncertainly. 'Perhaps he thought he could carry it off.'

A businessman built like a heavyweight boxer, Rawling had no time for anyone, not even the police when they were looking for his assailant, resenting Marnie's questions as he lay in his hospital bed, gold wedding ring worn like the single portion of a knuckleduster.

'I'm not talking about a professional job,' Fran said. 'This was done crudely, and not with a hollow point needle or a piercing gun. A tapestry needle, possibly. And it was done on the night of the assault, the wound was bleeding when they brought him in.' She rubbed a hand at her spiky blond crop. 'Everyone was busy fixing the facial injuries and this was nothing, probably healed itself in a couple of days, but it's the *deliberateness* that caught my eye. Like Kyle's burn. The rest of it could be written off as a random attack, any lunatic with a blunt instrument and a head full of pills . . . But a cigarette lighter, and a needle? That's personal. That's nasty.'

'Rawling didn't bring it up,' Marnie said. 'When we interviewed him.'

'Look at the press coverage from the trial, the *detail* in it. When he beat his wife he never broke bones or left bruises where they'd be seen. He pulled out her hair. Hanks of it, until she ended up needing a wig for work. On one occasion?' Fran tapped a finger on the table. 'He ripped out her earrings, tore both lobes in the process. I'm not surprised he didn't mention the amateur piercing.'

Marnie's scalp bristled.

'They *burned* Kyle.' Noah leaned forward, his face thinned. 'Is this—?'

Personal. Vengeance.

43

Marnie looked at Fran. 'Go on.'

'That's all I've got.' She reclaimed the mug, standing and going to the corner where the kettle was kept. 'It's niggling at me, though.'

'Carole Linton.' Noah linked his hands, tension in his shoulders.

'Carole. Yes.' Fran didn't wince as the team at the station had, but she hesitated again. 'She was stabbed three times in the abdomen and stomach, and then stamped on. Hard enough to rupture an ovary, and her spleen. Her skirt was set on fire.'

'The worst attack,' Marnie agreed. 'Until Kyle.'

'Because he died? I'm not sure I'd downgrade what happened to Carole on that basis. And Rawling could've suffered a stroke. Head trauma is unpredictable.'

'If we're looking for a connection,' Noah said, 'something personal – nasty – that happened to Carole? Take your pick. But she wouldn't talk about it, not even the obvious injuries. If we're looking for something smaller, damage we couldn't easily see? I don't think she'll give it up.'

'She kidnapped a toddler.' Fran was making a fresh mug of tea. 'Held him for a month. Hurt him. Bullied him . . . But the ruptured ovary was part of an indiscriminate attack. I'm not sure we can call it payback, not of the kind we're looking at with Stuart and Kyle.'

'Very little of what Carole did was made public,' Marnie said. 'If our vigilante did something subtle then it could mean he has access to court records.' Colin's unpopular theory. 'Or he was there, eleven years ago.'

'Ollie Tomlinson,' Noah said.

Ollie was the toddler kidnapped and bullied by Carole. He was fifteen years old now.

'If the ruptured ovary was deliberate then it could be

punishment of the kind we're talking about. Tying the assault directly to the original conviction.' Noah rubbed at his cheek. 'Punishment, or justice. Whatever our vigilante imagines he's meting out.'

'We should speak with Carole and Stuart again.' Marnie stood. 'See what secrets they've been keeping. Other than the ID on our suspect . . . Neither of them would describe their attacker.'

'The head trauma,' Fran said as a parting shot. 'Stuart may not have seen much. Blunt trauma doesn't need to be life-threatening to throw your vision out of whack.'

'That doesn't explain Carole's silence.' Noah buttoned his coat. 'The attacker stayed away from her face and head. She's keeping secrets. If the attacks are personal, if there's a dialogue involved? Torture, punishment . . . Maybe that's why she's so terrified.'

'We should re-interview the pair of them.' Marnie nodded at Fran. 'Good work. We have a stronger case for connecting the assaults now. It's not DNA, but it's distinctive.'

'I've got the easier job,' Fran said. 'Interviewing the corpse. Kyle will give up his secrets, eventually. Good luck getting what you need from your two.'

'She's right,' Noah said, as they were driving back to the station. 'How're we going to handle these new interviews with Carole and Stuart? Do we say we think their attacker killed Kyle? If the assaults are personal . . . I'd ask for protection, wouldn't you?'

Marnie took a moment to answer, her eyes on the traffic. 'Kyle's death was an accident. You heard Fran. Any one of them could've died the same way. Our vigilante's not on a killing spree. He wants these victims to live. Far easier to kill them, less chance of being caught, or ID'd.'

'D'you think they know him?'

'Possibly. We've been assuming it's the same attacker because we saw a pattern. Fran's given us a new reason for seeing one. Burning, piercing . . . But there's still no DNA. If our vigilante is getting up close and personal, I'd have expected *something*. Some trace evidence to link the crime scenes. We know there's no connection between the victims, no shared experience before the assaults. None of them served time together, none of *their* victims have anything in common.'

'You think we're looking for more than one vigilante?'

'I'm wondering if we need to widen our net. I'd like to take another look at *their* victims, even if only to rule them out. Rawling's ex-wife. The boy Kyle burned. The child Carole took—'

Her phone rang. She took the call hands-free, with the speaker on. 'DI Rome.'

'Sorry to be calling so soon.' It was Harry Kennedy. 'I need your help with something. In Lancaster Road.'

Marnie kept her eyes on the traffic, hyper-alert to the cars ahead and behind. Aware of Noah at her side, sitting with his head turned away, giving her space for the conversation. 'Can it wait? My GBH is a murder now.'

'Of course. Whenever you have time.'

Her thumbs pricked. 'Is it worse than you thought? Alan and Louise. Still GBH or—'

'Still GBH. No better, no worse. It can wait.'

'I'll call you.'

'Thanks. Good luck.' Kennedy rang off.

The traffic kept her busy, saved her from landing too hard on the idea that he wanted her inside the house. Her mouth dried. She couldn't do that – break the promise she'd made to herself never to go back there. Without even Welland to understand, or to stop her. She couldn't.

'That was DS Kennedy,' she glanced at Noah. 'With Trident. Do you know him?'

'No.' He moved his right hand, but didn't touch her. 'No, I don't think so.'

'You heard about the break-in at my place.' She wanted to make this easy for Noah, or as easy as it could be. 'That's what Kennedy's investigating.'

'Yes, I'm sorry.' He took a breath. 'I should've said, when you asked about my chat with Welland—'

'I'm glad you didn't.' She found a bright smile from somewhere. 'I'd prefer to keep this on a professional footing. Luckily DS Kennedy's picked up on that vibe . . . Let's talk with Kyle's mates from the office, find out why he was in Page Street last night.'

'He should've been on a train home according to his mum. But he kept irregular hours. They weren't surprised when he didn't come back.'

Noah's phone played the theme tune from *The Sweeney*.

'DS Jake. Yes, we are . . . No, that's okay, go ahead.' He switched to conference call, thumbing at the volume control.

Ron was saying, '. . . porn mags, like we thought. And torn-up letters. A *lot* of torn-up letters. And did I mention the smartphones? Take a punt at how many his mum and dad junked in that bin.'

'From the Christmas-came-early vibe,' Noah said, 'I'm guessing it runs into double figures.'

'Close. *Seven*. Seven smartphones. Old models, but only just.'

'SIM cards?' Marnie asked.

'Intact.' Ron sounded triumphant. 'Colin's taking a look right now.'

'What about the letters?'

'We're seeing how much we can salvage. Might take a while.'

'They didn't want us to read them, or to find the phones.' Noah frowned. 'But they can't have been that scared about the content or they'd have burned the letters and flushed the SIM cards.'

'You're thinking like a detective,' Ron said. 'They're thinking like a mum and dad. They didn't know we'd intercept their bin. They were expecting the council to get shot of it all.'

'True,' Noah conceded.

'Good catch,' Ron said. 'We'd have missed this little lot if it wasn't for your eagle eyes.'

Marnie nodded at Noah. 'We need to speak with Evan Lowry,' she told Ron. 'The cabbie who found Kyle. And do we have the list of his drinking pals?'

'I'll text it over.'

'Thanks. And ask DC Tanner to dig out the files on the first victims. Rawling's wife, Valerie. Ollie Tomlinson. Mazi Yeboah. I want current contact details, and whatever else she can find.'

Three victims of the vigilante.

Three victims of the *victims*.

The case was growing heads, like a hydra.

10

Finn heard the key in the front door and even though he'd heard it tons of times in the last ten weeks, the sound made him freeze up, goosebumps pinching his skin. He looked round the kitchen, checking everything was in its place. The bin by the back door, oven on, supper cooking. His throat was scratchy when he swallowed. He wanted to say he'd caught a cold, but he knew it was fear making his tongue fat, stopping him from saying anything that might get him punched, or worse. The goosebumps were another warning, his skin's way of screaming at him not to get hurt.

'There you are.' Brady had a carrier bag from the Spar.

Hundreds of Spars all over London. Finn had stopped trying to figure out where this house was. He knew Brady drove a long way because he'd been hungry by the time he was let out of the car, and he'd really needed a piss.

'Put this away, will you?' Brady handed Finn the bag. He'd brought the cold in with him, a smell like iron railings, litter and grit.

Milk in the bag and bread, grapes, Doritos, bog paper, wine. The usual shopping. No receipt to give any clue to where the Spar was, just a warning printed on the plastic bag about the dangers of suffocation. Finn put the shopping into the fridge and cupboards.

'What's for supper?' Brady wanted to know.

'Pasta. The one you like.'

Brady looked round the kitchen, taking his time, before fixing his stare on Finn. 'Have you showered?'

'Not yet. I wanted the hot water for the washing-up. I'll have one later.'

'You'd better,' Brady said. 'You stink.'

He pulled a grape from the bunch and threw it up into his mouth. Tipped his head back down and grinned with his wonky teeth. Ugly fucker. Scary, too. His teeth cast shadows.

'Sorry,' Finn said. 'I'll shower now, before supper.'

He ducked sideways, towards the stairs, fighting the urge to run, and the urge to check over his shoulder that Brady wasn't following.

Brady wasn't his real name, just the one Finn gave him that first night when he woke up here with his stomach growling because they'd driven miles from where Brady found him. He must've carried Finn into the house. He was squatting at the side of the bed when Finn woke up. The first things he saw were those wonky teeth grinning down at him.

Dad had taught him about perverts. Men who stole kids off the streets and did sick stuff to them before burying their bodies where they wouldn't be found. 'Fucking Brady,' Dad had said and it'd stuck in Finn's head afterwards when he was on his own, which was how Brady found him.

In the bathroom, he turned on the shower but didn't get undressed, standing with one foot propped to the door because there wasn't a lock. He hadn't washed that first week, thinking that's when Brady would do it, waiting until Finn was naked, with the water running to get rid of the mess. His heart ran a race whenever he was in the bathroom, even when Brady was out of the house. This was where he'd do it. Rape Finn and cut him into pieces to be put out for the bin man – that bastard in the beanie. It'd been ten weeks and Brady had shown no interest in seeing him naked, but that didn't change how sick he felt being in the bathroom, his tongue fatter than ever, stoppering his throat like a wet wad of meat.

Pasta for supper. *His* favourite. Finn wished he had the guts to spit in it, or piss in it. Dad would've done that. But Brady made Finn take the first mouthful ever since that time he added bleach to the stew. He'd thought it'd poison Brady, that he'd fall face-first into his supper and Finn'd be able to grab the keys and get free. *Stupid*. That's how he got the bruises. That was the night Brady made him kneel so long on the kitchen floor he couldn't hold it in and wet himself and even then Brady made him kneel, stinking of his own fear and thinking what Dad'd say if he was here, what Dad would do—

He'd nut Brady, for starters. Break his teeth, crack his skull open. No one fucked with Finn's dad, least of all a filthy pervert, a kiddy fiddler.

Steam crowded the bathroom, making him cough. His foot was jammed to the door. He should get it over with, strip and get in the shower, get clean as fast as he could. Couldn't go back downstairs until he was clean. Brady wasn't coming up here, didn't care whether Finn had his clothes on or not, only cared if he stank. And if the supper burned.

He took his foot away from the door, tripping out of his jeans and boxers, dragging his T-shirt over his head and getting into the shower, yelping because the water was running cold. He grabbed the shampoo and squelched it into his hand. Rubbed it everywhere and kept rubbing until the water washed it away.

He avoided looking at his body, at the bruises and the skinny whiteness, all the evidence that he was weak, useless, a stupid ten-year-old kid.

Shook himself like a dog and scrubbed a hard towel at his skin before dressing again, hopping on one foot when his jeans snagged, sobbing under his breath, tears coming from nowhere, making his nose burn and his throat close up worse than ever.

'Just fucking *let* me . . . Just come *on*!'

His shoulders hit the door. He dragged at the jeans, panicking, wishing he'd never taken them off. Stupid Gucci jeans that cost Dad a fortune and didn't fit any more and stank of piss even though he'd washed them twice, shrunk them probably, but he weighed less than he had ten weeks ago even with all the pasta, because he puked most days, mostly from fear, he was so scared—

'Just . . . *Please* . . .' He rubbed his eyes on his shoulder, new goosebumps there. This place was a prison, shitty food and threats, cold showers and clothes that didn't fit, didn't feel like yours. Being bored all the time, being scared.

'You're a stupid piece of shit.' He kicked at the empty leg of his jeans, feeling savage, feeling small. 'A stupid, worthless piece of *shit*.' Snot came out of his nose, salty on his top lip.

When he had it under control, he straightened and reached for the jeans, trying again to get dressed, slower this time, chewing the underside of his lip in concentration.

No good being angry. No use. At least being scared made him careful. Kept his head down, kept him wide of Brady's feet and fists, no matter how much he wanted the fucker face-down in his supper, choking. All that would have to wait. It would all have to wait.

He hauled the T-shirt over his head, shook it into place.

Lifted his face and looked in the mirror.

Steam had softened the glass, running into a mesh of streaks, like grey bars.

From downstairs, the sound of a cork coming out of a bottle of wine.

Suppertime.

11

In Lancaster Road, one of the street lights guttered like a candle. The Audi parked under it blinked from red to black as the light struggled off and on.

'Thanks for coming.' Harry Kennedy was waiting by the car in his grey suit, white shirt. 'I appreciate it.'

Marnie nodded, pulling her coat closer. 'How can I help?'

'The house. It's a mess. Hard to say what's been taken. If we could question Alan and Louise, it'd be easier. But neither of them's in any shape for it yet.'

Marnie turned to look at the house. Taped off, the way it had been six years ago. No frost then, just rain. Weeks and weeks of rain. But that day . . . the sun came out. Shining on her dad's car, and on the knife in the SOCO's poly bag. The pictures were like Polaroids in her head, freshly taken Polaroids; she had to shake each one to make it come into focus.

'You want me to check inside the house. See what's been taken.'

When Kennedy didn't speak, she turned to look at him.

'You've not been here in years.' His eyes were black in

the half-light. 'And in any case, I wouldn't ask you to do that. Crime scene photos, maybe. But not that.'

She waited for him to say what he did want. Why he'd called her here at the end of the day when the light was gone and it was hard to see – anything. In the houses across the street, slabs of yellow marked the lit rooms, carving pictures from furniture and the blue pulse of televisions, breathy patches of condensation on the windows. She should check on her flat, the place she rarely visited now that she was with Ed, make sure the heating was clicking on twice a day to keep it from turning into a block of ice. Places needed people living in them to keep the brick breathing and the air circulating, to stop the doors from swelling shut.

In Lancaster Road, all the houses were lit, save one.

It was going to freeze tonight, the cold like teeth against her cheek. The Audi's windscreen was already icing over. She shivered. 'I bet it's warmer, inside.'

Kennedy didn't have a coat. If he'd meant this conversation to take place out here, he'd have put on a coat. He wanted her inside the house, he just didn't want it to be his idea. Welland would never have allowed this to happen, not on his watch. He'd have physically blocked her view of the house with his bulk. But he wasn't here. Just Harry Kennedy, shivering because he'd left his coat in the car, expecting it to be warm inside the house. Fear circled its shark's fin in her blood. No good. She needed something better. Anger. This house had reverberated with her anger, once.

'You have the keys.' She moved in the direction of the police tape. 'I'm guessing.'

He followed, ducking under the tape when she held it for him. 'Yes.'

The gravel rolled under their feet, the way it had when

55

she was fourteen and trying to sneak home without waking her parents. Perfect perimeter security, better than a dog because gravel didn't sleep. She resisted the instinct to duck when she passed under the hanging basket above the front door, its smell – peaty, acidic – scratching at the exposed nerve of her memory.

Inside, shadows stirred, peeling away when the light clicked on, to crouch in the corners of the hall and at the closed doors to the living room, and kitchen.

He'd killed them in the kitchen.

If she could avoid going in there, she would.

'They came in the back door,' Kennedy reminded her. 'We've fitted a temporary lock.'

She nodded, not speaking. The stairs stretched up, their treachery still mapped in her head, the steps that creaked and the ones that groaned, making a pantomime of her ascent.

Six years ago, Stephen had sat on the third step – one of her safe, silent steps – red to the elbows with their blood. And his own; his right palm sliced open where the knife had jarred against her mother's breastbone, making his grip slip from handle to blade. They'd stripped him at the station, peeling off clothes that shed flakes from their already-drying blood. It can't have felt real to him, what he'd done. If it had felt real, he'd have been screaming, thrashing. He'd sat on the third step quietly, waiting for the police. Hearing – what? Mrs Poole, the neighbour, shouting in the street. The dinner burning on the stove. Blood stretching across the tiled floor, did that make a noise? In her head, it did. But perhaps Stephen only heard his own blood beating with whatever imagined threat or danger had driven him to kill the two people who'd tried hardest to help him.

'Sorry about the smell,' Kennedy was saying. 'Someone's coming to sort it out.'

It prompted her to breathe. She'd been holding her breath since the hanging basket. Faeces and urine. *That* kind of burglary. No stains on the hall walls, or carpet. No stains on the stairs. The agency had re-carpeted, six years ago, painting over the stains before putting the house on the rental market because she wasn't ready to sell, dogged by the idea that it held clues she'd missed. Alan and Louise Kettridge had been living here ever since.

'Which room were they attacked in?'

'Alan was on the landing. He confronted them, that's how it looks. Louise was in the back bedroom.' Kennedy paused. 'No sexual assault. Just a beating, the same as Alan got.'

Marnie nodded, but didn't move. In her head, the Polaroids kept popping, like pins. Vicious little bursts of light and dark. Memories, on the blink. She wanted to reach for the wall, something to hold onto just for a second, until she got her balance back. Stupid—

Six years. It had been six years. But he was there on the stairs, a skinny fourteen-year-old with their blood all over him. And she was the same age, trying to sneak home. Tasting of tequila and cigarettes, a half-prepared lie in her mouth, in case she was caught.

Kennedy touched a hand to her elbow, static tightening the skin inside her sleeve. 'Are you okay? We can—'

She broke the contact by moving a step deeper into the hall. 'What did you want to show me?'

'Upstairs. Look, this was a mistake.' His eyes darkened. 'I'm sorry—'

His remorse brought her anger into focus, like turning a dimmer switch the wrong way.

'You wouldn't have brought me here if you didn't need me.'

He searched her face, shook his head. 'No . . .'

'So show me.' She moved past him. Through the blood-soaked ghost on the stairs, and up. To the landing where Alan Kettridge had been beaten unconscious.

Spatter on the walls. A reek of faeces from her parents' bedroom at the back of the house. Her chest hurt, over-crowding with nostalgia. Six years ago: a white waffled bedspread, her mother's jewellery on the dressing table, Dad's red cardigan on the wardrobe door, and photos everywhere, her three-year-old face looking back at her from their bedside cabinets.

Kennedy stopped her going into the bedroom. 'Not there.' He nodded towards the bathroom.

She turned and saw the ladder. Dad's heavy-duty loft ladder, standing in position outside the bathroom door. The kind you pulled down on a pole, its steps leading up into the attic where she'd stored the boxes which she hadn't wanted in a warehouse. Clothes, and books. Nothing valuable, just things she wasn't ready to look through and make decisions about. The agency had said it was fine, they'd tell the tenants not to use the attic, but—

'They went up there?' An alien sensation, her skin stiffening, resisting the pressure of the air from the hole above her. 'The gang . . . They went into the attic?'

'That's how it looks.' Kennedy kept his distance. 'Fingerprints on the ladder that match our gang's. And footprints up there.'

'Did they take anything?'

'That's what we don't know. The Kettridges didn't use the attic. No pressure marks on the carpet,' he pointed, 'and fresh plaster dust where the ladder came down.'

'The pole . . .' She looked for it.

'In the bedroom. They used it to hit Louise. Their prints are on it, the only fresh prints.'

'What were they after?'

'We don't know. We don't know what was up there.' He paused. 'They didn't take anything from down here. Both smartphones left in the bedroom. Televisions, laptops. Good stuff, expensive, and two of everything. They left it all.'

'Then it wasn't an initiation.' Marnie turned to look at him. 'It wasn't young kids.'

'The prints belong to kids. But they didn't come here to steal, or not the usual stuff. They came to beat up whoever was living here, and to make as much mess as they could.'

'Kids would take phones if they were in plain view. Don't you think?'

'Something's off,' he agreed. 'I've seen this sort of break-in before, but usually? It's a warning. And it's always personal. Blood, mess, fear. Marking their territory. If the Kettridges were rival gang members it might make sense. But they work in finance, and marketing. They're upwardly mobile thirty-somethings . . .' He stopped.

Blood, mess, fear.

Like a summing-up of her life. She felt his stare on her face and turned towards the ladder, remembering her father's advice to always wear gloves in case it trapped your fingers. The gang hadn't worn gloves. They hadn't come here to steal.

Usually a warning. Always personal.

Like the damage done to Kyle, and Stuart, and to Carole. Nasty. Private warnings whispered just for them, pierced through cartilage, burnt into eye sockets—

The ladder was sixteen steps of shiny aluminium, reaching into the dark.

What was up there? Nothing of value. Things only *she* cared about. Personal belongings. Why had the kids gone into the attic? Beating her tenants unconscious, defacing the walls, soiling the bedroom. For what? For *her*—?

'Talk to me.' Kennedy's voice was taut. 'Tell me what you're thinking.'

'I need to see up there.' She set her teeth. 'I need to see what they took.'

'Okay.' He pulled two pairs of crime scene gloves from his pocket. 'I'm coming with you.'

12

Dan was in the kitchen, taking steaks from the fridge, a cold bottle of Becks in one hand.

Noah watched him drink a mouthful, feeling thirsty. 'I hope there's another of those.'

'Here.' Dan snapped the cap on a second bottle. When Noah crossed the kitchen to take it, Dan caught his arm and pulled him close enough to kiss.

Noah held him off with his elbows. 'Eau d'morgue. I need a shower.'

'Hard day?'

'I've had better.' He'd had worse too, but the burn inside Kyle's eye had got to him. Torture. He knew how that felt, how scared Kyle must've been, how easy it was to fear for your life when a madman, or woman, had you trapped with no intention of letting you go. Did Kyle know he was going to die? Did the vigilante say as much when he struck the flint of the lighter?

Evan Lowry, the cabbie, hadn't been able to give them anything new. Kyle was bleeding when he'd found him. In shock, incapable of speaking and Evan didn't ask questions, busy calling for an ambulance and trying to keep

Kyle alive. He'd cried when Noah told him that Kyle had died. 'Poor sod, he was no older than my youngest. Thank God he didn't have kids . . . Tell his mum and dad I'm sorry, yeah?' A hard day, for everyone.

Dan was propped against the kitchen counter, one hand holding his blond fringe from his forehead, worry in his blue eyes. Wearing his favourite red T-shirt, faded to pink at the shoulders, tattered Levis slouching at his hips. 'We're going out later, yes? Only you look—'

'Bad day.' Noah put the Becks down, and smiled. 'Help me wash it off?'

Afterwards, as Dan was frying the steaks, Noah asked, 'No Sol tonight?'

Dan shook his head. 'I tried to get hold of him, but guess what? He's got another new phone. Old number's dead. Are you sure your little brother doesn't have shares in Sony?'

Noah cut lemon wedges for their plates.

Sol's sixth phone in a month. Upgrades, or something worse? Gang members changed their phones daily, afraid of surveillance. Eight months ago, Sol had said he was getting out, shaking off the last ties to the gang he'd run with since they were kids. What would Trident's DS Kennedy make of Noah's brother? Was Sol on his radar? He'd been close to any number of crimes, always swearing he stood wide of the serious stuff. Thank God he'd never served a custodial sentence, since their vigilante appeared to be targeting Londoners with violent pasts.

'Eat,' Dan instructed. 'You look wiped out.'

Noah did as he was told, reminding himself that he didn't do this – bring his work home with him. Except this was different. This was Sol.

'D'you want to talk about it?' Dan asked.

'Sorry.' He shook his head. 'I'll be better after I've eaten.'

'Okay.' Dan spun a sprig of watercress between his fingers. 'But you can talk. I do listening as well as cooking.'

'I know you do. You're a man of many talents. I noticed that in the shower.'

'Nice detective work.'

The gleam in Dan's eyes lifted a weight from Noah's shoulders.

'This?' He held up a forkful of steak. 'Is amazing. Sol doesn't know what he's missing.'

Scarfing a burger somewhere, probably. The finer things in life had never held much sway over Sol. Still, as long as he was safe and staying out of trouble.

'How was *your* day?' Noah asked. 'Still heading off early tomorrow?'

'Train's at six-twenty.' Dan was curating an art exhibition in Manchester. 'I'll bike it to the station.'

'I can give you a lift.'

'Thanks, but I need the bike at the other end. And I wouldn't want you to be late for DI Rome.'

'Marnie,' Noah amended. 'Seriously. If we're going drinking with her and Ed, it's Marnie.'

The four of them had a long-standing drinks date. Marnie's idea but the date kept changing, not easy to find a chink in their wall of work for letting off steam.

'You wouldn't rather have them round for dinner?' Dan drank a mouthful of beer. 'I could cook us something so amazing she'll want to promote you.'

'I know you could. But then she'd have to return the favour, and she doesn't cook. I don't think Ed does either. They live off Kettle Chips as far as I can tell.'

'Maybe we should get them together with Sol.'

'If we knew how to get hold of *him*.'

'DI— *Marnie* could trace his latest phone.'

Noah shook his head. 'Not her style.'

'Bet she knows someone who could, though.'

True. Harry Kennedy would be all over that. He'd wanted Marnie in Lancaster Road. Was she there now? Noah steered his thoughts in another direction.

'I'll wash, you dry.'

'Like the shower?' Dan shone a smile at him. 'You're on.'

13

'Nothing?' Kennedy stood with his head bowed under the pitch of the roof. 'You're sure?'

'No, I'm not sure.' Marnie looked again at the boxes stacked in a barricade around the opening to the attic. 'It was a long time ago, and I had a lot on my plate.'

'At least they didn't make a mess up here.' Kennedy waited a beat before adding, 'I wouldn't have put you through that.'

'You wouldn't have had a choice. This is a crime scene. It was then, and it is now.' She turned before he could answer, climbing back down to the landing.

Kennedy followed, peeling off the gloves when he was at her side. Marnie kept hers on, moving past him, towards the back bedroom. This time, he didn't try and stop her. She knew she was giving out a spiky vibe. The boxes in the attic— Smelt of her mother's perfume, her father's books.

She wanted to see what the gang had done here last night. Focus on the new crime, one which might be solved with or without her help. She wanted the past back in its box where it belonged. This wasn't her parents' home any longer. It was Alan and Louise's.

The back bedroom was in chaos, glass on the floor from a ruined dressing table, wardrobe tipped and spilling clothes onto the stained floor. Ripped curtains at the windows, holes kicked in the bedside cabinets, stains on the walls. A light icing of forensic powder over everything. Her pulse slowed, seeing the mess. It made sense, in a way the attic's untouched boxes did not. Burglary. Brutal, mindless. It followed a pattern she recognised, and understood.

'You said you found two phones in here.'

'Yes.' Kennedy came to stand at her shoulder. 'One on each night stand.'

'Did they smash the phones?'

'No. They were on the floor, but the screens were intact.'

'They smashed everything else.'

'Yes, they did.'

Like Marnie and Noah's vigilante. Smashing bones and faces but taking nothing, making it easy for the police to identify the victims. Wanting the victims known.

'How many kids were involved, do you know?'

'Five separate sets of prints.'

'And you're sure they were kids?'

'Small prints. Five sets of trainers, the biggest a size six. That's small, unless they were girls.' Kennedy brushed dust from his dark hair. 'I don't think girls did this.' He meant the smell, the spray pattern. 'It explains why there was no sexual assault, if the boys were pre-pubescent; older kids would've done more damage. In that sense, your tenants were lucky. They took a battering but it's nothing that won't mend. In time.'

'May I see their medical reports?'

'If you think it'd be useful.'

'It's your investigation,' Marnie said. 'I'm just curious

about the motive here. No theft but a warning, you said. Personal.'

'That's how it looks.'

'Show me the other rooms. Or is all the mess up here?'

'They wrecked the kitchen, and the living room. Smashed the mirrors in the bathroom. The only room they didn't touch was the front bedroom.'

Her room. And Stephen's. Pain tugged its long leash, making her fingers twitch. So much for the past staying in its box. The house had put its ears back when she'd entered, the way it had always done. She'd always hated this house, and the feeling had been mutual. Even her bedroom with the wall she'd painted red one winter, making a bad job of it because she was angry—

'Let's start there.'

The red wall had been whitewashed, the shadow of her bad paint job sitting stubbornly under the new topcoat. A shelf still ran above the bed. The tenants had put up a trio of canvases printed with yellow sunflowers. The bed was a sofa now. A desk by the window, with a lamp and a square vase filled with red beads. Perhaps it was the beads making the wall glow pink.

'Spare room,' Kennedy said. 'Not much here worth wrecking. Or they ran out of time.'

Or they were told not to touch this room.

Whole days when she'd not moved from the bed, watching time come and go on the other side of the window. Rigid with wanting to get up, get out. Numb with misery. Tracking the shadows across the ceiling, waiting for the moment when the light hit the crack in the window and dazzled a kaleidoscope of colour into the room. Stephen had slept here, opposite the wall she'd painted in a fury. Under the shelf with her books and boxes, the things she left behind when she got away.

They were told not to touch this room.

She switched off the thought, going ahead of Kennedy, back down the stairs.

The sitting room was a jumble of overturned furniture, books thrown from shelves, framed prints pulled from the walls, a leather sofa ripped open by a knife. In here, the vases had been smashed, glass beads flung to the far corners of the room.

The kitchen—

She had to summon anger to get herself through the door. Into the room where their bodies had been found. Soapsuds on Dad's clothes, his sleeves rolled up from washing the car. The base of a saucepan burnt out on the stove; Mum's supper a charred, sticky mass.

Nothing as terrible as that, now. Just glass and china, a microwave heaped full of its own broken door. Food pulled from the fridge, a low tide of sour yoghurt and milk. She'd expected to see the back door reinforced with metal sheeting, but its glass panels were intact. Of course, Kennedy had said the gang crowbarred it.

Standing under the bright ceiling lights – too many, too hot – she felt her pulse slowing again. Because it was possible to stand here without breaking down? Because she'd survived as something other than a victim? As a detective. No, it was more than that.

No one was dead. Alan and Louise had taken a battering but they'd heal, in time. If they were lucky, even the nightmares would fade. The house—

A lot of the furniture would need replacing. New paint, new carpets. The place looked mugged. Ugly. That brought its own relief, bittersweet and sharp. Six years ago, she'd wanted to take a hammer to the walls to uncover the reason for what Stephen had done. Last night's gang had done what she could not. Their destruction, their *hate* was how she'd felt six years ago and it felt good, now, to see the house so injured. Evidence everywhere of the violence committed. No mockery of order, no sneering tidiness. She *preferred* it like this, stinking and ruined. It was honest. A truth she'd always felt but could never see, until now. Growing up—

How often had she wanted to wreck the place? Kick holes in its walls, break the smug lines of its face. Her gaoler, her enemy. The gang's radical makeover was like a lost puzzle piece, the bit that made sense of all those years of misery, rage, impotence.

As if the house was showing her its true face, finally.

Walking back to their cars, Marnie asked, 'The gang you're after. Do they have a name?'

'The Crasmere Boys.' Kennedy shivered. 'If I'm right. We're hoping for some help from Zoe Marshall's lot on that front.'

'Zoe Marshall?' Marnie didn't recognise the name.

'She works for Ground Up. Private mediation company with strong links to local communities, open lines of communication . . . They pitch in when the people we need to talk to don't trust us. Which is all the time. Zoe's great. Young, smart, takes no prisoners. Bags of compassion, too. Kids love her, even the bad ones.' He shivered again. 'Especially the bad ones.'

'You think she'll know who did this?'

'It's a long shot. Fingerprints gave us nothing. Another reason the gangs use young kids. No criminal record, first offence.' He didn't shrug, looking serious. 'We've got about two hundred gangs active in London right now, with

SARAH HILARY

around four thousand members. Plenty of them flossing
– showing off their Rolexes to recruit new blood.'

'You've got a job for life.'

He acknowledged her irony with a quirk of his mouth.
'Thirteen hundred arrests in under two years. Less than
a hundred firearms, not even a quarter of a million in
cash. Tip of the *Titanic* stuff. On the other hand, don't ask
me for statistics on teenagers killed in knife attacks.'

'No need, I know them by heart.' She paused. 'I want
to visit Alan and Louise, tell them how sorry I am this
happened. Would you have a problem with that?'

'None whatsoever.'

'Thanks.' She nodded. 'I'll be in touch.'

They scraped ice from their windscreens, the house
standing in darkness at their backs, its empty eyes watching
as they drove in opposite directions, away.

14

Finn scraped the plates into the bin, shaking sticky red tubes of pasta from the fork. His stomach heaved, but he kept it down. He'd puke later, when Brady was sleeping. He was at the table now, finishing off the wine. Finn had to keep his glass topped up. A test, to see if he'd make a mess. Then Brady'd have an excuse to punish him. He liked an excuse to do that, pretending it was Finn's fault, that he'd brought it on himself. Twisted, but that's who Brady was.

Finn tried to think what Dad would do, right this minute. It was a game he'd played at home: 'What would Dad do?' Usually, Finn ended up arguing, shouting. That helped for a bit, felt like he was filling the hole in the house. Loads of times he'd covered his ears and hidden under the duvet when Dad was kicking off. But after he'd gone, Finn was the one shouting, because the house felt wrong. Too quiet, too *normal*. Because it was up to him to fill the Dad-sized hole.

No point doing what Dad would do here, with Brady. He'd get the belt again – and who hit anyone with a belt? When Dad hit, he used his fist. Quick and hard and then it was over and everyone was sorry, could say sorry, and get on.

Brady taking the belt out of his trousers? Went on forever. Unbuckling, pulling it out a loop at a time, doubling it over in his hands, tugging it flat. And looking at Finn all the while, pointing him at the floor, to his knees. That wasn't normal. That wasn't *losing-your-temper*. It was slow and cold and a million times worse than Dad who only ever did it when he wasn't thinking and who'd always been sorry after. Brady wasn't sorry. Brady wanted to do it again.

Watching Finn refill his glass, waiting to see if he'd mess up. He didn't, even though his hands were sweaty like his armpits. He hated the hard stink of the wine. Kept his eyes off Brady's face. Thinking of the sea, that time Dad took him down for the day, 'That's where we used to park our bikes,' showing him the pier and the new paint for the cycle lane that hurt Finn's feet because he'd taken his sandals off too soon, couldn't wait to get down onto the beach where the pebbles hurt worse but then Dad scooped him under one arm and ran with him, bellowing, down to the sea, 'Sink or swim!' launching him in, saltwater burning Finn's nose until he laughed it back out again, Dad's hands slapping the water and Finn slapping back so the whole sea was rocking around them before they started to swim, smoothing it flat with their arms. The dull grey roll of it like the whale that got stranded and couldn't turn itself in time so those men came and tore out its teeth for trophies. 'Dirty bastards,' Dad said, and they were. The sea wide and grey and rolling but never quite far enough, always back for more the next day. Finn with his blue bucket and spade, Dad in his tennis cap with the green visor. Sun behind the clouds but hot enough to burn, his legs too tight inside their skin, freckles all over Dad's nose.

'Close the bin.' Brady, at the table, drinking wine. 'It stinks.'

Watching Finn, hoping he'd cry. He'd cried on the third day. Not the first, or the second. He'd been too weirded out, and stupid from the stuff Brady gave him to make him sleep. Thinking it was a game, even thinking it was a foster home. He didn't ask any questions, not the right ones, just stuff like, 'Where's the toilet?' and, 'Can I call my mum?'

On the third day, he realised what Brady had done. Kidnapped him. Taken him off the streets where he'd been with a bunch of mates just hanging out, smoking, some cans maybe. Nothing serious. Not like a *gang* or not really. Just kids, they were all just kids. But only Finn got lifted. One of the others must've seen something. Okay, so they'd been drinking but they weren't falling down. Someone must've seen something and known it wasn't right. One of them must have told someone, not the police obviously but *someone*. On the third day he cried because he knew what it was and he was scared Brady was going to hurt him, cut him up, kill him. Brady sat and watched him cry and didn't try and stop him, didn't say stuff to make him feel better. Finn had thought he'd try that, lies to keep him quiet. Or else threats, to make him shut up. Instead he just sat and watched Finn with snot coming out of his nose, wiping at himself, *begging*—

'Get the washing-up done,' at the table now, drinking wine, 'then you can go to bed.'

Finn jerked his head in a nod, keeping his back to Brady.

He wasn't scared of being jumped, not any longer.

He was scared of Brady's eyes, the way they watched.

Like those men on the beach who'd waited for the whale to die.

Watching for hours and hours.

Waiting to dig out its teeth as trophies.

15

Valerie Rawling had olive eyes and a pale mouth, sleek black hair cut close to her jaw, feathered over her ears. From what they knew of her husband's cruelty, Noah guessed it was a wig. In the photograph taken for her firm's website, she was smiling, lips pressed shut.

'She's a marketing manager now,' Debbie said. 'For a beauty company. Lives in Lincoln, I've got an address and phone number. So that's Stuart's victim, eight years on.'

She moved to the next photograph, of a good-looking young African man.

'Mazi Yeboah was fourteen when Kyle set fire to his blazer. He suffered second-degree burns to his back and shoulders, needed a skin graft. He's twenty-four now, living in Barnet with his girlfriend and working for a local charity.'

The photo showed Mazi at a fund-raiser, grinning broadly. He wore a red tracksuit zipped to the neck, hiding the damage done a decade earlier by Kyle, and Jack Goodrich.

'That leaves Ollie Tomlinson.' Ron nodded at the third photo. 'Did we ever find out the full extent of what Carole did to him?'

Debbie glanced at Marnie who nodded. 'Go on. You know as much as any of us.'

'Ollie was taken ten days before his fourth birthday from a supermarket car park in Harrow. His mum had strapped him into the child seat while she was returning the trolley. She only glanced away for a second, but when she looked back he was gone. She doesn't remember seeing anyone near the car, or following them in the supermarket. She was sure Ollie would've shouted if it was a stranger, because she'd taught him to do that. But he didn't make a sound, not even when she called his name. He'd have shouted back if he'd heard her. Unless someone had a hand over his mouth.' Debbie stopped, blinking at the board. 'So she thought it must've been someone he knew, or someone who'd planned it. He was a strong little boy; she had trouble getting him into the car seat if he didn't want to go. He'd kick and shout at her. She couldn't believe he hadn't kicked and shouted at Carole.'

Fifteen-year-old Ollie glared at them from the board, crop-headed, sloe-eyed. High cheekbones and a Viking nose, mouth thinned to a dark, contemptuous line. Nothing like the cherubic toddler whose face had been shown to the public eleven years earlier.

'He was with Carole for four weeks before the police traced him. She'd fed him on raw pasta and tissues. He was malnourished, dehydrated, anaemic. Bruises around his wrists and ankles where she'd tied him down. No sexual assault. Paramedics described him as spacey but not obviously traumatised. He wasn't crying or shaking. He let them check him for injuries and evidence of abuse. Thorough checks. The medical report called him a very passive, pliant little boy, keen to do as he was told. Wanting to be told what to do.'

Debbie studied the picture of Ollie. 'As if she'd trained him, that's what his mum said. As if Carole had taken her kicky little boy and trained him to be obedient, the way you'd train a dog.'

'He grew out of it.' Ron folded his arms. 'The obedience. He's been in trouble of one kind or another for the last four years. Excluded from school for chucking chairs at staff. Nicked for shoplifting, kick and run, you name it. I can see him setting fire to Carole's skirt, no trouble.'

'And he's in Islington,' Debbie said. 'The Jonas House estate, not too far from where Carole was attacked. How he knew she *was* Carole is another matter. From what the psychiatrists said he'd no memory of those four weeks. She'd moved away, altered her appearance. Ollie's off the rails right now but there's no sign he's capable of that kind of detective work, or even motivated to do it.'

'Jonas House's a ghetto, full of thug life. Any one of them could've attacked a single woman walking alone at that time of night.' Ron pointed a trio of fingers at the board. 'This's my problem with the whole thing. These three were all in dodgy parts of town after dark, alone. Harder *not* to get attacked when you treat London like some massive after-hours playpen.'

'Page Street isn't dodgy,' Noah said. 'And the way our victims were hurt? Burning, piercing . . . We've got a better reason now for seeing a link to a vigilante, or a group of vigilantes.'

'Arseholes R Us?' Ron wasn't convinced.

None of them were, except Noah. Marnie was going to have to fight to keep the team together on this, especially with Welland out of the picture. He might not have agreed with her vigilante theory, but he'd have backed her to the hilt.

'Can we have an update on Kyle's smartphones?' she said. 'The ones his parents threw out?'

'Some interesting texts.' Colin took a set of print-offs from his desk. 'About meeting up, partying. I've printed what I could get.' He handed out the copies. 'Nothing that's jumping out as a motive for his murder, or even a solid reason for him to be in Page Street last night.'

Marnie scanned the data in silence. They all did.

'I've put a list of numbers on the same page,' Colin said. 'Some names there, but not many. No surnames. An Adam and a Tina, couple of Jacks. Nothing that's lighting any databases yet. I'm cross-checking with the other victims, and everything else we've got.'

'Wasn't Jack the other kid who set fire to Mazi's blazer?' Ron looked up from the list. 'The one Kyle's dad called a thug?'

'Jack Goodrich.' Debbie nodded. 'Did they keep in touch? His parents said not.'

'If he was running with Goodrich he'd have kept it a secret, at least from his mum and dad.' Ron picked up the pen and wrote *Jack Goodrich* on the whiteboard. 'Gerry was sure he'd learnt his lesson, but maybe Kyle liked being in a bad crowd. We know he was travelling, clubbing.' He nodded at Colin's list. 'That fits with what you've found on the phones.'

'I'm assuming he had apps on the phones,' Noah said. 'Can you print me a list? And match it to the phones and texts, so I can see which apps he was using on which phone?'

Colin nodded. 'I can do that, easily.'

'Any idea why he had so many handsets?' Marnie asked. 'I can see he might've wanted a number his parents didn't know, but seven phones? Eight, counting the one we found on him.'

'Overkill,' Colin agreed. 'And the style of the texts is different. On one phone he's using emoticons, on another he's not even using text speak – spelling everything out very precisely. It makes me wonder if the phones belong to other people, and Kyle was just holding them.'

'Or he nicked them,' Ron said. 'That'd be our first thought, bagging a stash like this. The only reason we've not thought it's because Kyle's dead and we're coming at it from the victim angle. But maybe he was sending threats, blackmailing people.'

It was becoming harder and harder to like Kyle Stratton. Stuart had been bad enough, a bully and a wife beater. And Carole, who'd kidnapped a child and treated him like an animal. So much easier to work on cases where you had sympathy for the victims.

'Any luck making sense of the letters?' Marnie asked.

'His dad did a good job of shredding them.' Colin polished his spectacles with his tie. 'All in the same hand-writing, though. I'm still piecing them together.'

'Blackmail,' Ron said, 'maybe.'

'Or love letters?' Debbie suggested. 'Wouldn't his dad have said if letters kept turning up for him? And if they were threatening letters, he'd have handed them to the police, not torn them up.'

'Ask them. I'd like to know whether we're digging at a dead end.' Marnie nodded at Debbie and Colin. 'Good work. Text me the photos and addresses for Ollie and the others. DS Jake and I are going to talk with Kyle's workmates about what happened at the pub last night.'

Outside, the cars were frozen shut. Noah couldn't remember a winter as hard as this one. He scraped the windscreen while Marnie tackled the locks with a cigarette lighter. The cold clutched at everything. Behind them, the police station twinkled madly, a penitential ice palace.

Noah's breath hung in the air, like Marnie's. He watched her work the lock free from ice, alert for signs of stress, given what was happening at her house. She hadn't talked about Harry Kennedy and whatever he'd wanted from her last night. Noah hoped she was talking to Ed, not keeping the stress to herself. This case was tough enough without that. The team fractious, unsure which direction to take. Marnie would keep them on track, he knew, but it wouldn't be easy.

'The texts,' he said when they were seated in the car, waiting for the heaters to clear the windscreen. 'Those names. Adam, Tina, even Jack—' He stopped.

'I wondered about Tina. Street name for methamphetamine, isn't it?'

'And Adam's MDMA. Jack could be heroin.'

'Captain Jack,' she murmured. 'What Colin would call pre-*Torchwood* appropriation.' She turned to look at Noah. 'You think Kyle was a drug dealer?'

'Not necessarily. But we should get a full tox screen from Fran.' He rubbed the cold from his hands. 'In a couple of the texts he spelt parTy with a capital T. I'm guessing . . . PnP. Party and play. Kyle might have been into the gay scene. Chemsex, even.'

'Educate me?' Marnie negotiated the thinly salted tarmac to exit the car park.

'The short version? Two or more of you hook up on a dating app for a party involving a lot of drugs, usually crystal meth or mephedrone or GHB, and a lot of sex.'

'That's why you asked Colin for the list of apps,' Marnie deduced. 'Is there a particular app we should be looking into?'

'That'd be nice and simple, wouldn't it?' Noah shook

his head. 'I can name six, without trying too hard. And I don't keep up to speed with this stuff.' Having Dan, he meant, being monogamous. It was a long time since Noah had been on the dating scene. 'Clubs are closing all the time, with everything moving online. Dating, drugs . . . Chemsex can be risky. Health officials woke up to it late, but there's been a lot of alarm in the last year or so. Some of it's unwarranted, but not all. The argument veers between hedonism and disinhibition. I've got friends who think it's set gay rights back by half a century; a lot of homophobia's built into the hardcore dating apps, boxes you can tick to set the levels you find acceptable, and the ones you won't tolerate. Still . . . there's no evidence Kyle was partying like that.'

'Except the texts.' A frown hollowed Marnie's cheek.

The traffic was painfully slow, an ice-bound creep towards Westminster. Pedestrians in extra layers picked their way up gritted pavements, looking stunned by this long spell of winter.

'When you were with his parents,' Marnie said, 'did you get any sense they might've known he was taking the partying too far? You said his dad insisted he'd learnt his lesson after Mazi.'

Noah thought back to the conversation in Kyle's bedroom. Gerry's anger just below the surface, the strange tension in the house, resisting their questions. 'It could be as simple as them not liking the fact Kyle was gay. Not wanting us to see his phone records, or read his letters.'

'Could it explain eight smartphones?'

'Not unless he was hooking up with people he couldn't shake off, and that's not PnP as I understand it. It's more a question of being lucky if you see the same face twice, or if anyone remembers your name. Assuming you gave it out in the first place. Plenty of people like the freedom of that anonymity. Eight smartphones might mean Kyle was playing at being eight different people, for eight strangers. Not necessarily sinister.'

'No other clues at the house?' Marnie flexed her fingers at the wheel. 'In the light of the texts?'

'Nothing. But he wasn't living there, just using it as a hotel.'

'Let's see what his workmates have to say. Even if he wasn't over-sharing, they may've picked up on something. I'd like to know how closely our vigilante was watching him.'

'Ron was right about one thing,' Noah said. 'All our victims behaved recklessly. With Stuart, we could put that down to arrogance. But Carole? You'd think she'd know better.'

'That could be the legacy of her time inside.' Marnie's cheek hollowed again. 'Everyone imagines prisoners are hyper-alert, but emotional disconnection is a decent survival strategy.'

'And our victims weren't exactly made of human kindness to begin with . . .' Noah watched a couple of kids march past, hooded heads down, phones clutched in gloved hands. The cold made everyone move faster in a bid to keep warm. 'We're assuming our vigilante was a victim at some point, but perhaps he's emotionally disconnected too. Someone who wants to lash out, choosing ex-cons because that's how he justifies the violence to himself.'

'Perhaps. But let's rule out the obvious candidates. Anyone with a personal grudge against our victims.' She parked up outside the sleek plate-glass office block. 'Starting with Kyle.'

Kyle had worked in an office designed, Marnie imagined, for optimum productivity. Windows sealed shut and tinted

81

to keep out distracting views. Ambient air, colourless, odourless, tasteless. Desks in a complicated configuration which a consultant had doubtless prescribed for a happier, more engaged workforce. Posters added slabs of colour. Pot plants were a concession to nature negated somewhat by the sheen of furniture polish on their leaves.

Kyle's manager was thirty-something in a Hugo Boss suit, comb tracks in his gelled hair. He'd set aside a meeting room for the interviews. 'Such a shock, for us,' glancing at his wristwatch, an Omega Seamaster as modelled by James Bond. If only everyone were as easy to read.

The meeting room smelt of stale coffee and stale air. Pop art prints of Battersea Power Station prompted memories of the crime scene which she and Noah had investigated eight months ago, back when London was thin rain and sunshine. It was nearly impossible to remember a time before this crippling cold. The sleek silver coffee machine was patchy with fingerprints. A clutch of remote controls – for lights, for sound, for air? – lay alongside. Everything adjustable, controllable.

The first person through the door was a carbon copy of the manager. Same gelled hair, same suit and watch (a fake, surely?), same words out of his mouth, 'Such a shock.'

Marnie had the sinking feeling that they were going to learn nothing here, other than how to clone a management consultant. Her phone buzzed before they'd reached the first question.

'Boss?' It was Ron, sounding urgent. 'Carole Linton.'

'Yes?'

'She's missing. Not answering her phone, not home. Neighbours haven't seen her in days, but they remember someone hanging around her place last week. Creepy, a couple of them said.'

'Description?'

'Yep. And guess what?' He wanted a prompt.

'Go on.'

'The creep's an absolute dead ringer for Ollie Tomlinson.'

Ron sucked a breath. 'I'd say we've found our vigilante.'

16

Finn couldn't stop shivering. His head was swimmy, making the room rock like he was in the haunted house at a funfair, one of those with the girls painted up the sides, big tits in tight bikinis, rocket launchers on their hips. 'Bacon butties,' Dad had said. 'Come on.'

The whole fair was lit blue and orange, stinking of fried fat and sugar, electricity burning so fast it made the ground buzz under Finn's feet. The noise was amazing and so were the butties, hot and greasy. They sat on the grass and saw a ride called the Sledgehammer smashing up and down with all the people caged inside screaming. Finn propped his elbows on the grass, skin stained blue, head pounding in time to the Sledgehammer. He was so happy. Itching all over from the grass and the colours that kept hitting him, but happy.

The ride brought the cages down, screaming faces right next to his, before scooping them back up, away. 'We should move,' Dad said. 'If they puke, it'll land right on us. Come on, I'll win you one of those big cats.'

Finn followed him through the crowd, towards the arcade. Three men at the rifle range, inked fingers, cropped heads. Soldiers. Arms slung around each other's necks, beer bottles hanging from their fingers. Finn felt clumsy, watching them. The noise of the fair rattled from his teeth to his feet, making the rack of prizes bounce, plastic eyes jiggling in the stuffed toys.

Dad won him the blue cat he wanted. 'Ghost train,' he decided next, passing Finn the prize by the scruff of its neck, googly eyes turned up like it'd died.

The ghost train was brilliant. 'What's red and green and silver?' Dad said. 'Zombie with forks in its eyes.'

Spray-on cobwebs stuck to Finn's hair. Halfway round the ride, a dummy lurched out in a black suit with bolts through its neck, arms glued round another dummy in a white coat, their faces melted together. 'Frankenstein,' Dad said. 'That's what you get for making monsters.'

When the ride stopped, they climbed out. Dad first, Finn following, lurching like the monster, his balance shot, ears wailing and popping.

'Mark Maples,' Dad said. 'First person to die on a Disneyland ride. Silly fucker stood up on the Matterhorn.' He was full of facts like that. Dead clever, Finn's dad.

Back in the caravan, Finn could see the funfair when he shut his eyes, neon pinwheeling through the black. Their clothes stank of onions and candyfloss. That was it. The last time Finn could remember being happy.

Never mind he was a prisoner now, trapped here with Brady.

He'd not been happy since that holiday, the haunted house, Dad winning him the big cat. He'd wanted to bring the cat with him when he ran, but it was too big. So he'd left it with the rest of his stuff in the house that'd been too quiet and empty since Dad went. In here—

Brady's house was hot, and cold.

Finn couldn't stop shivering. He didn't even care if

Brady thought it meant he was scared. He felt sick. Sweaty, his head swimming, a dead taste in his mouth. If he wasn't the one cooking all the food, he'd think Brady had poisoned him. But it wasn't drugs or poison or anything other than fear; he couldn't eat or drink without puking it back up because his gut was knotted so tight.

Brady had gone out, the way he always did, but Finn was too sick to try the locks in case this time he'd left the doors open. Brady had two keys for each door, locking the house back and front from the outside. Every day for the last ten weeks, Finn had checked both doors after Brady left, thinking maybe *this* time he'd forgotten—

Brady never forgot. Perverts were too careful. Finn had tried telling him, in those first few days, that he wasn't what Brady thought. He looked older than ten, he'd always looked older because he was skinny and tall and he had Dad's nose. He could pass for thirteen, easy. He'd thought if Brady knew he was just a kid, not even eleven, he'd let him go. Looking back, he didn't know why he'd thought that. It's not like perverts were picky. 'I'm only ten,' he'd said. 'I should be home with my mum. She'll be going spare.'

That was a lie, for starters.

Brady ignored him anyway, let him cry it out. When he stopped crying, Brady sat him down and gave him this set of rules, made him read it aloud to show he understood. Shit like—

If the house isn't clean, no food.

If I try to leave, the belt.

Twelve rules, all shit like that. Threats. 'You're lucky,' Brady said, 'I could put you in a fucking cage. I won't, though, as long as you follow the rules.'

Finn hadn't believed him until that first time with the belt, kneeling on the floor. Then he'd believed. He made himself repeat the rules under his breath when he was cleaning, and it was like that time Uncle Regan trained his dog until it rubbed its own nose in its piss without Regan having to do anything other than stand and watch. Finn used to cry for that dog, burying his face in the blue cat Dad won him, calling Regan a bastard, crying until the cat's fur was wet. That was a long time ago. The dog was dead by now. Regan would've drowned it. He was always threatening to drown it.

Dad said, 'Don't get mad. Get even.'

Whenever shit happened, bullies, threats, Dad said, 'Get even.'

Finn shivered, pulling his sleeves over his hands. He was behind with the cleaning, with everything. The bath dug in his chest when he leaned over to scrub it, pressing at him like an iron bar. He started shaking and the bath was full of black spots except it wasn't, it was just his eyes, burning. He opened his mouth and everything slid out, pasta and milk and toast and tea, slopping into the bath and splashing back up, specking his face.

He turned on the taps and watched the puke dilute, washing further into the bath, too far for him to reach without moving and he couldn't move because of the iron bar in his chest.

Hot water brought it all back to life, like the worst Pot Noodle ever.

He turned off the taps and pulled a towel from the rail to make a pillow on the floor.

His head was spinning, everything squirming.

The heating had clicked off ages ago.

It was cold on the floor, but Finn felt hot. Sick.

If Brady came home to a bath full of puke, he'd kill him. Then how would he ever get even?

17

'Ollie Tomlinson hasn't been to school in eight weeks,' Ron said. 'He's not home, no one's home. We're trying to reach his mum at work, and we've let the community support units know we're looking for him. So far no sightings since this one at Carole's last Saturday.'

'The neighbours who saw him hanging around there,' Noah said. 'How reliable are they?'

'I'd call it a hundred per cent.' Ron rapped a knuckle to Ollie's photo. 'That nose is distinctive. They didn't know who he was, of course. We've kept names out of it.'

Fifteen-year-old Ollie stared back at them from the board. At nearly six feet tall and broad-shouldered, by any physical standard he was an adult. Marnie studied his eyes, the contempt in his stare. It'd taken Stephen until the age of twenty to bulk up the way Ollie had, but his eyes were the same, had been for years. God knows what was going on inside Ollie's head. If he'd found the woman responsible for humiliating him eleven years ago, training him the way you'd train a dog—

'Let's find him,' she told the team. 'Speak with his

mum, see if he has an alibi for last night. And the other attacks. Even if he's tracked down Carole, it doesn't follow that he's involved in the other assaults. We have a murder investigation on our hands. Let's not get too distracted too soon.'

'Well said.' A woman was standing in the doorway, her head cocked. Fifties, silver-blonde, in a black trouser suit over a red shirt that matched her lipstick. 'DCS Ferguson.' Northern accent but she clipped it back. 'I'll be standing in for Commander Welland.' She came into the room. 'Carry on. I'll catch up.'

Noah glanced at Marnie. Was Welland sick? He'd looked dog-tired when he'd given Noah the news about her tenants. Marnie had pinned a polite smile in place, but he knew her too well to mistake the brief flare of hostility – or was it fear? – in her eyes.

'You were talking about our murder investigation. Kyle Stratton.' Ferguson was half a head shorter than Marnie but solidly built, carrying her age like an advantage. 'How's that looking?'

'We've recovered a number of phones, and correspondence which we're checking for evidence to suggest he was in contact with his killer, or engaged in anything likely to have provoked an attack. We have the initial post-mortem findings, and will have a full tox screen soon. His colleagues describe him as someone who liked a good time but kept it within limits. Never late for work, never less than reliable.' Marnie's dry tone said she hadn't taken this version of Kyle at face value.

Noah shared her scepticism. The management consultants had all hit the same note, between fun guy and fast-tracker. Kyle the careerist didn't ring true, given what else they knew.

'These are the colleagues who were drinking with him?'

DCS Ferguson nodded at the pictures of Kyle's shattered face. 'Did none of them leave with him?' She swung her eyes towards Noah. 'DS Jake, perhaps you could field that one?'

'They went their separate ways, ma'am. Kyle wasn't the first to leave, or the last. He was headed home, that's what they all believed. They saw him walking in the direction of Victoria Station. The last train to Reigate was eleven-forty p.m. The pub closed at eleven and he'd left five minutes earlier, in plenty of time to make that train if he'd wanted to. Page Street was a detour.'

'What's door-to-door throwing up?' Pivoting to the right. 'DS Carling?'

'We've got a team at it, ma'am, in Page Street. So far, nothing.'

Ferguson considered the photos on the incident board. 'Beaten with a blunt instrument brutally enough to cause fatal injury, and yet no one saw or heard anything?'

'Not until the cabbie,' Ron said. 'And he didn't see anyone running off.'

'So what theories do we have, aside from the vigilante?' Curling her lips on the last word.

'It could've been a random attack.' Ron straightened. 'That time of night, that part of London . . . It could've been kids, even.'

'But he wasn't robbed. Kids would've robbed him, unless you have nicer ones round here than we do in Manchester.' A smile like a footnote on her face. 'Do you?'

Ron shook his head. 'They might've got scared, run off—'

'Scared of what? If someone saw something, why hasn't door-to-door winkled them out?' She clicked her tongue. 'No recent texts to suggest he might've been on his way to meet someone? I know you're having fun with the older texts.'

If Marnie's tone was occasionally dry, Ferguson's was arid. Noah wondered if this was her way of making a forceful first impression. Had Marnie known she was being drafted in? Welland would have wanted her forewarned, surely. After the break-in at Lancaster Road this was the worst time for her to be without her chief ally. DCS Ferguson didn't look like anyone's ally.

'No recent texts,' Marnie said. 'But we'd like to question his parents about why they threw out the phones and destroyed the correspondence.'

'If he courted this trouble,' Ferguson put her brows up, giving herself a temporary facelift, 'how does that hang with your vigilante theory?'

Before Marnie could answer, she said, 'Come and update me later. I'll be in my office.'

Welland's office, she meant.

'I'd like to see some names on the board by the end of the day.' She turned on her heels, red-soled Louboutins with silver toe-studs, and made an exit that left Noah's teeth aching in his head.

All the eyes in the room moved to Marnie.

'Commander Welland is taking four months away from work for health reasons. DCS Ferguson is standing in.' She gave her steadiest smile. 'DS Carling, I'd like you to check in with the house-to-house unit, see where they're up to. DS Jake, let's ask some more questions in Reigate.'

'What about Carole, boss?' Debbie shook her head. 'If she's missing—'

'Let's establish that. From what the neighbours said she's often away from home. I don't want to jump to conclusions given our limited resources. Find out what

Ollie's been up to. See if you can get hold of Lisa Tomlinson. But the murder takes priority.'

She nodded at Colin. 'Work through the rest of whatever's on the phones, and do what you can with the letters. I'll ask Fran to fast-track the full tox screen. DS Jake?'

They were headed out when they were stopped by a couple coming into the station.

'I was hoping to catch you,' the man told Marnie. Tall and dark in a navy peacoat, his collar turned up against the cold. Carrying a plastic bag, its contents box-shaped. 'This's Zoe Marshall.'

Zoe held out her hand then said, 'Sorry,' pulling off a red mitten and offering the hand again. Her face was half hidden by a woolly hat, but she looked about Noah's age. An inch over five feet tall and slight, wearing a khaki parka and black biker boots.

'You must be DS Jake.' The man shook down the collar of his coat. 'Harry Kennedy, Trident.'

More handshaking. Harry had long fingers that went with the rest of him, lean and hard. He swapped the carrier bag to his left hand, holding it the way you held evidence, carefully.

Cold came off the pair of them.

Marnie said, 'I'm afraid we're on our way out.'

Noah heard the resistance in her voice and wondered if Harry knew her well enough to hear it too. She was good at compartmentalising, but it was impossible to do that when someone was standing between you and the exit holding what looked like evidence and with reinforcements, albeit in the small form of Zoe Marshall.

'Two things,' Harry said. 'Zoe's working with kids over in Islington.' He nodded at her.

'You're looking for one of them.' Her accent was north London. 'Ollie Tomlinson? Community Support asked if I'd seen him. I'm working with the kids at Jonas House. I've been worried about Ollie for a while.'

'When did you last see him?' Marnie asked.

'Three weeks ago, and he'd been in a fight. Cut knuckles and that . . . *swagger*, you know?' Zoe rubbed her nose. 'I knew he'd been up to something from the way he was strutting around, taking a swing at stuff. He'd nowhere to go after he got banned from the sports centre, which's a shame because he was letting off steam there. That's half the fight with these kids.'

'Why was he banned?' Noah asked.

'Stuff went missing. Footballs, golf clubs, gym kit.' She put her hands in her pockets. 'Basically anything not nailed down, and saleable. His mum always said if he'd got money he'd be up West spending it, but I don't know. He's one of those kids who likes to stay on his own patch. I'm worried no one's seen him in a while.'

'When was he banned from the sports club?'

'A couple of months ago? Maybe a bit longer. Around the time he started skipping school.'

Ten weeks ago Stuart Rawling's jaw had been broken by a golf club.

'And the other thing?' Marnie looked at Harry Kennedy. 'You said two things.'

He held up the carrier bag, its contents shaped like a shoebox. 'From Lancaster Road. I'm sorry, but you need to see this.'

18

In the interview room, Zoe pulled off her woolly hat and stuffed it into the pocket of her parka. Chestnut-brown curls, cut short, frizzed around her face. She pushed the curls behind her ears, wrapping both hands around the cup of coffee Noah had made. 'Thanks.'

'Don't thank me until you've tasted it. Station blend.'

They exchanged a smile.

'It's hot, that's all I care about.'

No rings on her fingers. Her ears were pierced but she wasn't wearing earrings, or any other jewellery. Her clothes were like Marnie's, gender-neutral, a long-sleeved grey jumper over black jeans and a white T-shirt that looked like it might be thermal underwear. Nothing showy, nothing for kids to grab at. If she was working at Jonas House, grabby came with the territory.

Noah said, 'Tell me about Ollie.'

She drank a mouthful of coffee before she answered. 'I'm supposed to say he's not a bad kid. That's how these statements usually start, and it's my job to see the good in them. But since Harry said you're handling a murder investigation, I don't want to waste your time.'

'You work with him a lot? DS Kennedy.'

'All the time. Ground Up's a mediation service but really it's about finding a way round the barriers these kids put up.' Her green eyes lighted a little. 'Not just kids, but that's the way it's been headed for a while now. Younger and younger. Ollie's one of the older boys. Fifteen's almost retirement age in gang terms.'

'How long's he been in a gang?'

'As long as I've known him. So nearly three years.' She drew the cuffs of her jumper over her hands. 'Okay, he *was* a good kid back then. A bit lost, you know? Looking for a place to fit in. His dad's gone, Mum's working hard.'

'What's she like?'

'Two kinds of mums. Those who cope, and those who cop out. Let the kids come and go while they get on with their own lives. Ollie's mum is a coper. Keeps the fridge full, cooks his favourite food, rolls with the punches.'

'Literal punches, or figurative?'

'Figurative as far as I know, but copers are good at covering up.' She sipped at the coffee. 'Three years ago, Lisa was tearing her hair out trying to keep Ollie on the rails. He was her good little boy and she didn't want to lose him to a gang.'

'Her good little boy,' Noah repeated.

Did Zoe know what'd happened to Ollie eleven years ago? How Carole took Lisa's child and trained him like a dog to be obedient? How long had the effect of that lesson lasted? Until he was twelve and running with a gang? How had it felt to see her kid turn kicky again? Was there a moment when Lisa was glad to have her rough little boy restored to her?

'He was an angel according to Lisa.' Zoe hooked her thumb at the lip of the mug. 'Never any trouble, always at her side. A shy boy, sensitive. I never saw that version of him. By the time I met Ollie, he was already kitting up. Scoping out the street, looking for a way in with the hardest gangs, carrying a knife—' She stopped. 'No, I'm wrong. The knife came later.'

'When did he start carrying a knife?'

'A year ago? He showed me. "Look, Miss. I got this for my birthday." He was pleased, had an ear-wide grin. I remember thinking, "You're lost," but I expect he didn't feel lost. He felt found.'

Talking about the knife had brought a grimness to her face. 'That's what it's like for these kids. A gang feels like family. They don't see the damage that's done, the broken ties, sometimes broken bones. They feel *whole*, for the first time. Trying to get them out when they're like that? Well, I don't know if you've ever tried to take a clingy child from its mum, but . . .' She shook her head.

Carole took Ollie from Lisa's car, silencing his shouts with a hand across his mouth.

'Lisa hasn't reported him missing,' Noah said.

'Possibly because she knows he isn't. If he's going home to be fed, or to wash . . . He might not be living there in any proper sense, but as long as she sees him often enough to be sure he's in one piece that might be enough. Copers hate involving other people. Lisa wouldn't go to the police unless she was scared something had happened to Ollie.'

'Only then? He's been carrying a knife for over a year. Isn't she worried he might be hurting other people, getting into that sort of trouble?'

'How would she know? If he came home covered in blood?' Zoe stopped, struggling for the first time with what she was telling Noah. 'All right. Let's be honest. Lisa's more than just a coper. She's a tiger mum. If Ollie came home covered in blood and none of it was his? She'd clean him up, and shut him up. I know that sounds bad, and so we're clear – pure speculation on my part. The worst I've seen her do is stick up for him when the neighbours said he was bullying younger kids. But she did it fiercely, way beyond protective. I remember thinking she'd stick up for him no matter what. So, no. I don't think she'd call the police unless she thought *he* was the one getting hurt. As long as he's okay, she'll keep quiet. Maybe she believes he's still her good little boy underneath it all.'

'But you don't.'

'I can't,' Zoe corrected. 'I wouldn't be doing my job if I indulged in that kind of fantasy.'

Noah saw the steel in her for the first time. She'd looked soft in the woolly hat and red mittens, like a young woman who might volunteer on the weekends, run charity races, talk about going to the jungle in Calais. But she wasn't soft. She had a runner's build like Marnie, slim and strong. Even the chestnut curls had a steely quality. 'Did you report the knife, when he showed it to you?'

'Yes.' She was unblinking. 'That's my job.'

'And you've not seen him in three weeks?'

She shook her head.

'Tell me about the sports centre,' Noah said. 'What exactly was taken, and why wasn't he arrested?'

'You'd have to ask them for a list. I don't know why they didn't press charges. They were sure it was Ollie and his gang, but I suppose they'd no evidence. It was a shame, even *they* said that. He'd been joining in, helping to organise a little league team.'

Little league. When Fran suspected a baseball bat was the weapon used to kill Kyle.

'His gang,' Noah said. 'How many other kids are involved?'

'From what I've seen? Three or four at most. That was a while back. The last few times I saw him, he was on his own. Ollie likes to keep things tight.'

'Anyone he's especially tight with?'

'It's hard enough to win these kids' trust.' Zoe looked wary. 'If they think I'm handing out names like pizza flyers . . .'

'All right. But you said you were worried about Ollie. Just him, or any others? In his gang, or on the receiving end of it?'

She considered Noah for a long moment before saying, 'You know about gangs. Let me guess – kid brother? Or sister. More and more it's sisters.'

Noah smiled. 'I know about gangs because I'm a detective and this is London.'

She flushed. 'Sorry. That wasn't—'

Because he was black? Political correctness was a minefield. 'It's okay.' He shook his head. 'But tell me about Ollie's gang. If there's someone he's especially tight with, we need to know.'

A new image in his head: Ollie swaggering, swinging a golf club. A friend, off-camera, keeping Stuart Rawling distracted. The assaults were far easier for two people to carry out.

'There were a couple of kids.' Zoe pushed her hair behind her ears. 'Younger than Ollie, but full of themselves. A bit of hero worship in the mix from what I saw. Ollie treats them like shit, of course, but that's how gangs work. These kids would crawl over broken glass for him.'

What else would they do with broken glass?

'Names?' Noah asked.

'I'd have to check my notes to be sure. Like I said, the last few times I saw him he was on his own. My information's out of date.' She rubbed at her wrist. 'It's always out of date. These kids grow up so fast.'

'How about Ollie? Anyone *he* looks up to? Or anyone he's got a particular grudge against?'

'You think he's mixed up in this murder.' Her stare was shrewd. 'Is he your only suspect? Because I don't see it. Not murder, not Ollie.'

When Noah didn't speak, she sat back, blowing a breath. 'Shit, this's the bit I *hate*. The kids trust me, that's why Trident uses me. Betraying their trust is what pays my wages. Of course first I have to win it, and since these kids smell bullshit from a thousand feet that means I have to *really* win it. No faking allowed. Not that I'd want to fake it.' She pushed the heel of her hand at the table. 'You think your job's a head fuck? Try mine for size—'

Noah waited, not speaking.

'Okay, I retract that.' She lifted both hands in a gesture of surrender. 'My job's got nothing on yours. If Ollie's in your sort of trouble I should shut up or put up, I know that. It's what I tell my team every day. There's a line.' She drew it on the table with the heel of her hand. 'We can walk right up to it, and talk right up to it. But when a kid crosses it? We're done. That's your territory, and I respect it.' She brought her hands together slowly, aligning them at the lip of the table. Lines on her face, bracketing her mouth. She looked around the room before her eyes returned to Noah.

'You asked if he has any special grudges?'

She bit the inside of her cheek. 'Where do you want me to start?'

19

'Violence,' someone had once told Marnie, 'isn't what you think it is. It isn't someone bursting into your home in the middle of the night. It's a soft knock on the door in daylight. A knock that tells you the person outside has brought the worst possible news. News that's going to change your life forever. Violence is *waiting* for a knock on the door, and realising your whole life is that knock.'

Harry Kennedy had taken the shoebox out of the carrier bag he'd brought into the station. He'd put it on the desk in her office. A battered white box with a black lid and a picture of a boy's school shoe, size three. She'd never seen the box before but from the gentle way Kennedy lifted it from the carrier bag, she *knew*— She knew what was inside.

'Tobias Midori,' Kennedy said. 'He's part of the gang we suspect of the break-in at Lancaster Road. His mum found this in his bedroom in the early hours. He wouldn't say how he came by it, so she called us. She's worried out of her wits about him.'

'Tobias Midori.' Marnie was stalling for time. 'How old?'

'He's nine. His mum didn't hear him go out but she

heard him come home at three a.m. He was showering. She heard crying. The bathroom door was locked, so she looked in his bedroom and that's when she found this.' He moved his hand close to the box, but didn't touch it.

A smudge of blood on the lid, under a sticky dusting of fingerprint powder. At some point and for a long time, the box had been crushed, deep creases in its sides. Pushed somewhere, hidden.

'Nothing else from the house?' Marnie didn't want this to be it – the only evidence that Tobias Midori had been in Lancaster Road. It wasn't enough. It was too much.

'Nothing from the house. But his mum found blood on his clothes and trainers. We're running tests.' Kennedy was trying to help. 'He's on the list Zoe gave us of kids recruited into local gangs, running with the Crasmere Boys. Zoe wasn't surprised when I told her that Mrs Midori had called. Sad, but not surprised. We're checking on the rest of the gang. Tobias isn't talking but I'm hopeful that with Zoe's help, maybe even a positive ID from Alan or Louise, we can nail this quickly.'

The taking of the shoebox was nothing in the scheme of things. The real damage had been done to the Kettridges. Aggravated burglary, category one. But the shoebox made it theft. Black leather boy's shoes. The first pair her parents had bought for Stephen?

'Do I need gloves?'

DCS Ferguson would have approved of the dryness in her voice. Damned if she was letting Kennedy see how much she hated him bringing the box here, putting it on her desk. Did he even know what he'd done? Or had she impressed him so much last night, going ahead of him into the house, that he imagined she was invulnerable?

'You don't need gloves.'

Violence is a soft knock on the door.

Marnie removed the lid and set it to one side. Then the light was inside the box, moving over everything, bringing the contents to life, staining it to treasure, ruby and jet and silver—

Her charm bracelet. She reached for it instinctively.

How many times had she searched for it? Knowing Stephen had taken it, thinking it lost for good. The bracelet was lighter than she remembered. She counted its charms, each one tarnished by the black air inside the box. The birdcage with its silver chip of a bird, the gypsy caravan with the wheels that turned. The fan with a miniature heart cut into each leaf, the fish with articulated scales. And her favourite, the horseshoe, its curve smooth enough to rub against her six-year-old lips. She pooled the bracelet gently, and placed it inside the upturned lid of the box.

What else? What other treasure had Stephen stashed in here?

Notebooks. She recognised her handwriting. Red, and black. Her skin cringed with memory, imagining the secrets Harry Kennedy had read when he'd opened the covers. A camera—

Dad's camera that went missing the winter before the murders. She lifted it out, heavy in her hands, a brick by modern standards. He hadn't wanted to upgrade to a digital model, loved his old Nikon. The frame counter said 24. She clicked it open and found the finished film inside the case, wound tight on its reel. What would she uncover if she queued one lunchtime at a counter for a paper wallet full of shiny prints? Photos of Stephen and her parents or older ones, of her?

A photo was tucked under the notebooks at the very bottom of the box. She slid her thumb under its stiffly curling corner to lift it out into the light.

A boy of eight in blue jeans and a green T-shirt, bare

feet on bleached grass. A garden swing in the background. The boy was standing in front of a young woman with red curls in a crisp new police uniform. Her arms were around his neck, held there by his hands as if she was a scarf he was trying to knot into place. The sun had wiped their faces blank, but the boy was smiling and so was she. Behind them, the swing's cross-beam stood as solid as a gallows.

Violence isn't what you think it is. And punishment isn't prison. It's waiting for that soft knock on the door. It's never being free.

Marnie put the photo down. Wanting Kennedy out of her office and her station. 'Thank you, this is all mine. Do you need me to sign for it?'

When she looked up, he glanced away, shaking his head. 'No need. I kept it wide of the record. I'm sorry—'

'Don't do that.'

He met her eyes. 'Do what?'

'Keep things wide of the record imagining you're doing me a favour. It's a crime scene. Write it down. I don't want anything left off on my account.' She put the lid back on the box and set it to one side. 'Alan and Louise. How are they doing?'

'Getting better.' Kennedy smiled, too brightly. 'We might be able to interview them later today.' He wiped the smile, taking a step back from her desk. 'Look, this was out of line. I needn't have brought it here. I could've texted, or asked you to come to my station. I'm sorry.' He stood with his eyes dark on her face. 'That's a professional apology. I'm not usually an arsehole. Zoe wanted to tell you about Ollie, and I had the shoebox in my car. I should've left it there.'

She nodded an acceptance of his apology. 'That's good news about the Kettridges. Hopefully they'll be able to give you a description of the other kids. Assuming Tobias doesn't get there first. You said Zoe knows him. Does she know his standing in the gang?'

'We haven't spoken at any length yet. I told her your investigation takes priority.' He rolled his neck. 'She doesn't think Ollie's in that league – murder – but I told her to give you what she'd got. I hope it helps. We'll be interviewing Tobias together.'

Marnie nodded. 'That's good.'

'The notebooks,' he said suddenly. 'I didn't read them. I wouldn't – I saw they were private, and I made sure no one read them.'

As far as she could tell, he was speaking the truth.

'One thing.' She touched the shoebox. 'This was well hidden. I searched that house six years ago.' She hadn't intended to say it, but his apology looked sincere and she needed to make peace between them for what lay ahead. 'It's the reason I didn't sell, because I was afraid there might be clues – things he'd left behind. This was too well hidden for Tobias to have found it by accident.'

'So then . . . Someone told him where to look? This was burglary-to-order?'

'I wouldn't go that far.' Not yet. 'But I thought you should know. When I say I searched the house six years ago, I mean it. Fingertip search, every room.'

Kennedy nodded, a frown marking the bridge of his nose.

She opened a drawer in her desk, shutting the shoebox inside. 'Let me know how the interviews go.' She straightened, aware that he'd kept his eyes on her. 'If you're able to do that.'

'It's your house. They're your tenants.'

'Your investigation.' She moved towards the door, prompting him to do the same. 'Have you met DCS Ferguson? She joined us this morning.'

'Not had that pleasure.' He used a neutral tone which told Marnie he'd heard how much of a pleasure lay in store for him.

'I'd introduce you, but I'm running late. She's working out of Welland's office.'

'How is he?' Kennedy asked.

'Bored, I imagine. He hates being dry-docked.'

In the corridor, they said goodbye. She watched him walk in the direction of the office that DCS Ferguson had commandeered for the next four months. He moved like a swimmer, hard lines under the dark coat, hands empty at his sides. Marnie turned the other way, towards the incident room.

Ron was on the phone. 'That's great, mate, if you can.' He caught her eye and gave a thumbs up. 'Yeah, ask for DS Carling at the front desk. I'll pop down. Cheers.' He hung up, swinging his chair back from his desk. 'Eyewitness. At effing last!'

'From Page Street?'

'One of the flats at the front, eight floors up, but he caught the start of the assault. Didn't stop to watch the whole thing, assumed it was the usual kicking-out-time crowd. Then he saw the crime scene tape this morning. He's been slow off the starting blocks, but I reckon he's on the level. Pat Hammond. He's coming in to make a statement.' Ron reached for a marker pen. 'Best part?'

He wrote on the board, stepping back to let Marnie see what he'd added.

'*Two* attackers. One a lot bigger than the other. Add that to what Zoe Marshall just told Noah – I'd say we're looking at Ollie and one of the youngsters who thinks the sun shines out of him.'

'Where is DS Jake?'

Debbie answered, 'Front desk called. Someone asking for you, boss. Noah took it.'

'Let me know when Mr Hammond gets here. Any luck getting hold of Lisa Tomlinson?'

'She does a lot of shift work, service stations, that sort of thing. We're trying to find out where exactly she's working today.' Debbie pulled a face. 'None of the places her neighbours suggested have her down on a rota this week. Her phone's switched off, too.'

'Keep trying. Where's Colin up to?'

'He's locked himself away with the phones and letters. Trying to piece it all together.'

'All right. Keep me posted on that.'

Her phone thwapped: a text from Noah.

Stuart Rawling, interview room 3. Bring body armour.

20

Rawling had resented Marnie's presence at his hospital bedside ten weeks ago, and he didn't like her any better in the police station now: 'Thought I'd be fobbed off with your boy here all morning.'

Noah's hands were folded on the metal table, his shoulders set, all the tension tucked away at the back of his neck where Marnie could see it but Rawling couldn't.

'Mr Rawling.' She drew out a chair, sitting at Noah's side. 'How can we help?'

'You can start by telling me why the maniac who broke my jaw isn't behind bars yet.' He moved his face into the light, showcasing the handiwork of his surgeon. Jowls the colour of corned beef, eyes like milk-blue marbles. Fleshy lobes to his ears, the helix too deeply curved to see whether the vigilante's piercing had left a scar. Wearing a blue pin-striped shirt under a navy mohair suit, gold clip across a plush purple tie. Smelling of something spicy that might have been last night's curry or this morning's aftershave. He curled his shoulders as he sat, letting the light find his bald patch, an aggressive oval of scalp. A big man in a foul mood. Marnie's least favourite type.

'Our investigation is ongoing,' she said. 'We're happy to keep you updated on our progress, but I'm guessing you have a specific reason for visiting the station this morning?'

'I read the papers.' He let her see his hands, the knuckle-duster on his ring finger. 'Is that specific enough for you?'

Did his ex-wife still wear her wedding ring? Valerie was a marketing manager, living in Lincoln now. How long had it taken her torn earlobes to heal?

'Kyle Stratton. Broken face, broken bones. Now he's dead.' Rawling stroked the gold tie clip, managing by luck or talent to make the light strike off it into Marnie's eyes. 'I hope you're not about to tell me to count my blessings.'

His blessings? That would be a long list, beginning and ending with the short prison sentence his lawyer had negotiated a decade ago; they'd be here all morning.

'I wouldn't ask you to do that. Do you have information about Mr Stratton's murder?'

'That's your job, isn't it?' Nodding his head at Noah. 'Or your boy's. I'm here to ask when you intended telling me this maniac is targeting ex-cons.'

The ceiling hissed with light, dust spitting inside fluorescent tubing.

'What's this, police blockade?' Rawling looked from Marnie to Noah, and back again. 'If some freelance journo can figure it out, I'm sure you two can manage it.' He fingered his right ear. 'Three assaults in two months. You're waiting for him to hit his stride, is that it?'

Under the sarcasm, he was scared.

Marnie said, 'I don't know which papers you've been reading, Mr Rawling—'

'I'll save you some time.' Reaching into a calfskin brief-case, slapping a broadsheet onto the table. 'Tabloids, I could think it was conjecture. But the editor of this clearly thought it was worth paying for. Even if he kept it off the front page.'

The piece was buried on page five, under a story about a council estate with a worse reputation than Jonas House.

'Serial assaults end in murder,' Rawling summarised while they read. 'Police consider issuing a warning to those paroled in the Greater London area. What I'd like to know, what my *lawyer* would like to know is when you're going to stop *considering* issuing a warning and actually issue it. Too late to save me the plastic surgeon's bill but perhaps some other poor bastard can be spared the humiliation I went through.'

Humiliation? Ten weeks ago, from his hospital bed, he'd described the assault as an 'unlucky thumping'. Nothing in the statement he'd given had hinted at humiliation. But perhaps he was talking about the jaw wires, speech therapy.

Marnie folded the paper and passed it back. 'This is imaginative, but it isn't accurate. If we were issuing a warning you would have heard that from us, not read it in here.'

'Not accurate?' He pointed at the scars on his jaw. 'Does this look *not accurate* to you? Maybe I should be in a morgue drawer like Stratton. Not dead enough for your pay grade, is that it? So you palm me off with your pretty boy here. No offence.'

'None taken,' Noah murmured.

'Three assaults in two months. One of which ends in murder. When the tabloids get hold of this they'll have a permanent hard-on. Stratton served time for aggravated assault, although it doesn't seem to trouble this maniac whether or not the convictions were sound. How's he choosing us?'

'Mr Rawling,' Marnie said, 'there are assaults every week in London. The fact that this reporter thinks he's identified a pattern—'

'All I want to know is do I need a bodyguard when I step outside? Too late for Stratton.' He pushed two fingers at the paper then looked in disgust at the fingers, as if the newsprint had left a stain. The collar of his shirt was jaundiced; he'd sweated into the starched cotton.

Whether or not the convictions were sound.

Still pleading his innocence, but he was scared enough to have come here and not because of the story in the paper, which was the thinnest evidence imaginable.

'What is this really about?' Marnie asked. 'Assaults happen in London all the time, and papers print speculative stories. As you've pointed out, we're in the middle of a murder investigation. I'd prefer not to think that you're wasting our time. So why are you here? Have you remembered what your attacker looked like? Perhaps he, or she, said something to you during the attack which you'd forgotten but now you've remembered and you'd like to make an additional statement.'

'He – or she?' Rawling repeated. 'You think a woman's capable of doing this?' Jabbing at his jaw again, eyes sunk in the meat of his face, neck stained red. 'You think *you're* capable? Or your boy here? Do I look to you like someone who can't take care of himself?'

'In my honest opinion? You look scared.'

It reduced him to a stare.

'You have my sympathy. What happened to you was frightening. You believe it was deliberate. You were targeted because of your time in prison, that's what this paper's speculating. A vigilante attack. Not unlucky. Deliberate, targeted. Why would you think that, unless

110

your attacker said or did something to make you think it?'

'You've got Stratton's corpse. That's not enough for you?'

'Have they been in touch?' Noah asked.

Rawling batted the question away with his fist. 'Stratton's dead, for Christ's sake!'

'Not Kyle. Whoever broke your jaw. Have they been in touch? Is that why you're here?'

'Are you accusing me of withholding evidence?' His expression didn't change, but his face thickened. 'Only that's the sort of thing my lawyer'd be keen to hear.' He jerked his head at Marnie. 'Is your sergeant accusing me of withholding evidence?'

'Not if you've brought it with you,' Noah said lightly. 'Have you?'

Like the skin setting on custard, the way his face thickened. 'If you're hanging yourself, you'll want a longer rope . . .'

'Mr Rawling,' Marnie said, 'you're wasting our time. I'd be happy to explain that to your lawyer in terms he'll understand, but I'd rather you tell us what's going on. Let us help.'

Finally, acceptance shouldered its way onto his wide face. He reached inside his jacket and removed an envelope, tossing it onto the table. A plain white envelope, letter-sized, too flat to be holding more than a single sheet of paper. A second-class stamp under an illegible sorting office mark. His ex-wife's name and company address in Lincoln, handwritten in blue biro, all capitals. The envelope had been torn open.

'Sent to Val at her office. With a second-class stamp, as if it didn't matter when she got it.' His contempt shifted down a gear to make space for an angry species of worry.

'You can't read where they posted it, I've tried. And it'll have at least four sets of prints on it. Val showed it round the office before she passed it my way.'

Marnie took two pairs of crime scene gloves from her pocket.

When they'd gloved up, Noah turned the envelope to the light. 'They've used wax. Crayon, maybe. A white wax crayon over the stamp. To stop the postmark from setting.'

Rawling shifted in the chair, folding his arms, turning his face away.

'You don't recognise the handwriting?' Marnie asked.

'I don't recognise anything, other than the stamp. Second-class.'

Noah eased the contents from the envelope.

A pair of newspaper clippings.

The first dated from the time of Rawling's conviction, reporting the two-year prison sentence passed down after he was found guilty of assaulting his wife. The second clipping was ten weeks old, stating that a fifty-five-year-old businessman had been attacked in east London and taken to hospital with facial injuries. Nothing else in the envelope. Nothing was underlined or highlighted in either clipping, although the letter C was written in blue biro at the base of each story.

'When was this delivered?' Marnie asked Rawling.

'A week ago. Val sat on it for a few days, showed it around, nearly threw it in the bin but then decided to send it on to me.' His jaw clicked. 'In case it was important.'

'She doesn't recognise the handwriting?'

He shook his head.

'No theories as to why it was sent to her?'

'You'd have to ask her. I imagine they found her address

on the internet. They'd have sent it to her home address if they had it, so that's something. Maybe Stratton's girl-friend'll get a sick little note of condolence.' He pointed at the envelope. 'Sending it to my ex-wife? That's passive-ag-gressive. But this,' showcasing his scars, 'is the real thing. So I'm asking again why I wasn't warned this maniac is targeting people, *killing* them now.'

'You're assuming this was sent to your ex-wife by whoever attacked you,' Noah said.

'You want to put a positive spin on it, sunshine? Go ahead. I could do with cheering up.'

'Why didn't you tell us,' Marnie said, 'about the ear piercing?'

Rawling sat back, showing his teeth like a cornered dog. 'What?'

'Whoever attacked you tore a hole in your right ear. You didn't mention it when we interviewed you at the hospital. You said you couldn't describe your attacker, even though he was close enough to do that sort of damage.'

'My face was full of blood.' He stared her down. 'I was fucking *blind*.'

'An unlucky thumping . . . Why didn't you mention the piercing, Mr Rawling?'

'Because it was humiliating.' His shoulders squared. 'Have you ever been humiliated? How about your boy here? Ever had someone kneel on your chest and spit in your face?'

'They spat in your face?' Noah echoed.

'In my *mouth*.' A pulse beat blood-red under his eye. 'In my *fucking* mouth. You're looking for maniacs. Sick little *fucking* maniacs.'

Marnie waited for him to calm down. Then she said, 'Plural?'

'What?' Thrusting the word through his teeth.

'You said *they* knelt on your chest. And you said little. In your original statement, you told us it was a single assailant. Big. Now you're saying . . . what exactly? That it was children?'

Like the ones who stole the shoebox from Lancaster Road, knowing exactly where to find it. Burglary-to-order. Assault-to-order?

Rawling blinked before he composed his face. 'Two of them. In ski masks. One was a big bastard, but the other was just a kid. Little *shits*. And, yes, they punched something through my ear, but in the scheme of things? So what. They broke my face, smashed me up. The ear was a postscript, didn't even hurt.'

He flexed his jaw until it crunched. 'How hard can it be for you lot to catch them, that's what I want to know. This isn't a criminal conspiracy. It isn't even grown-ups.'

He pointed a finger at Noah, then stabbed it at Marnie. 'It's fucking kids.'

21

HMP Cloverton was built a decade before Marnie was born. Search the floors and walls and you might find thumbprints from the men who'd mixed the cement, perhaps even initials scored here and there. But mostly it was graffiti, and failed attempts at whitewash. Every so often, a public petition called for prisons like this to be made more human, inmates to be given light and space, even a patch of earth to plant vegetables or raise chickens. Cloverton boasted vinyl flooring, decent insulation, what the architects called 'softening devices'. Regardless, it had the worst reputation of any prison within a ten-mile radius of Greater London. Holloway had chickens. Cloverton had self-harm, and suicide. It also had Stephen Keele.

Marnie was made to wait in a room carpeted, as if from free samples, in ill-assorted green squares. The last time she'd visited Stephen he'd been the inmate of a juvenile detention centre with his own room, a sports centre, and vending machines that belched out Mars bars and Dr Pepper. Here, posters gave instructions for escalating a complaint to the prison ombudsman, and the official procedure for mandatory drugs testing.

Cloverton had set a room aside for the interview. It was a police matter, she'd explained. Stephen was the only person before Tobias Midori who'd known where the shoebox was hidden in Lancaster Road, the only person who could possibly have told the Crasmere Boys where to find it. Two people were in hospital as a result. She was glad of the wait since it gave her the chance to sort her feelings into order, shuffle the fear and anger to the bottom of the deck. She checked her phone for messages from Noah and the team – she was less than an hour from the station – but there was nothing. No news on Ollie or Lisa, or Carole. No developments following Stuart Rawling's revelations. The visit to Reigate to see Kyle's parents could wait another day. Nothing to distract her from here. Now.

In the interview room, Stephen sat with his dark hair buzz-cut to a bruise on his scalp. Hands linked on the table, shoulders broad enough to hold the shadow of his head. Dressed in a tight white T-shirt and grey sweatpants, his arms bare below the elbow, every muscle sleek as a dancer's. She looked for the ghost of the boy she'd lifted onto the swing in Lancaster Road, but he was gone. Overwritten by this grown man with the strong pulse moving smoothly in his throat.

'I have the shoebox.' She drew out a chair to sit facing him. 'Thank you for that.'

'Thank you,' he repeated. His voice was deeper, more nuanced. The muscles in his neck were slim but defined, like those in his arms. He could bench-press his own weight now.

'You told someone where to look for it. Instructed them to take it from the house. I'm here to find out why you did that.'

Just for a second, she thought she saw surprise on his face. But it must have been the unfamiliar lighting in here because—

'You wanted it.' Dark eyes, unblinking. 'Didn't you?'

So it was true. Burglary-to-order. Her fault. *Hers.*

'The kids who took it wrecked the house and hospital-ised two people to get it.'

'Your tenants.'

They looked at one another through silence thinned by static.

Marnie thought of the photograph, his hands pulling her arms around his neck. She could have snapped it in that moment, his neck. It would've been easy. Or later, an accident with the swing. Accidents like that happened all the time. Instead, she'd walked away. Leaving him in her parents' house like a ticking bomb. He'd killed two people, and hospitalised two more with whatever instruc-tions he'd managed to get out of here to Tobias and the Crasmere Boys.

'How did you do it?' Cloverton's visitor list held no clues. But someone had sent him food parcels when he was in juvenile detention. Someone was looking out for him, despite everything he'd done. 'Who are you in touch with out there?'

His stare flickered, but didn't leave her face.

'You should talk to me,' she said. 'I'm all you've got. That's what this is about, isn't it?'

'That house.' He leaned towards her, bringing his shadow onto the table. 'Did it feel good, seeing it wrecked? I bet it did. I wish I'd seen it.'

She waited, counting out the beats in her head until he spoke again.

'It had to feel good, seeing it like that. That *fucking* house.'

The room was filled with reflective surfaces that duplicated his smile, sending it back at her no matter where she put her eyes. That much was the same, but something was different. Not just his physical appearance. In the tone of his voice, and in his eyes. He was radiating hostility, but at an altered frequency. Because of this place? The walls were older, thicker. The juvenile detention centre was tiled in polystyrene. Cloverton was stone and cement. Behind him, the prison beat its blunt tattoo of noise, punctuated by the occasional shrill of a buzzer. Marnie had been in lots of places like this, over the years. But Stephen hadn't. This was his first time in an adult prison. Twenty years old, looking the way he did, dossing down with the lifers and wife beaters, drug addicts and arsonists. He had to be feeling vulnerable. Was that what she was hearing in his voice, seeing in his eyes? The balance of power between them, always fragile, trembling in her favour?

'Why?' she asked him.

How many times had she asked that question? Too many to remember. The only answer he'd ever given her was a lie: 'I did it for you.' She expected him to repeat that lie now, but he didn't.

'You only ever ask that. Why did *I* do it?' He thinned his lips. 'You never ask what *they* did. Or do you know?'

'What *they* did?' The tips of her fingers fizzed. 'They gave you a home, their love—'

'That fucking house? You're calling that a home?' The words fell out of him, easily. Before, she'd always had to win each one. 'You couldn't live there any more than I could.'

Now, the skin clenched at her wrists.

They were doing this. Having this conversation, finally.

He was going to give her the answers she wanted. *Needed.* Was he?

'You don't kill someone because you're unhappy in their house. You could have run away.'

'Like you did?' He wanted something back from her, a measure of understanding.

It was a dance between them, it'd always been a dance.

'Like I did,' she conceded.

'You hated that house. We both did. And it hated us.'

'I ran away,' she agreed.

'I slept in your room,' Stephen said. 'You were there with me. The two of us, the same.'

'No.' She wasn't giving him that. 'We're not the same. I ran, you stayed. If it was the house you hated, why didn't you wreck that? You could've kicked holes in the walls, torn everything down. Burned it to the ground. But you didn't touch the house. You killed *them*. Why?'

He shoved back in the chair, setting the heels of his hands at the lip of the table. Bruises on his knuckles, blood under his nails. She had to blink to be sure she was seeing it, that it wasn't a flashback. Retinal ghost. The long shrill of a buzzer cut through the wall behind them and he flinched, eyelashes shivering, cheekbones lengthening. He was angry, and afraid.

He was *afraid*.

This place – God knows what it was doing to him, what these people were doing to him. Locked up with lifers, men who had nothing to lose and too much time on their hands. On their fists. Some of them, the worst, had probably given him a hundred reasons to be afraid.

Marnie let this new fact settle in her skull.

'Why?' she repeated then.

He clenched his teeth at her. 'They fucked with me.' He knew that *she* knew how scared he was. 'They brought that bitch back into my life.'

'What are you talking about? What bitch?'

119

Hate came off him in waves. Always before, he'd hidden it. She'd known it was there but she'd never seen it – *felt it* – like this. Hot waves of hate, breaking over her.

'Stella,' he spat the name.

Stella Keele, his mother.

'How did my parents bring your mother back into your life? They *saved* you from her—'

'Can you forgive her, Stephen?' He mimicked her mother's voice, curling his mouth around the words. 'She's so sorry, about everything.'

'They didn't do that.' The mimicry was too good, making her throat throb. 'They wouldn't. Apart from anything else, Children's Services would never have allowed it.'

'Children's Services?' he sneered. 'You mean those morons who told them I was harmless? Those morons who told *you* I was harmless?'

Nausea lodged its dry spike in her sternum.

Stephen shifted his shoulders, watching her. This was better; he'd tipped the scales back in his favour, put her on the defensive, made *her* afraid. 'You didn't know,' he said, as if he was handing out a consolation prize. 'They didn't tell you.'

He was getting better at lying, more cunning, more cruel.

This place had taught him new tricks.

Well, all right. She had some tricks of her own.

'She's on your visitor list. Stella. Are you missing her care packages? You need all the chocolate bars and tinned tuna you can get in a place like this. For currency.'

'Piss off.'

Better.

'Tell me how you got the information to the kids who stole the shoebox.'

'Tell me you didn't know about their truth and fucking reconciliation campaign.'

'You're stalling, I get it. You're not in a hurry to be back in your cell. Scary, isn't it, prison? Not like that soft-play centre, Sommerville.'

'They hated you.' He sat back, enough for the tide of his shadow to retreat. 'Your mum and dad. They hated you.'

The light struck the table, bruising Marnie's eyes.

'You put them through hell. Always running out, getting drunk, kicking off. They fostered me because you were such a disappointment they had to try again, see if they couldn't get it right second time around.' Snaking his dark lips. 'They'd never have fostered me if it wasn't for you. They'd be alive *right now* if you weren't such a fuck-up as a daughter. And a detective.'

Pointing two fingers from his eyes to hers.

'You had *six years* to see what was under your nose. I was in that house for *six years*. But maybe you saw, and you just didn't give a shit. You'd got away and that's all that mattered.'

She stayed silent, waiting for it to be over. For him to burn through the hate and come out the other side. But there was no other side with Stephen, she knew that. She'd come here knowing it.

'Tell me how you got the information to the kids who broke into the house.'

'To make your job easier?' He laughed, a grown-up sound unlike any she'd heard from him before. 'You've never known which questions to ask, have you? Never asked any about me, not until it was too late. Where I'd come from, what I'd been through to get there. Why they wanted me so badly.' His eyes became hooded. 'What went on in that house before I finished it.'

'You're trying to excuse what you did—?'

'I don't need an excuse.' He put his hands in plain view.

'I'm serving my time. You're the one who needs an excuse. That's why you keep coming back. Or maybe you just like prisons.' Dipping his head at the shove of sound through the wall. 'Because this is where you belong, because you know you fucked up. You left the three of us alone in that house. *You* couldn't live there. What made you think I could? I had to look at that wall you painted every day, every night.'

She saw it in his eyes, the wall, the colour of a blood-stain.

'I was sleeping with your ghost,' Stephen said, 'with everything you left behind. Shall I tell you how it felt, the morning I killed them?'

No. Don't tell me. I don't want to know. Stop talking now, just— Stop.

He leaned in, nailing his stare to her face. 'It felt like your hand on the knife. Under mine. *Your* hand. Putting that knife into them, again and again and again—'

'That's enough.' Somehow her voice came out quiet and low. 'It's enough.'

'No wonder you can't stay away.' He straightened and sat back. 'You should be locked up, just like me. But you are, aren't you?' He drilled a forefinger to his temple. 'You're locked up here.'

Her chest was packed with pain.

She had to get out, away.

'Are you done?' she asked.

'I'll never be done. *We'll* never be done.' His stare on her again, swarming with hate. 'You're a piss-poor excuse for a detective and you always will be, until you start asking better questions. Proper questions. The ones you never asked.'

He stood, lifting a hand for the CCTV lens in the corner of the room.

'I'm going back to my cell now. You?'
Curling his mouth at her.
'Can go back to yours.'

22

'I'm a prisoner. I'm Finn Duffy. I've been kidnapped by a pervert and I've puked in his bath. He's going to kill me. I can't clean it up, I can't do anything because I'm sick. I'm sick and stupid and I'm just a kid, not even eleven. I was going to see Dad, but that's finished now. He's got me, fucking Brady's got me. I tried to poison him but he gave me the belt. If the house isn't clean, no food. If I try to escape, the belt. If I make too much noise, duct tape. Brady's joke, "Silence is golden. Duct tape is silver." I hate him. And I'm scared, I'm really scared.'

Finn stopped. He scratched out the last two sentences so hard the paper tore. Wrote—

'Don't get mad, get even. It's down to me now, not Dad. But I'm sick. My puke's in the bath and it stinks. I've made the whole house stink. I wish I'd puked on *him*.'

He squinted, trying to make sense of the words he'd written which were dancing like ants across the piece of torn wallpaper. No notebooks in the house, no books of any kind, but he'd moved the wardrobe a bit, upstairs. Picked at the edge of the wallpaper until he was able to tear away this piece before pushing the wardrobe back in place. He'd kept the pen he'd used to write the message for the bin man. A blue biro, blotchy, but it worked.

'I'm Finn Duffy,' he wrote, 'he took me in Camden. I was with Ollie and the rest, we were hanging out up at Jonas House, not doing anything, just a couple of cans. Brady had a car. I couldn't see its plates. Big boot, that's where he stuffed me. Big car, think it was silver.'

Using his neatest handwriting, making it small to save space. Some of the words in his head he didn't write down because it wasn't meant to be his life story or something they could sell to a newspaper like that mate of Uncle Regan's did. This was to help the police catch Brady. He'd written, 'Wonky teeth. Adidas trainers. Smells of curry.' When he screwed up his eyes to try and get a better picture, he just got red squirming across black. Like the funfair. Cartoon faces, googly eyes, zap of static from the blue cat Dad won.

'House across the street has a yellow door,' he wrote. 'Curtains always closed. I've watched for hours and seen no one. No one comes up this street except the bin men and they hate me. Beanie Hat could've saved me, but he didn't. It's Raccoon City out there, he'll leave my body to rot or take it someplace else. But I think he'll leave it here. I still don't know why.'

He stopped to cry for a bit. It was easy to cry because he felt so sick. After puking in the bath, he didn't see how he could make it any worse.

'He won't tell me why. If he's a perve, he hasn't touched me. Not yet. He doesn't even like me, tells me all the time that I stink. He doesn't fancy me so why's he keeping me here, I don't get it. It's like Uncle Regan and that dog. He hated it, called it a bitch. She was so scared, shaking all the time, this grin on her face, trying to please him.

Creeping up close, whining for another kick. He's a proper bastard, Dad said. He grew up with Regan and it wasn't just dogs he kicked. I asked Dad why he had a dog when he hated it and it cost so much, he was always on about the money, like Brady buying cheap pasta, telling me how much I'm costing him, so why doesn't he just let me go?'

He stopped to cry into the crease of his elbow, wiping snot from his nose.

'Except Regan got a kick out of seeing the dog crawl so maybe it's that. Maybe Brady needs someone crawling to him because his life's shit. Dad says Regan was pushed about at school, at work. He says you pass it down the line, there's always someone who'll take it, Dad says, and if you don't like it *you* pass it down and so I think I'm Brady's dog, that's why I'm here. Regan drowned his dog, I think he drowned her. I know he put her into fights with other dogs, invited his mates to watch. Dad says there's always someone happy to watch a fight like that, up West or in Camden under the market. He showed me a way in, we're not supposed to know about. Dad knows all the secret places round there. If this was Camden, I'd know how to hide. Under the canal in that tunnel where the Crasmere Boys went, where Ollie wanted to hang out that time.'

He wasn't writing. His hand was slack, blue stains on his fingers. Lying on the floor, talking at the tiles. He didn't have any paper and there wasn't any pen, leaking or otherwise. The stains on his fingers were from that tablet thing inside the bog; he'd clawed at it when he was puking that last time. Pebble-dashing the porcelain, Dad called it.

'Ollie must've seen something,' he wrote, fingers twitching out the words on the cold floor. 'He was with us that day, he wanted me for the Crasmere Boys because of who Dad is. Should've gone with him, should've thrown a C-sign, whatever shit he wanted. Gang stuff. Dad says to step wide of that, it'll suck the skin off you, stay wide . . .'

Blinking at the white chill under his cheek, gob at the edges of his mouth, tasting like blood.

'Dirty house . . . no food. Escape . . . the belt.'

Reciting Brady's rules, learnt by heart, ticking the list with his fingers, folding each one on the tiles, except they wouldn't fold, too stiff, knuckles swollen like Dad's.

'Make a noise . . . duct tape.'

He could feel it tight and sticky on his face, dragging his lips back into his teeth, tongue trapped at the back of his mouth, impossible to swallow.

Tears burned in his nose. 'Tell anyone . . . the river.'

A whale came up the river once. Dad showed him where. It took the wrong turning like those that died on the beach. Uncle Regan put his dog in the river, tied a rock to her lead and kicked her in. Finn had imagined it so many times he didn't know whether the pictures in his head were real or not. The dog whining at Regan's feet, still looking for ways to please him even after all the kickings. The rock from the beach, that strip of sand and gravel London calls a beach, and mud that sucks at everything, your shoes, your toes, your fingers if you reach for a pebble.

'It sucks.'

And Dad laughing, his throat pointed at the sky. 'That's London for you . . .'

The splash when the dog landed. The hole it opened in the water, brown.

Then the hole sucking shut and the river running on like nothing happened.

Like there never was a rock, or a dog, or Finn to see her die.

23

The station's heating had packed up, again. Everyone was shivering in their coats, huddled by the whiteboard, hands wrapped around hot coffees.

'We're looking for Ollie and anyone close enough to be called his friend,' Marnie said. 'We know he had a gang, and that it was close-knit. Zoe gave us a couple of names, but neither boy has seen Ollie recently. Stuart says his attackers were children, one large, one small. We know Ollie was popular with younger kids, ten- and eleven-year-olds.' She stopped.

Noah wondered whether Ron and the others could see how worn out she was. Her eyes gave back the light from above the whiteboard as if she were translucent, her lips colourless. She'd disappeared for a couple of hours – seeing Welland? Or Ferguson.

'We need to find whoever sent the clippings to Valerie Rawling,' she said. 'If our vigilantes want recognition for their work then let's hope they've left a trail we can follow. DC Tanner's leading on that. DS Jake and I will visit Ollie's home and speak with Lisa, assuming she's back from work.'

'Why did Val send the clippings to Stuart?' Ron slurped at his coffee. 'Like she wanted him to know he was attacked because of what he did to her. Rubbing his nose in it.'

'Or she was warning him,' Debbie said. 'We don't know she's glad he was attacked. She put up with him battering her for twenty years. It's probably more complicated than it looks. Kids wouldn't understand that.'

'The vigilantes wanted Val to know the two things were connected,' Noah said. 'They sent the clippings to her, not him. In their heads, this's about justice. They needed her to know they'd done what the courts couldn't – punished him, properly.'

'Where did Ollie get hold of the newspaper story about Rawling's trial?' Colin chafed his hands together. 'That story's seven years old. Ollie was only eight at the time.'

'Let's find out if Mazi Yeboah was sent clippings about Kyle,' Marnie said. 'And let's not make any assumptions about Ollie. DS Jake, you spoke with Zoe Marshall?'

'She liked Ollie, once upon a time. It wasn't easy for her to betray his confidence, but she told me some interesting things.' Noah looked at the mugshots on the board: Ollie as a toddler, and a teenager. 'When he turned twelve, he started keeping lists in old diaries. He showed Zoe a couple, when she was first working with the kids on his estate. He kept the lists in date order, very neat for a kid who didn't like school, but Zoe said not to read too much into his truancy; lots of kids can't be in school for lots of reasons. Often it's the bright ones or the quiet ones who find it hard to be in mainstream education.'

'Which was Ollie?' Ron wanted to know. 'Bright, or quiet?'

'Both, back then. He made lists of everything. The lists he showed Zoe were of things he loved, and things he hated. Food, clothes, music. People. He had a diary filled with lists of the people he hated. And what he'd like to do about it.'

Ron's face sharpened. 'Such as?'

'Zoe says she'd have reported it if he was a danger to himself or others. She wondered about abuse in the family. A lot of the punishments he wrote down involved being locked up. In cupboards or car boots, or cages. She made a point of getting to know Ollie's mum. His dad was out of the picture. What she saw of Lisa reassured her, but she worried that Ollie would find a gang, somewhere to belong. And she worried about the lists.'

'I'll bet she did,' Ron said. 'I don't suppose he had Carole's name written down?'

'Zoe can't remember details. It was three years ago. The only names she remembers were celebrities or school-mates, anyone who'd run up against Ollie's tendency to judge you on the basis of your taste in music. Once she'd ruled out abuse, she didn't think any of it too troubling. But Ollie started hanging out with the wrong crowd, throwing up gang signs in the street, acting tough . . .'

'That's when the penny dropped.' Ron drank more coffee. 'Sounds a real charmer, even at twelve. Now wouldn't it be great if Zoe recognised *his* handwriting on the envelope sent to Rawling's wife? Better still, we get hold of his notebooks and match the writing from those.'

'Did Zoe feel threatened by him?' Debbie asked. 'That's usually a good indicator of how serious those sorts of problems are, or the direction they're headed in.'

'She didn't feel threatened,' Noah said. 'But she's a tough cookie. She's sure the better part of it's swagger, doesn't believe Ollie's capable of doing serious harm to anyone, except possibly himself if he keeps running with the wrong crowd.'

'Does she know what Carole did to him?' Ron asked. 'And what was done to Carole?'

'No. And I didn't enlighten her.'

Ron's phone rang. 'DS Carling . . . Thanks, I'll be down.' He hung up, nodding at Marnie. 'That's our eyewitness from Page Street. Shall I show him Ollie's mugshot?'

'Play it by ear,' Marnie said. 'If he didn't see faces then don't show him faces. It would be too easy to jump to the wrong conclusion from Ollie's stone-cold-killer impersonation.'

'At least we've got a name.' Ron reached for his jacket. 'For DCS Ferguson. And it's making the vigilante theory look solid.' He grinned. 'I might even start buying into it myself.'

Jonas House was iron-clad in cold, its breeze blocks finished by a bad paint job with more wrinkles than a smoker's skin. Eight months ago, Marnie and Noah had found a girl's body on a high-rise estate in south London. This was north-east London, an experiment in low-rise living, but no less depressing. Jonas House was built as post-war housing for single people and couples, but most of the one-bedroomed boxes were crammed with families. Small surprise the kids wanted out, even if only to the narrow strips of grass segregating the eight blocks.

The estate's low sprawl limited the prospect for dead space, but a knot of kids had found a spot where the grass had frozen with a ferocity that said this particular strip didn't ever get the sun. Two of them were stabbing at the ice with broken selfie sticks, the others standing shoulder to shoulder, smoking e-cigarettes. None of them looked older than twelve. Three boys and a girl, dressed in the uniform of the school that Ollie hadn't attended in eight weeks. Despite the cold, not one of them wore a coat. Their breath was the same colour as the grass.

'Makes you wonder what their homes are like.' Marnie shivered inside her scarf, wound high around her throat. 'That they'd rather be out here on a day like this.'

'Are you okay?' Noah asked.

She glanced at him, and nodded. 'It's been a long day.'

'The light will be gone soon.' He looked to their left where the eighth block stood derelict, its doors and windows boarded up. 'I'm surprised they've not found a way inside there.'

'Perhaps social cleansing has sapped their sense of enterprise.'

That was better; she sounded more like herself.

'The regeneration generation.' Noah followed her across a lethal stretch of ungritted tarmac, towards the block where the Tomlinsons had lived for the last ten years. 'Lisa moved here when Ollie's dad moved out. Bit of a comedown from Harrow.'

'You have a gift for understatement.'

Inside, Jonas House was a degree colder. Smelling of chip fat and orange ammonia. The lift had been out of order long enough for someone to spray 'I'm fucked' on its doors. Each block was four storeys high. A long climb for a pensioner, or a family with a pushchair and the week's shopping to bring home. Lisa and Ollie lived on the third floor at the far end, their door painted blue. Curtains drawn at the window, but that wasn't unusual. All the windows they'd walked past were the same. Apart from anything else, it was a heat-saving measure.

From the walkway, Noah could see the kids congregated below, their shadows stretching as the day shrank to darkness. Four miles away, Westminster throbbed with callous heat and light. The derelict block was floodlit, possibly as a precaution against trespassing. Had Lisa watched Ollie in a group like the one below? Close enough to keep an eye on him if she'd felt the need to do that. Hard to imagine how she couldn't, after what'd happened eleven years ago.

Carole had been attacked not far from here. Walking home alone, a route she took when work kept her late. Like Lisa, she worked shifts, minimum wage, unpredictable hours. Rawling was in hospital drinking through a straw when Carole was attacked. If Ollie and one of his friends were responsible for these assaults then they'd decided not to start with the woman who'd taught Ollie about violence, given him a fixation with punishment and captivity. Cupboards, car boots, cages.

Marnie knocked on the blue door. When there was no answer, she stripped off her glove and knocked again, louder this time. No sound from inside the flat, her knuckles raising an echo that said it was empty. Then the grating of a key in a lock from the flat next door.

An elderly Sikh in grey flannels and an Aran jumper nodded a welcome. 'She's not home. You're the police?' Looking at Noah then Marnie, nodding at their badges. 'It's good you've come. I'm concerned about her, and the boy.' He held his door wide, inviting them inside.

They followed, into the living room that adjoined Lisa's hallway. A bright little box of a room, smelling of roses and radiators.

'You will want my name. Himmat Singh. Sit, please.' He settled in a high-backed armchair facing the sofa, red slippers on his feet. 'I last saw Lisa three days ago. The boy? A fortnight or more. Lisa works long hours, often all night. It isn't unusual for two days to go by when I do not see her, but three?' He shook his head. His face was long and lined, his eyes bright and brown. 'Now I am worried. She is very quiet, like a mouse, a good neighbour. But even when I do not see her, I hear her. These flats . . . You hear everything.' He spoke softly, in a voice that wouldn't have sounded out of place on Radio 4; received pronunciation, a voice from another generation.

At his elbow, a low table held a lamp and a paperback book. *Lord of the Flies*. A silk tapestry hung on a slim brass pole, its picture of a Sikh priest reading the Granth. One wall was crowded with photos of Himmat and his family. As a young man in uniform about to go to war; with children and grandchildren on his knee. An orange tufted rug warmed the floor. All the furniture was old, but had the patina of pieces well chosen and loved. Noah hadn't expected to feel so comfortable anywhere on the Jonas estate, but Mr Singh had succeeded in shutting out every last trace of the bitter chill, transforming this municipal box into a real home.

'Three days she hasn't been here. I wonder, is she looking for the boy? He has been gone two weeks or more.' He cupped the side of his face with one hand. 'I am not a nosy neighbour, just concerned. The boy and I were friends once. I miss him. And I worry, for her.'

'Do you have a key?' Marnie asked.

'Yes.' He touched his hand to his trouser pocket. 'I haven't used it. I heard her go out three nights ago. She hasn't come home. The boy is too loud to be home without me knowing it.' He smiled, but his eyes were sad. 'Clumsy, and loud. He never used to be that way. He would sit where you are sitting and ask for stories of the war, the desert where I fought. He was a quiet boy. They all grow up clumsy for a time. But Oliver has stayed that way. And angry now, also.'

'Why is he angry,' Noah asked, 'do you know?'

'At that age, living here? Who needs a reason?' But he shook his head, as if he didn't understand Ollie's anger. Lisa hadn't told him, about Carole and the cage.

'We heard he's friends with some of the younger boys. Have you seen them recently?'

'Yes, when I am shopping. I try not to be in the shops when they are out of school.' Touching the tips of his fingers to the white turban he wore. 'On Monday, I see them smoking.' He mimed vaping. 'The little silver pipes.'

'But Ollie wasn't with them?'

'Not in a long while. I would see him on a Friday, by the swings. Not so long ago I would get a nod. But even that has become too much trouble. He has his new friends, new rules . . .' His eyes moved to the door and lit with a smile. 'Ah! *Now* she comes. Say hello to our visitors.'

A cat walked across to where Himmat was sitting, offering her chin to be rubbed. Long-haired, about seven years old, her face white on one side and tabby on the other. 'This is Bess. She isn't as snooty as she seems, just a little wary of strangers.'

'Ollie's new friends,' Noah said. 'New rules. Do you mean a gang?'

Himmat nodded. 'So many of them have gone that way. Last summer, two stabbings.' Putting his fingers in a prayer shape. The cat leaned into him, making a low chirping noise. 'That is what I fear for the boy. His mother fears it too.'

'Have you talked with her about Ollie?'

'Often, but not lately. She is busy with work, trying to pay bills. She lost one of her jobs, and there are fines from the school because of truancy; always something to be paid. She works nights as well as days. I cook for her and Oliver, it's all I can do. She lets me make meals for the freezer. She's proud, won't ask for help, prefers to give it. She wants always to do something in return, so I invent little jobs. She mended a shelf in my bathroom that needed a ladder. Even when the boy and I were friends, she did not like to take advantage. But she knew he was safe here.'

He leaned forward a little, his eyes bright with concern. 'You will hear bad things about him, if you ask questions around here. An angry boy, a violent boy. Angry at the whole world. But this is only recently. Less than a year ago he would sit where you are sitting, asking me questions.' He knuckled the cat's head. 'Bess liked him, and she chooses her allies very carefully. He is a sweet boy, under all the showing off. They must all show off now. Oliver, he carries the weight of the world with him, I have seen it. But a good boy, underneath it all. Remember that. Too few of them will ask questions but he was curious, always after answers. Of course he grew bored as he grew up. All stories are boring, at that age.' He smoothed a hand to his cheek. 'Even ones about war.'

'I think we should borrow your key.' Marnie stood up. 'And take a look next door.'

The cat turned its head, staring her up and down.

'You will tell me?' Himmat dug the key from his trouser pocket and held it out. 'When you find her and the boy, you will tell me?'

Bess moved from Himmat's feet to Marnie's, purring up at her.

She took the key and crouched to touch the cat's head, as if for luck. 'Yes.'

Lisa's flat was the same size as Himmat's but felt bigger because it was empty. Not just of people, of things, all the little touches that make a house a home. Leaves and litter had blown in from the walkway and been left to straggle the length of the hall. A row of pegs hung with coats, several pairs of shoes kicked off just inside the door; women's shoes, except for one oversized pair of muddied trainers. The sitting room had a black leather sofa, scuffed all over, and a TV on a plastic stand. Damage to the wall showed where a much larger TV had once been bracketed. Shoved down behind the sofa was a duvet and a pillow. Ollie's bed, when he was home? DVDs in a metal rack in one corner. Carpet stained by what looked like spilled cups of coffee, or cans. A grey T-shirt on the radiator, its hem as stiff as cardboard. Unlike next door, the cold had been allowed to creep inside the Tomlinsons' flat. The curtains, pretending to be velvet, were drawn across the window but light fell through in wet-looking patches.

Noah followed Marnie to the kitchen which smelt of un-emptied bins and long-ago-burnt toast. The kettle stood with its lid propped open. Half-empty jars of jam, Marmite, peanut butter. Boxes of kids' cereal, frosted flakes, chocolate coatings. A loaf of bread was going green by the side of the toaster. The pedal bin was overflowing. At its side, a black plastic liner lumpy with rubbish, a neat knot tied in its neck. Noah opened the fridge, recoiling from the stink of rancid milk. He put his hand inside. Like Marnie, he was wearing crime scene gloves. 'Fridge's dead. Try the lights?'

She flicked the switch by the door. Nothing happened.

'The electricity's been cut off.' Noah shut the fridge. 'One bill too many?'

Zoe had said Ollie's mum kept the fridge full.

Lisa was a coper, a tiger mum.

Where was she?

In the room at the back of the flat: a double bed and a cheap metal clothes rail.

Marnie crouched to look under the bed before straightening.

'Himmat said three days.' Noah watched her checking the clothes on the rail. 'It feels longer since anyone was in here.'

'Could be explained by the shift working. Maybe.'

They moved to the bathroom where the shower unit was scaly and the toilet lid was missing, a scum of grey on the surface of the water. A plastic bucket filled with half-empty bottles of shampoo and shower gel stood inside the unit. Water was coming from the shower head in a steady trickle, splashing up from the dimpled plastic floor. A pair of toothbrushes at the side of the sink, their bristles splayed with use. The sink was stained with paste and traces of dried blood, the kind you might spit out if you had bleeding gums.

'Where are they?' Noah looked at the blood, feeling a snag of fear. 'You don't think—'

'We need to call a team in here,' Marnie said. 'Something's not right.'

She turned back to the kitchen where she removed her coat, hanging it on the door. Removed her suit jacket too, rolling up the sleeves of her jumper and shirt as she walked to where the pedal bin was leaking its sour smell of fish and rotting fruit. She put it to one side, concentrating on the bag of rubbish placed next to the bin, its neck knotted tight.

'How did Carole end up living half an hour from here?' She worked at the knot patiently, not tearing the bag. 'Someone should have joined the dots between her and Ollie. She should never have been allowed to settle so close.'

'You're thinking he saw her, on the street? *Recognised* her—?'

'I'm thinking out loud.' She untied the final knot in the bin liner. 'Ollie was four years old when he last saw her. She's changed. New hair colour, new address . . .'

She opened the neck of the bag.

Noah had expected an extra dose of olfactory overload, but the contents didn't smell.

'What's in there?' He crossed to Marnie's side.

She held the bag's neck wide so that he could see what she was looking at.

Torn newspapers. Some with clippings cut out. Magazines, of the kind Ron had suspected the Strattons of dumping – porn, but men not women.

Something heavy was weighting the bottom of the bag, making it knock against the side of the pedal bin as Marnie lifted the liner.

She reached in. Moved the magazines and papers to one side.

Ticking, at the very bottom of the bag.

The heavy weight was a baseball bat.

Ticking against it—

A disposable lighter.

24

Finn knew this face. He knew it. Not Brady—

A big nose like Dad's. Like Finn's would be one day.

Big nose and purple eyes. Smoker's breath, yellow. Not Brady. Brady was wine and fat red pasta. Grapes tossed up into his open mouth. Bad, bad teeth.

This face was cigarettes, and threats.

A hoodie, like Finn's.

He wasn't that much older than Finn.

Always hanging around Jonas House.

Living there, like the Crasmere Boys.

Oh, he was—

Ollie.

The face belonged to Ollie.

That was when Finn started screaming.

25

It was late and she was bone-tired, but Marnie wasn't ready to go home. With Noah, she'd filed the paperwork from Lisa and Ollie's flat, meticulously, because while the task lasted she wasn't required to think about what came next.

After dropping Noah at his place, she drove a short distance and parked up. Locking the car and standing by its side, defeated for a moment by the thought of how quickly its locks would freeze. Then she turned and walked away. Wanting to move, if only to keep warm. The cold crowded in, chilling her face and the slim margin between her sleeves and gloves. Was this punishment? Six years ago, she'd slept on the station floor, believing she deserved the ache in her bones. 'Go back to your cell,' Stephen had said. As if she was as much a prisoner as he was.

Ed's was her safe place. Warm, quiet, a world of comfort in its cluttered rooms. Why then was she denying herself what she needed so badly?

'Do you?' a voice niggled in her head. 'Is that really what you need?'

She drew a breath of freezing air – knives in her lungs – turning towards the river.

Walking is the repeated act of saving yourself from falling. Where had she read that? In one of the books Lexie, her therapist, gifted to her six years ago. Moving forward was momentum, you just had to keep doing it. She could smell the river suspended ahead, London on all sides pulsing with sound, car horns and tyres. Music coming from the west, voices from the east. It was quiet at Ed's. No, more than that. It was silent. Ed hated talking about Stephen. Hated *Stephen*—

Not only for what he'd done six years ago. For what he was still doing. Baiting Marnie, bringing her back to him, again and again, making her stick her hand in that fire of guilt and loss.

'They'd never have fostered me if it wasn't for you.'

Nothing Stephen had said was any worse than the voices inside her own head.

But hearing him say them—

'They would be alive *right now* if you weren't such a fuck-up as a daughter. And as a detective.'

Hearing him say the words was much worse. She could never repeat them to Ed.

'You had *six years* to see what was under your nose. I was in that house for *six years*. But maybe you saw, and you just didn't give a shit. You'd got away and that's all that mattered.'

She needed to let it go, move on. Not that Ed would ever use platitudes like that, but she had to accept she'd never have the answers she wanted. Stephen wasn't a child any longer. She wanted to talk to Ed about how it felt to look into Stephen's eyes and see fear for the first time. And how it felt to know that he was right when he said she hadn't asked enough questions, about him. Back when it mattered, when it might have made a difference. Was that why he hated her so much? Because she should've dug at the truth of what'd happened to him? As a detective, as a daughter. It hurt, to go digging. When Harry Kennedy made her go inside that house and later, when he brought the shoebox to her office, she'd been furious with him. But he was just doing his job, the way she'd failed to do hers.

'Never stop asking questions,' Welland had told her on their first day together. 'A detective who doesn't ask questions is less use than a waterproof teabag.'

Stephen was scared. Barely twenty years old in an adult prison with an appalling reputation for brutality. He was the victim now, not her. He'd spit out his own tongue before asking for her help, as a sister or a detective. But he was vulnerable, in there. Could she ignore that? Could she explain to Ed why this wasn't about shoving her hand back into Stephen's fire? This tangled mess of regret and guilt and this – need for redemption, for the pair of them. She couldn't just let it go. Could she?

'It's too late,' the voice niggled. 'You saw him. It's too late.'

However it got there, the violence was inside Stephen. And that meant he shouldn't be let out of prison, not now, probably not ever.

Street lights yellowed the pavement's frost, setting its glaze to the black patches which would conspire against the morning's commuters. Right around her, London wrapped its soundtrack. She didn't want silence; perhaps she never would. This wasn't punishment, it was – *change*. A shift in her, like ice breaking free from a rock to move upstream.

She'd reached the Thames. It shifted delicately, persistently. Centuries ago it'd frozen solid in winters much worse than this. Solid enough for fires, and to walk from one side to the other.

Stripping off a glove, she touched the iron bar which ran along the wall separating the embankment from the water. The iron was a different kind of cold to the air. Blunter, softer. She wrapped her fingers around it, letting the bar burn into the palm of her hand. There are degrees of pain, just like degrees of cold. It was easy to forget that.

A barge sounded its horn, the noise rippling out across the water in rings. Hot breath rose from its funnel, from the funnel of every boat down there. Her breath was clinging to her lips like smoke. For a second, she ached for a cigarette, her skin clenched with nostalgia for the wild girl who'd grabbed at life with both hands, punching and shaking to try and make sense of it—

Car horns barked behind her.

She should go home. Even if she couldn't talk to Ed, she could sleep. There was work to do tomorrow. There was always work to do.

Her hand gripped at the bar a moment longer before she pulled away, seeing the heated imprint of her palm shrink slowly as the cold took back custody of the iron.

It was nearly 9 p.m. by the time she reached Ed's place. She was forced to park a street away; a short walk but she felt every step of it, thinking of Carole and Kyle and the contents of the bin liner found at Ollie's flat.

The heel of her boot caught a patch of ice and the shoebox in its carrier bag swung, striking her shin. She'd brought the box with her, not wanting it in her desk drawer. She'd hide it at the back of the wardrobe, a place she knew Ed wouldn't look.

He was heating chicken soup in the kitchen, wearing decimated cords and a red fisherman's jumper, odd socks on his feet, bed-head brown curls in his eyes. She shed her coat and scarf, resting her eyes on him because it felt good to be this far from dead bodies and DCS Ferguson, and stolen salvage from her childhood.

'Good timing.' Ed turned from the stove to smile at her. 'This's ready.'

His eyes flickered to the carrier bag, only briefly, but she'd lost her chance to hide it. She set it on the floor beside the sofa as Ed brought the soup bowls with bread hot from the oven. A good meal, exactly what she needed to get the day's cold out of her bones.

After they'd eaten, Ed made coffee and they sat together, her head on his shoulder, his hand at her hip. Six years ago, she'd thought herself unfit for intimacy of any kind. But here she was sharing his tiny flat with the Buffy DVDs and the David Lynch posters, fitting right in.

'What's in the box,' he said, 'new shoes?'

'It's from the house in Lancaster Road.' She leaned down and scooped it up. 'They found it when they were clearing up after a break-in last night.'

Ed didn't move, but his hand lifted a fraction as if her words had slid a sheet of paper between his touch and her skin. An onlooker wouldn't have noticed, but she ached for the loss of contact between them. Ed didn't judge and he didn't pry but her secrets scared him, she knew. He'd defend her right to them with his last breath. Perhaps that was why they scared him.

She felt it again – ice breaking away; a change coming.

Police sirens swept up the street, pulling the night into the flat. Just for a second, she was Detective Inspector Rome and Ed was Victim Support Officer Belloc. London leaking through the walls, bringing the baseball bat and cigarette lighter in here when she'd needed a moment to explain how much (and how little) the contents of the shoebox mattered. She wanted Ed to be the one to take the lid off the box, as if he might cancel out the fact of its having been handled by Harry Kennedy. But Ed wouldn't do that, invade her space, so it was up to her to take the lid off for the second time in the same day, letting the light in to stir at the mean little litter of Stephen's stealing.

'Can you imagine me wearing this?' The charm bracelet.

She intended it as a joke, to defuse the static which was making her conscious of the chaos around them – the curling edges of Ed's posters, slippery towers of his CDs – but her hand fitted inside the bracelet as if she was still eight years old and in love with the ridiculous rattle of its silver charms. She found the horseshoe by instinct, its cool curve slipping like a ring around the tip of her little finger. Ed's eyes were in the shoebox, on the notebooks. The camera.

She lifted out the photograph of her and Stephen. 'I was so proud of that uniform . . .'

Ed took the print when she held it out for him. 'How old are you here?'

'Twenty-two? Twenty-three.'

Stephen's smile, his hands holding her arms around his neck. He looked happy. Eight years old, newly fostered, still learning to call her *sister*.

'It's funny, I don't remember him smiling. Not then.' She forced herself to concentrate on the moment captured in the photograph, not what came later, not what'd been said between them earlier today. That moment, in the garden. She reached a finger and touched Stephen's smile. To show Ed that she wasn't afraid of hearing her skin sizzle. 'He must've been happy, back then.'

Ed kept hold of the photograph. She wanted him to speak, but he didn't. Stephen's hands around her wrists, holding her tight to his back. It'd been chilly that summer, the heat coming and going with the sun behind the clouds. She'd been glad of the uniform. Goosebumps—

Stephen had goosebumps on his bare arms. If she concentrated, she could feel the way they'd caught at her wrists, pricking. He'd shivered and pulled her close like a coat. She felt the small bones in his fingers, sharp blades of his back like folded wings. A pang of pity for him . . . Was that what made her shiver? A skinny, silent child trying to keep warm in a strange house. He'd liked her uniform. Her parents had worried that it might make him nervous, in case he'd seen too much of the police back at the foster home or in his real home. He'd been sitting on the stairs when she'd opened the front door with her key, wanting to surprise her parents with the new uniform. She'd put her finger to her lips when she saw him and he'd stared intently for a second before his smile came, lifting his left index finger to his lips, copying her. Sharing her secret.

'The notebooks should be fun.' She reached into the shoebox, blinking heat from her eyes. 'God knows what teenage angst is scribbled here.'

Ed put the photo aside, reaching for her free hand, taking some of the chill away with the warmth of his fingers.

'You'd better not read them.' She wasn't ready to be comforted. 'I'm serious. There are song lyrics in here, maybe even poetry. Angry teenage poetry. You're not ready for that, Belloc.'

'I'll raise you. *Romantic* teenage poetry.'

'You aren't serious.'

'Does it look as if I throw anything away, ever?' He nodded at the insulating wall of books and boxes. 'My first set of dental braces is hiding somewhere in this lot.'

'All right, you win.' She smiled, returning the notebooks to the box.

The charm bracelet wouldn't slip off her hand the way it'd slipped on. She surrendered her wrist to Ed who released the clasp, pooling the bracelet in his palm before placing it inside the box.

Marnie lidded the thing, and set it aside. 'More coffee? And tell me about your day.'

They talked for a while, Ed keeping it light with a story about a broken kettle bringing his office to a standstill. Too much of the day's noise was hammering in her head, a hot spot at her feet where she'd placed the box. Not just bad lyrics in the notebooks. Lists. As a teenager, she'd kept lists of everything. Music she liked, food she wouldn't eat, places she'd rather live than at home. Ollie kept lists too. A way of taking back control in a life that felt chaotic, or claustrophobic, or both.

'We're looking for a fifteen-year-old,' she told Ed when it was her turn to talk about her day. 'Ollie Tomlinson, the boy who was snatched as a toddler. He looks like being a suspect in the attack on Carole Linton. And the others, maybe. Kyle Stratton died. Ollie's a murder suspect.'

It sounded cut and dried, but it wasn't.

'How's his mum coping?' Ed asked.

'She's missing too.'

'With Ollie?'

'It looks that way. She cleared out his stuff just like Kyle's parents did, except Ollie's stuff included a weapon.' Marnie drank a mouthful of coffee. 'Something interrupted her. She left the evidence in the kitchen, as if she had to go in a hurry.'

'D'you think she's hiding him?'

'Honestly? I don't know. It would make sense, given their shared history. She lost him once before, which would make any mother over-protective. But Ollie's running with a gang. He's been drifting away for a long time. She's up to her eyes in debt, working all hours just to pay the bills, and the fines for his truancy. That must have changed the dynamic between them.'

'What else?' Ed asked, seeing her frown.

'We can't find Carole. She's not answering her phone, and she's not been home in at least three days. The same three days that Lisa's been missing.'

'You think—'

'This is about revenge. Not just punishment or vigilantism. Revenge. We don't know how many others are caught up in it. Ollie kept lists. We searched the flat, but didn't find them. A baseball bat, newspaper clippings about the recent assaults, but no lists. Ollie must've taken them with him, which might mean he's not done yet.' She shook her head. 'Their neighbour tried to help. They weren't alone, not in the usual way. But they're gone. They must've been really scared . . .'

'You're tired.' Ed kissed the corner of her mouth. 'Let's go to bed.'

Bed was good, but it was a mistake to fall asleep.

The dream came instantly, as if it'd been waiting behind the lids of her eyes. She recognised its colours, pink and grey, like the glimpse of something softly living inside a hard shell.

She was lying in a narrow airless space, black on all sides, the dimensions of a coffin.

It wasn't a coffin. It was a crate, like the ones used by the firm which put her parents' belongings into storage so that she could rent the house to the Kettridges. Everything put away except the few boxes she'd stored in the attic where Tobias and his gang had climbed, finding the shoebox stashed by Stephen six years ago. Stealing it

149

away, as if it was the only thing they came for. As if the house was theirs and they could take what they wanted, and leave the rest burning behind them. Not with fire, with rage.

In the dream, Marnie felt the fever of their loathing. She was wearing her father's wristwatch, tacky with his blood. Desperate to get out, wake up. Dead air eating her lungs, panic crowding her head, her body fighting the cramped angles of the crate. *Stephen—*

Stephen was packed next to her. Their bodies crushed together, the bones in his shoulder and ribs, hip and thigh, slotted into hers, all the way down to where their ankles were pressed so tightly she couldn't tell where he ended and she began.

The whites of his eyes shone at her in bursts, like stars blinking, dying. He smelt of bleached grass and creosote and the cold metal links of the swing where she'd lifted him, still in her police uniform, that day Dad took the photograph.

Stephen's breath at her cheek, sweet and pink, smelt of candy shrimps, childhood.

Under the press of their bodies, a smaller sensation stabbed the base of her spine where the charm bracelet was buried, its little knots of silver sharp as pins. She tried to reach it, but it was buried too deep between them.

She kept fighting although there was no room, all the space and air crowded out by her and Stephen, and the bracelet's bright stabbing in her back.

Cold scent of metal and his eyes sparking, breath heating her cheek.

Tears running into her ears, the way they do when you weep lying down.

Every cell in her body fighting to get out – *wake up –*

but she wasn't moving and nor was he, crushed up against her, all sharp bones and body heat and sweet pink breath.

He had a hand on her wrist, holding her when she tried to fight her way out.

'Not yet,' he was saying, kept saying.

'It's not time yet.'

26

Noah woke early from a confused dream where he was dancing on stage in a confederate uniform to a frantic hip hop soundtrack. He rolled sideways, to kiss Dan's shoulder, before remembering Dan was stuck in Manchester after missing the last train home. He stretched in the too-empty bed, blinking at the mean pinch of light behind the curtains. Today was the day they'd find out whether the baseball bat in Ollie's flat had been used to kill Kyle Stratton.

He was showered, shaved and dressed by 7 a.m. Breakfast was toast eaten in the kitchen while reading Dan's good morning texts. He was smiling by the time he left the house.

In the street, his phone buzzed with a fresh text and he opened it, expecting another message from Dan but getting, *Where's your brother?*

Number unknown. Dad, most likely, using a work phone. Before Noah could respond, a second text came through—

Where's your fucking brother?

Okay, not Dad. Noah held the phone the way you'd

hold a lit candle, sheltering the screen with his free hand as if the day's cold might snuff it out. Shrugging his coat up around his ears, his breath coming in clouds. The phone fizzed in his fingers a third time, making him flinch.

Fancy a lift? I'm 2 mins away. The new text was from Marnie.

Noah looked up the street, thumbing back, *Great*, seeing ranks of parked cars each with its windscreen glinting under the street lights. The day tasted of grit and salt, burning the back of his throat. He scrolled through the texts before checking his call log for anything which might tell him who was after Sol. It had to be someone Sol felt safe giving Noah's number to. Five calls in the log belonged to different phones Sol had used over the last few months. Noah rang the most recent number, getting the familiar message: 'The person you are trying to reach is not accepting calls.'

Where's your fucking brother?

He shivered, pocketing the phone and rubbing his hands to get the warmth back into his fingers.

Tyres picked at the road's grit as Marnie pulled up, double-parking alongside a frozen Lexus. She'd scraped her windscreen clear of ice, but it clung to the roof and doors. Noah struggled with the passenger door until she reached across and popped it from the inside.

'Good morning.' She smiled. 'I was hoping you'd be up early.'

'Strange dreams . . .'

'You too?' She glanced in the wing mirror, a new thinness in her face. 'Fancy a coffee before we get started?'

A week ago they'd have grabbed takeaway coffees on their way into the station but the prospect of DCS Ferguson, surely also an early riser, made a café stop not only tempting but essential.

Marnie parked at the side of her favourite place in a space marked 'Private' which the owner let her use because, Noah suspected, he was a little in love with her.

Kim was a big blond Dane with a square chin and stormy eyes, hands the size of side plates. Dressed today in khakis and a white wool jumper that smelt of oil lamps, he led them to Marnie's favourite table, clicking on a couple of lights to take the dark from the back of the café. He didn't smile at Marnie but his eyes softened as he drew back her chair, waiting for her to be seated. She turned her head to thank him and Noah saw that thinness in her face again, marking out the cleanly vulnerable angles of her cheek and jaw.

'How's Ed?' Noah wanted to ask if she was okay, but this was an easier question.

'He's good, thanks. How's Dan?'

'In Manchester. He got stranded overnight. It's even colder up there.'

Warm in the café, though. Wood-lined, with a gentle pulse of heat from old school radiators. The tables smelt of soap and beeswax. Kim kept the place spotless.

'When's he back?' Marnie asked.

'Today, I hope. Trains keep getting cancelled. Frozen tracks. It's all a bit post-apocalyptic . . .'

Noah watched Kim behind the bar, frothing milk, steam curling around his wrist. 'Do you think he'd let us hole up here if the world ends?'

'Worse places to be stranded,' she agreed.

The coffee came, bruised black in big blue cups. No fancy barista art, just hot milk in a separate jug, lidded. At the side of Marnie's saucer, a tiny meringue-topped biscuit which Kim called *ingenting* and translated as 'nothing'. She thanked him, smiling until he responded with a rare smile of his own before leaving them alone.

Noah wrapped his hands around the cup, letting Marnie add the milk as she had the knack of smoothing the bitter edge from the coffee.

'I was thinking,' she said, 'last night. About Mr Singh.'

'I liked him.' Noah nodded. 'Such a good man.'

She replaced the lid on the milk jug, propping her elbows on the table. 'How many Londoners have a neighbour like that? Someone close by, who wants to help.' She sipped at her coffee. 'Who *does* help. Cooking meals, looking out for Ollie.'

'Not many. I'd say he's one in about four million.'

'And yet Lisa didn't tell him about Ollie, about what happened when he was four.'

'It was a long time ago. Bad memories.'

'She works shifts, places she can get to on foot.' Marnie rested the blue cup on the back of her wrist, holding it steady. 'Carole's the same. And they live less than half an hour apart. What are the chances they've met?'

'In London? Slim.'

But she was sitting too still, looking too serious.

'Shit,' Noah said. 'You think *Lisa's* our vigilante?'

'She'd have recognised Carole if they'd met in the street. I'm not sure that's true of Ollie.'

'So the baseball bat and the lighter are Lisa's.' Noah frowned at the window where steam had painted patterns in the frost. 'Not Ollie's?'

'It's possible, don't you think? Or she could be cleaning up after him, protecting him.'

'Tiger mum, that's what Zoe called her. She said Lisa stuck up for Ollie when he got into trouble, no matter how serious.'

'That's understandable after what they went through eleven years ago.'

'It doesn't explain Rawling, or Kyle.' Noah put the span

of his hand across his mouth, pressing his thumb and fingers to the ache in his cheekbones. 'Lisa, I mean. If it's Lisa doing this.'

'No.' The cup had left a red mark on the back of Marnie's wrist. 'I don't want my nasty mind leading us up a blind alley. And Rawling said *kids*. Let's look in the logical directions.'

'Carole,' Noah said. 'If Ollie attacked her, he'd have let her know why. I don't see a fifteen-year-old doing something as savage as that in silence. He'd *want* her to know why he was doing it. But if *Lisa* met Carole and recognised her, despite the new hair colour . . . I'd recognise someone who'd put me through that. And with Ollie heading off the rails, getting into trouble?'

They paused for Kim to bring a refill of coffee, before he retreated to the kitchen.

'The gang,' Noah continued. 'The way Ollie changed. Swaggering about, staying away. That must've felt like he'd been stolen all over again. If it touched a nerve and if Lisa saw Carole—?'

Walking to whatever low-paid work she could get, worrying about her son all over again, then seeing the woman who'd put her through weeks of hell, forced them to move from Harrow, caused her marriage to break up, fuelled her son's fantasies about punishment. Tiger mum, knowing her son had spent weeks in Carole's cage.

'We need to find Carole.' Marnie added hot milk to their cups. 'And try to find someone who knows where Ollie is.'

'He's with Lisa, isn't he? Having no car limits their options. They left in a hurry, though. No time to get rid of the baseball bat or the other evidence.'

'DCS Ferguson would remind us we have a murder to solve. Without a solid reason to suspect Ollie of attacking

Kyle, we should delegate in the direction of Missing Persons. Until or unless Forensics tell us that the baseball bat has Kyle's DNA on it.'

'If our killer's a vigilante then it makes sense to keep the cases together. And you're right about Rawling, he said it was kids—'

Noah's phone thwapped: another text. He'd almost forgotten the earlier two.

This one had no words. Just—

A picture of Dan, carrying his bike onto a train.

Taken from a distance but close enough for Noah to see the sheen on Dan's cheekbone. A mountain bike, high spec. Noah's birthday present to him. It weighed 14.4 kg. That was the thought flashing in his head as he looked at the picture. The bike weighed 14.4 kg.

'What is it? What's happened?' Marnie touched his wrist. 'Noah?'

'Nothing. At least . . .'

The phone jolted with a new text.

Where. Is. Your. Fucking. Brother.

Chair legs scraped as he stood.

Kim turned from the bar to look at him.

Marnie kept her hand on his wrist, her voice very steady. 'Noah, what's happened?'

'Just— Give me a minute.'

He turned his back and walked to the front of the café, speed-dialling Dan's number.

He dragged the door open to a shock of cold air that felt good, needful.

The number rang. And rang.

Shit, Dan, pick up. Don't let me—

Voicemail: 'This's Dan's phone. Leave a message.'

'Call me back?' He tried to keep the fear from his voice. 'I need to know you're okay.'

He texted the same thing with a slick taste in his mouth as if he was about to vomit.

Someone was looking for Sol.

They'd followed Dan to the station yesterday. Had they got on the train with him? No – forty minutes ago, Dan had been sending smutty texts. Texts that could only have come from him. He was safe in a hotel in Manchester. Noah should've asked him which one, but it hadn't seemed important last night. He could be calling the hotel right now, checking that Dan Noys was in his room. In the shower, that would explain the voicemail. He'd have been out late last night. Canal Street, clubbing, refusing to hide in his hotel room the way the world wanted him to—

Since Orlando, Dan had been defiantly demonstrative, needing to be part of the scene in a way neither of them had in years. Dan was grieving, wanting to celebrate what they had and to show two fingers to the corners of the world where hate still lived. Noah understood, but it exhausted him. Not just the clubbing and late nights when he was working but the worry, private and personal, for Dan's safety. The worry rubbed at the edges of everything.

He scrolled back to the photo.

Virgin train. Dan in black jeans and a zipped squall jacket, blue beanie, Osprey rucksack. His cold weather clothes. The photo must have been taken at Euston yesterday morning as he was boarding the train to Manchester. He'd arrived safely. Forty minutes ago he'd been sending filthy good morning texts. He was okay, he had to be.

Where. Is. Your. Fucking. Brother.

Noah sucked in the cold air – like breathing icicles – and shivered.

Behind him, the café pulsed with heat. How was he going to explain this to Marnie? It would mean admitting his kid brother was caught up in a gang, like the one that broke into her house, or the one Ollie was running with. Gangs were meant to be on the other side of their desks, not living in their homes, sleeping on their sofas. He'd have to admit he had no idea where Sol was or what he was up to. Worse, that he'd let Sol use his flat as a base, his phone number as a contact. But none of that mattered, not really, as long as Dan was okay. And Sol. Let Noah look a fool, let him lose his job, as long as they were safe.

He stared at the phone, willing it to ring.

The cold was inside his head now. He could feel his skull contracting.

It was freezing out here; he'd left his coat over the back of his chair in the café.

In a minute he'd go back inside. Get warm. Explain himself to Marnie.

He just—

Needed to stop shaking first.

27

Marnie watched Noah standing out in the cold, his head bent over his phone. If he didn't come inside soon, she'd take his coat to him. She could do that much.

'Give me a minute,' he'd said. Whatever had happened, whatever message was hollowing his face with hurt, he needed a moment alone with it.

She stood, counting out cash to pay for the coffees before pulling on her coat and scarf. Taking her time, to let Noah do the same. They needed to be at the station soon, or else incur Ferguson's wrath. Not that wrath was in her repertoire, yet. Marnie felt a pang as sharp as toothache for Tim Welland. She should call him, see how things were. He'd appreciate the distraction. She could take him a couple of books—

'You've paid.' Noah reached past her for his coat. 'What do I owe you?'

'No need.' She caught the grey chill of outdoors from his skin. 'You can get the next ones.'

'Thanks.' He pulled on his coat, keeping his phone in his hand. 'I'm waiting for a call from Dan. It's probably nothing.' He moved his mouth into a false smile. 'We should go.'

She held him still with a real smile. 'You said probably nothing. What might it be?' She read wariness in his face, and guessed its cause. 'I'm asking as a friend, not a boss.'

He didn't let go of the phone, just raised his free hand, spanning the narrow width of his face with his palm, the way he had earlier. 'It's Sol. And Dan.' His eyes were hot. 'It might be Dan.'

'Tell me.' She nodded for him to sit back down.

'Can we move? I'd rather be moving.' He checked his watch. 'We need to get to work.'

'With you like this?'

'I'm okay. I'll be okay. It's just—'

His phone rang, and his eyes snapped back into focus. 'Dan? Hey . . .' He straightened, nodding relief at Marnie. 'That's good. No, it was just . . . Yeah. Me, too.' His smile was genuine now. 'Where are you?'

Marnie gestured with the car keys, wanting to give him space to talk.

At the bar, Kim was polishing cutlery. He'd have customers soon, the first of the office workers, those not lured by the brighter lights of the coffee chains. This place was a well-kept secret.

'Thank you,' she said. 'For the coffee, and the parking space.'

'Of course.' His fingers moved smoothly, bringing up a shine on the steel bowl of a soup spoon. 'Come again soon.'

'We will.'

She waited in the car for Noah. Thinking about Kyle, and Ollie and Lisa. Their good neighbour, Himmat. Had he seen Ollie's notebooks, or his knife? Fran's team were checking the contents of the bin bag for DNA. No visible blood on the bat, suggesting it'd been wiped clean. But Himmat would have heard Ollie coming home in the early hours of yesterday morning; the walls were thin in Jonas House, and Ollie was a clumsy kid. So who brought home the baseball bat, if not Ollie?

'Sorry.' Noah got into the car, fastening his seat belt. 'Thanks for waiting.'

She started for the station, not asking any questions.

Noah would tell her or he wouldn't, but she trusted him to make the right decision. He wouldn't hold back information which might affect his work, or hers. He'd put his phone away and lost the worst of the tension in his face, but he was wound tight enough to twang if she touched him.

He looked dead ahead for a short time before scratching his cheek. 'Sol's in some sort of trouble.' Using his interview voice, neutral. 'He gave my number to someone who's threatening Dan. At least . . . I think that's what's happening. Dan's okay. He hasn't spotted anyone hanging around. Someone took a photo of him yesterday morning, getting on the train to Manchester.'

'That was the text?'

'One of them.' He moved his jaw. 'The others were asking where Sol is.'

'And you don't know who sent the texts,' Marnie deduced.

Noah shook his head. 'I can't get hold of Sol. He's changed his phone five times in the last few weeks. It's been a fortnight since I spoke with him properly; we're never home at the same time. Mum and Dad haven't heard from him, they thought he was with me. He's staying at my place, or he was. He's not been home in a couple of nights. That's not unusual. That's . . . Sol.'

'So these texts weren't from friends of his.'

'Sol wouldn't give my number to just anyone.' Noah rubbed his right thumb at his left palm. 'So I'm thinking they *were* friends but something's happened.' He drew a short breath. 'He told me he was trying to get out, but he's been in a gang on and off for the last ten years. Harry Kennedy's probably got him on his radar. I should've told you this sooner. I'm sorry.'

'You did tell me.' Marnie was waiting for a traffic light to change. 'Just not in as many words.'

Sol was trouble. Noah had dropped enough clues to that in the time they'd worked together.

She felt the weight of worry in his stare and moved her head to meet it, unblinking. 'Did I need to know details, before now?'

He shook his head, hot-eyed again, his face as open as she'd ever seen it. Laid bare by this worry for his brother, and for Dan. For his job too, or that part of it which relied on their working relationship. Noah had his secrets, everyone has secrets. But he didn't lie, or dodge, or boast. He was one of the most honest people she knew.

'There was no reason for you to tell me until now.' She released the handbrake, drove on. 'What did you advise Dan to do?'

'Watch out for trouble.' He rubbed the heel of his hand at his eyes. 'Stay in a group, avoid being on his own. And I told him to keep in touch, text me every hour.'

'Good.' She nodded. 'How are we going to find Sol?'

'I can try Dad again, but I doubt he's gone there. He wasn't home two nights ago. I checked.'

'Do you know the gang he was trying to leave?'

'No. I only know the one he used to run with. I wasn't joking about Harry Kennedy; Trident probably has eyes on this gang right now.'

'Ask him,' Marnie said. 'From what I've seen of DS Kennedy, he's decent. Discreet, too.'

163

'I'm not looking forward to telling DCS Ferguson . . .'

'We'll tell her when we need to, *if* we need to.'

Noah's phone chimed. He dug it out as Marnie took the turning into the station car park.

'DCS Ferguson,' he said. 'She wants us in her office.'

'Good timing, in that case.' Marnie parked up. 'Let her know we're on our way up.'

DCS Ferguson had made herself at home in Welland's office. His calendar was on the wall but everything else had been put into boxes and stacked in corners. His desk had been swept clean, and polished and laid with her things: a rose-gold MacBook Air, glossy black fountain pen, laminated world map doubling as a mouse mat, potted miniature narcissus.

World domination and a potted narcissus; as an analysis job for a psychologist, it was hardly worth getting out of bed for. Noah wondered if the woman knew the signal it sent out and liked it that way, a short cut to impressing on you just who was in charge here.

'DS Jake. DI Rome.' She stayed behind the desk. 'I was hoping you might have started early today, given the week we're having. Then I wouldn't have needed to sort out an interview room for Kyle Stratton's parents.'

'They're here?' Noah was surprised. They'd set out early from Reigate to reach London before 8.30 a.m. 'We didn't ask them to come in, did we?'

Ferguson chipped a smile from her mouth. 'I was hoping you'd have the answer to that.'

'We didn't ask them to come in,' Marnie said. 'But we were going to visit them yesterday, before events overtook us. We need to interview them about the phones and the letters they threw out from Kyle's room.'

'Serendipitous, in that case.' Ferguson touched her

fingers to the MacBook, angling it away from Marnie and Noah. 'They're in interview room two.'

She ran her eyes over whatever was onscreen. Her Tumblr, possibly. Bodies of her enemies stacked up in the back streets of Salford. 'Interview room one being occupied by Mazi Yeboah.'

If she'd hoped to take Marnie by surprise, she was disappointed. Not much surprised Marnie, as Noah was learning. Not even admissions about your family's gang connections.

'When did he arrive?' she asked evenly.

'Oh, they came together,' Ferguson said. 'A road trip from Reigate with the young man their dead son set on fire eleven years ago.'

Welland would have made a joke about them cheating Mike Leigh out of a job.

Ferguson just said, 'Interview rooms one and two. All yours.'

28

Mazi Yeboah wore a navy logo-less tracksuit and mid-price running shoes, sitting with his forearms flat to the table, his spine straight in the chair. Twenty-four years old, a second generation Ghanaian living in Barnet with his girl-friend, Debbie had said. Good-looking, narrowly built with clean fingernails, no rings, no wristwatch. Noah looked for evidence of his close encounter with Kyle back when they were both schoolboys. There – at the throat of his tracksuit, a thread of pink where his skin was otherwise black. Under the tracksuit he was wearing an orange running vest.

'Are they okay?' East London accent. 'Kyle's mum and dad? They're okay, yeah?'

Noah pulled out a chair and sat. 'You travelled with them, from Reigate. How'd that happen?'

'I went to their house.' Mazi spread his hands on the table. 'I didn't mean to freak them out, just wanted to know they were okay.'

'You knew where they lived?'

'Yeah. Yes.' He met Noah's gaze, didn't flinch or look away. 'I heard what happened to Kyle and I wanted to say sorry, and see if they were okay.'

'You wanted to say sorry.'

'About Kyle, yeah.' He sat back in the chair.

He'd been running, Noah could smell it on him. Clean sweat, not cortisol.

'I didn't mean to freak them out. I guess they didn't know.' He pulled the tracksuit cuff over his hand, using it to wipe his top lip. 'Anyway, bad idea. So I'm sorry about that too.'

'About freaking them out.'

'Turning up at their house. I'd have called, but they're not in the phone book and Kyle says they're weird about letters so—' Wiping his lip again. 'Said. He *said* they were weird about letters.'

The sound he made was beyond distress. His fingers twitched on the table, light picking at the pink thread on his neck.

Noah waited, knowing that Mazi would talk without the need for questions.

He'd come here to talk, words crowded behind his teeth, waiting to get out. And Noah knew what they were, some of the words at least.

He knew what Mazi Yeboah was going to tell him.

Gerry and Brenda Stratton sat under the stewed light, looking uptight. Brenda wore a turtleneck jumper two shades paler than her tan, and white skinny jeans with heeled black boots. Her husband was in a red velour V-neck and pressed grey suit trousers, no shirt under the V-neck, just grey chest hair. They'd dressed in a hurry.

'You're interviewing him then.' Gerry tucked his chin to his chest. 'Is he telling you why he doorstepped us at that hour? Insisting we drive him here like we're a taxi service.'

167

'Kyle thought we were a taxi service.' Brenda sounded stunned. 'To and from the train station, until we told him no. We like a glass of wine in the evenings. Well, he did too.'

'Not wine.' Gerry folded his arms. 'He liked something a lot stronger.'

The room was too hot, but they looked cold.

'He turns up on our doorstep saying he's heard about Kyle and he's so sorry. He'd been running. In this weather! At that time of day.' Brenda put a hand to her throat. 'The sun wasn't even up.'

'Freezing out there.' Gerry glared at the door then switched his stare to the radiator. 'Not much better in here. Who the hell goes running when there's black ice?'

'He's standing there,' Brenda said, 'dripping with sweat and he's saying, "Sorry, I'm so sorry," and then he insists we get in the car and drive here. "We need to tell the police," as if he knows better than we do what should be done about Kyle.'

'I said I'd take him to the station, he could get a train home.' Gerry turned his face away, jaw bunching. 'He wasn't having any of that. Oh no. *He* knew best.'

Marnie waited. There was no need to ask questions. Sometimes there were no questions you could ask. You just had to sit and see what came out of people who were grieving or raging. She wondered if it was the same next door, whether Mazi was boiling over with words.

Brenda said, 'He'll be telling you all sorts, we know that. It's written all over his face. Soon as I opened the door, I knew. We both did. That's why we came. Not because he insisted, but so you didn't get one side of the story and not the other.'

'You need both sides to a story.' Gerry didn't look at

Marnie or his wife, fixing his stare on the wall. 'That's what I said to the school the first time Kyle was in trouble, before it ever blew up. I said, there're two sides here. It's all very well shouting about bullying but have you looked at it from both sides? Have you taken a long, hard look? They hadn't, of course.'

Brenda searched inside the sleeve of her jumper for a trio of gold bangles, bringing them into the light with a look of relief, as if she'd retrieved her dignity in some small measure.

'A lot of shouting,' Gerry said. 'But you need to stop and look at the facts, quietly and squarely.'

'Even when it's awful.' Brenda turned her bangles, appealing to Marnie with a sudden desperate stare. 'Even when it's the last thing you want to hear.'

'He hated me at school.' Mazi moved his shoulders as if the skin graft was too tight, or the memory too vivid, of what Kyle and Jack Goodrich had done. 'That's what everyone thought. That's what *I* thought, for a bit. He hated me.' He looked down at his hands then up at Noah. 'He didn't, though.'

The light hummed over their heads, not liking the cold. Nothing in the station did. The heating had come back, but reluctantly. The station stank of stewed tea, packet soup and wet sheep – from the jumpers they were all wearing under their suits.

Mazi hadn't worn a coat to visit Kyle's parents. He hadn't planned the trip or he'd have dressed for it. Reigate wasn't any warmer than Barnet. He'd run to keep warm.

Noah passed him a bottle of mineral water.

Mazi held the bottle between his hands. It set blue shadows on the table. 'His mum and dad are pissed off, I get that. But they had to know. His dad thought he'd

169

screwed up. Kyle said he was getting grief for it even after ten years. They thought he was a thug. And they were embarrassed. They're decent people, I didn't want them thinking—'

Noah waited.

'What happened to Kyle?' Mazi touched his fingers to the blue shadows. 'I didn't want them thinking that was *justice*. Karma. That he'd run into trouble again, the way he did before. He said his dad never stopped watching him for signs that he was still a bully. That's what they thought, that he was a thug and a bully. Yeah, and a racist. But that was the least of it, you know?'

He looked up at Noah. His eyes were huge, hot.

'I didn't want them thinking that he got what he deserved.'

'These facts,' Marnie said, 'that you want us to look at squarely and quietly. Are they connected to the letters and phones you threw away?'

Gerry's stare swivelled from the wall to his wife.

Marnie would've preferred to interview them separately, but for now they were a team. DCS Ferguson had put them in here. Victims, not suspects.

'Seven phones, in working order. That was an odd thing to throw out.'

Brenda shook her head. 'We don't know what you're talking about.'

'I'm afraid in that case we will need to make this a formal interview.'

'God's sake!' Gerry rolled his neck. 'We didn't want you chasing up the wrong road, all right? There's nothing on those phones or in those letters that explains why he was killed. *Brutally*. By a *maniac*. Not some smutty date he'd fixed up out of curiosity or boredom – whatever it was.

Did you see the mags he was reading?' Lifting his chin. 'If you found the phones, you found the mags. It was all an adventure. A *game*. He didn't travel, not like us, but he explored all right. Oh he was a first-class explorer was Kyle! No stone left unturned. Experimenting all over the place.'

'With people? Or did you mean some other kind of experimenting?'

Gerry wouldn't answer.

'He was twenty-six,' Brenda said. 'He wasn't a child any more, but it was our home. We didn't kick him out, or even ask him to leave. Lots of parents would've done that. While he was under *our* roof, he played by *our* rules.'

She stiffened in response to an angry movement from her husband. 'He *did*. That trouble at school . . . He'd put us through enough. He wasn't going to put us through any more.'

Her eyes were pale in the tanned skin of her face. 'Enough's enough. He knew that.'

'It wasn't exclusive,' Mazi said. 'Kyle wasn't— That wasn't his thing. He said he got enough domestic bliss at home. A whole world out there, that's what he said, waiting to be explored.'

He held onto the bottled water, blinking. 'He liked parties. New people, different. Strangers he'd never see again. I said I thought it was fucked up, but he didn't care. "Of course it is," that's what he said. "Of course it's fucked up. That's the point." I learnt to keep my mouth shut.'

He linked his fingers around the neck of the bottle. 'Chemsex. You know what that is?'

'Yes.'

Mazi raised his eyes, scanning Noah's face in recognition. 'You'd think Kay invented it, the way he went on.'

171

Kay. Kyle.

'I asked him once if he wanted me to go with him. If that's what he wanted, the pair of us at a party some-where, maybe a different party every night. He had a good laugh about that. "Like an old married couple? Fuck off." So I did.' Blinking. 'I fucked off.'

Noah waited, holding in the questions he needed to ask. Whether Mazi knew why Kyle had gone to Page Street that night. Whether there was anyone in particular he was worried about, strangers Kyle had screwed around with, or who hadn't wanted to back off. Enemies he'd made while he was popping pills in houses he'd never been inside before, or since.

'Shit.' Mazi wiped his nose with the heel of his hand. 'This isn't— Not why I came here.'

'That's okay. Take your time.'

'Take my time?' Opening his eyes wide. 'He's dead. We don't have any *time*. I wasted it writing letters when I could've gone round there. Being pissed off because of the pills and the girls and the stag parties in search of his missing—' He stopped, kicking a foot at the table leg. 'Shit, man. Don't talk to me about *time*. Okay? Just don't.'

'All right, I won't do that. Tell me why he was in Page Street. Tell me why you think he died.'

Mazi bent over the water bottle, picking at its paper label with his thumbnail. His shoulders shook. The pink thread of the skin graft ran deep into the neck of his vest, to a river of welts where Kyle had burned the skin from his back. 'Me . . .' He wept, raw in his chest.

His hands opened, fingers dancing with distress.

'What do you mean – me?'

'It was me.'

He lifted his head, face streaming tears.

'Because of— It was *me*. I killed him.'

29

Marnie closed the door to her office, nodding at Noah to sit down. She moved her chair so that they were shoulder to shoulder, looking at the newspaper clippings.

'These.' Mazi had dug the clippings from his pocket, pressing them to the table in the interview room. 'That's how I know it was me.'

Yesterday's date and a photo of Kyle taken just after he'd been found guilty of racially aggravated assault. He was fifteen, all scared eyes and cheekbones, about to spend three months in a secure unit. An old photo, but the story was up to date: Kyle's assault in Westminster, the fatal injuries from which he'd died.

'It was me.' Mazi had covered the clippings with his hands. 'He died because of me.'

The second clipping was the report from eleven years ago, of Kyle's conviction. Two faces, side by side. Kyle and Mazi, just boys. One white, the other black. Fifteen and fourteen years old, in the same school uniform. Of the two, it was Kyle who looked scared. Mazi was smiling, pre-assault; the reporter had failed to get a photo of him on the burns ward of the local hospital.

'These came in yesterday's post,' Noah told Marnie. 'To Mazi's home address. He worked late, didn't find the envelope until he got home around ten p.m. Couldn't sleep, went for a run, ended up getting the first train out to Reigate to see Kyle's parents. He was scared they might've got the same post. That they'd be thinking the same thing he was, that Kyle was killed because of what he did to Mazi, eleven years ago. Even though Mazi had forgiven him, and Kyle knew that.'

'How recently did he forgive him?' Marnie asked.

'Three years ago. Kyle saw his name in the paper after a fund-raiser, got in touch via the charity Mazi works for. They went for a drink, then back to Mazi's place.'

Noah rubbed at his temple. 'He'd figured out that Kyle liked him, back in school. And he'd liked Kyle. But it was impossible. The kind of school they were at, the mates they had . . . He wasn't surprised when Kyle went the other way, started hanging out with Jack Goodrich who *did* hate Mazi. Then there were Kyle's parents . . . How're they coping?'

'With their son's death? Better than you might expect. With his boyfriend turning up on their doorstep with these clippings? Not so much. His dad's refusing to believe it. Two sides to every story, he says. He thinks Mazi meant something else when he began blaming himself.'

Marnie's eyes darkened to ink-blue. 'And I quote: "That sort are always only one step away from doing something dangerous." He thinks Mazi was confessing to killing Kyle.'

'Mazi loved him,' Noah said. 'That's what makes it tricky. Gerry could understand the experiments, even the sex. It was the love he couldn't get his head around.'

'Define experiments.'

'What we thought when we looked at the phones. Chemsex, pills, strangers. Not just men. Women too. Kyle liked to keep his options open. Gerry approved of the women, and Kyle liked his dad's approval, that was a big part of the problem. Gerry stood by him when he went to prison, even when the neighbours got snotty. A lot of it was Gerry wanting to lecture him about his mistakes, but not all of it. Mazi says Kyle couldn't make up his mind whether he wanted to rub his dad's nose in it, or keep his promise to reform.'

'Does Mazi have any ideas about who killed him?'

'Beyond blaming himself? No. I asked about the phones. That was Kyle compartmentalising – different phones for the different people he was trying to be. Worried about the data trail once he'd used the apps too often, for sex or pills. And paranoid about getting calls from people he didn't want to see again.' He shook his head. 'Everything was a one-night stand with Kyle. Mazi said a new phone meant a clean leaf when he started to feel too dirty. He wasn't surprised Kyle kept the phones rather than throwing them away, but he was surprised Kyle kept his letters.'

'Brenda found them,' Marnie said, 'inside one of the magazines they threw out. She thought they were from a girl because of where she found them. Then she read Mazi's name. They couldn't make sense of it. The forgiveness shocked them as much as the love. "After what Kyle did to him," that's what they kept saying. The idea of Mazi wanting revenge makes sense, but not the idea that he was able to forgive Kyle.'

She touched a hand to her neck, nursing an old ache there. 'There's nobody in Page Street that Mazi thinks Kyle might've known?'

'They broke up three weeks ago,' Noah said. 'Mazi'd had enough of worrying where Kyle was, or whether he was coming home.'

'Explain that to me. We thought Mazi lived with his girlfriend in Barnet. And Kyle was in Reigate with Gerry and Brenda. So where was home?'

'Barnet. Mazi shares the flat with a friend, but she isn't his girlfriend. Kyle had slept over so often he had clothes there, and books. He didn't want any of it back when they broke up. Mazi thought that meant they'd probably get together again. It'd happened that way before. He'd given up on ultimatums, but he hoped Kyle would get tired of the parties and pills, and pretending to his parents that he was getting something out of his system before he settled down.' Noah crooked his mouth, not smiling. 'No one expects grandkids these days, and Gerry and Brenda are too wedded to their lifestyle. Holidays, cruise ships. They wouldn't want to give that up for babysitting duties. But they wanted Kyle to bring home a nice girl. Proof that he'd calmed down. Made good.'

He put his thumb on the newspaper clippings. 'I gave the envelope to Ron for Forensics. Same handwriting, though. And the same trick with white wax to cheat the postmark.'

'Our vigilante wanted Mazi to know why Kyle was killed. Unless this is about more than justice then whoever's doing it didn't know that Mazi and Kyle were in a relationship.'

'They didn't care.' Anger altered Noah's voice. 'Kyle or Carole or Mazi – they're all faceless. Not human enough to matter. Our vigilantes are pretending this is about punishment, setting the record straight, evening the score. But they've hurt Mazi in ways Kyle never did. This?' Pushing his thumb at the clippings. 'Is just an excuse for what they want to do, which is hurt people. Break their faces, their legs. Set fire to their skulls. *Kill*—'

He looked at Marnie, fierce-eyed. 'Gerry's right. We're

looking for a maniac. Not a vigilante. Not anyone who cares about justice, not really. Someone who loves violence and hates people.'

He pushed back from the desk. 'A killer. We're looking for a stone-cold killer.'

30

Duct tape tastes like its colour. Not silver, not sharp enough for that. Dull and grey like having a mouse pressed into your mouth, a dead mouse with glue and blood in its fur.

Finn's lips were bleeding where he'd tried to tear them free from the tape. The tip of his tongue had swelled up and he was scared to swallow. People died from swallowing their tongues, plus it felt like his throat was full of fingers but he couldn't cry because his nose would fill with snot and he could hardly breathe already because of the fingers and the way his tongue was swollen.

The tape was wound right around his head.

Ollie had wrapped it tight, stretching it before he tore it with his teeth and pushed two fingers at Finn's forehead, shoving him back into the corner between the bog and the bath. 'He's done.'

He'd looked up as he said it, and Finn had seen fear in his eyes. Ollie's eyes were purple and he'd never seen any special look in them other than *pissed-off* or *fuck-off*, but just for a second—

Ollie looked scared.

'He's done.' He knelt on the towel that Finn'd been shivering under until they made him move.

Ollie's hood was down, letting the light all over his head, his lashes long as a girl's. He spat a piece of duct tape into his hand, looking at it then looking at Finn. 'Now what?'

Purple eyes. Scared, like Finn. Or just pissed off that he was being made to do this – wrap duct tape around Finn's face, and whatever else he was about to do.

'His hands and feet.' Brady, in the doorway. 'Do it.'

Ollie reached for the roll of tape.

Finn shook his head, making it spin. He was going to puke, he was going to drown in his own puke. This was it, where they raped him and killed him and cut him up in the bath—

He kicked out, catching Ollie's hand.

'Come here, you little shit.'

Ollie grabbed him by an ankle and one wrist, hauling Finn into his lap until his spine was up against Ollie's chest and Ollie's arm was across his shoulders. He let go of Finn's ankle, reaching for his wrists and crushing them together with a single hand.

Finn kept kicking even though there was nothing to kick except the bath and the bog, but he didn't stop, twisting like a fish in Ollie's lap.

'Fuck's sake.' Ollie used his chin to catch Finn's forehead, holding hard until Finn's hair tore from struggling. 'Let me do it,' he hissed. 'Just – let me do it.'

His arm was across the front of Finn's shoulders and there was a different pain to the bones in his wrists being ground together and the hair being torn out of his head—

Ollie's fingers were squeezing his left arm just below the shoulder.

Squeezing him tight, the way you'd hold onto something to keep from drowning or falling.

Like Ollie was the one about to die, and Finn—
Finn was the only thing keeping him safe.

31

'Mazi Yeboah was sent clippings, just like Valerie Rawling. Two clippings each, linking these assaults to the earlier crimes. Our vigilantes want the original victims to know what they've done.' Marnie indicated the photocopies on the evidence board. 'Forensics are looking at the enve-lopes.'

'What's with the C?' Ron pointed at the letter written in the corner of each clipping. 'It's on everything, like a copyright symbol. Their way of owning what they've done? Or a clue? It's pretty arty, the way they've done it. The Cs on the envelope don't look like that.'

The tips of the C were squared off, shaped into short vertical lines.

'Could be a gang sign.' Noah picked up a pen and replicated the C on the whiteboard. 'Crasmere Boys are one of the newer gangs. I asked Trident for a list after Rawling said it was kids that attacked him. Crasmere Street's only a quarter of a mile from Jonas House. We need to find out whether Ollie has any connections to the gang. I've put in a call to Zoe Marshall.'

'Pat Hammond said kids too. He's our eyewitness at

Page Street, but he couldn't ID either of them. Hoodies and trainers, he *thinks*. Couldn't even give me colours.' Ron looked disgusted. 'I'm crossing him off the list. CPS won't touch him with the sharp end of a shitty stick.'

Debbie said, 'The sports centre confirmed they had a break-in two months ago. They said it was kids from Jonas House, sent a list of what was lifted. It's basically our vigilantes' shopping list. Golf clubs, baseball bats and a croquet mallet.'

'Play a lot of croquet in Camden, do they?' Ron scoffed.

'A promotional gift from a local business, apparently.'

'Ollie and co found a better use for it . . .'

'Do we know that for certain?' Noah asked. 'That it was Ollie who broke into the sports centre?'

'They didn't press charges,' Debbie said, 'because their security was on the blink and they'd no proof but yes, they're certain it was him. Officially he was banned for anti-social behaviour.'

'Where are we up to with CCTV at Page Street?' Marnie asked Colin.

'Last sighting is Kyle crossing Victoria Street just after he left the pub. He's looking at his phone. Call log says he got a text alert from an app. A hook-up. The app was using relative distance info so there's a chance Kyle's location was flagged for our killer to see.'

'How?' Ron asked. 'You mean the killer was using the same app? The killer was the hook-up?'

'Not necessarily,' Colin said. 'Any app that uses relative distance data carries the risk of your actual location being determined, but generally it's by someone who knows how the tech works and can access the app from multiple locations while you're standing still. I checked and this app has an option to turn off the "distance from" info.

But even if Kyle had turned it off, his profile would still appear in the cascade of users.'

'Well that's clear as mud,' Ron muttered. 'He was using this app to pick up strangers for sex, that's about the size of it, right?' He looked across at Noah.

Marnie said, 'Is there any value in asking the app for a password to Kyle's account?'

'We could ask.' Colin looked doubtful. 'But if we think it's kids then I don't see them using an app like this. Or hacking his location for that matter. If you're smart enough to do that then you're smart enough not to attack him in the street. They could've waited until he got home.'

Marnie looked at Debbie. 'Any luck getting hold of Carole?'

'Still not answering her phone. Same with Ollie and Lisa . . . I've been trying to find out where they might've bumped into one another. There's a service station where Lisa worked late shifts, and Carole has a car. That's as close as I've got. Sorry, boss.'

Marnie's wrists itched. Too many loose ends. Too many coincidences and not enough hard evidence. DCS Ferguson was going to walk all over the little they had.

'Kyle's tox screen came back,' Ron offered. 'His liver took a pounding from methamphetamine. That fits with what Mazi told us, but it doesn't get us any closer to who killed him.'

'The newspaper clippings,' Noah said. 'Not the ones from the last ten weeks. From seven and eleven years ago. How did our vigilantes get hold of those? Kids wouldn't bother tracking down old newspapers. They might've told Val and Mazi that they'd paid a debt on their behalf, but clippings? I'm not sure kids even know newspapers exist, do they?'

'Ollie's vanished off the face of London,' Ron reminded

him. 'And his mum too. Maybe Ollie doesn't read papers, but Lisa does. In any case, we've got the bin bag from their flat. Why aren't we talking about that? The baseball bat, the lighter. Porn mags, and not the sort sixteen-year-olds look at.' Another glance at Noah. 'Lonely housewives might like that stuff, though.'

'We're not talking about the evidence from the Tomlinsons' flat,' Marnie said, 'because we're waiting on Forensics. It's too convenient that we've struck what looks like the evidence lottery right on the doorstep of two missing persons with a motive for attacking Carole Linton—'

'Convenient?' Ferguson was in the doorway. 'I'm not sure I believe in evidence that's too convenient. I believe in offenders who fuck up. We get plenty of those in Manchester, where we've an aversion to looking gift horses in the gob.' She nodded at the evidence board. 'Are you sure you're not overcooking this? From where I'm stood, it looks more complicated than it needs to be. I'd like to establish a baseline going forward. Keep it simple.'

'A fresh pair of eyes is always welcome.' Marnie stood back from the board. 'Please.'

Ferguson crossed the room, picking up a marker pen as she passed Ron's desk. 'What's this?' Pointing at Noah's replication of the letter C from the clippings. 'DS Carling?'

'It's what our killer put on the newspaper stories, ma'am. The ones he sent to the victims.'

'An ownership stamp?'

'Or a gang sign.' Ron nodded at Noah. 'Trident gave us a list.'

'How many gangs of two people – *kids* – do you have in Greater London right now?'

'Might not be the same two kids every time,' Ron said. 'Different pairs, maybe.'

'How many gangs send newspaper clippings? Or operate as vigilantes?' Ferguson drew a line through Noah's sketch. 'If we're barking up a tree, let's at least pick one that's indigenous.'

She capped the pen, holding it between her hands, eyes on the room. 'Kyle liked a lot of sex and he took drugs to speed things along. DS Jake, what's your take on that?'

'The sort of sex we're talking about takes place behind closed doors.' Noah used his neutral voice, with just a chip of ice in it. 'If his death's linked to the app he was using then there was no need to kill him in the street. That was noisy, and it was risky. Added to which we know the attack was connected to what happened eleven years ago because the killer sent a message to Mazi.'

'Are we taking a full statement from Mr Yeboah?' Ferguson swung her stare to Marnie. 'Kyle's parents seem to think it worthwhile.'

'They brought him here in their car. I doubt they'd have taken that risk had they truly believed he was their son's killer.'

'Are we charging *them*—? They disposed of evidence. That's obstruction. DC Pitcher, how long did you spend trying to piece together the love letters they were too embarrassed to let us read?'

Colin blinked, but the question was rhetorical.

'We could charge Kyle's parents,' Marnie said, 'although the CPS might raise an objection. They're victims, and they've lost their only child. I'd prefer to focus on finding Ollie and Lisa.'

'How about finding and re-interviewing our other victim?'

Ferguson pointed the pen at Carole's face on the board.

'Now that Mr Rawling has told us it was kids, and our eyewitness in Page Street corroborates that, maybe Carole can be ruled in or out of our conspiracy theory once and for all.'

She nodded at Marnie. 'It would be nice to cut some of this complexity down to size.'

'At least she called it *our* conspiracy theory,' Noah said, as he and Marnie headed out of the station. 'We get joint ownership of whatever happens next.' He checked his phone for Dan's latest text.

It was there, on time. Dan was fine. No new demands from whoever was after Sol. Noah let out the breath he'd been holding, rubbing his thumb at the phone's screen.

'What did DS Kennedy have to say about Sol?' Marnie knew what was going through his head.

'He's calling me back once he's asked around.' He pocketed the phone. 'I think I can forget about it for a bit. Concentrate on cutting our complexity down to size.'

They were headed for Carole's place. It couldn't be coincidence that she'd been missing for the same three days as Ollie and Lisa. Whatever Ferguson said, this case was complicated. Pretending that it wasn't wouldn't get them any closer to the truth.

Marnie was thawing the car's frozen lock when her phone rang.

She handed the lighter to Noah, and took the call. 'DI Rome.' Noah held the lighter to the lock, thinking of the burn to Kyle's eye.

Whoever did that had pretended they were paying tribute to Mazi. They couldn't imagine a scenario in which Mazi had not only forgiven his tormentor but fallen in love with him. *Life* was complicated. Their vigilantes, like DCS Ferguson, were wrong.

Marnie held out the car keys, listening to whoever was

on the other end of the phone. The car crunched as it opened, reluctant to give up its new layer of ice. Noah held the door for her, swinging it shut before walking around to the passenger side.

'Change of plan.' Marnie had pocketed her phone and was shivering in the driver's seat.

Noah tried for optimism. 'Carole's turned up?'

'Another assault.' She started the engine, letting it idle while she cleared the inside of the windscreen. 'Ferguson is going to think we're making this up . . .' She put the scraper away and set her hands on the wheel before turning to face Noah. 'This one happened behind bars.'

'In *prison*?'

'HMP Cloverton.' Her irises burned black, making the whites of her eyes very bright. 'Ask me how I know it's our vigilantes.'

'How?'

'The victim, Jacob Collins, has a skull fracture and five broken bones. That's nothing this prison hasn't seen before. It has one of the worst reputations in the country.' She spoke as if she knew HMP Cloverton intimately. 'But Mr Collins? Is asking for us.'

'Us? You mean the police or—'

'You and me. He reads the papers, watches the news. Other than that, he keeps his head down, working out his sentence. Sixteen months for using a dog as a weapon. His victim lost five fingers.'

'Another of life's charmers . . . And he's asking for us. Why?'

'It's unclear, but the attacker . . .? Carved the letter C into his shoulder.'

The windscreen had misted over again.

Marnie cleared it, again.

'You're right,' Noah said. 'Ferguson's going to think we're making this up. We know our vigilantes aren't inside. Which means whoever did this has contacts in prison. That might stack up if it's a gang, but it can't be kids. Even if Ollie *is* involved, it goes deeper than a couple of kids.'

'I want you to stay here,' Marnie said. 'Pick up the search for Carole, and the others. Our latest victim isn't going anywhere.'

The thinness was back in her face.

'Find Ollie, if you can. I'll see what our dog handler has to say.'

32

Prison changes people. Some shrink, others bulk up. Jacob Collins had worked out. To fit in, or to stay safe. In the photo from his trial three years ago, he'd been narrow, made narrower by an ill-fitting suit. Now he filled the prison issue grey sweats, even without the added bulk of bandages and plaster casts. He shifted in his bed, acknowledging Marnie with a quiver of his battered, black-stitched face. One eye was swollen shut, his lips split, nose broken. Right hand in plaster, ditto his left leg. Under the pills and surgery, he smelt of prison soap, cheap and pungent.

'You're not her,' he said. 'DI Rome. You're not old enough.'

Marnie showed her badge. 'You asked for me, by name. Why?'

'You were in the papers, in charge of finding whoever killed that desk jockey in Westminster.'

'Kyle Stratton.'

'Yeah.' He rubbed the heel of his hand at his chest. 'Aidan said you were the one I needed.'

'And Aidan is?'

'Duffy. He's the one making sure the trains run on time

189

round here.' Collins looked her over. 'He said I should ask for DI Rome. I thought you'd be older.'

'Aidan Duffy. He works here?'

Humour pulled his face into a new shape. 'Ow . . .' He petted his stitches. 'Don't make me laugh.' Smoothing his thin hair with the hand that wasn't broken. 'Aide's an inmate, same as the rest of us. Well, not quite the same. Like I said – trains.'

Deals, he meant. Wheels within wheels. All the small fires that kept a place like this burning with bargains and factions, envies and loyalties and grudges. Which meant Aidan Duffy was a bully with the clout to make those around him jump in any direction where a tall wall wasn't in the way.

'Aide never said you were a redhead.' Collins itched the skin on his chest. 'Think he might've mentioned that. He's borrowed my porn enough times.'

Six years ago, when she first became a prison visitor, Marnie had consulted a pamphlet written by an old lag for inmates and their loved ones. A survival guide to prison life. Advice on everything from diet and hygiene to the etiquette of visits. Inmates would be high on sweets and fizzy drinks, the pamphlet said. It warned that prisons used lip readers, so you should cover your mouth unless you wanted your conversation to be caught and recorded. If you ever cut a visit short you'd be searched, as the prison would assume your meeting was a dead drop. The pamphlet didn't have any guidance for visiting your parents' murderer, nor was it very strong on ways to question inmates with broken faces who thought they could wind you up with their porn preferences.

'Was it Aidan who broke your fingers?' she asked.

'I said don't make me laugh.' He touched the dressing on his left shoulder. 'Aide's a mate. Straight up.'

'In your statement you said you didn't see who attacked you.'

'That's right.'

'So why am I here, exactly?'

'Shit, love.' He ran his eyes over her. 'Your bedside manner needs some work.'

'So I'm told.' Marnie glanced at her watch. 'If you've nothing for me, I have things to do.'

'Hang on.' He rolled his shoulders. 'You're looking for this nutter, right? The one who's dishing out punishments on your patch.'

The legacy of the prison was written all over him. He might like to pretend he was a hard man, but even his fingers looked defeated. He'd been someone on the outside, striding around with his pit bull on a short chain, threatening anyone who didn't show respect. Prison had introduced him to a whole new hierarchy of bully. He was outclassed.

'Aidan says you're looking in the wrong places.' He ran his thumb down the stitches in his face. 'Says you need to be checking a bit closer to home.'

Marnie moved her mouth, flatlining a smile. 'Is he wasting my time, like you?'

He scoped the space behind her then lifted his hand to his left shoulder, unpeeling the tape that held the dressing in place, to uncover the wound it was hiding.

Carved black and bloody into the deltoid—

The letter C, at an angle. Not like the clippings, and not like the version that Noah had drawn on the evidence board. Seen from this angle, it wasn't the letter C at all. It was a horseshoe.

Collins flexed his arm. 'For luck.'

The wound was drawn with the ragged tip of an improvised knife which'd flayed the skin as it carved out the shape, no wider than his thumbnail.

A horseshoe. Like the one on her bracelet. She'd taken apart every room in the house, hunting for it. The day came back, savage in its detail. Searching until her fingers were full of splinters, her throat sandpapered by dust. Grit at the skin of her scalp, under the strap of her watch, in the toes of her boots. A thin abrasion every time she moved, rubbing, wearing her away.

'A horseshoe.' Collins scratched at his chest. 'Yeah?'

A dimension was missing, making a woodcut of his broken face.

She blinked and he came into focus, behind the heated gleam of her tears.

'For luck, Aidan says.'

He taped the dressing over the wound.

'You want to be looking closer to home.'

33

Carole Linton's address was a basement flat in a cul-de-sac flanked by a main road to the east and a salvage yard on the west. The yard was packed with cars, burnt out or smashed up, stacked in pyres to be stripped down for parts before being crushed into disposable cubes. Noah could smell petrol and melted plastic. He went down the ungritted steps to Carole's front door, knocking twice in the hope she'd answer quickly so he could get indoors. Ever since this cold snap started, all of London was icy windswept corners where litter froze like his feet.

No answer to his knocking. No window in the brick wall running the length of the footwell. The flat was a cheap conversion, stopping south of planning regulations. Carole had been living here since she came out of prison. She'd dyed her hair, altered her appearance, moved into this basement next to a scrapyard of wrecked cars. Her own car was parked outside, had been for days judging by the windscreen's triple coating of frost, beads of ice as big as garden peas.

Noah checked his phone. Dan's latest text was lyrics

from their favourite song, signed off with a taco emoji and, *I'm starving*. He was on his way home, sticking to public transport and broad daylight. No word from Sol, but Noah hadn't received any further demands for information as to his whereabouts. He was hopeful Trident would have a lead, if not on Sol then on the gang he'd been running with. He tried Carole's door one last time before climbing back up the icy steps.

Someone was waiting at street level.

Noah got a glimpse of grey, swinging—

A baseball bat coming straight for his head.

He swerved but not fast enough and the bat bounced—

Hitting his shoulder hard, coming back round to its original target.

An explosion of stars, red.

His hand grabbing for the rail, feet out from under him thanks to the ice, falling too fast for it to end any way but—

This. *Hard*.

Three, four bruising blows to his ribs – not the bat but the steps as he fell, landing in the right angle by Carole's door with a faceful of litter and his eyes full of blood.

Booming in his head, or—

No, that was boots coming down the steps. That was the bat being swung from a gloved hand so that it clattered against the railings coming down to where he was lying, trying to get up.

Nothing would cooperate. Not his feet, not his hands. The ice made a worse joke of his struggle, sending him in every direction but up—

Up, up and away. *Away*. His head was ringing, pitching his brain too close to his skull, blood bumping in his temples, red and wet in his eyes.

Standing over him, bat swinging—

He tried for a description but it kept sliding away. No colours, no details. Just monotones wrapped in layers, not tall but *big* with layers, spreading in all directions thanks to the concussion, a giant, no, a dwarf with giant's hands and a face hidden by a balaclava—

He lifted his left arm, thinking—

This is how he broke them when they tried to stay alive.

Impossible not to, though. He couldn't see colours or details, couldn't move his legs but his arm came up to protect his head by pure instinct. Survival—

'Ollie?' He tried to get words out, but his mouth was slack.

Something stuck to the side of his face. A frozen crisp packet. He'd seen one when he was knocking at the door. He was getting a closer look now that he was down here with the litter.

The bat rattled the railings again then reached in to stir at his ribs.

He couldn't stop any of it.

'Ollie . . .' His left ear was crammed full of car horns, sirens, people shouting, but it was just the damage done to his head, sounds shoving inside his ear where the bat had hit.

He stayed on the steps. Ollie or whoever it was stayed right there on the steps with the bat and it couldn't be the same one, not the bat they found in his flat, because Fran had that. She was scraping it for Kyle's DNA. This was a different bat. A second one for her to scrape.

What was he waiting for? Ollie.

Why wasn't he finishing it while Noah was like this, too hurt to fight back?

He'd have to come down the last couple of steps, though. He'd have to get close enough for Noah to reach out and grab one of his legs. If he could manage it; his hands felt huge, and a long way away from the rest of his body. He was shivering so hard his teeth jarred.

He tried his voice again: 'Police . . . I'm . . . DS Noah Jake—'

Something falling, heavy, on his face.

He couldn't work out if it was snow or litter or the baseball bat.

But whatever it was his world was shrinking.

Going, going—

Gone.

34

Aidan Duffy wasn't what Marnie had expected. A man of Jacob Collins' age, she'd assumed, balding and bulky. But Aidan was in his thirties with a boyish head of black curls, cool grey eyes and a Viking nose. The nose was unbroken like the rest of him, which was slim and tight and smooth with muscle. He didn't look her up and down the way Collins had, just took the seat in the visitors' room, folding his hands on the table between them. No tattoos on his fingers, and no visible scars. He kept himself clean. Others did his dirty work.

They were the only two seated here. A couple of guards at the door, fulfilling regulations. Marnie hadn't missed their deferential body language when they'd escorted Duffy – moving like a dancer, loose in the hip – in here. Collins wasn't the only one outclassed by Aidan Duffy.

'You advised Mr Collins to ask for me by name. Perhaps we can start there. With how you know my name and why you gave it to Mr Collins after he was attacked.'

Aidan wrinkled his straight nose. 'I'd rather start with something else.' A lilt in his voice, southern Irish, soft as a cat's paw. 'Forgiveness, can we start with forgiveness?'

197

'Whose? And of whom?'

'For the sake of argument and because I don't want to be missing my lunch, can we say it's yours? And of Stephen Keele.'

He had her full attention, and he knew it. Taking his time, lifting a hand to knuckle the bridge of his nose, rubbing his fingers through his black curls. Confident that he looked good, and was saying words she had to hear. She couldn't stand up and go, not now he'd given out Stephen's name.

'They moved him here, oh it's going on for five months ago now. Nice-looking boy like that, even after he put himself to the trouble of looking less nice, shaving his head, getting the six-pack.' Aidan broke out a grin, fresh and white. He had very good teeth. 'Not that the six-pack goes amiss in a place like this. Well, in a place like this, you know?' Lilting his voice, slurring his words a little until they ran into one another. 'Even the little four-packs have something going for them and your boy's got himself the full six. In he comes, that head of his held high and I'm for calling it *killer instinct*. Because he's nice-looking and he's got the brains to match. Barely twenty years old and he's circling with the sharks. No more juvie with your daytime telly and your Pot Noodle, no. This's the real thing.' He dropped his head to the side, smiling at her. 'He's lining them up and he's potting them down and I'm right away thinking, "Oh, you're a bright boy, you're smart enough to be scared, and clever enough to hide it," and I'm for taking him under my wing because it's nice to do that from time to time, to have a brave bright boy by your side.'

He stopped, keeping the smile switched on. He was very good.

Marnie looked for a chink in his armour, but she

couldn't see one. Not a single red thread on his face, no hint of pink or yellow in the whites of his eyes. Clean-shaven, smelling of green fern, expensive. He didn't use the prison soap; he'd got his hands on something better. How many of the men in here were under his long thumbs? Was Stephen?

'Five months ago, then, I'm for taking him under my wing. Tucking him in, keeping him safe. You don't want to know what happens to a nice-looking boy in here when he's not being kept safe.'

'Can we dispense with the prison mythology?' Marnie said. 'And skip to the part where you gave my name to Jacob Collins?'

'You'd not have come if I'd crooked my little finger. Not even if I'd said his name. Stephen Keele.' Drawing out the syllables, rolling the first off his tongue. 'Stephen Patrick Keele.' Widening his eyes. 'Oh you didn't know the middle name? Patrick, that's a good Irish name. Saintly. That's a sense of humour someone had, calling him Patrick.'

'All right.' She smiled back at him. 'Mr Duffy. You're very clever and charming, and you're very used to getting your way. I can see that. It's boring in here, so I do sympathise. But if you don't cut to the chase in the next minute? I'm going to stand up and walk out.' She leaned a fraction closer to him. 'I'll send a constable to take your statement, as I'm sure you have a lot to say. But you won't be saying it to me.'

His eyes gleamed. 'I'll cut to the chase, Marnie Jane Rome.' Leaning towards her by the same small fraction. 'Your little brother's in a fuck-load of trouble and it's all your fault.'

'How is it my fault?'

'You're the one let him down. The one who lied, pretending she didn't know why he did it.'

This again. A girl in Sommerville had said Stephen blamed Marnie for his incarceration. Stephen himself had said, 'I did it for you.' There was nothing new here, just the same old lies repackaged with a white smile and a pair of cool grey eyes.

'Mr Duffy—'

'Aidan,' he said softly.

Then, 'You're the one broke his heart.'

Her teeth ached where she'd clenched them.

'You broke his heart, Marnie Jane Rome.'

Aidan tipped his head, the light lying along the high bone of his cheek.

'And now everybody's paying for it.'

35

'Safe. Take it easy, yeah? I called an ambulance. You need checking over.'

No argument there. Noah sat with his head in his hands, nursing the first lump's new friend, the pair of them conspiring at the side of his skull to make everything hurt. His fingers came away tacky with blood, but he was alive. The world had come back from the pin hole where concussion had sent it. He was breathing, and he was in one piece. Propped upright, more or less, in the litter trap outside Carole's front door. No new bruises, other than the ones left by the steps; Ollie hadn't hit him while he was unconscious.

Sitting on the steps was a black woman of about his age, with a nose stud and braided hair. In a fake leopard-skin coat over a red jumpsuit and blue snow boots. Her hands in her pockets, shoulders up around her ears. 'I'd give you my coat but I'm freezing my tits off already.' She stamped her feet on the step. 'Should've gritted your yard.'

'Yes . . .' His ears were ringing, but it was a hundred times better than before. He felt out the bones in his face – nothing broken.

'Safe,' she said. 'You're still beautiful.'

Her grin was the best thing he'd seen all day.

'*You're* beautiful,' he managed. 'I'm just lucky.'

His voice was slurred, but not much.

'You fell down your steps and you're bleeding all over your nice coat. Not my idea of lucky.'

'Did you . . . see anyone? Else. Anyone else.'

'Just you, lying down here.'

He felt in his pocket for his phone. It was in one piece, showing Dan's latest text.

'What's so funny?' She stamped her feet, breathing a cloud of cold.

Noah put his aching head back against the brick wall. 'Taco emoji . . .'

'Taco . . . You're funny when you're bleeding.'

He wiped the side of his head with his sleeve, squinting at the screen. He needed to call Marnie. And Ron. He'd lost time. Not long, but—

'Here.' She pulled her hand from the pocket of her coat. 'Give me that.'

He should've put up a fight. The phone had personal stuff on it, not to mention police stuff. But he held it out and she shuffled down a step to take it.

'What number? You're trying to ring someone. Taco emoji? What's her number?'

'His . . .' Noah was still stupid from the baseball bat.

She grinned, her fingers poised over the keypad. 'Number?'

He gave her Ron Carling's number, watching as she punched it in.

'Hey, Taco. I've got your boyfriend here. He's in need of some loving.' She scooted down the step to hold the phone to Noah's ear.

Ron was saying, '. . . *taco*—?'

'It's me. I found our vigilante.'

'Sounds more like *he* found you.' Ron's voice was sharp. 'Where are you? Are you okay? Who's that with you?'

'Carole's place. Not really. And I don't know.'

'Have I got to come and get you?'

'There's an ambulance coming.' He looked up at the woman, who nodded down at him. 'I'm okay. Baseball bat, but he only got my head.'

'Only?' Ron repeated.

'I saw him.' Noah shivered.

He was starting to feel sick.

'It's Ollie. I think— It's Ollie.'

36

'The poison and the antidote are brewed in the same vat. Have you heard that saying now?' Aidan Duffy linked his hands behind his head, leaning back under the light that was bruising Marnie's skin. 'The poison and the antidote,' running the words together, 'brewed in the same vat. Tell me you know what I'm talking about so we can get to what's really going on.'

'You're quoting creed from the Forgiveness Project. What's really going on?'

'Anger.' He shifted his hands to the crown of his head. 'Locks you in a cage.'

At the inside of his right wrist: a word. No, a name. Inked in black. *Finn.*

'But then forgiveness?' He was showing her the tattoo. He wanted her to see it. 'Forgiveness is a great big act of betrayal to many. I've known families broken up by it, into little bits. Do you know what it is to be broken into little bits, Marnie Jane Rome? Of course you do.'

Finn. Who was that – a brother? A lover? A child?

'They say a guilty conscience needs to confess. They say that now, don't they? And a work of art's a confession.'

He dropped his grey gaze to her hips, as if he could read the words inked on her skin, her teenaged tattoos. 'According to your man, Camus.'

'Who's Finn?'

His eyes darkened, warningly. Too soon. This was running to his timetable, not hers. She didn't want to sit here with a man to whom Stephen had told God knows what lies about her, and God knows what truths. How much did Aidan really know? About Stephen, about her?

'You know about prisons,' he was saying, 'I know you know about prisons. How you have to make friends in here, a whole new life for yourself because no one can live out in the cold for long, not for long. You fit in, find your place. Rub along. You call it survival, but it's living. Life. Then there'll be a lockdown, there'll always be a lockdown. Alarms ringing, your cell searched for drugs, weapons.' A movement of his shoulders, acknowledging the guards by the door. 'Everything turned upside down and stamped on all over again. And you're sick for days afterwards. Not just because they reminded you where you were, how low you'd sunk. You're sick that you let yourself start *living* in here. Now your life's in pieces all over again, but you pick them up because you have to. Every time, you pick them up.' He stopped, asking a question with his eyes.

'Give me a name.' She was calm now. She didn't even know why, but she was calm. 'You want my help, that's why I'm here. Give me a name.'

'You're here because he's here. Your boy's here, and you can't stay away.'

He dropped his hands to the table, wrists flat to its surface. His face hollowed suddenly. 'I had him under my wing, tucked in tight. Oh, he was like a little bird and I had him safe . . . But it's hard, you know? To stay safe. And now he's asking to be out, now he's lost and there's this unholy fucking *fireball* all around him, between him and me, and I'm damned if I do, damned if I don't.'

He was scared.

It hit her like a jolt under the ribs.

Aidan Duffy was *scared*.

Of what, or whom, she didn't know. Not yet.

'Give me a name.'

'Carole Linton. Stuart Rawling.' His eyes shone at her. 'How many names do you need? Kyle Stratton.' Scared, and angry.

'Give me the other name. The one that can make it stop.'

Laughter left him in a short burst. He put both hands into his hair, burying his fingers in his black curls. 'Oh Marnie Jane Rome! I've been giving you that name since we began. It's *yours*. You're the one started this and you're the one can make it stop. The only one.'

'How?'

'By finding the bastard who's having so much fun for your sake, in your name. Leaving the little presents all over London. Teeth and bones and eyeballs like some pagan fucking ritual.' The Irish accent was stronger now, no spark of a smile left on his face. 'My brother had a dog used to bring him dead frogs, but you! You take the fucking biscuit.'

'Who attacked Jacob Collins?' She held hard to the panic which was stuttering its way from her sternum into her throat. 'That wasn't the same person who killed Kyle Stratton.'

Aidan shook her question away as if it were a wasp. The expensive cologne wasn't working, not now. She could smell stress under the green fern.

'They drew on him, did you not know that? His ma and da. Drew on him with their fingers.' He put his hands into a prayer shape. 'Finger-painted dirty words everywhere on his little body, even the places he couldn't see without a couple of good mirrors. His ma was the worst for it, a filthy mind and a temper to match. You never bothered looking in those corners, though, did you? Too busy wading through your own mess to think about his.'

Stephen. He was talking about Stephen.

'You were putting on your lovely blue uniform while he was learning how to stand in the snow barefoot without weeping, because his ma hates a crybaby.' Aidan hardened his eyes at her. 'And the whole house's a fucking museum of what's wrong with them, it's receipts and bills and it's gadgets turned into torture devices. A whole sick-in-the-head existence with no neighbours near enough to care, just bad noises and nice smiles when anyone gets close enough to interfere. Think of that, think what it's like to live with the *throb* of the city outside and life going on like nothing ever happened, cars going past and lights like the funfair's in town – like the kids are running sticks along the railings and shouting for sheer joy while he's in there with the Franklin fucking Mint on the walls, gilded plates and silver thimbles, and he's trying so hard to work out what she's written, what lies she's told to his skin, or maybe they're truths. He doesn't know, he doesn't know.'

When he stopped speaking, silence rushed to fill the gap left by his words.

He had his eyes on her, daring her to speak.

Daring her to ask, again, for the name. Any name.

'I knew a boy once,' he said, when the silence had saturated the room. 'He was with his ma like Stephen was, because they'd decided his old daddy was a bad man. His whole family got moved to a safe house while the police investigated. His da was locked up, but his ma? She was right there with him.' He drew a heart on the table with his thumb, tracing over it. 'She's as bad if not worse than the other and she's *right there* with him in the safe house, put there by the police because they think it's all about the da. They think that boy's safe.'

'Are you talking about Finn?'

His head tipped back until his eyes were on her. 'You took that house apart, a murder house. Police ripped it out brick by brick, poured cement to stop it coming down around them while they dug and dug to see what horrors they could find. You weren't even in your lovely blue uniform then, still at school. They burned everything. That's what you do, isn't it, with a murder house. You're for burning it all up, making it disappear. Except it never does. You can dig it up and pull it down, feed it into incinerators and crush it into cubes, crush those into smaller cubes until it's all just dust to blow from your fingers.'

He put his palm up and blew across it, into her face. His breath smelt of cherries. 'All you've done is make a big hole where it used to be. And *you* try not looking at a big hole when it's carved in the middle of your life because someone stole the thing that matters most. Came like a thief in the night to take it and you know he's crying, you know he's scared but you can't reach him.'

He blinked. 'All you can do is listen to the wind whistling through like it's your *heart* with a hole in it. You'd plug that hole, wouldn't you. Any way you could, with whatever you could lay your hands on. So don't sit there and tell me you're on top of this. That you're *whole*. Don't be telling me he can't hurt you locked up in here, just the same as he could out there, filling your house with whatever he needed to do to forget.'

'Are you finished?' The itch of her watch at her wrist, taking time away. 'Or is there more?'

'There's a boy,' he said abruptly. 'Wakes to the sound of sharpening knives. Duct tape on his mouth. God knows what round his wrists and ankles. They put him in a bath. He's cold and scared and sick – and they've put him in a fucking bath.'

'Finn.' She nodded at his wrist. 'Your boy?'

Aidan moved his jaw, but didn't speak.

'Really? You give me the long talk about murder houses and prison and finger-painting, as if someone's paying you by the word to keep me here, but you can't tell me what I need to know to get your boy out of the bath and into an ambulance?'

His eyes sparked responsively. 'Arrest me.'

'What?'

'Arrest me.' He put his hands on the table, wrists together. 'Take me in your nice police car out of this pit to somewhere we can talk properly.'

'You're afraid.' She looked him in the eye. 'Who are you afraid of?'

'Right this minute?' He crooked his mouth. 'I'm afraid of you.'

It was the truth. She could read it from his face.

'Because he's right. You're a stone-cold heartbreaker, Marnie Jane Rome. You've got gravel in your veins, and ice in your blood.'

He tipped his head at her, grey eyes unblinking. 'You've brought the winter in here with you and it is long and cold and it's going to kill us all.'

209

37

Ron was smoking in the station's car park when Marnie got back from Cloverton. She hadn't known that he smoked. He stubbed it out when she parked up: 'Trying to keep warm, boss.'

She moved her head in a nod. 'How's Noah?'

Ron had texted while she was driving back. Noah had been attacked with a baseball bat, outside Carole Linton's flat. He was in hospital, bruised but not badly. It could have been so much worse.

'Concussion. They're keeping him overnight. I reckoned you'd want a catch-up before DCS Ferguson gets on our case.' Ron peered at her. 'You okay, boss?'

'Who was it? Did Noah say?'

'Ollie, he thinks. But he's not a hundred per cent.' Ron jogged his shoulders, trying to dislodge the cold that'd settled there. 'What d'you find at Cloverton?'

'Nothing good.'

How was she going to explain herself – to Ron, to Noah, to her team? Ferguson would need to know the worst of what Aidan Duffy had said. Marnie had called her from the prison, giving the skeleton facts, enough to outline the seriousness of the situation, but Ferguson would have lots of questions. She was going to be holed up here for a long while.

'Do me a favour?' she asked Ron.

'Of course, boss.'

'Check on Noah. Let him know that I'll see him as soon as I can, but it might not be today.'

Ferguson would pull her off the case, that's what she feared most. When she heard what Aidan had said, she'd pull Marnie off the case.

She looked up at the window of Welland's office where ice had laid its web across the glass, just as it had over the tarmac under her feet. Black ice, resisting the best efforts of the salters. What was the word favoured by the weathermen? Treacherous.

She tried to see Stephen as a small boy made to stand barefoot in the snow. Finger-painted, Aidan had said, by his parents. Lies written on his skin by the woman who'd been his mother in name only. The woman he'd accused Marnie's parents of bringing back into his life.

And now this other boy, Finn. Aidan's son. Tied with duct tape, terrified.

Marnie's breath came in clouds as she stood seeing the pictures Aidan had put in her head.

Not knowing which, if any, were true.

Lorna Ferguson was waiting in Welland's office.

Marnie didn't shut the door, expecting to be moved to an interview room. The thought of giving a statement made her sick, but it was necessary. Stephen had made it necessary.

'Sit down.' Ferguson reached a hand into the drawer of Welland's desk, bringing out a bottle of Lucozade. 'Blood sugar. You look like you need it.'

Marnie took the drink, her chest tight with tears. 'Thank you.' She hadn't expected sympathy from this woman, wanting Welland – someone who understood how deep this went.

'Aidan Duffy,' Ferguson said. 'How much do you trust him?'

'Not much.' She unscrewed the lid from the bottle and drank a mouthful. 'He's scared for his son. That was real. The rest of it? I don't know.'

'All right. Let's start with his son. We'll take it a step at a time.' Ferguson closed her laptop, setting it aside. She looked up when Marnie frowned. 'You thought I'd have you in an interview room, taping the whole thing?'

'Yes.' It came out too bluntly. She softened the word with a smile. 'Yes.'

'In fact I'm a bit of a bitch.' Ferguson tucked her hair behind her ears. 'Usurping his office, challenging your team. That's what you think.'

'You've got a job to do. I respect that.'

'You can stop being so careful, that's what I'm getting at.' Ferguson sat back. 'I'm a bitch because it gets results from people. But not from you.'

'It's true I'm missing Welland,' Marnie offered, 'as a friend.'

'Of course you are. Well . . . Let's shove on, shall we? Just remember I'm a Northerner. That means blunt speaking, no bollocks, but I can hand out hugs when I need to. Most days I'm having trouble holding them in.' She straightened, her voice crisping. 'How's DS Jake?'

'Concussion. They're keeping him in overnight, but DS Carling says he's okay. He got a look at our vigilante. Not a good look, but enough to think it's Ollie Tomlinson.'

'How does that fit with what Duffy told you?'

212

'It does and it doesn't.' The brisk questions helped; solid ground under her feet. 'We could *make* it fit. That's the trouble. I'm not sure how much of what he said was rubbish. Clever rubbish, but rubbish.'

'Well, here's what we'll do. We'll pick apart what he said and set it against what we know. What doesn't stand, we set to one side. But I'll tell you what I'm not having.' Ferguson thumbed a speck of mascara from under her eye. 'I'm not having some sick little sociopath running *my* cases or pointing his fingers at *my* detectives. I don't care how pretty he is.'

A jolt of dismay – did she mean Stephen?

'Aidan Duffy.' Ferguson curled her lips around the name. 'I looked him up. Those Irish eyes and the holy black curls, like him off the telly forever pouting round Cornwall on his horse . . .'

'You should see him in action.' Marnie smiled. 'He's good.'

'Not so good he isn't slopping out with the rest of the scumbags.' Ferguson eyed her. 'He pressed your buttons, and that's no easy thing. Tell me about his son.'

'I was hoping you could tell me, if you've seen his records.'

'One dependant. Finian Paul Duffy. Eleventh birthday coming up. Another one his dad won't see, being in prison.' Her voice was hard, careless. 'Finian lives with his mum in north London. I've written down the address.'

'We should contact her, to check Finn's safe. There's nothing in Misper.' Colin had looked while she was driving back from Cloverton. 'But we should make sure.'

'Because you believed that bit.' Ferguson studied her. 'What makes you think it wasn't button-pushing like the rest?'

'Aidan was scared. He says ten weeks ago Finn was

213

lifted off the street by people who're holding him, as leverage to make Aidan carry out threats inside Cloverton.'

Ferguson flexed her eyebrows. 'These kidnappers, who are they?'

'He doesn't have names, he wasn't given any. At first he thought it was the men he'd embezzled from, revenge of some kind. But the things they're demanding make no sense . . . The kidnappers want him to get close to Stephen Keele. He thinks they must've known he was already close. He'd singled Stephen out as soon as he arrived at Cloverton, as someone he could use.'

'Empire building,' Ferguson said.

'He didn't put it like that, but yes.'

'So when did these mystery kidnappers get in touch?'

'Ten weeks ago. A message was passed to Aidan by Jacob Collins who says he was handed it by the visiting healthcare team.' Marnie put down the Lucozade, knotting her hair behind her neck. 'Aidan destroyed it because that's what you do with messages like that in places like Cloverton.'

'Convenient.'

'Oh there's every kind of convenience in his story, and no evidence unless Finn *is* missing—'

'He is.' Ferguson served the words like punches, two short jabs from behind her desk.

'What?' Bile burned in Marnie's throat.

Ferguson watched her reaction with interest. She'd let her sit here for six minutes, *hoping* for six minutes that it was all a fantasy spun by Aidan.

'There's no Finn Duffy in the Missing Persons database—'

'No,' Ferguson agreed. 'But I rang his mum while I was waiting for you to get back here. She thinks he's been staying with his uncle Regan for the last ten weeks. Uncle

Regan has no idea where his nephew is, and cares less. It's one big happy family. Be glad you're not part of it.'

Marnie couldn't speak. She didn't trust herself. Under the lip of Welland's desk, she clenched her hands so hard they hurt. A child of ten was missing, and it was on her account.

'There's something else.' Ferguson spoke as if she was reading her cues from Marnie's face, taking stock of the buttons she could press, an arsenal of her DI's tells. 'Finn's at school with Ollie Tomlinson. The pair of them hang out together. He should've been in our sights right from the start.'

The radiator whined, unhappy because Welland liked it at full blast while Ferguson played with the temperature according to her mood. Right now she was giving out a cold front as treacherous as the black ice in the car park.

'So now we know our scumbag's telling the truth about his missing son.' She smiled at Marnie. 'What else did he have for us?'

Us? Nothing. Aidan's confidences had been for Marnie's ears. Perhaps she should demand a formal interview, and a solicitor. One thing was clear – she needed to tread very, very carefully with Detective Chief Superintendent Lorna Ferguson.

'He had Jacob Collins beaten up. Because he wanted the police to come to the prison, but he couldn't be the one asking for us. That would've got back to the kidnappers, and put Finn in worse danger. So he had his friend attacked, and told Jacob to ask for me.'

'That's a lot of sneak, even for a sociopath. What's Duffy's end-game?'

'I'll write it up, but this part may be fantasy. Aidan knows about the assaults. He knows we're looking for vigilantes who are targeting ex-cons. He wants us to

215

believe that our suspects and his son's kidnappers are one and the same. It's . . . complicated.'

Ferguson's face was a reminder of just how much she hated complication. 'And this leverage inside Cloverton, whatever it is the kidnappers are asking Duffy to do. How does that fit with our investigation?'

'Which version do you want?' Marnie asked. 'His fantasy, or my speculation?'

'Start with the fantasy, and we'll work from there.'

38

Dan sat at the side of the hospital bed, reaching for Noah's wrist. 'Hey . . .'

Noah pulled his hand close enough to kiss. 'God, it's good to see you.'

'You too, but I could do without the bruises.'

'They don't look heroic to you?' He smiled, wanting to take the worry from Dan's eyes. 'You should've seen the way I went down those steps – that was some serious triple lutz action.'

'Triple klutz, I think you mean.'

'That, too.' He pushed his fingers inside the sleeve of Dan's jumper, finding the hard shape of his elbow. 'C'mere.'

'All right, Eric Radford, you win . . .'

After the kiss, Dan stayed close enough for Noah to feel his heart beating. He hadn't realised until this minute how afraid he'd been for them both, after the morning's texts and the afternoon's assault. 'Have you been back to the flat?'

Dan shook his head. 'I came straight here after DS

Carling called. I was expecting Marnie to be the one telling me you'd landed back in here.'

'She's stuck at the station, Ron says. She's dropping by later. I'm here for the night.'

'On account of the lumpy head.' Dan nodded. 'You know I'd sleep in the chair if they'd let me.'

'They won't. And I need to know if Sol's home.'

'This isn't down to him, is it?' Dan stopped short of touching the baseball bat's bruise, setting the ends of his fingers to Noah's temple. Tension in his voice, and his touch.

'It's not down to Sol.'

'Good. Because I like him, but I'd turf him off the sofa in a second if I thought he was a danger. We've got enough of those without family pitching in. And you've got it worse than I have.'

Not just homophobia, he meant. Racism. Noah had kept the worst of it to himself, but London had changed in the last year, too many people believing they'd won a mandate for their prejudices.

'It's not Sol, just the weather. I'd have stayed upright if it wasn't for the ice.' He smiled. 'Go home. Let me know if you find him on the sofa.'

'I'll text you either way.'

Dan turned Noah's hand over in his, opening its palm for a kiss and closing Noah's fingers to keep it there. 'Before you say it, I'll stay safe. Can't have two of us taking up bed space in here.'

'Do something for me?' Noah smiled up at him.

'Anything.'

'Order tacos and eat my share?'

It was 10 p.m. by the time Marnie reached the hospital. She parked up, checking her reflection for evidence of her close encounter with Ferguson. The day was written all over her face. Much the same as Noah's, but at least her day had only featured metaphorical baseball bats.

A full minute passed with her too weary to climb from the car, wanting nothing more than to drive home to Ed. Less than forty-eight hours ago, she'd questioned the value of the silence that shaped their closeness, but silence was what she needed. An end to the day's questions and noise, the pictures in her head of a four-year-old boy finger-painted with obscenities and a ten-year-old boy bound with duct tape, out of her reach.

Tomorrow they'd start hunting for Finn Duffy. Marnie didn't want to wait until tomorrow. She wanted to be hunting now. Her whole body burned, from her ankles to her ears, with the need to rescue Finn. 'Go home,' Ferguson had said. 'Get some rest. Child Protection can take the night shift. We'll regroup in the morning.'

She hadn't taken Marnie off the team, but she had to be considering it. The idea of this mess, of any part of this mess, having been made on her account was bad enough. But to be taken off the team responsible for putting it right? That was unbearable.

She was locking the car when her peripheral vision gave her the lurker, standing to the side of the hospital entrance in a grey hoodie and track pants. Not smoking, just the cold turning his breath white. Noah's height or nearly. Same build, same way of standing with his hands shoved into his pockets, shoulders up.

She walked towards the entrance without looking at him, changing tack at the last second so that they were face to face. 'It's Sol, isn't it? Hello. I'm Marnie.'

Noah's brother stared at her, on the brink of an instinctive denial.

'I could use a hot drink,' she said. 'You?'

Sol could use a square meal. Hollow-cheeked, with the glassy eyes of someone who'd been running on empty for days. Unshaven, unwashed. He had to unlock his chattering teeth before he could answer her. 'Is he okay?' His eyes flickered to the hospital entrance. 'Noah. S'why I'm here.'

'They're keeping him overnight, but he's good. Visiting hours are over, though. There's a late-night place round the corner. Fish and chips, if you fancy it.'

Sol blinked. Nodded. 'I'll check it out.' He turned on his heel.

'I'm headed there myself,' she said.

He kept his face averted, but his shoulders were shaking.

She fell into step at his side, not touching and not looking, letting him walk with her without the need for any show of bravado.

When they reached the café, Sol came to a standstill. 'No cash on me.' The neon striped his face blue and white. He tried a smile. 'Have to owe you, yeah?'

Under better circumstances, she bet, that smile could win wallets. He had his brother's good looks plus a rakish edge that was being undermined just for the moment by hunger.

'My treat.' She let him open the door for her. 'Cod and chips, and tea. How does that sound?'

'That's . . . Yeah.' He nodded.

She brought the meals to the table he'd chosen at the back of the café, with a clear sightline to the door. Wooden forks, but he got stuck in with his fingers.

'This's cool. Thanks . . .' He brightened almost imme-diately, like a flagging child transformed by food. 'So you're his boss . . . He *loves* you, man.' Eyes shining as he sucked hot tea from the cup. 'Can't believe he got busted. But it's not bad, yeah? You said he's okay.'

Marnie nodded. She was hungry, and the food was

good. Hot, salty flakes of fish, fat, vinegary chips. 'He's been worried about you.'

'Yeah.' Sol sucked grease from his knuckles. 'Me too.'

'You've got some tricky customers on your tail.' She kept it casual, eating with her fingers the way he was eating, keeping wide of an interrogation. But she'd not forgotten Noah's eyes when he'd received the threatening text in Kim's café at the start of the day. If she could do nothing else, she could put Noah's mind at rest, or try to.

Sol played with the wooden fork, bending it between two fingers while his other hand went on feeding chips into his mouth. Resisting her statement. No, it was more than that. Antipathy, and not just to her. To what she represented. Authority. Sol, she was sure, had sixty names for the police and not one of them complimentary.

'I was with him,' she said. 'When he received the text sent by whoever you're hiding from.'

'Yeah?' He hooded his eyes, pushing the carton of food away.

'Eat it. You need it.'

He splintered the fork between his fingers, blinking at the broken bits of wood. His jaw was one long clench, eyes scaring to the door every few seconds.

Marnie was tired of sitting with men who pretended to be brave, pretended to be hard, simply because they were afraid.

'Whoever it is you're hiding from . . . Are they dangerous? Or just playing at being dangerous?'

'Visitor hours are over, yeah? I can get this shit from my brother.' He looked at the food. 'Don't need it from you.'

'Finish that. Who knows when you'll get another free meal, since you're clearly not keen on going home.'

'They don't need my shit on their step.' He started

eating the chips, hunger trumping hostility. 'Noah showed you this text he got?'

'He hasn't reported it, not yet. But he was upset. Whoever you're hiding from has threatened Dan Noys.'

Sol's hand stopped moving between the carton and his mouth. 'For real?' His eyes were huge.

'That's why I'm asking how dangerous they are.'

'Dan's okay though, yeah?' Genuine fear, and concern. 'He's okay.'

'For now. Maybe it's not a problem if your friends are just flossing. But I'm guessing you're sleeping rough for a reason.'

'I ain't sleeping rough.'

'You're not sleeping at home.' Or anywhere with hot running water. 'Noah's worried about you. And about Dan.'

Sol broke the fork into smaller pieces, his bottom lip shiny from the chips. He was just a kid, she realised. A spoilt kid. With none of his brother's courage, or strength.

'How did you know he was in the hospital?' she asked, more gently.

He didn't answer for a long minute. Then he said, 'That's where they put him.'

'Who're they?'

'I ain't giving you names. Bad enough I'm sitting here eating this shit you paid for. You think I'm giving you *names* . . .' He rubbed at his eyes with the back of his hand. 'You think they're *flossing*—? They fucked him up. With a *bat*. Next time they'll take his head off. Next time—'

'Wait. You think a *gang* did this?'

Ollie, Noah had said. Not a definitive ID, but he'd been sure that it was Ollie who'd hit him, and left him for the paramedics. Now Sol was saying—

'You think your gang attacked Noah?'

'They fucked him up.' Sol jabbed the broken fork at the table, between misery and anger. 'But it could've been worse, could *be* worse. If I don't sort it out.'

'How will you do that?'

'By staying wide. No one needs my shit in their life.'

'Noah needs you. You're his brother. Whatever trouble you're in—'

'I ain't *in*. I'm *it*. I'm the trouble.' Not just self-recrimination. Pride, too. This was his role, the trouble-maker, Noah's off-the-rails kid brother.

'You think this is your fault.'

'You—' He blinked at the table. 'You don't get it.'

'I get it,' Marnie said. 'You messed up and you thought you'd put it right, but someone else has a better idea, or thinks he has.'

Sol looked up at her, fretting at the splintered fork. 'That . . . Yeah.'

'You need help sorting it out. I don't see how running away is going to do that.'

'It's all I got.' He put his hands up, as if she'd told him to do it, splaying his fingers. 'I got nothing. I'm – *nothing*.'

'You're Noah's brother. And you have something, other-wise why are these people threatening him and Dan?'

'They want me back.' He linked his hands on the top of his head, pushing with his palms until tears came. 'That's what this's about. I ain't going back. Shit I've done—' He shut his eyes. 'No way I'm starting back up.'

'You've drawn a line. Good. Now we just need to get the other side to do the same.'

The breath left him in a laugh. Tears travelled down his face and he wiped them with the cuff of his hoodie. 'Thanks for the food, though. For real.'

He was exhausted, needed to sleep, get clean, recharge. Maybe then he'd be able to talk about this properly, see something other than stone walls everywhere.

'You could do me a favour,' she said.

'Yeah?' He opened his eyes, warier than a cat. 'What's that?'

Noah was awake, propped by pillows in the narrow hospital bed.

'I'm breaking the rules.' Marnie sat by his side. 'But they've allowed me five minutes on account of the badge. How's the headache?'

'What headache? I'm a hundred per cent meds, blissed out. Weird dreams, though. Rather be awake.' He searched her face. 'What's happened?'

'Too much to tell you about in five minutes, but I wanted you to know Sol's safe.'

'He's—'

'Safe.' She steadied him with a smile. 'He's at my place. I needed someone to keep the flat from freezing, and he needed a place to crash. It's fine. He's safe.'

'I don't . . .' Noah's face blanked with confusion. 'What?'

'He was hanging around outside the hospital, looking like he'd not eaten in a week. I fed him chips and he told me a few things, not much. He needed a place and mine's going begging. I've been worried about it being empty during this cold spell. It's fine, honestly.'

'That's not . . .' Noah put his knuckles to the bruised side of his face. 'Okay, but I'm not sure it's a great idea. Sorry, I don't mean – I'm grateful. But it's your home. Sol isn't— He's my problem, not yours.'

'Oh I think there's enough problem to go around. It's a temporary solution, I didn't give him a key. If he walks, he can't get back in again. But it's a chance for him to have a hot shower, and to get some sleep. He needs to stop running so he can think about what to do next.'

'He *talked* to you?' Noah looked stunned.

'I fed him fish and chips. We chatted a bit, not much. I wanted you to know he's okay. You can stop worrying about him for a while. I gave him a phone, just a cheap one, pay-as-you-go. Told him to call you tomorrow.' She nodded at Noah's iPhone. 'I can put the number in there, if you'd like?'

'Thanks . . .'

She fed the number in, then stood. 'Dan's all right?'

'Yes.' He reached for her hand. 'Thanks. Thank you.'

'Get some rest.' She pressed his wrist. 'I won't expect to see you tomorrow, so take it easy.'

'We've got Ollie to find.'

And Finn Duffy.

And whoever was hunting Sol.

'You need to be on top form. I'll call round when I get the chance, bring you up to speed.'

'Something happened, didn't it?' He was watching her face. 'I'm pilled to the eyelids, but I can see that. Something's happened.'

'I'll tell you when you're well enough. Get some sleep, get better.'

He nodded. 'Thanks, again. For Sol.'

'One thing.' She couldn't leave without asking. 'How sure are you that it was Ollie who attacked you?'

Noah took a moment then said, 'It was him. I'm pretty sure—'

He nodded, looking unhappy. 'It was Ollie.'

39

'Are you going to keep quiet?' Ollie scuffed a foot at the bathroom floor, his trainers making the tiles squeal. The towel was in the corner where he'd kicked it. 'Are you?'

Finn didn't understand the question. He'd been quiet for hours. Ever since Ollie did his ankles and wrists with the tape. Just lying here, blinking at the bath, swallowing the spit in his mouth when it built up the way it did at the dentist. His hands felt huge, taped in front of him, like he was wearing boxing gloves. Everything kept going black as if someone was pouring hot tar into his ear until his head filled, until it reached his eyes and he stopped being able to see. Then his feet kicked and his head emptied a bit so he could make out the bath and the tiles and Ollie sitting there keeping guard, before the tar started pouring in again and it all got swallowed up.

'Shithead.' Ollie kicked at his ankles. 'Are you going to be quiet?'

Finn blinked, nodding. It made the tar go into his eyes and he couldn't see as Ollie shuffled across the floor and got him under the armpits, pulling him half onto his lap.

Finn didn't fight, the way he had before. Ollie held him the same way, one arm across his shoulders, saying, 'Keep quiet, you'd better keep quiet,' and he started hitting the side of Finn's head.

No, not hitting. It hurt like that's what he was doing but he was picking at the end of the duct tape, trying to get it loose. Finn's head rocked on his neck, like it belonged to Ollie now.

'Fuck's sake. Come on . . .' Ollie's fingers slipped, the bone in his wrist hitting Finn's nose.

He tried to lift his hands but Ollie batted them away, struggling with the tape. It hurt, dragging at his hair, and the tar wasn't tar any more because it was too thin, slopping in his skull like petrol. His head was full of petrol and Ollie was going to set it alight if he didn't stop shaking him. They'd die in a fireball, melted together. They'd be a headline in the newspapers but Ollie'd get the blame, because he was the oldest. Finn was just a kid and he hadn't duct-taped himself—

He thought, 'That's what you get for making monsters.'

His head fell forward, knocking his chest with a *chunk*.

The tape was off. Something wet crawled out of his mouth and down his chin. A red snake slipping down his T-shirt, spreading itself out. He panicked, tried to hit it away.

Ollie held him hard. 'Shut up or it goes back on.'

Finn sobbed. There was a fucking *snake* on him—

'What's your problem?' Ollie was squeezing his arm again. 'Can't you do as you're told? You used to be able to do what the *fuck* you were told. D'you want to go back in the cage? You'll go back in the cage and I'll kick it, I'll kick it across the fucking floor, you little shit.'

Finn squinted down at his chest where the snake was

wide and red and keeping very still, its head pointing to where his jeans were wet again.

'You stink.' Ollie sounded different, not as angry. 'Did you piss yourself?'

'Snake . . .'

'What?'

'There's – snake.' He tried to shake it off him, but it clung on.

'There's no snake.' Ollie propped his chin on Finn's head. 'It's blood. You bit your tongue.'

Finn squinted at his chest. Blood was trailing down his chin. His lips stung and when he licked them his tongue stung too, gluey and disgusting. He'd pissed himself over his own blood coming out of his own mouth. Pain grabbed at him where Ollie had unwound the tape. It was on the floor, a long loop of grey with bits of his skin and hair stuck to it. He tried to stop sobbing but it was hard, his chest hiccuping, mouth gulping. He wiped at his face with white fingers, blue under his nails because of the tape round his wrists. He could bite through it now his mouth was free, he'd bite through it when he'd stopped crying.

'It's okay,' Ollie was saying, 'it'll be okay.'

He was rocking Finn, rocking the both of them.

Finn wanted him to stop. He was going to puke if Ollie didn't stop. 'Don't . . .'

It was worse than when Ollie was hissing at him and tying him up, because it made no sense. Finn had known Ollie was hard – you didn't fuck with Ollie – but he hadn't known Ollie was mental and this was mental, rocking Finn like he was a baby.

'Get off me, yeah?' He pulled free, twisting round on the tiles.

Ollie kept rocking, his eyes fixed on Finn, but it was

like he was seeing straight through him to the wall behind. Finn pulled his knees up, holding his bare toes with his fingers. He could unpick the tape from his ankles, bite it off his hands. That's what Dad would do, if he was here.

Ollie kept rocking, kept staring.

'Where is he?' Finn rubbed his toes to get rid of the blue. He was shivering but the petrol had stopped slopping in his head. The only fire was over his right eye, burning.

Ollie stared straight through him. He looked drunk, eyes big and black, glittery like Dad's when he'd been on the whisky.

Finn started picking at the end of the tape around his ankles. 'There's two of us now.' He shook his hands to get the blood going, wiping the sweat from his fingers onto his jeans before trying again with the tape. 'We can get out of here . . . Help us, would you?'

Ollie stopped rocking, but didn't speak or look at Finn.

'Fine, don't help.' He'd found the end of the tape and was pulling it free, one awkward loop at a time, passing it under his legs. It kept catching on everything. 'I thought you were with him but you're not. It's okay now there's two of us. We can fight him. You can fight anyone . . .'

'Get in the bath.'

'Piss off . . . I'm nearly done.'

Ollie was joking, that's what he thought. He'd taken the tape off Finn's mouth and why would he do that unless he was on Finn's side? But Ollie said it again: 'Get in the bath.'

'Why?'

'Just – do it.'

Ollie had a plan, that was it. He was going to get Brady in here and nut him, and he didn't want Finn in the way. 'I can help.' He dragged the last bit of tape from his ankles, wincing. It was worse than taking off a plaster. 'Let me help.'

'Get in the bath.' Ollie started rocking again. 'They told him you were in the bath.'

Finn brought his wrists to his mouth, searching with the sore tip of his tongue for the place where he could start unpeeling the tape. 'Told who?'

'Will you get in the fucking bath?' Ollie spoke through his teeth like he was being pulled back into the room, dragged here against his will, the way Finn had been.

'Why? You said they told *him* – who?'

'Your dad.'

'What?' Finn felt punched. 'They told my *dad*—?'

'Who d'you think this is for?' Ollie smacked his hand against the side of the bath, making it shout. 'All this shit. Who else gives a fuck about you?'

'Brady hasn't— He never said—'

'Your fucking dad,' Ollie gritted the words through his teeth, 'all this shit's for him. To make him do as he's told. And it's working, so, yeah. Get in the bath before I tape you shut again.'

Finn climbed to his feet. He stumbled towards the bath, remembering how he'd puked in it, feeling the stinging wetness of his jeans, hating the stink of himself. Scared of Ollie, scared of Brady. So scared he couldn't see straight.

Ollie shoved a foot at him to hurry him up. He was rocking again, arms round his knees, eyes off. Black and shiny, staring through the wall.

Finn put his taped hands on the curled lip of the bath. It was cold and hard. He balanced on one foot, lifting the other over the lip. Blood rushed to his head and he tipped forward like he was going to land face first in the bath, except Ollie's hand shot out and caught him by the knee of his jeans, holding him steady.

Finn looked down at him sitting there, and he couldn't make sense of Ollie, why he was here or what he was thinking. He hated Finn, but he'd helped him. He'd let Finn take the duct tape off his ankles, but now he was yelling at him to get in the bath. Because of Dad, he said—

He imagined lying down in there, by the plughole where the icy air came in. Not being able to see the door, not being able to get away and it was always going to be the bath where Brady did it – cut him up. Killed him. 'I – can't. Don't . . . Don't make me get in there.'

'You're in the bath,' Ollie said. 'That's what he thinks. He's thinking of you right now. He's doing what they say because of you, because he gives a shit.' His voice broke. 'You've got someone who gives a shit about you so be thankful and get-in-the-fucking-bath.'

Finn climbed in, standing with his feet shrinking from the squeaky cold inside the tub, holding its hard lip, not able to let go.

'Lie down,' Ollie said. 'He's thinking of you lying down in there.'

'What's Brady making him do?'

'Lie down.'

Finn lowered himself. 'Is he making him hurt people?' His voice was odd, echoey, down inside the bath. It was like lying in a space capsule or that machine where his gran went for tests before she died. He put the ends of his fingers to the overflow, feeling the cold running through its grill. Days ago he'd liked doing this, feeling the outside getting in. Not now. 'Ollie?'

'What?' He sounded a long way away. Quiet again, though. Not angry like before.

'Is Brady making him hurt people? My dad.'

'Yeah. But he likes it, doesn't he? That's what they said.

He likes hurting people. They're only asking him to do what he likes doing anyway.'

Finn curled on his side, facing away from Ollie.

Everything was white now.

No more tar, no more black.

White and hard and so cold he couldn't feel his toes.

He could unpick the rest of the duct tape with his teeth, but what was the point?

Dad was seeing him like this.

Lying here in the bath.

He should stay where Dad could see him.

40

Kim's café was a warm refuge from another bitter morning. Marnie nursed a cup of coffee, watching the door. It wasn't yet 7 a.m. but she'd wanted a head start on the day, knowing what it was likely to bring. She'd slept with Ed at her side after sidestepping his questions last night, remembering his reaction to the shoebox and needing the chance to put her thoughts in order; Ed was too important to be a dumping ground for the mayhem in her head.

The café door opened, letting in a razor-edged chill and Harry Kennedy in his peacoat, its collar turned up. He made his way to the table where she was sitting.

'Thanks for coming at stupid o'clock.'

'It was my turn.' He looked around. 'Great place. If I want coffee, do I order at the bar?'

'It's coming.' She smiled. 'You can sit down.'

He shrugged off his coat, putting it over the back of his chair. Grey suit, white shirt, no tie. He rubbed a hand at his head, bright-eyed from the cold start. 'How's Welland, have you heard?'

'He's going into hospital next week.'

'Let's hope for good news.'

'Yes.' She waited while Kim brought the coffee. 'Milk?'

'Thanks, just a splash . . .' He took the cup from her, wrapping his lean fingers around it. 'This smells good.'

'Tastes better.'

They shared a moment of silence.

'Tobias Midori,' Marnie said then. 'Has he given you anything more about why he took the shoebox from Lancaster Road?'

'We're interviewing him this morning. Zoe'll be the appropriate adult.'

'Any news from the hospital about Alan and Louise?' That should have been her first question, after he'd asked about Welland. 'I've not had the chance to visit them myself.'

'They're getting better, but still not ready for questions. I'm thinking we crack Tobias, we get the gang. They left enough DNA to make the rest of it easy.' He gestured contritely. 'When I say "crack Tobias" I am of course talking about the sensitive handling of a nine-year-old by a trained professional. Zoe's got the gift with these kids. They trust her. They talk to her.'

'I have questions I need to ask Tobias,' Marnie said. 'I'm happy for Zoe to ask them, but if there's a chance I could sit in . . .'

He studied her face before saying as Noah had last night, 'Something's happened. Are you able to tell me what?'

'I need to tell you. It has implications for your case . . . More coffee?'

They waited while Kim refreshed their cups. Kennedy betrayed no trace of impatience. Zoe might have the gift with kids, but Harry wasn't without talent of his own when it came to winning trust.

'I was in Cloverton yesterday,' she told him. 'Speaking with an inmate, Aidan Duffy. He's keen for me to see a connection between the break-in at Lancaster Road and the vigilante assaults we're investigating.'

'Why?' He frowned. 'And how?'

'A couple of caveats. Aidan Duffy's a con man. We need to take everything he says with a large dose of salt. And he's sharing a cell with Stephen Keele. So . . . that's salt enough to grit the M6.'

'They're playing you,' he deduced. 'Are they?'

'It's a strong possibility.'

Harry rubbed at his head again, more slowly this time. 'I can guess at Keele's game. But this con man— What did you say his name was?'

'Aidan Duffy.'

'Aidan Duffy. What's he after?'

'He has a ten-year-old son. Finn. He says Finn's being held hostage by the people responsible for the break-in at Lancaster Road.'

'And these are the same people behind the vigilante assaults?'

'According to Aidan. He knows names, dates. Details I can't ignore. And his son's missing. So you see my problem.'

'You're screwed.' He scratched his eyebrow. 'Sorry, that's unhelpful. I meant—'

'No, you're right. Thank you.' She was relieved. 'I didn't want to waste time dancing around what's at stake. Finn's missing and Aidan knows too much about what we're both investigating for it to be guesswork. He knew about the shoebox.'

She hadn't shared this detail with DCS Ferguson. Harry was the first person to hear it.

He drank a mouthful of coffee before asking, 'What exactly does he know?'

'That it was taken from Lancaster Road, and what's

inside. The charm bracelet. You saw it?' He nodded. 'There was a horseshoe.' She held up her hand, making the shape of the charm with her thumb and index finger. 'Aidan wants me to believe that's what our vigilantes have been writing on the newspaper clippings sent to the victims. I don't mean Rawling or the rest. The original victims, the ones our vigilantes are avenging. We thought it was a copyright symbol or a gang sign, but Aidan says it's a horseshoe. He arranged for someone to carve it into the shoulder of a friend of his in Cloverton, Jacob Collins. It looked like the work of our vigilantes, so I got a call. Duffy says he set Collins up because he needed to get me to the prison.'

'He had his friend attacked? Nice. What does he do to his enemies?'

'I'm not in a hurry to find out,' Marnie agreed.

'His son.' Harry frowned. 'Finn Duffy?'

'You know him?' She hadn't expected this.

'The name's familiar. Is he local? I'm assuming he's in Greater London.'

'Camden. We think he knows Ollie Tomlinson, who's also missing and allegedly connected to our vigilantes. Certainly connected to one of the victims, Carole Linton.'

'Damn.' Harry rolled his neck, holding it in the crook of his hand. 'Okay. Where d'you want to start? With Tobias?'

'I want to find Finn, and whoever killed Kyle Stratton.' She set her cup back in its saucer. 'Whether I'll be allowed to stay with the investigation's another matter.'

'You're the best detective they have. Ferguson's a fool if she thinks otherwise—' He stopped, still holding his neck, the skin flushed under his eyes. 'That came out stalkerish, but so you know? Toby Graves is a mate of mine.'

Toby Graves was a hostage negotiator. Marnie had

worked with him more than once. The last time had involved the rescue of two frightened teenagers from a site near Battersea Power Station. It felt like a lifetime ago, but it was less than nine months.

'Toby's a fan,' Harry said. 'So you know.'

Marnie's smile was reflexive. 'Aidan said the same about our vigilante. It's why I'll be taken off the case. Because someone out there thinks it's fun to have my attention, and this is the way to get it. By attacking people. Breaking bones. Killing.'

She'd been afraid of Ed's reaction to this part of the story she'd been spun at Cloverton. The stunned look on Harry's face was a clue, and he hardly knew her.

'It was bad enough,' she said, 'being reminded how it felt to be a victim, back inside that house – but the shoebox? That's when I knew it was personal. I'd half-suspected it, seeing the mess in there and knowing they'd been in the attic. When you brought me that box, I *knew*—'

She straightened, sitting back from the table. 'So, yes, Aidan's a con man. And he may well be playing me. But whether he is or he isn't, I won't be on the case to find out. I won't be rescuing his son, or arresting Kyle's killer. Ferguson may even put me on special leave.'

Harry let his breath out, looking at her for a long minute. 'How much of this does she know? Ferguson. What've you told her?'

'All of it, except the shoebox. I said I think a lot of it's fantasy spun by Aidan, with or without Stephen's help. But I let her have the lot.' She touched her fingers to the empty cup on the table. 'Can't have detectives withholding evidence, that would signal the end of days.'

Like hers, his smile was reflexive. 'If she has any sense, she'll keep you on the case.' His eyes were dark. 'How else's she going to solve it?'

'My team's good. DS Jake's one of the best detectives I've worked with.'

'If this's about you,' Harry said tightly, 'then you need to be on the case. And if it's a wind-up? You definitely need to be on the case.'

It sounded simple when he said it, but it wasn't.

For one thing, if Aidan was telling the truth, there wouldn't be a case but for her.

Harry moved his hand, stopping short of touching her wrist. 'Tell me the questions you want to ask Tobias.'

'I need to know who told him to steal the shoebox. Where he found it, how he *knew* where to find it. If he tells us who gave the gang their instructions, we'll be a step closer to finding Finn.'

'Let me speak with Zoe and confirm the timing of the interview. What else can I do?'

'That's it, for now. But thanks. I needed to talk this through with someone who wasn't DCS Ferguson.' Marnie checked her watch. 'I should get to work. You too.'

They stood, pulling on their coats.

Harry took out his wallet, but she shook her head. 'I've got this.'

Outside the café, Harry turned up the collar of his coat.

'Drop you at the tube?' Marnie offered.

'Thanks, but I'll walk. Need to process the caffeine . . .' He buried his hands in his pockets. 'What does DS Jake make of all this?'

'I haven't told him yet. He spent the night in the Whittington after a close encounter with a baseball bat.'

Harry lost the smile. 'But he's okay?'

'He's okay.'

'He asked me about his brother. Sol, is it?'

'Sol's safe,' Marnie said. 'I'm not so sure about the gang

he was running with, or from. Any help you can give would be appreciated, I know. Noah's out of hospital this morning. I told him to stay home for the day.'

'I'll check in with him later.' Harry narrowed his eyes at the road then looked at her. 'Someone's really gunning for your team.'

'That's how it feels, yes.'

'You're staying safe, though.' It wasn't a question, but he was concerned.

She nodded. 'No more solo patrols. Tricky, with resources the way they are, but I'm not taking any risks, especially after Aidan's story. Fantasy or otherwise, we know there's a killer out there.'

A killer, and a ten-year-old boy. She had to head off that collision, one way or another. Having blood on her hands was part of being a detective, but this was different, this felt as if—

Finn had crawled inside her to hide. She felt him as a physical pain, a thing she'd swallowed. A stone fed to her by his father. Along with a pack of lies, she was sure of that, but Aidan had needed her to feel this pain – *his* pain – for Finn.

Tied with duct tape, locked in a stranger's house.

Afraid for his life.

She had to find Finn and make him safe.

Whatever else happened, she had to do that.

41

DCS Ferguson was wearing her red shirt, red lipstick, killer heels. She'd wheeled in a new evidence board, parking it alongside the existing ones.

Marnie stripped off her gloves. 'Good morning.'

Ferguson gave a nod but otherwise ignored her. She'd cleaned the new board with hairspray, getting rid of every last mark from the old case scribbled there.

What was it Welland had said? 'She favours a frigate, type twenty-three . . . They call her *H.M.S. Dauntless*.' And Marnie had pointed out that *Dauntless* wasn't a frigate, it was a destroyer.

'We're a team short.' She was lining up marker pens.

'They'll be here,' Marnie said. 'I've told DS Jake to take a day to recover. He's certain it was Ollie who attacked him. Given where it happened, I'm wondering if we've overlooked the obvious.'

She walked to the new board, which was gleaming so fiercely she could see her face in it. Picking up one of Ferguson's new pens, she wrote a capital letter C.

'For Carole. Linton.' She capped the pen and put it down. 'Noah was attacked at Carole's flat. We know she controlled Ollie once before. He isn't smart enough to have masterminded all this mayhem, but perhaps he's part of it. Because Carole needs him to be.'

'You've been doing a lot of thinking.' Ferguson appraised her. 'Did you sleep at all?'

'Very well, in fact.' She smiled. 'Here's the team.'

Ferguson swivelled on her heel as Ron and the others came in, shedding their coats before gathering around the evidence boards, looking alert.

'How's Noah?' Debbie asked.

'Much better. I spoke with the Whittington an hour ago. They're discharging him. He's staying home today, but we should have him back with us tomorrow.' Marnie paused, to give Ferguson the chance to take command, but the woman just nodded at her to continue. 'We have a new priority. Finian Paul Duffy.' She pinned Finn's photo to the board. A good-looking boy, as handsome as his father, with cropped black curls and soft grey eyes. 'Finn. He's ten years old. We think he went missing from the Jonas House estate ten weeks ago.'

'We *think*?' Ron echoed.

'There's some confusion in the family as to exactly how long he's been missing. I'll make the calls needed to clear that up. Finn goes to the same school as Ollie. They may be friends. We're getting a warrant to search Carole's flat.'

'So that's . . . four missing persons?' Ron grumbled. 'Ollie and his mum. Carole. And now Finn Duffy. Why's he our priority and not Misper's? Sorry, boss, but haven't we got a murder to solve?'

'That's a good question,' Ferguson said coolly. 'DI Rome?'

'We've been given information to suggest Finn's disappearance is connected to Kyle's murder.'

Marnie waited until the room was quiet, all eyes on her. Ferguson was watching too. Waiting for her to get this right, or wrong.

'The source of the information is problematic, so we're going to proceed with caution. I'll be working with DCS Ferguson to establish a baseline going forward.' Using the woman's own words, a trick she'd learnt from Welland. 'That's what the new board's for.'

She nodded at the team. 'This is a ten-year-old. If we can find any one of our missing persons, great. If we can find Finn quickly, even better. But let's not get distracted from what we already know. DC Pitcher, anything from Forensics on the evidence found in Ollie's flat?'

'I'm chasing them this morning,' Colin said. 'And for the handwriting analysis on the envelopes and clippings.'

'What about our new victim?' Ron asked. 'From Cloverton.'

Ferguson nodded. 'DI Rome?'

'Jacob Collins is part of the baseline we'll be establishing. For now, we're keeping him to one side of this.' She took a step back. 'You may have something to add, ma'am?'

All eyes in the room shifted to Ferguson. 'You heard DI Rome.' She gave a red smile. 'Lots to do. Let's make a start.'

'Aidan Duffy asked you to arrest him.' Ferguson closed the door to Welland's office, nodding Marnie at a chair. 'Why didn't you?'

'No grounds.' She sat. 'He was nowhere near Jacob Collins when he was attacked. Aidan should have got his hands dirty, then I'd have been able to make an arrest.'

'So he's still sharing a cell with Stephen Keele.'

'As far as I know.'

Ferguson eyed her. 'And you still think the larger part of what he told you is misdirection?'

'Or fantasy. Yes, I do. He wants us to find his son. He's clever enough to realise that making me feel guilty is a great way of incentivising that outcome.'

'I'd like to interview him, all the same.' Ferguson opened her MacBook. 'You said he knew details of the assaults on Rawling and the rest.'

Marnie didn't dispute it. 'Someone feeding him information, that's clear.'

'And that someone might be our killer. Right. Fix up an interview at Cloverton. You and I can ask awkward questions, see how far his Irish charm gets him.' She glanced up. 'Why don't we see Stephen Keele while we're at it? Divide and rule. I'd like him in a separate cell afterwards. Or bunked with someone less indulgent of his charms.'

'You don't think giving the pair of them our attention is exactly what they're after?'

'Oh I don't think Keele's ever had to work very hard for your attention. Has he?'

Marnie's smile was involuntary, her only defence against the woman's new angle of attack. 'Are you planning to put me on special leave? Ma'am?'

'Not a chance of that. So long as you're not showing any signs of cracking up, I need you here for the head count.' She frowned at her MacBook, nodding a dismissal. 'Let me know when DS Jake's back at his desk. We're thin enough as it is, given the shambles we're trying to sort out.'

She didn't look up, clicking her tongue at whatever she was seeing onscreen. 'I didn't think I'd be saying this so soon, but I'm missing my neck of the woods. Up the Curry Mile they just brick or bottle you. You've introduced me to a whole new level of scumbag. Congratulations.'

Noah was eating toast when his phone rang. Sol, calling on the number Marnie had put into his phone at the hospital last night. 'Hey, Sol.'

'It's me.'

'I know.' Noah smiled at Dan, who'd come through from the kitchen and was frowning at the interruption to his bed-rest regime. 'Hey, Sol.'

'You okay?' His brother sounded nervous. 'They let you out, yeah?'

'I'm fine. I'm home.' Noah reached for Dan's hand, pulling him down onto the sofa next to him. His ribs twinged, but not much. His headache was clearing. 'Dan says Hi.'

'Yeah?' More than nervous. 'He's okay?'

'We're both good.' Noah put his free hand in Dan's fringe. 'How about you?'

'For real? I'm freaking out.' He heard Sol switch the phone to his other hand. 'This's fuckery.'

'Where are you?'

'Your boss's place. She told you, yeah?'

'So you're safe.' But Noah let go of Dan and sat forward, unnerved by the fright in his brother's voice. 'Sol? You're safe?'

A beat before, 'He's been out there hours. Like *hours*—'

'Who?'

'This is *fuckery*, man.' He sounded as if he were pacing. 'You gotta tell her.'

'Tell who? Sol, what's going on?'

'Your boss. Someone's outside her place *right now*. Been there hours. In his car, just watching the place, he's watching—'

'You recognise him?' Noah stood. 'You need to give me a name. I know you don't want to, this is gang stuff and you think you have to deal with it on your own, but you don't. You can't.' He touched his knuckles to the bruise left by the baseball bat. 'Give me a name. Let me help.'

His brother made a sound between laughing and sobbing.

'Sol—?'

'Not me, bro. This's her shit. It's *hers.*'

'What? You're not making any sense. Calm down and tell me what's going on.'

He heard Sol set his teeth. 'Outside her place, yeah? *Right now.* Not one of my boys, not *any* bad boy. This's hers. She's got a stalker, your boss. He's out there like he's front row *seating,* eating fucking Doritos.'

Noah ran it back: 'Someone's parked up outside DI Rome's flat, eating Doritos. Why're you freaking out? You've got weirder habits than that.'

'Because he's *watching.* You think I don't know what that looks like? He's staking the fuck out of your boss's flat, and *shit*—' Sol broke off.

Noah turned full circle, catching the look of worry on Dan's face, waiting for his brother to say something more.

'Sol?'

'He's outta the car,' whispering, 'shit, he's coming up the steps.'

The rattle of metal on metal.

Noah's neck clenched, the phone greasy in his grip. 'Sol, talk to me. What's going on?'

'He's— Fuck, he's put something through the door.'

'Through the letterbox? What is it?'

'Hold up . . .' Sol was breathing fast.

For a long minute all Noah could hear was Sol breathing through his mouth, short breaths, too much adrenalin.

Then he said, 'Okay . . . It's just a letter for her. Marnie Jane Rome.'

The sound of the envelope being turned over in his hand. 'Not much in here, maybe just a fan letter. He's got shit handwriting . . . C for creep, yeah.'

Noah propped a hand to the wall. 'There's a C on the envelope?'

'On the back, yeah. Right where he's sealed it. And some crap on it, like food or shit . . .'

'Wax. Is it white wax?'

'I guess. Yeah . . .'

'Is he still there?'

'Went back down the steps after shoving this through.'

'Is he in his car? *Sol*. Go and look. Now.'

He counted seven seconds before Sol said, 'He's there, but he's got the engine running. Yeah, he's fucking off.'

'Take a picture,' Noah snapped. 'Take it now, before he goes.'

'No camera, man. This phone's a piece of shit. No offence to your boss, but she's—'

'What's the registration?' Noah gestured to Dan who was ahead of him, already holding out a pen and pad. 'I need the make of the car, the registration, anything else you can give me.'

'He's fucking off. Hang on.'

'*Don't*— Sol, stay in the house. Don't let him see you.'

Silence. The sound of his brother breathing and under that, very faint—

The spit of tyres on a gritted road.

'Sol?'

'Yeah, man. I got it.' Sol gave him a registration number. 'Shitty silver Astra, sticker in the back for Battersea Dogs Home.'

'Did he see you?'

'No. I can describe him, though. You want that?'

'Save it for the station,' Noah said. 'I'll send someone round, but Sol?'

'Yeah?'

'This time, you stay put. You're a witness. We'll give you protection if you need it but you *stay put*. I get to the flat and find you gone? There'll be a warrant out for you. I'll issue it myself.'

42

Tobias Midori was nine, but looked younger. All eyes and outsized trainers that snagged on the interview room's rubber floor. Dressed in school uniform, a white polo shirt under a bottle-green blazer, black trousers too long for his thin legs. Licking his lips where a crust of milk and oatmeal had dried, the good breakfast his mother had insisted he eat before coming here to be interviewed by Harry Kennedy and Zoe Marshall. Zoe wore a dark green sweatshirt and black jeans; the clothes made her look like an older student from the same school. Tobias trusted her, Marnie saw that straightaway. He trusted Zoe, but not Harry and not Marnie.

Harry ran through the introductions, keeping it gentle, not scaring the boy despite the gravity of the charges. Marnie tried to place this frightened child next to the wreckage in Lancaster Road, the blood and broken glass. She'd seen Mrs Midori outside, waiting in her best coat, her face collapsed by sorrow and shame. A respectable woman, trying to hold her head up.

'We know you took a shoebox from the house.' Harry had removed his jacket, sitting in shirt sleeves. 'We don't know why. Can you tell us?'

Tobias shifted in the chair, shoulders twitching. His eyes were all over the room.

Zoe said, 'It's okay. We know this wasn't your idea. Sometimes stuff happens and you get caught up in it. You don't mean to but it catches you and it's really hard to step off.' Her voice had a rhythm, calming. She'd angled her body towards the boy.

After a beat, Tobias stopped fidgeting and sat still.

Zoe glanced at Harry, who nodded for her to continue. 'This's a chance to give your side. You're the only one who can do that. Harry – DS Kennedy – needs to know what happened so he can make sense of it and clear everything up.'

Tobias was rocking to the rhythm of her voice.

'I didn't hurt them.' His voice was thin, like the rest of him. 'That wasn't me.' He shot a scared look at Zoe then across the table at Marnie. 'I just got the box.'

'Where did you find it?' Harry asked.

Tobias licked at the crusted corner of his mouth. 'Tanker cupboard.'

'Tanker cupboard?'

'Where the water's kept.'

'The water tank,' Harry said. 'Where was that?'

Tobias raised a hand above his head. 'Up the steps.' His eyes flickered to Marnie then away. 'In the attic.' He brought his hand down, making it flat. Fingers closed, thumb tucked in. He propped the hand sideways, his little finger on the table. 'Behind the tank, pushed in. Tight.'

His hand was narrow, like a knife. Smaller than Marnie's hand, smaller than Stephen's now. But not then. He'd been a skinny child, like Tobias. Behind the water tank in the attic, that's where he'd stashed the shoebox. Pushing it tight, hiding it where it would take a child's hand to reach it. Marnie had pulled that house apart, but she'd not thought to put her hand behind the water tank.

'That's a good hiding place,' Harry said. 'How'd you know the box was there? I'm guessing someone told you.'

'Yeah, but I don't know names.' Tobias wet his lips. His eyes flickered left, then right. 'I'm not giving you names.'

'Because you're scared what'll happen?' Harry nodded. 'I saw the house, and the people who live there . . . That was very nasty. I'd be scared of whoever did that.'

The boy's narrow chin came up. 'I ain't scared of shit.'

'All right.' Harry looked surprised, and impressed. 'Good for you. So who was it? Who told you where to find the box? Who told you to take it out of the house?'

Silence.

Harry nodded again. 'I get it. It's scary—'

'It was a *letter*, yeah?' Tobias kicked at the leg of the table. 'I don't know who sent it. Just a letter and some shit about Crasmere, 'bout my boys. No one takes shit like that. You take it, they take *you*. I got it because they *needed* me to get it. And yeah it's cos I'm small, but that's why they need me.' He made his hand into a knife again, pointing it at Harry, at Marnie.

'I'm their *key*.' Tilting his chin. 'I open all the doors.'

Marnie had turned her phone off during the interview. She switched it back on as Harry walked Tobias to where his mother was waiting. Zoe zippered her coat, taking the red mittens from her pockets. 'Sorry. I wish I could've been more use.'

'He talked,' Marnie said. 'I doubt he'd have done that without your support.'

'He's a good kid.' Zoe freed her hair from the coat's collar. 'I know it's my job to say that but it's true. One of those you wish you could take out of London someplace he could grow up without a gang breathing down his neck. Kids are sponges; they soak up so much.' She rubbed the heel of her hand at her nose. 'I've got a nephew his age in Kent. Small towns are boring, but safe.'

'I'm sorry, I need to make a call.' Marnie was reading a text from Noah. 'Thanks for your help.'

'Any time.' Zoe held out her right hand, keeping the mittens in her left.

Marnie shook her hand, turning away as the call connected. 'Noah? What's happened?'

Harry was coming up the stairwell as Marnie headed down.

'We should talk,' he said, 'about what happens next.'

'Later.' She nodded. 'We have a lead on our killer. I have to go.'

He stepped out of her way. 'Anything I can do?'

'I'll let you know. Thanks.'

'Are you safe to drive?'

The question was asked so bluntly, she stopped and turned to face him.

'Are you?' He was standing two steps above her, a frown in his eyes. 'Only you look like someone hit you with a hard object.'

'There's a witness waiting. In my flat.'

'In your *flat*— What happened?'

'I'm safe to drive. That was your question, wasn't it?'

'I can give you a lift.' He rubbed a hand through his hair. 'Seriously. The offer's there.'

'Thanks, but I've got this.' She started back down the stairs. 'I'll call you, about Tobias.'

* * *

251

In the car, she checked her reflection to see what had spooked him. Her face was pale, but she was always pale. It irked her that he'd seen beneath her mask. On the other hand, 'Like someone hit you with a hard object,' summed up the situation neatly.

She started the engine. Set her phone to hands-free. Rang Noah.

'Sol's here,' he said. 'We've got a description. He was wearing gloves, or I'd get Forensics to dust the door. Colin's running a check on the registration. Do you want me to open the letter?'

It was going to take Marnie forty minutes to reach the flat. At least forty minutes. Even if they moved Sol to the station – they'd lose time if they waited for her to be the one to open the letter.

'Do it,' she told Noah.

Traffic had brought her to a standstill. She blinked at the brake lights of the car in front, flexing her hands at the wheel. Each of her fingers was gripped by cold.

The careful sound of the envelope being opened by Noah—

'Okay . . . It's clippings again. Two of them, but these are photocopies.'

He spoke very clearly, without emotion. She was grateful for that.

'The first one's from six years ago. Lancaster Road. Exactly what you'd expect.'

'And the second?'

'There's no date—' Noah stopped.

In his silence, she heard a world of doubt and worry. 'Tell me.'

'It says an inmate at Cloverton was found hanged in his cell. The third death in six months . . . As with all deaths in custody,' he was quoting from the clipping, 'there will be an investigation by the independent Prisons and Probation Ombudsman. A spokesman for the coroner's service said a post-mortem examination had yet to be carried out on the twenty-year-old male.'

Warning posters in the waiting room, those mismatched green carpet squares, the shrill of an alarm making him flinch— His fear. His fear like a snake under *her* skin.

Marnie's eyes felt glued open, fixed on the breathy exhaust of the car in front. 'That's it?'

'The inmate was moved to Cloverton from a juvenile detention centre in the South-West five months ago.' Noah stopped. 'That's it.'

'No name?'

'No name, no photograph.' His voice tightened. 'I'll contact Cloverton. Shall I?'

'Yes.'

'I'll call you straight back.' He rang off.

Dead ahead, the car's brake lights died.

Blare of a horn behind her—

The traffic was moving. She released the handbrake, raising her left hand in an apology.

A rushing noise in her head—

The heater. She reached to switch it off and the cuff of her coat snagged on the gears. She struggled, dragging it free. Another blare from behind. When she looked in the mirror—

Her eyes were wild.

She signalled left, looking for a space to park up, seeing—

A static row of frozen cars, each roof glittering, every space taken.

43

Sol was on the sofa with his eyes shut, shaving foam drying behind his left ear. He'd slept where he was sitting, the shape of his head in the cushions, a neat pile of bedding unused at the side of the sofa. He'd showered and shaved but he looked whip-thin, burnt-out.

Noah turned to watch the street through the shutters, his phone in his hand. He was waiting for Cloverton to return his call. The photocopied clippings were inside an evidence bag, back to back so that he could read each one without opening the bag.

'Greg and Lisa Rome, Lancaster Road . . . Fourteen-year-old in custody.'

'Post-mortem . . . yet to be carried out on the twenty-year-old male.'

Noah's head ached, nothing to do with yesterday's concussion; he was angry for Marnie. Whoever was playing this sick game had made him part of it, reading out the clippings, hearing the hurt in her voice. He'd checked the internet, failing to find any recent news reports that matched the second clipping, but he needed confirmation. He couldn't call back with half a reassurance.

A car crawled past outside, its driver not trusting the council to have salted these streets. Fewer and fewer residential roads were being treated, because supplies of salt were rationed now.

He gripped his phone hard, willing it to ring. Whatever had happened at Cloverton, Marnie needed to know. Waiting was almost worse than the pictures in his head – in *her* head – of Stephen hanging in his cell. She was waiting for Noah's call, imagining a post-mortem, enquiry, funeral. Her brother. Her parents' killer.

Noah started texting an explanation for the delay, wanting her to know that he was waiting for the prison to call him back.

From the sofa, Sol said, 'This's fuckery . . .'

'Yes,' Noah agreed shortly, 'it is.'

His phone rang: Colin Pitcher. 'The Astra's registered to Elliot Pershall. Seventy-three years old, address in Feltham.'

'He's not the driver.' Noah glanced at the description Sol had given. 'We're looking for a man in his thirties.'

'No report of the car being stolen. But I'll put a call through.'

'Can you text the DVLA details? I'm waiting for a call back, need to keep this line clear.'

'Will do.' Colin rang off.

Noah studied the text when it came. Elliot Pershall looked every one of his seventy-three years, with fleshy ear lobes and a fleshy nose. 'Is this anything like the man you saw?' He walked to where Sol was sitting.

His brother squinted at the driving licence. 'No way. This's *old* . . .'

'I know it's not the man you saw, but could they be related? Can you see *any* similarity?'

'Like this's his dad? Nah. Maybe.'

'Nah, or maybe?' He didn't have time for Sol's games. 'Which is it?'

Sol looked up at him then back at the photo. 'Maybe, but I don't think so.'

'Give me your phone.' Noah held out his hand.

'I don't—'

'DI Rome gave you a phone. I need to borrow it.'

Sol dug it from his pocket, handing it over with a look of surrender. 'Chill . . .'

Noah dialled the station. 'Find out if Elliot Pershall has a son. If so, he may be a suspect. If it turns out the car's stolen, we need to know when and from where. Run it through the systems for everything you can get. I'm waiting for the boss, we'll be back within the hour. Someone needs to organise an e-fit from an eyewitness. If DCS Ferguson wants an update, get her to call me. But the Astra goes on the board.'

His phone was ringing.

Cloverton, calling back.

'I have to go.'

44

Marnie locked the car and stood at its side. She'd cursed the slow journey getting here, but now it was too soon. She wasn't ready to be inside, hearing what Noah had to tell her.

Everything hurt, from her throat to her feet. She checked her pockets, one after the other, as if she could locate the precise source of the pain. At least she knew Ed was safe. She'd texted when she was stuck in traffic, and he'd texted back. She hated not knowing how long their vigilante had been watching her, how much he knew of her private life. He'd thought that she was living here, at the flat where Sol had spent the night. Which meant his information was out of date, by months. Her phone was ringing. She looked at it—

Noah, calling to say whether or not it was true.

Whether Stephen was dead. Murdered.

She pushed the phone back into her pocket, wanting to do this face to face. It'd been hard enough on Noah having to tell her about the clippings. This time she could at least meet his eyes, let him know how sorry she was that he was caught in the middle of this mess.

He opened the front door as she climbed the short flight of steps to the flat.

She stopped him before he could speak. 'Let me get inside.'

He stepped back into the narrow hall, closing the door behind her. She could smell shower gel, and dust from the radiators. The flat felt empty, but it wasn't. Sol was here, and Noah.

'All right.' She turned to face him, armed with a smile. 'Tell me.'

'He's alive. It was a lie.'

Nothing. Not relief, or disappointment.

Just the same pain, everywhere.

It was a lie.

If he'd said, 'It's true. Stephen's dead,' would it have been different? A different pain, surely. Or none at all. Could he have done that? Their vigilante, *her* vigilante. Excised her pain by punishing its perpetrator? No. She thought of Mazi's tears. Whoever was doing this wasn't interested in the excision of pain, only in its escalation.

'I suppose that's why he used photocopies,' Noah was saying, 'so that he could mock it up to look like a real news story. But it's a lie. Cloverton's confirmed it.'

'Good. That's – good.' She nodded at the bruised side of his face. 'Are *you* okay?'

'Yes.' He touched a hand to her elbow.

She kept the smile in place. 'Sol's here, yes?'

'On the sofa.'

'What exactly did Cloverton say?'

'No deaths at the prison in six months. Stephen's in his cell, they checked. We have a name for the owner of the Astra, but he's not the man Sol saw. Elliot Pershall, a pensioner from Feltham. We're trying to find out if his car was stolen, and if so when and where.'

'Sounds as if you're on top of things. Any word from DCS Ferguson?'

'Not yet.'

They went through to where Sol was sitting on the edge of the sofa, his elbows on his knees, head hanging. He looked up when they came into the room.

'I'm starving,' he said. 'Can we get some breakfast?'

At the station, Noah took Sol to where the e-fit expert was waiting. When he reached the incident room, Ron was pinning a photo of the Astra to the board, alongside an enlarged copy of Elliot Pershall's driving licence.

'Says his car was nicked while he was at a hospital appointment two days ago,' Ron told them. 'Poor sod spent forty minutes searching for where he'd parked it before he gave up and got the bus home. Memory's going, he said. Not the first time he's lost his car. Left the keys in it, too.'

'Which hospital?' Marnie asked.

'Hillingdon. Uxbridge. Nowhere near any of our victims.' Ron scratched the back of his head. 'We're drawing a bit of a blank. Sorry, boss.'

'Is he on his own?' Noah asked. 'Mr Pershall.'

'Widower, no kids. So, yeah. He was on his own. We've asked for CCTV footage from the hospital car park, should be with us soon.'

'Any news on Lisa,' Marnie asked, 'or Carole?'

'Nothing, boss.'

'And nothing on Finn.'

'Only that he's definitely not been seen in ten weeks. Child Protection have sorted the paperwork and put out the alerts.'

'All right. Let's find whoever stole Mr Pershall's car. And let's find Ollie. Anything connecting him and Finn.'

She looked across at Noah. 'You should be at home, resting.'

'I'm fine. If I start feeling stupid, I'll go. Let me help until then.'

Before Marnie could argue, Colin arrived.

'Forensic report on the stuff from Lisa's place.' He handed Marnie a sheet of paper. 'Fran's team found *two* blood matches. No fingerprints. Not on the bat or the lighter. And not on the bin liner. Whoever used the bat, and whoever binned everything afterwards, wore gloves. But Fran got bloods from the bat.'

'This should get us an arrest warrant.' Marnie studied the report. 'For Ollie.'

'It's Kyle's blood?' Noah's head throbbed, blackly. He looked at Colin. 'You said *two* matches.'

'Kyle's blood on the bat,' Marnie said. 'No question this is our murder weapon. But, yes. There's another blood match. And Fran thinks it's fresher than Kyle's.'

'That means—'

'After Kyle was attacked, the bat was used again.'

'Fran's matched the blood already?'

'She didn't have to look very far,' Colin said. 'Same case file.'

Noah was watching Marnie. 'Whose blood is it?'

She looked up. 'Carole Linton.'

Her eyes burned in her face.

'It's Carole's blood on the bat.'

45

Ice was melting, trickling to where Finn lay curled on his side where they'd buried him, in the snow. White on all sides but it wasn't cold, not really. Not real snow. Just that the bath was white. The ice wasn't real either, only water from the taps and he was glad because he was thirsty and when he pushed his tongue out he could taste taps, pipes, the bleach he'd used to clean where he was lying with his hands taped, feet free, mouth gummy from the glue.

'Ollie?' The name rattled round the bath like a pebble, his voice weird and washed out. His head was burning, but he was freezing cold. 'Ollie?'

'What?' Like he was a long way away, in another room.

'I feel shit.'

'Yeah.'

'Is he coming?' Brady, he meant.

'Yeah.' At least Ollie wasn't angry.

Finn moved his fingers, pressing at the sides of the bath. It felt soft but it wasn't, that was in his head, that was just his fingers being too numb to feel properly. 'Is this really about my dad?'

'Yeah.'

'Why?'

'I told you.' Ollie sucked at something, maybe just air. 'Because he gives a shit.'

'Will he let us go? After Dad's done what he wants, if he does what he wants. Will he?'

After a bit, Ollie said, 'He'll let you go.'

'Why not you?'

'I've done stuff.'

'What stuff?'

'Can't you shut up?'

'I'm cold. My feet are cold.'

The squeal of Ollie's trainers on the floor, his shadow blocking the light. He wrapped a hand towel round Finn's feet then covered the rest of him with a bath towel.

'Thanks . . .' His teeth chattered.

Ollie sat back down.

'What stuff've you done?' Finn asked after a bit, mostly to make sure Ollie was still there.

'Nothing. Forget it.'

'You can tell me. I won't say anything.' He put his hand on the side of the bath. 'I'm going to tell them how you tried to help, you gave me these towels.'

'Yeah?' Ollie didn't believe him. 'You going to tell them about the duct tape too?'

'What'd you mean when you said that thing about a cage?' He spread his fingers on the white wall between them. 'You said you were going to put me back in the cage and kick it, but there wasn't any cage.'

'Not for you.'

'What?'

'You want to know what's funny?' Ollie sounded worn out, like a little kid. 'They all said I didn't remember. My mum always told everyone, "Thank God he doesn't remember," like that made it okay. I had to tell her to stop saying it. She'd have told everyone, "Thank God he doesn't remember," when what kind of moron doesn't remember being shut in a cage?' He knocked at the side of the bath. 'You'd remember, wouldn't you?'

'Yes.'

Ollie was talking about something that'd happened years ago, he had to be. He was too big to put in a cage now. This'd happened ages ago, when Ollie was little. Littler even than Finn.

'You'd remember being made to eat your food like a dog, down on your hands and knees. Not even real food. Screwed-up tissues she'd used to clean her face with, and that curly pasta straight from the packet. Not even cooked. Dry pasta. She wouldn't let you soften it with water or your spit, made you eat it while she watched, seeing the way it scraped the skin off the inside of your mouth, made your throat bleed. Only if you cried, she'd kick the cage and keep kicking it, for hours sometimes.' A squeaking sound, like his feet couldn't stop moving on the floor.

Finn wanted to ask who did it, and why. It made him ill to think of anyone treating Ollie that way – treating *anyone* that way. But he was afraid to speak in case Ollie got angry again. Shame could make you angry, Finn knew.

'Sickest bit?' Ollie said. 'I missed it when I got back home. Being told what to do. All those therapists getting me to draw pictures of my *feelings*, not one of them was any use. I wanted *rules*. If no one gives you rules, you can't make sense of *shit*. So yeah, I was glad. When *she* showed up. I was glad.'

He sucked at snot in his throat, snot or tears. 'No one else was any use to me except Mr Singh and I couldn't keep seeing him, not with the Crasmere Boys calling him a towel-head and worse. I was going to get him hurt. She says that's what happens near me, and she's right.'

She? The woman who'd put him in a cage had come back? Finn couldn't make sense of what Ollie was saying. Surely if there were therapists and his mum telling people he didn't remember stuff then that meant they'd caught whoever did it. And if they'd caught her, they must've locked her away. But maybe she was out now, the way Finn's dad would be one day. Maybe they'd let her out of prison and she'd gone looking for Ollie. Finn shivered under the bath towels.

'Mr Singh was my friend.' Ollie's voice cracked. 'But she warned me what'd happen if I tried to have friends. I'm fucked up inside. She *knew*. I was going to get him hurt. Only one way to get well, that's what she said. That's what she showed me.' His heart was beating too hard.

Finn could hear it through the side of the bath and okay maybe it wasn't Ollie's heart, maybe Ollie was knocking his feet on the floor or his head on the wall, but it sounded like his heart and it sounded too hard, like he was going to have a heart attack. Finn had to get him to calm down.

'Why're you here?' he whispered. 'If this's about my dad, about me. Why're you here?'

Ollie didn't answer.

'What did you do? You said you did stuff—'

'I killed someone, okay?' Ollie thumped the bath.

Finn curling tighter under the towels. It wasn't true. Ollie wasn't a killer. He was a kid who'd been kept in a cage by someone who'd come back to fuck with his head. You didn't fuck with Ollie, not unless you wanted trouble. Ollie was *hard*. 'You didn't—'

'Yeah? You happy now? I killed someone. Smashed

their head to shit. Broke their fingers, broke their *fucking* nose. Blood everywhere. You should've seen the blood, I was *slipping* in it, *tasting* it. I could see his brain inside his face and she made me— She had a lighter and she made me—' He stopped, sucking at the air. It sounded like sobs, like Ollie was sobbing. 'And it wasn't true. *Only one way to get well.* It wasn't true. Because it didn't make me better, it just made me a killer.'

He'd really done it. Killed someone. Beaten them to death.

Finn couldn't breathe, couldn't see, even with his eyes wide open. He couldn't see.

'So yeah.' Ollie knocked his hand at the bath again but softly, like he'd spread his fingers, starfished on the walls between them. 'I'm not going anywhere.'

46

The steps to Carole's flat were icy, ungritted. Noah's ribs twinged with memory as he followed Marnie down. The front door had been unlocked by the landlord, a thickset man with a fistful of keys who did as he was told and stayed out of their way.

No change in temperature as they stepped inside, just a deadening in the air. No smell – the cold playing its part. Noah had been in worse places, but not recently. The flat was damp and it was dark, carpet decaying along with the window frames. Black everywhere from untreated mould. Pieces of furniture, cheap and scarred, peeling wallpaper. A square box of rot; stage-set for the world's most depressing kitchen sink drama. 'A studio,' the landlord called it, meaning the bed pulled out from the sofa and the kitchen was a plug-in hot plate, the bathroom a cupboard fitted with a chemical toilet and a shower that dripped into a tiny sink. Nowhere to hide a dead body, barely room for a living one. Noah's fingers pricked inside the crime scene gloves.

Marnie opened the minibar-sized fridge. A week-old pint of milk had separated into water and cheese. No storage space in the studio, just uncovered shelves where Carole kept clothes and make-up, a handful of books. Picture books, for kids. No television, no computer. A trio of plastic handbags hung from a peg by the door. Marnie opened each in turn, before taking down a black quilted bag and emptying its contents onto the shelf where Carole kept her hairspray.

Wallet. Car keys. Lipstick, hairbrush, painkillers. In the wallet, a creased ten-pound note and some loose change. Credit cards, bank card, driving licence. Paperwork from a job agency, loyalty cards for a couple of coffee chains. House keys.

Marnie put the two sets of keys side by side.

'Her car's outside,' Noah said. 'Frozen shut. It's not been driven in days.'

Carole's blood was on the baseball bat used to kill Kyle.

She'd left her car keys, house keys, wallet.

'She's gone,' Noah said. 'Isn't she?'

Dead, he meant. Murdered, like Kyle. 'Or else that's what she wants us to think.'

'We need Forensics in here.' Marnie made the call, standing with her eyes on the windowless wall. Then she pocketed her phone. 'Come on.' She headed out of the flat.

The landlord was vaping; the red smell of raspberries stung Noah's eyes.

'Not a lot of room in there,' Marnie said. 'Did Ms Linton rent storage space from you?'

'Round the back.' He searched the fistful of keys. 'I suppose you'll want to see . . .'

He led them through the salvage yard, past the burnt-out cars to a big garage with a roll-up metal door that he dragged up and open. Cold air sucked at them from inside. The garage was piled with possessions. Crowded, but dry. Better living conditions than the flat.

'This doesn't all belong to Carole Linton,' Marnie said. 'Presumably.'

The landlord pointed to the far corner. Light ran in, finding the reflective surfaces of crates and plastic sheeting that divided the space into sections.

Marnie and Noah picked their way to the back where a grandfather clock was wrapped in a blanket, a noose of rope round its neck. A set of drawers with fancy handles, an ornate mirror. Furniture from a different life to the one lived in the studio, its edges protected by blanketing.

'The attack on Carole,' Marnie said. 'We knew it was different to the other assaults. No marks on her face, and a knife not a blunt weapon. Her skirt set on fire . . . It stood out, right from the start.' Her eyes flashed in the dim light. 'Carole was different.'

'Her crime was different too.' Noah thought of the abandoned keys in the studio flat, and the blood on the baseball bat. 'She was hiding information about the attack, we both thought that. Should we have been watching her? If we'd asked better questions, kept her under surveillance . . .'

'We were busy. The attacks were escalating. Carole wasn't the only victim.'

The letter C on the clippings, and carved into the shoulder of the inmate at Cloverton. Had they missed a trick? Had this been about *Carole*, right from the start?

'Noah . . .'

Marnie reached a gloved hand for the blanket covering what looked like a trunk.

It wasn't a trunk. It was a cage.

A black wire cage with a shallow plastic tray as its base. Large enough for a big dog, or a small child.

'This isn't—'

'Not the cage she kept Ollie in. The police seized that.'

Marnie's voice was taut. 'She went out and bought another one.'

She dropped the blanket back over the cage, crouching to uncover the smaller items stacked on the floor. Boxes, mostly. Photographs, all pre-dating the time when Carole took Ollie from the car park in Harrow. Books, newspapers. Buried underneath, a scrapbook with its blue pages swollen inside an orange cover.

Marnie opened it. On the first page, glued in place—

A child's face looking out from the bars of a cage like the one behind them. Vacant eyes, a pink mouth slick with spit, small nose caked with mucus. Long black eyelashes, each one wet and separate. Damp curls sticking like feathers to his little head. Ollie Tomlinson, his black eyes ringed by purple, the irises all but lost to shock and fright.

Marnie turned the page to more photos. Ollie lying on his side in the cage, fingers pushed through the wire. Sitting up in nothing but a nappy, face pressed to the bars.

'The police didn't seize this?' Noah felt a pulse of anger at the thought of Carole looking through these pictures after she'd been released from prison, long after her punishment was over.

'They didn't know about it.' Marnie turned another page. 'No mention of a scrapbook in the police report, or the records from the trial.' She stopped.

A single photograph on the blue sugar paper. Faded, old. Not Ollie.

This child had pale eyes and pinkish-blond hair.

The same age, three or four years old.

In a cage, alone.

'She took *more* kids?' Noah's throat closed in protest. 'That's not Ollie.'

'No, it's not.' Marnie turned the page to more photos of the same child.

Small fingers pushed through black bars.

Noah was afraid, as the pages turned, that he'd see the faces of more trapped children. But it was only Ollie, and this other child.

'How did we not know about this?' he demanded. 'Carole was on trial. They searched her house, took everything. How did we not know?'

Marnie didn't speak, studying the face of the nameless child. Impossible to tell if it was a boy or a girl. Not cherubic like Ollie. Those pale eyes—

Noah couldn't look away. 'Who is it? And what happened to them?'

'I don't know.' Marnie straightened slowly, holding the scrapbook open in her hands. 'But we need to find out.' Her breath was white. 'We're looking at someone your age, or mine.' She pointed at the photos. 'These were taken twenty or thirty years ago. Look at the quality, the discolouration. Whoever this is? Carole took them years before she took Ollie.'

Pale eyes stared up from the scrapbook, colourless in the lock-up's semi-light.

'Whoever this is,' Marnie said, 'they're not a child any longer.'

47

'This is who our witness saw delivering the latest set of news clippings.'

The e-fit showed a man in his thirties, oblong face, thinning fair hair. Sol had given a detailed description, right down to the blackheads on the right side of the man's nose. Noah had been complimented on his brother's acuity: 'I wish all witnesses had his eye.'

Their suspect was wearing a black fleece-lined anorak over bleached jeans, white trainers, 'But more like grey. Dirty.' He'd picked at his teeth with his thumbnail as he'd climbed the steps to Marnie's front door. 'Ugly, ugly teeth.' Sol hadn't missed a beat.

'We've shown this to Elliot Pershall, but he's none the wiser,' Ron said. 'No matches in our system. CCTV at the Hillingdon shows the Astra entering and exiting the car park, but no eyes on the driver. Col's running the e-fit against CCTV from their front desk.'

'Mr Pershall's memory's going,' Debbie said. 'He's been passed around a few places before landing up at the Hillingdon.'

'If he was visiting other hospitals,' Noah said, 'let's find

271

out which ones. It's possible our suspect saw Mr Pershall on an earlier occasion, the way he parked, leaving his keys in the car . . . This might not have been opportunistic.' He glanced at Marnie, who nodded for him to continue. 'Carole works shifts as an auxiliary, at more than one hospital.' He pinned up the job agency paperwork from her handbag. 'There could be a link between her and our suspect. If so, we need to find it quickly. In terms of motive—'

'Shall we save the psychology for the interview,' Ferguson interjected in her arid way. 'We've a warrant for Ollie Tomlinson. That's plenty to be going on with.'

'Carole's five foot one,' Debbie said. 'And she's really skinny.'

'Your point, DC Tanner?'

'She could pass for a kid.' Debbie hesitated.

Marnie said, 'Go on.'

'We know Ollie's big for his age, and she's tiny. We've been looking for two *boys* but with their shared history—'

'And our car-jacker with the bad teeth?' Ferguson asked. 'How does he fit in?'

'Like DS Jake says, ma'am, if she's working at hospitals, maybe *he* is too . . . She could be using him, the way she's using Ollie. Our eyewitness in Page Street said the same as Stuart: *two* kids, one big, one small. If the small one's Carole then she could be in charge. It wouldn't be the first time she's told Ollie what to do.'

'DI Rome.' Ferguson turned on her heel. 'What do you make of this new theory?'

'It's plausible. Carole went missing around the same time as Ollie. And DC Tanner is right to point out their shared history, which was rooted in violence and control.'

'So she faked her own assault?' Ferguson said. 'Set fire to her skirt, ruptured her own innards?'

'No. But she's a part of this,' Noah said. 'And not in the same sense as Stuart, or Kyle. Carole was always different—'

They all turned when the door opened.

'We have a name,' Colin said, 'for the man who stole the Astra.'

He held up a print-off. 'From the Hillingdon. I ran the e-fit and got a match.'

Marnie pinned the new photograph to the board.

Everyone gathered closer to study it. Noah blinked. The likeness to Sol's e-fit was uncanny, right down to the blackheads clustered to the right of the man's nose.

'That's not a CCTV still,' Ron said.

'No,' Colin agreed. 'It's a staff ID. He's a paramedic.'

A *paramedic*?

Like the ones who'd treated Kyle, and Stuart, and Carole.

'Huell Gareth Bevan. Thirty-five years old, lives in Feltham, works out of Cressey Road ambulance station in Camden.' Colin rubbed a mark from his spectacles. 'That's as far as I've got.'

'I'll make some calls.' Ron wrote the contact numbers on a scrap of paper and moved away.

'We need a record of Bevan's shifts,' Noah said. 'If he was in Holloway at the time of the assaults, or in Westminster earlier this week . . .'

'I've put in a request.' Colin glanced at Marnie, asking a silent question, wanting a moment of her time, alone.

Ferguson intercepted the look. 'There's something else, DC Pitcher?'

'No, I just—'

'Is it connected to the investigation?'

'Yes, but—' Colin looked cornered.

'Go ahead.' Marnie smiled at him, disliking Ferguson's

tactics to divide-and-rule her team. 'Good work on finding Bevan.'

'Thanks, boss. It's just . . . he's on a visitor list.' Colin cleared his throat. 'At Cloverton.'

'Bevan is on the prison visitor list?'

'I ran his name through the system as soon as I had it,' Colin said. 'No criminal record, but he's twice visited an inmate at Cloverton in the last ten weeks.'

Marnie held hard to the smile, afraid to let it slip. 'Which inmate?'

'Jacob Collins.'

Not Stephen, not this time.

'Collins . . .' Ferguson looked at Marnie. 'You met him, didn't you?'

'I did, yes.'

'A friend of Aidan Duffy's, although perhaps Mr Collins should take that under advisement given the nature of their friendship just lately.'

'Then Bevan's the one,' Debbie said. 'The one who gave Collins the message about Aidan's son. He has to be. If he's the one who took Finn—'

'Have there been any sightings of Finian Duffy?' Ferguson demanded. 'DC Pitcher?'

Colin shook his head. 'Nothing on CCTV, or not yet.'

'His friends haven't seen him in weeks,' Debbie said. 'They thought he must've moved away. When we asked about Uncle Regan they all said Finn would never've gone there unless he was desperate. He sounds like a nice kid. Ollie wanted him in his gang because Finn's dad's famous for being a hard man. No one believed it when Finn turned Ollie down. You don't say no to Ollie and Finn's just a little kid, not even eleven. He stood up to Ollie. They all said that took guts.'

Ferguson straightened, nodding at Marnie. 'You and

I are going to Cloverton first thing tomorrow to interview Jacob Collins and Aidan Duffy, and anyone else
we think may have information pertinent to this investigation.'

'Is there a reason we can't go sooner?'

'I've arranged the interview for tomorrow morning. It's
been a long day and I was hoping, perhaps optimistically,
that we'd be busy arresting Ollie Tomlinson with what's
left of it.'

Ron returned from his desk, saying, 'Bevan's not
been home since he took off from your place, boss. He's
not due at work until ten p.m. We've got eyes on the
ambulance station, and his flat. No reason to think
he's absconded, unless he knows he was seen this
morning.'

'Bevan didn't see Sol,' Noah said. 'He was watching the
flat for a while before he posted the envelope through
the door. He must've thought the coast was clear.'

'Are we still keeping these cases separate?' Ron asked.
'If he's threatening you, boss—'

'He didn't threaten DI Rome.' Ferguson checked her
watch. 'Any more than he threatened Valerie Rawling or
Mazi Yeboah. He was paying tribute, that's what he'd like
us to call it. The threat implied by the faked newspaper
clipping was directed at Stephen Keele.'

Stephen's name had never been spoken in front of
Marnie's team.

Welland would have bitten through his own tongue
before he did that.

Ron and Colin looked sideways, at the board. Only
Noah met her eyes, disliking Ferguson's tactics as much
as Marnie did. She'd told him about the conversation at
Cloverton with Aidan, given him the same information
she'd given to Harry Kennedy. It was stripping her bare

to keep telling everyone her business. Perhaps that was Bevan's intention. And Ferguson's too.

'We should look for Finn in Bevan's flat,' she said. 'Since he's our chief suspect.'

'We'll get a warrant,' Ferguson agreed. 'In the morning.'

'Tonight,' Marnie said. 'Why not right now?'

'Insufficient grounds. So far all we have is the envelope of clippings, and a stolen car. We can link him to the assaults, possibly even to the murder. But we've nothing to suggest he's involved in the kidnap or false imprisonment of a child.'

'His connection to Jacob Collins,' Noah said, 'suggests it to me.'

'We'll find out, first thing tomorrow.' Ferguson clapped her hands at the team. 'Good work, everyone. Get some rest. We'll start over in the morning.'

Marnie said, 'Let me give you a lift home.'

Noah didn't argue, wanting the chance to talk with her about what had unfolded at the station. 'We didn't tell her about the scrapbook. The other child in the cage.'

'I didn't think it was the right moment to add a new mystery face to the board.' Marnie ran the heater, turning out of the station car park in the direction of Noah's flat. 'How's Sol?'

'Hungry. Dan says he's eaten his way through the fridge already. We could order Chinese, if you'd like to hang around for that?'

'Thanks, but I need to get home.'

To Ed, not to the place Huell Bevan thought was *home*.

'Her tactics are all wrong.' Noah rolled his shoulders. 'Ferguson's. She's going to mess this up if she isn't careful.'

'Or she'll shake something loose,' Marnie said equitably.

'At Cloverton, I meant. From what you've told me

about Aidan, he's smart enough to play her. He'll probably enjoy it, too.'

'Perhaps. But she won't be happy until she's satisfied herself on that score.'

'Never interrupt your enemy when she's making a mistake.'

'Napoleon?'

'Hmm. The Louboutins were the giveaway.' He put his head back against the seat rest. 'She's punching above her weight.'

'I'm worried she hasn't got started yet. That this is just a warm-up bout.'

'I told Welland I had your back.' Noah touched the bruises on his face. 'He might have warned me what was incoming, though. She takes no prisoners.'

Unlike Carole, with her caged children.

And whoever was holding Finn.

Marnie was watching the car's mirrors. Noah was watching, too. For Huell Bevan because he wasn't at home and they didn't know what he wanted, not really. Only that he was after victims to appease, and to punish. Ferguson imagined that this ended when they had him behind bars, but she wasn't tuned to the city's heartbeat the way Noah was, and Marnie.

All of London strummed with show-offs and strays, fear and bravado. What Bevan was doing hadn't started with him, and it wouldn't end there. Pain didn't stop because you benched its latest player. Bevan had passed it up the line, that's all, a new friction plucking at the city's strings, the whole of London one long dirty neon bruise, aching and echoing to this new tune.

Ed was on his way out when Marnie got home. 'Work, sorry . . .' He pulled on his coat, his face drawn with worry for someone else he was trying to help. Not enough Ed to go round.

'I'll be fine,' Marnie told him. 'Go.'

Alone in the flat, she sat in her usual spot and roll-called her blessings, bringing them close enough to people the empty space at her side. After a while, she reached for her phone and dialled Sean Welland's number, hoping for news of his dad.

'He's here,' Sean said, 'if you'd like a chat.'

'Only if he's okay with that. I wasn't expecting to speak with him.'

'You'd be doing me a favour. Stir-crazy doesn't start to cover it.'

Marnie waited while Sean handed the phone to his father.

'I'm in a holding pattern,' Welland grumbled, 'for the surgeon with the steadiest hands. Cheer me up and tell me about someone else's shitty day.'

He sounded so like his usual self that Marnie shut her eyes, smiling. 'How long have you got?'

'For you? All night. How're things in the trenches?'

'Don't you mean on the high seas? Frigates and destroyers, remember?'

'You're under fire,' he deduced. 'That didn't take her long. How's the team holding up?'

'We miss you. *I* miss you. Sorry to be selfish, but I really do.'

'Nice to be wanted by someone who isn't wielding a scalpel . . . How's DS Kennedy?'

He was asking for an update on Lancaster Road. What could she tell him? Not about the shoebox, or Aidan Duffy, or Stephen. She didn't want that sort of worry in his head.

'Harry's good. You said he would be, and you were right.'

'Harry?' Welland echoed. 'That schoolboy charm has a sell-by date, just so you know.'

'I'll try to remember that.'

'I heard about Kyle Stratton. Hope you're getting re-inforcements in the hunt for your vigilante.'

'Vigilantes,' she amended. 'Stuart Rawling made a fresh statement, and an eyewitness says two people attacked Kyle. We have a suspect, Huell Bevan. But he's gone to ground.'

'Let's hope you find him before anyone else becomes intimately acquainted with his assorted weaponry . . .' Welland paused. 'You sound like you've been on the blunt end of it yourself.'

'Those honours went to Noah. He's on the mend, but assorted weaponry is right. And we think whoever's doing this has Ollie Tomlinson involved.'

'The kid from the cage?' He breathed a heavy sigh. 'You've got your work cut out.'

'I'm keeping busy,' Marnie agreed.

'Tell DS Jake he has my sympathy, as someone else about to take up space in our overcrowded, underfunded health service.'

'I've not forgotten about the whisky,' she promised. 'Get Sean to send smoke signals as soon as you're ready for visitors.'

'I will. And in the meantime? Do what you do best, Detective Inspector.'

Sol was taking up most of the sofa when Noah got home, one hand buried in a bag of popcorn, the other propped behind his head. Eyes on the TV but not watching, flicking to Noah then past him, to the hallway; he'd moved the sofa, to have a clear sightline to the door.

'Dan's out. That's cool, yeah?'

'It's cool.' Noah had asked for a couple of hours to speak to Sol alone. Dan was out with a group of friends who'd see him home safely. No one was taking any risks. 'Have you eaten?'

Sol shook his head. 'Just . . .' Holding up the popcorn.

'Give me a hand in the kitchen?'

'Sure.' Rolling upright, planting his bare feet on the floor. He was wearing a clean set of sweats, looking less burnt-out than he had at Marnie's place.

In the kitchen, Noah made turkey sandwiches while Sol took the tops off a couple of beers.

'I've been hearing compliments about you all day. That e-fit you gave us? Oscar-winning.'

'You caught him, yeah?'

'Not yet, but we've ID'd him. Thanks to you. You want mango chutney on this?'

'Yeah.' Sol sucked beer from the backs of his fingers, watching Noah. 'Your boss okay?'

'Yes.' He passed one of the plates to his brother, taking one of the beers in return.

They ate at the kitchen table.

Sol picked his sandwich apart before putting it back together and taking a big bite. Noah kept his phone at his elbow for texts from Dan, but it was more likely the gang was watching the flat now, if they'd seen Sol return here earlier in the day.

'You let Mum and Dad know you're okay?'

Sol nodded. A mouthful of beer, another of turkey, wiping his mouth with his thumb.

Noah let him eat most of the sandwich before he asked, 'So is it drugs?'

Sol dropped his head forward, showing the bony back of his neck. The hand that wasn't full of sandwich reached for his beer.

'Or money?' Noah moved the bottle closer. 'Or is it both? Did you steal someone's stash?'

'This's your boss asking?'

'It's your brother. It's me. I need to know what's going on. I want to help.'

'You could leave it,' Sol said. 'That'd help.'

'Wouldn't help Dan. Someone followed him, took a photo as a threat. Who's looking for you?'

'You *know* who.'

'Your gang,' Noah surmised. 'I don't know names, you've never given me names.'

'Yeah?' Sol took a swig of beer. 'Wonder why.'

Noah looked at the photos on the fridge. Snaps of him and Sol as kids, all wide white grins and skinned knees. Sol's smile was irresistible, always had been.

'Remember Rojay, your best friend when you were ten? You said it freaked you out what happened to him. Watching him getting run into the ground. Used up and spat out.'

Sol blew a tuneless note from the neck of the beer bottle. 'Rojay was a fool.'

'He wasn't even twenty.'

Another tuneless note, indifferent. 'Died doing what he loved, though.'

'Dealing drugs and getting slapped around?'

Sol shrugged, as if Noah had put a hand on him and he was shaking it off. Noah didn't want to put a hand on his brother's shoulder, but he was close to wanting to put a fist in his face.

'Look. You've got out. That's what you told me, and I believe you. Only they're not happy. You've pissed them off and they're taking it out on me, and Dan. *Your* mess, but we're in the middle of it. So. Help me sort it out.'

Sol finished his sandwich and his beer. Then he shoved his body back in the chair, feet sprawled under the table. 'You were the one said I'd to come back here.' Spoiling for a fight now.

'To sort it out,' Noah enunciated each syllable. 'We're sorting it out.' He thumbed the screen of his phone until it brought up a notepad. 'Give me names. Addresses if you have them. And give me the reason. Drugs or money, whatever it is.'

'I ain't doing it,' Sol said. 'I'll fuck off, yeah? I'll do that. But I ain't playing your game.'

Police informant, was the game he meant.

'I'll help you. But you have to come in.'

'I ain't doing it. You'll have to arrest me, man.' He laughed as he said it, but not with his eyes.

'Tell me what laws you've broken, and I'll do that. Arrest you.'

'Yeah? Then what – phone Mum and tell her you did it?' Daring him. 'Tell Dad?'

'They don't like what you're doing any more than I do.'

'They don't *know*, any more than you do.'

Stand-off. Like they were kids again, squabbling over sweets stolen from their mum's secret jar. But Sol had a point; Noah knew what their parents would say. He'd grown up being lectured on the value of family. You always *always* put family first, no matter how rotten. A bad family's better than an empty sty. You don't cut off a stinking finger.

Sol was remembering the lectures too. He locked his

hands loosely, showing their shape to Noah. 'This's *family*, man. You ain't breaking this.' He dragged his hands apart, a knuckle at a time, before laying them palm-down on the table. 'No way.'

'You'd be good,' Noah said. 'You've got the eye. I wasn't kidding about that e-fit. It wouldn't all be snitching. There could be a future in it. No future in what you're doing right now.'

His phone rang, before Sol could respond.

Noah stood up to take the call. 'DS Jake.'

'Bevan was working every night there was an attack.' It was Ron Carling. 'His shifts match the assaults *and* their locations. At the time of the first two, he was in or around Holloway. Then he moved across town. Best of all? He was *in* St Thomas's the night Kyle was taken there.'

Sol stayed at the table, pushing crumbs around his plate with the ball of his thumb.

Noah walked the call into the sitting room. 'Does the boss know?'

'Her line's busy. I'm going to try again in a bit. But Bevan's our vigilante, got to be. Just wish we knew where he was.'

'He didn't turn up for work?' Noah checked the time: 9.50 p.m. 'He has a shift at ten.'

'No sign of him or the Astra. The boss was right, we should've busted his flat.'

'If he's taken Finn . . . We don't want to panic him.'

Ron sieved a sound of frustration through his teeth. 'All this hanging around's getting on my tits. I'd thought the DCS'd be packing her own Enforcer, what with coming from Manchester.'

'I wouldn't rule that out as a possibility . . . Still no sign of Carole?'

'Nothing. If she's pulling Bevan's strings, she's doing it from a distance.'

'I wouldn't rule that out either,' Noah said. 'Would you?'

48

'I ask you to find my boy.' Aidan Duffy looked Lorna Ferguson over from her dagger heels to her polished hair. 'And this is what you bring me? An ego in a shiny shirt.'

'I'm here to draw a line,' Ferguson said, 'under the game-playing, Aidan.'

He opened his throat at the ceiling, laughing loud and long. When he brought his eyes down, he didn't look at Ferguson. 'Oh Marnie Jane Rome! Has it come to this? This cunt telling you how to do your job.'

'We're looking for Finn,' Marnie told him. 'But we haven't found him yet.'

'Tell us about Huell Bevan.'

Duffy ignored Ferguson's question, his eyes fixed on Marnie. It wasn't forty-eight hours since she'd seen him but he'd lost weight; it showed in the bones of his face.

She said, as gently as she could, 'We're looking, but we need your help.'

Ferguson nodded. 'Huell Bevan—'

Aidan mimicked her nod, before turning it into a snarling shake of his head. 'Piss off, DCS Cunt, whoever

285

you are. Make this girl's life hell on your own time. I need her right now.' He locked his eyes to Marnie's. 'My boy needs her.'

'That,' Ferguson folded her arms, showcasing a gold watch, 'is exactly why you'll cooperate.'

Aidan leaned back, also folding his arms, giving her a full voltage blast of the Irish charm, black curls, stormy eyes, mouth softly smiling. 'Nice shoes. Did you pick them out yourself?'

Ferguson blinked. 'Why're you asking? Because you miss getting to pick your own clothes in here? A shame you didn't consider that before you embezzled close on a million pounds.'

He heard her out, his head tipped to catch every word. Then, 'I only ask because they make your feet look fat.' Each syllable smooth and round. 'Little piggy feet. Trotters.'

'I thought you wanted our help, Aidan. This is a funny way to go about getting that.'

He mirrored her body language but carelessly, as if it was an insult to his skill. To Marnie he said, 'You put up with this every day? How're you not reaching for the knives?'

Ferguson opened her mouth to speak but he cut her short, sitting forward with his teeth bared. 'What? WHAT?' Flinging the last word until it hit the walls and bounced.

Ferguson recoiled. Marnie willed her to be quiet, to let him burn through the anger and fear for his child. When he'd done that, he'd be able to talk to them.

But Ferguson wasn't seeing a frightened father. She could only see a con man and convict, her enemy. 'Was that a threat against a serving officer—'

There was a second when Marnie thought Aidan would lunge across the table.

Instead he pushed both hands into his hair and tilted

his head back as if it was someone else's. 'I wouldn't threaten you. You'd like it too much. You'd take it home and pet it, all night long. My *threat* . . .' Drawing out the sting from the honey in his words but slowly, slowly. 'You'd lie in your bed with it, making it last, making it my silver Irish tongue between your legs. Moaning your fucking lungs up.' He gave a laugh; he'd made her blush. 'You like men like me, dirty curls and white teeth, blood on our hands. You stupid, stupid cunt.' He brought his hands down to the table, folding them there. The weight loss was in his fingers too. His eyes shone with sleeplessness.

'This is what you're going to do,' he told Ferguson, 'and not because I say so, but because this girl's the best chance you have of making this madness stop. You're going to shut up. You're going to *stand* up, in those tottering tart's shoes of yours and walk out of here with your head held high for the guards who're pretending they didn't just hear me making you wet. You're going to stop driving this girl into the ground with your passive-aggressive bollocks, because *this*—? Is the detective.' Pointing his eyes at Marnie. 'She's going to solve this case because it's what she does, it's who she is. God help anyone, cunt or otherwise, who gets in her way.'

'You have a funny understanding of how a police interview works.' Ferguson's voice was clenched. 'However, in the interests of moving this along . . .'

She got to her feet, not looking at Marnie or Aidan. 'I'll be outside.' Her heels snagged at the floor as she walked from the room.

'Thanks be to fuck.' Aidan leaned back in his chair, loosening the fist he'd made of his hands. It hadn't registered with Ferguson, but he was frantic for news. 'Now tell me.'

'We think Huell Bevan has Finn. Bevan is a friend of Jacob's. He's the man who brought the message into here. The threat.'

'Huell Bevan.' Aidan tasted the name in his mouth. 'That's a Welshman?'

'He didn't turn up for work yesterday. We have a warrant for his arrest, and we think he knows it. We don't know how he knows it.'

'Oh no now, wait.' Lining his thumbs up on the table. '*Wait*. You've not given him a reason to panic. You've not done that.'

'No reason we're aware of. We want Finn safe. We want him found, and safe.' She paused, to give him space to calm down. 'Bevan was seen yesterday, leaving newspaper clippings. For me.'

He let out a long breath, turning his head until it clicked. 'Saying that Stephen Keele was found hanged in his cell.'

That pain again, everywhere at once. 'How did you know that?'

'Because those were my orders.' A muscle lengthened in his cheek. 'It's what I was told to do to keep my son alive. Your boy for mine, that was the deal. Only I broke it and now you're saying this bastard's gone to ground, under your radar.'

'We'll find him. I'll find him.'

'You will,' he agreed. 'Because no matter what words I said to get rid of that?' Nodding towards the door. 'If the stakes get any higher, I'll be improvising rope from whatever I can find.'

'That might be tricky.' She didn't flinch from his stare. 'DCS Ferguson's arranging for Stephen to be moved to another cell.'

'Don't tell me she's after interviewing him as well? How

many bad boy fantasies does that bitch need?' He showed his teeth in a savage smile. 'I'm not enough for her?'

'You'd think.'

He laughed. 'I like you, Marnie Jane. That's the trouble. I wish I didn't. It's just going to make what comes next really, really hard.'

More ultimatums. More fear masquerading as machismo.

'You're not going to kill anyone. Because you want to be able to look your son in the eye when I bring him to you. You don't want to be wasting precious visiting hours talking to your lawyer about extenuating circumstances.' She held his gaze, unsmiling. 'And in any case, you'd have killed him by now if you'd figured out a way to do that and still be a father to Finn.'

His face flickered, his eyes closing for a full second. 'I'm not good with threats, it's true. But you bring me my boy?' In his softest voice. 'I'll do it for you, as a gift.'

Marnie was silent, studying him.

'What? Oh you're thinking you should record that. Threatening behaviour.' He lifted an arm, draping it over the back of his chair, hanging his wrist. 'Maybe even charge me. Offences against the person, making threats to kill. You can't just accept it as a gift from me to you?'

'How is it a gift?'

'How's it not?' He wrinkled his straight nose. 'You're not telling me you're sorry for him after that story about his ma and da.'

'Was it a story? It sounded like the truth.'

'My Irish charm. We can weave a tale from a wisp of cloud.' He straightened in the chair. 'But say it's the truth, even so. He murdered your parents. Unless you're saving him for yourself, you should want him dead for that.'

'Should I? I want answers. I won't get them if he's hanging at the end of an improvised rope.'

'My boy's in pain. He's scared. For that alone I'd kill the bastard with my bare teeth.' He widened his eyes on her face. 'But you're better than me, Marnie Jane. Or you're harder. You can live with what he did. I couldn't. I can't.'

Because she was doing her job instead of lying curled in a corner somewhere, keening for her loss? He thought it made her hard. He had no idea.

'Help me to find Finn. I'm not interested in threatening Stephen, or anyone else. But I'm interested in your friendship with Jacob Collins, and his with Huell Bevan.'

Aidan scrubbed a hand at his head. 'Jacob said the message came through the healthcare lot, someone he'd never seen before.'

'Bevan works as a paramedic. He's on Jacob's visitor list.' Was she setting up Collins for another assault? More broken bones, or worse? 'You said you were given orders to put Jacob in hospital two days ago. Was that true?'

He looked at her, obliquely.

'Given what you've said about threats, I imagine it was a lie. You knew Jacob was connected to the blackmailer and you wanted to send a message back. Is that closer to the truth?'

'The only truth that matters is where my boy is. Jacob doesn't know. You can question him so you're blue in the face and you'll be no further forward. I was after saving you time.'

'Did Jacob give you Bevan's name?'

Aidan shut his eyes.

'He gave you Bevan's name,' she deduced. 'But you didn't give it to me. We could've arrested him two days ago. He could be in a police cell right now, telling us where Finn is.'

It explained Aidan's fury when Ferguson kept saying Bevan's name.

He'd known the identity of his son's kidnapper, and he'd kept it from the police.

'You thought you'd deal with this yourself, is that it? Friends of yours on the outside. The chance to flex your muscle, remind everyone not to mess with Aidan Duffy. For all we know *that's* what sent Bevan into hiding – your need to be in control.'

He moved his mouth tenderly but didn't open his eyes, or speak.

'Do you know what violence is?' Marnie waited for him to look at her. 'It's not broken bones or a face full of fist marks, or showing them who's *boss*. It's sitting in here keeping secrets to make yourself feel big and brave, while your child is out there alone.' She let him see her anger for the first time. 'Violence is me bringing you the news of what your secrets did to your son.'

Aidan propped the heels of both hands to the sockets of his eyes. When he spoke, his voice shook. 'Jacob doesn't know how to find Huell, no one does. God help me, they looked. They did. And that's on me.' He wiped at his eyes. 'He's a fucking ghost. No one—'

'He lives in Feltham and drives a stolen Astra.' Marnie stood up. 'You need better friends, or more faith in the police.'

'I've faith in you.' He looked up at her. 'I do.'

'Stay away from Jacob, and from Stephen.' She pulled on her coat. 'When was the last time you got a message from Bevan?'

'Two days ago. The hanging.'

So Huell had faked the newspaper clipping and delivered

291

it before he knew whether or not Aidan had carried out the kill order. He'd been sure of himself, confident he had Aidan in a corner, and that Aidan was a killer. He hadn't bothered waiting for the news to be published, in a hurry to let Marnie know what'd been done. Why? He'd taken his time to avenge Valerie Rawling, and Mazi Yeboah. What was making him panic now?

'Does he know Stephen's still alive?' she asked Aidan.

'I don't know, but Jacob won't have told him otherwise. I made sure of that.'

Threats, again. His one-time friend warned off.

'You're assuming Jacob is Bevan's only contact, that there's no one else passing information in or out.'

'There's no one.' Aidan blanked his eyes at the idea.

He stayed seated, looking up at her in her coat, ready to leave. He didn't want her to go, but he wouldn't ask her to stay. Out there, she could be looking for his son.

'So it was Jacob who gave you the details of the vigilante assaults?'

'Bevan, via Jacob.'

'And the shoebox,' Marnie said.

'The shoebox . . .' He shook his head. 'That was Stephen.'

'He told you where to look for it, or he told you what was in it?'

'Told me he'd hidden something in the house. A box's all he said. And where he'd put it.'

'And you passed that information to Huell Bevan.'

'He needed feeding,' Aidan said, 'have you never owned a dog? You have to feed them scraps between meals, to keep their jaws busy.'

Stephen hadn't hired Tobias Midori's gang to steal the shoebox. That was down to Huell Bevan.

'You thought you could fob him off with scraps, even

after he'd told you what he was doing, and what he wanted.'

'He wanted your boy in a corner. Like mine. The hanging . . . All that talk came later.' Aidan clenched his hands. 'I thought it was a game like any other. This place's made of the games you play to stay safe, get through. That's what I thought I was doing – *all* I thought I was doing, and I'm an arsehole, I know, an arrogant arsehole who can't keep his own child safe.'

Marnie looked down at him, feeling the hard pull of his pain. 'Tell me about Finn.'

'He's a fish. He's my little fish. Loves the sea, loves the sand and the waves, and the funfair. Fearless with it. Hates cruelty. Not— He's not like me. He's better than that, but it hurts him. The way he is, the way the world is. Like a layer's missing off him. I was after teaching him to toughen up, get his fists between him and the world, but he wouldn't. He wouldn't.' He pushed a hand deep into his pocket and even like this, grieving for his son, he knew how to pick his moment, conning the guards into looking the other way as he took out a scrap of neon-blue fur fabric so man-made it crackled with static. Stuck to the fur: two white discs with black dots inside. 'Googly eyes . . . This's how I knew they had him. I won this cat for Finn at the fair one year. He took it everywhere. Those bastards ripped it up.' He smoothed the fur between his fingers. 'They ripped it up.'

'Are you absolutely certain that Jacob doesn't know how to find Huell Bevan?'

'As certain as I am that you're standing there. He didn't know the bastard, only met him because he's asthmatic and has to see the healthcare team every once in a while. If I'd been short of breath then Bevan could've told me to my face what he'd done.'

'He wouldn't have done that,' Marnie said automatically. 'Too risky. He likes to keep things at arm's length. He's been very careful not to be caught, up until this point.'

'And now he's gone to ground. To wherever he's keeping Finn.'

She saw the heat of tears in his eyes. 'We'll find him. He wants attention, that's why he started this. He's not going to end it quietly.'

'You've got to give him hope.' Aidan returned the scrap of blue fur to his pocket. 'If he thinks it's over, he'll cut his losses. You have to let him hope that he can get what he wants.'

Marnie said nothing. She'd shared enough, to get the answers she needed, but she wasn't going to over-share. Not when a child's life was at stake.

'What're you going to do?' Aidan asked her.

'My job.' She looked down at him. 'You need to do yours.'

She didn't have to spell it out.

'Finn's dad,' he said softly. 'The only job worth a damn.'

Lorna Ferguson was waiting at the far end of the corridor. She looked Marnie in the eye and if her ego was demolished or even only bruised, she didn't let it show. 'One down.'

'I'd prefer—'

'To see Stephen alone?' Ferguson flicked her eyes to where Aidan was being escorted back to his cell, sketching a salute with her smile. 'I'll be in the car.'

Just like that. Marnie had thought it would be harder to shake her off. She'd been dreading the prospect of a three-way interview with her foster brother and her new boss. But Ferguson was choosing to make it easy, or at least less hard. Marnie was grateful, unable to imagine

Stephen's reaction to the woman. She'd tried to imagine it on the journey here but every time she put the three of them in a room together, the walls turned wet and red.

'I'll be in the car,' Ferguson repeated, walking away.

Wet and red, and Stephen picking his words like bullets to bring her down and bury her.

'Keep it as short as you can, DI Rome.'

Stephen was a woodcut in a white room. Marnie couldn't look at him, not right away. Her mind swerved from where he was sitting under the low light, showing her instead—

A seaside postcard her father had found years ago. She'd thought it boring, clichéd, but Dad said, 'It's hiding something,' and so she'd looked for the secret in the glossy card where the sky was pitched like a blue tent over the beach. 'Hold it to the light,' Dad said, and she did, and saw that it was covered in tiny pinpricks, like pores, thin sheets of coloured tissue between its front and back. Held to a strong light, the card became illuminated. Her father explained that these postcards were mostly in museums, but he'd found this one in a charity shop. 'Hold it to the light, Marn,' and she did, and the beach vanished into a black night lit by bulbs and fire. No more blue sky, just the pier lying its long lit skeleton out to sea.

'Tell me,' she said when she was able to speak. 'Tell me what they did.'

'They sat me on that yellow sofa.' Stephen shut his eyes then blinked them open on her face. 'The one with the stain on the arm. *She* sat in the armchair with the red cushion.'

'They let her in the house? I don't believe you. They wouldn't have broken a rule like that.'

Or any rule. But he was accusing her parents of worse than rule-breaking. Bringing his torturer, his abuser, back

295

into his life wasn't simply misguided or actionable. It was unforgivable.

'She said, "You have a lovely home."' Stephen moved his fingers on the table. 'They fed her biscuits, those ginger ones your dad loved. Coffee and biscuits and a glass of squash for me, like I'm a little kid. Like I was ever a kid after what she did.'

Marnie could see it, that was the problem. Her parents offering biscuits to a stranger in their home, determined to be civilised. They were great believers in civility, its power to surmount all problems. But not those of a damaged child. They can't have thought that. Can they?

'I'd have gone for her,' Stephen said, 'if I hadn't been so scared. I was fourteen, didn't think I was scared of anything any more. But *her*—? Sitting on that sofa, eating biscuits? The three of them smiling at me, talking about a *new chapter* in my life? I was so scared I nearly puked.'

He'd never admitted to any emotion before, least of all fear. She felt it again, moving like a snake under her skin. His fear. What'd they done? And why? He'd been their responsibility. They'd known about his mother, they must have known. Maybe there were gaps in their knowledge, but they'd known enough not to risk reuniting a vulnerable child with his abusive parent.

At the station, her team had been imagining Carole and Ollie in touch again after all these years. Wreaking havoc, destroying lives. Because no good could come of a reunion of that kind. Only bad, and worse.

'I'd have gone mad,' Stephen said, 'if it wasn't for you.'

He reached out and she flinched back but he stopped short of touching, his arm at full stretch under the light. She could see every rope and tendon, the blue tracery of veins at his wrist, the red dip of shadow at the inside of his elbow where a curved welt sat like an insect bite.

A burn mark, in the shape of a horseshoe. He'd—

Branded his forearm with her bracelet.

She blinked to clear her vision, making herself see what mattered.

Kyle's lips in the mortuary, bruised by blood. Finn with his hands tied, hearing the echo of his own heartbeat. Defensive wounds in her mother's palms, and on her father's body; all the ways in which they'd tried to save each other. Dark red handprints on the walls and floor. Alan and Louise Kettridge hospitalised, terrorised.

'Do you know a man named Huell Bevan?'

Stephen blinked away the question. 'I'd have gone mad—'

'Tobias Midori. Do you know him?'

'—without you.'

'Finn Duffy, where is he?'

His face was empty of recognition, as if she took up all the space in his skull. His eyes were filled with watching her, watching the girl he thought she still was.

His stare was a mirror, flattering in its way, the lighting just right to take the lines from around her eyes and the edges of her mouth. But she needed to stop looking, stop searching there.

'Your sanity,' she said slowly, 'was never in my safe-keeping. What you did, *you* did. If other people made mistakes then that's allowed, that's human. But *you* picked up the knife and *you* killed them. No one else did that. So . . . I'm stepping off this guilt trip.' She stood, pulling on her coat.

He watched her do it. 'If you're pretending you need proof, it's in the camera.'

She knotted her hair at the nape of her neck. Her hands were perfectly steady.

'They took pictures,' he said. 'They're in the camera.'

'Goodbye, Stephen.'

'Get the film developed, and you'll see.'

She turned her head away, waiting for the guard to let her out of the room.

'You'll see,' he called after her. 'I'm telling the truth.'

49

Noah was looking at the face of the first child caged by Carole Linton. He'd taken pictures on his phone of the pages in the scrapbook, not wanting to forget this piece of the puzzle. There were no clues as to the identity of this child, caged by Carole twenty years before she took Ollie. Children changed so much. Ollie had been blond and angelic. Now he was dark with indigo eyes and the chiselled features of a Diesel runway model. He and Lisa hadn't been seen in six days. The same six days that Carole had been missing.

In the Tomlinsons' flat: a murder weapon with Kyle and Carole's blood on it.

In Carole's flat: her keys and wallet, left behind when she went. Or was taken. Or wanted them to believe that she was taken.

Four assaults in ten weeks. One death.

Huell Bevan connected to the scene, every time. Even the assault inside Cloverton.

Clippings sent to Rawling's wife. To Mazi Yeboah. To Marnie. Huell was seen leaving the clippings for Marnie.

Now he was gone. Didn't show for his shift last night. Wasn't home.

The break-in at Lancaster Road. The shoebox stolen to order – by Bevan?

Finn Duffy taken ten weeks ago, held prisoner. By Bevan?

Who was Huell Bevan, and why was he doing all this? Noah had found nothing to explain it. No broken home, or childhood trauma. He'd never been in trouble with the police. The assaults and the break-in, child-snatching and threats . . . all of this had required meticulous planning. Nothing spontaneous or accidental, except perhaps the killing of Kyle. What was it Marnie had said after the post-mortem? 'He wants these victims to live. It would be easier to kill them.'

Bevan wasn't on a killing spree. It was quieter than that. In some ways, it was worse.

Leaving victims on all sides, living in fear, watching the shadows.

Why? What'd happened to Huell to make this an obsession? A compulsion.

Noah looked again at the man's face. Oblong, plain, small eyes, mouse-blond hair, bad teeth. He took out his phone and studied the face of the caged child, putting it alongside Bevan's.

No similarity, not even the ghost of one. If the caged child was Huell then the photo had been taken thirty-one years ago. Noah had found nothing in the man's history to suggest he'd been missing as a toddler. Should he dig deeper? Or was this a blind alley, no connection between Carole and Huell? Her blood on the baseball bat, yes, but that was found in Ollie's flat, not Huell's.

Noah's head ached. He needed to stop scrabbling around in the psychology and join the rest of the team working to trace the stolen Astra and Bevan's credit cards. They had two missing women to find. And Ollie, who was a suspect like Huell. They had Finn to find.

He reached for Finn's photo, putting the others aside. A good-looking boy, staring straight into the camera. Brave, his friends said, but off to one side. Where was he? And was he staying brave? Was that possible? Noah hoped so. He shut his eyes, hearing the sound of the bat striking the railings above him. What was Ollie doing at Carole's flat that day? She'd disappeared. Just like Ollie's mum. And Ollie himself. He'd seen Noah outside the flat of the woman who'd humiliated him. He'd known where Carole lived, and now she was gone.

Noah put the phone into his pocket and walked through to the incident room where Ron and Debbie were working on the credit card traces. 'Anything?'

'He spends twenty quid in the Spar,' Ron offered. 'Twice a week, sometimes three times.'

'Sixty pounds a week when he's living alone?' Bevan's flat had yielded no clues as to his whereabouts, or motivation. A bachelor pad with a DVD collection biased in favour of romantic comedies and tear jerkers, with just a couple of soft porn choices camouflaged in Disney cases. 'I don't remember a lot of food in there.'

'There wasn't.' Debbie looked up. 'We think he's shopping for Finn, and Ollie. That's assuming the three of them are holed up somewhere.'

'What about petrol? He isn't running the Astra on air.'

'He's not used his credit card at any petrol station since he stole it. Pershall says he thinks the tank was about a quarter full when he parked at the Hillingdon.'

'So he's still in Greater London. Where're the Spars he's shopping at?'

'Way ahead of you,' Ron said, 'but thanks.' He held up a map. 'Haringey.'

Noah studied it. 'Lots of empty houses around here.'

'Yep. And CCTV. We're on it.'

'Good job.' He handed back the map, walking to where Colin was working. 'Any news from the forensic search at Carole's flat?'

'No blood, but plenty of fingerprints. We're waiting on matches. Ditto the other DNA.'

'What about her car?'

'Didn't you say it was parked up outside?' Colin frowned. 'Hadn't been driven in days?'

'We should check it, even so. The keys were in the flat.'

'Forensics finished up there two hours ago. I'll put a call through, but it could take a while.'

'Let's you and I go there,' Noah said. 'We can check in with Ollie's neighbour, Mr Singh. See if anything's been happening at Jonas House in the last twenty-four hours.'

Same old cold, ice frozen into pea-sized pellets all over the car. Noah held his lighter to the lock on the driver's side, peering through the windows at the empty seats, dust on the dashboard. An A-Z was shoved down the pocket on the passenger side, its pages curling. Just the usual mess seen inside a car that wasn't used very often because fuel was expensive.

Colin stood on the pavement, a wool cap snug to his head, face turning the colour of the crime scene gloves they were both wearing. 'The stuff they logged in the lock-up. Why didn't Carole sell it? That grandfather clock was worth money. Why do people hang onto things? She's living in what's basically a squat, with thousands of pounds of furniture rotting in a lock-up.'

'Sentimental value?' Noah worked the lock with his hand, but the ice wouldn't let go. He reverted to the lighter, sheltering its flame with the angle of his body. 'Maybe it was worth more to her than money.'

'Maybe it was camouflage,' Colin said, 'for the rest of what she'd hidden in there.' The cage, he meant. And the scrapbook. 'Anyone breaking into the lock-up would've been distracted by the antiques. Useful when you're trying to hide another part of your past . . .'

The lock gave with a dull *thunk*.

'We're in.' Noah nodded.

He reached across to pop the passenger door, and Colin joined him inside Carole's car where an extra jolt of cold made them wince. Colin opened the glove compartment to a jumble of CDs, sweet wrappers, a plastic packet of tissues frozen into a brick. Noah ran his hands under the dash, finding the latch for the boot and pulling it, hearing ice protest at the rear of the car.

Nothing on the back seat but dust and scuff marks, the footwell full of leaves. Colin finished with the glove compartment and climbed out, leaving Noah to leaf through the A-Z for anything hidden in its pages.

'Boot's solid.' Colin ducked his head at the window. 'Can I borrow your lighter?'

Noah handed it across. Tucked inside the A-Z was an old passport-sized photo of Carole. Ten, maybe twelve years old. Not the face he knew from the evidence board. This Carole was younger, happier, holding the neutral expression demanded of passport applicants but with a smile just below the surface, as if a bubble of laughter was waiting to burst. This was the face Ollie had known, the face of the woman who took him from his mother's car and put him in a cage.

Noah turned the photo over in his hand.

The car rocked on its wheels.

'Oh, *shit*—' Colin, breathless, like he'd been punched.

Noah slid sideways fast, out of the driver's seat, into the road.

No one in a balaclava with a baseball bat. Just Colin standing with both hands raised. Staring into the open boot of Carole's car. Noah moved to join him.

Folded into the boot—

A woman's body.

Lying on her side, facing them, knees tucked to her chest, hands hidden between her thighs. Dressed in jeans and cowboy boots, a red plaid donkey jacket, plastic patches at the elbows. Blond hair grey at the roots in a frigid sheet across her face. No smell, no mess. The cold had done the job of a morgue drawer, preserving the body. She was tiny, not much bigger than a teenager.

'Call it in.' Noah reached a gloved hand and moved the frozen hair far enough to see her face.

Eyes iced shut, lashes stiff. Skin like bad bacon, yellow and pinkish-blue. Black where the blood had pooled in her jaw, resting against the carpeted well of the boot. No obvious cause of death. No blood outside the body, or none that he could see. She wasn't gagged, her feet weren't tied. Was she alive when she was shut in here?

'She's dead.' Colin was speaking into his phone. 'That's as much as we know right now.'

Noah crouched low, to look into her face.

She'd been here some time. Folded like this, her chin tucked to her chest.

She was here when he'd knocked at the door of the

studio flat, before the bat hit him for six. When he and Marnie were inside and the landlord was waiting with his fistful of keys, she was here. When they'd discovered the scrapbook in the lock-up. And the cage.

The whole time, she'd been here.

Tiny, frozen, her face turned towards the road.

Folded away inside the boot of her own car.

Carole Linton.

50

'Carole Linton.' Marnie pinned the photo to the board. 'Forensics are fast-tracking the post-mortem, but we think she's been dead at least six days. That ties with when Ollie went missing.'

'He did the pair of them,' Ron said. 'Kyle, and Carole. Then he went into hiding, with or without his mum's help. But where's the connection to Huell Bevan?'

Marnie waited until the room was quiet. Carole's killing had shaken them; she'd been so firmly fixed in their minds as a perpetrator, not a victim. 'DC Tanner?'

'The sports club that banned Ollie,' Debbie said, 'runs first aid training courses. Paramedics teach the kids about sports injuries and so on. Bevan was a regular there around the same time Ollie was. The manager said he saw Ollie with Huell, more than once.'

'Then which of them killed Carole?' Ron wondered. 'Or are they a double act? We thought Ollie didn't have any friends, not grown ones anyway. Just his gang.'

'I was *sure* Carole was involved in this, especially after

that second cage turned up.' Debbie shuddered. 'I can't believe she's dead.'

'We don't know that she was murdered,' Colin said. 'From the look of her she might've got into the boot to hide.' He took off his spectacles, blinking. 'Just to hide.'

Carole was his first dead body; Marnie understood his resistance to the idea of her murder.

Noah understood it, too. 'The car was locked and the keys were in her flat,' he said gently. 'Her blood was on the weapon found in Ollie's flat. It's possible she was made to get into the boot by someone who was planning to take her somewhere. Or perhaps they told her that was the plan. But they lied, or something happened to change their minds.'

'She was alive when she went into the boot?' Ron swiped at his mouth. 'That's cold. Not just literally, though if it wasn't sub-zero she'd have started to smell days ago and we'd be nearer to knowing what happened . . . I mean that's *cold*. Calculated. That's not a kid. That's someone who knows exactly what he's doing.'

'And *why*,' Noah agreed. 'But we still don't have a motive for Huell. Not one that explains all this planning, the care he's taking.'

'Never mind a motive,' Ron grumbled. 'I'd settle for an address. We know he's patronising the Spars in Haringey. Take your pick of empty houses round there. Narrowing it down's taking too much bloody time.'

Colin returned his spectacles to his face. 'CCTV still hasn't spotted the Astra.'

'His workmates were no use,' Debbie added. 'They just suggested we try his girlfriend, but none of them could give me a name. Huell isn't into sharing.'

'Unless it's the blunt end of his baseball bat . . .'

Marnie's phone rang. She took the call. 'DI Rome.'

'Are you at the station?' It was Harry Kennedy. 'I'm parking up. With Zoe.'

He sounded grim. 'You'll want to hear this.'

It was the second time Harry and Zoe had come into the station together. Noah wondered whether Marnie was remembering the first time, when Harry was carrying the shoebox from Lancaster Road. Zoe wore the same parka and biker boots but she'd removed the red mittens, or forgotten them. She looked cold and unhappy.

Harry shook down the collar of his coat. His hands were empty but he was bringing bad news, just like last time. Noah saw it in his face. Concern for Marnie, and something more—

Harry liked her. More than a little. Did she know?

Noah couldn't read anything other than professional courtesy in Marnie's manner as she led the four of them to an empty interview room.

Once they were seated, Harry said, 'I asked Zoe to look at the descriptions of Tobias Midori's mates. She knows the Crasmere Boys, or most of them. But that's not why we're here.' He stopped, nodding at Zoe.

'Huell Bevan.' She rubbed the end of her nose. 'You have a warrant out for him.'

'You know him?' Marnie asked.

Zoe nodded, her look of unhappiness deepening. 'He thought . . . I was his girlfriend.' She blushed then straightened, squaring her shoulders. 'I met him over at the sports centre near Jonas House, when I was first working with Ollie and the others. Huell was giving first aid training. We got chatting and he seemed to care about the kids so when he suggested a drink after work, I said okay.' She drew a breath. 'Big mistake. Big, big mistake.'

'When was this?'

'Two years ago? August bank holiday weekend.'

'Go on,' Marnie prompted.

'The next day he's texting me, but I hadn't given him my number. Ten minutes into the drinking session it was obvious he wasn't interested in the kids. Only in me. And he knew things.' Her face stiffened, defensively. 'Personal things. Including as it turned out my phone number, which I'd made a point of not giving him. The next day he texted about twenty times. I didn't reply to begin with, didn't want to give him confirmation of my number. I thought he'd get bored, or he'd assume the number wasn't mine. But he didn't stop.'

Her mouth was tight, as if her teeth hurt. 'The texts got more and more . . . personal. Obsessive. In the end I texted back and told him to stop. I said I'd report him to the police if he didn't.'

'But he did stop,' Marnie deduced.

'One last abusive text, calling me a heartless bitch. Then that was it.' She worked the clench from her hands with her thumbs. 'If it hadn't stopped there, I *would* have gone to the police. I was serious about that. Now I wish I'd reported it anyway because you have a warrant out for him, and for Ollie.' Her face changed, painfully. 'Whatever he's dragged him into, it's not Ollie's fault. Huell can be convincing. And Ollie's just a kid. He doesn't look it and he doesn't act it, but that's what he is. A kid.'

'Convincing how?' Noah asked.

'Plausible. Interested in you, lots of eye contact, lots of concern. Mirroring – I suppose they taught him that in training. It looks real, though. I'm good at spotting fakes, and I didn't spot him. Not until he was buying a second drink and touching my hand.' She grimaced at the memory.

'What did he know about you?' Marnie asked. 'Personal things, you said. You'll understand we need all the information we can get our hands on right now.'

Harry moved a fraction, enough for Noah to guess that Zoe had confided in him on their way over here. Whatever she'd told him, Harry hadn't liked it.

'He knew I'd been attacked.' Zoe put her hands on the table, rigid in the chair. 'Four years ago. A gang on one of the estates decided they'd had enough of me interfering in their recruitment process. I was out of the picture for a while, but I got better.' Her voice resisted questions, but she didn't stop speaking. 'It happened not long after I started with Ground Up. It was— Bad. They used knives. I was in hospital for four months. I thought about giving up the job; I was scared for a long time after it happened, really scared. But I like my job and the kids need people like me. That's not ego, it's maths. Not enough people want to do this work, and it matters. So, I went back.'

'I'm sorry,' Marnie said.

'That's not—' Zoe moved her hands. 'It's all right, I'm all right. I talk about it to parents and kids who've been victims of knife crime. I've not kept it secret. But what I don't talk about is the scars.' She stopped, but only for a second. 'I have scars. They're ugly. Huell knew where, and he knew how many. Details I'd not shared with anyone but my surgeon, and my mirror.' She'd pulled the cuffs of her jumper over her hands. Under it, she was wearing a white T-shirt.

Layers, Noah had thought, for the cold. He remembered her grimness when she'd talked about the knife Ollie had shown her. She'd known what knives could do, had the scars to prove it.

'Huell wanted to talk about my courage.' She looked nauseated. 'His texts were full of that. How brave I was, how I'd *survived*. Then they got more personal, more specific.'

'How did he get that information?' Harry asked.

'He's a paramedic, in Camden. I was in hospital there, he must've accessed my records.' She shook her head. 'I've tried to remember details of our conversation, wish I'd kept the texts, but I've had a new phone for over a year.'

'And you've not seen him since that drink two years ago?' Marnie said.

'Once or twice. At the sports centre, from a distance. I thought he was a creep. I wished he didn't have access to the kids the way he does, but I didn't think it was worse than that. If he tried any nonsense with Ollie I thought he'd find out the fast way what kind of kids he was dealing with.'

She rubbed at her nose. 'That sounds bad, but I'm sick of people who stand on the sidelines cheering me on, or make a big deal of my survival. I got on with my life, that's all. I was lucky to have a job to go back to, and I was sick of sympathy. And of good advice from friends and family about walking away. Moving on.' She shoved her curls behind her ears. 'If we all walk away from stuff like that who's left to do the real work?'

Huell had been right about one thing. She had courage, in spades. Noah had gone through training with a constable who was knifed in his first week on the job. He'd left the police to work in an office designing websites. Zoe had taken the hard path, and she'd played it down. She could've used the attack as a short cut during their conversation about the kids at Jonas House, but she hadn't. She'd stuck up for them, but not blindly. Doing her job even when she found it difficult, and with good humour too. Drinking the bad station-blend coffee, sharing a joke with him. All the time those scars underneath. No clue in the way she moved, just grimness when she talked about Ollie's knife. Attacked by a gang, but she was back out there. Fighting for kids like Ollie, whom everyone else considered long lost.

'When was the last time you saw Huell at the sports centre?' Marnie asked.

'Months ago. I can't remember seeing him recently.'

'But you definitely saw him with Ollie. When was that?'

'The first time? Two years ago, when he was friendly with everyone. But I've seen him with Ollie since. The last time must've been October half-term. School holidays are always tricky, the kids get bored. The sports centre liked Huell because he distracted them.' She shook her head. 'Maybe I should've told them about the texts, but I didn't think he'd be weird with the kids. If he'd been hanging around girls, I'd have said something. But it was just Ollie, and I knew he could take care of himself. Huell hadn't tried anything physical that night. He was . . . puppyish. Even his texts, until that last one.' She tipped her head, remembering. 'He was sick of seeing what violence did, that's what he said. Sick of patching people up after accidents and assaults. I thought he was a bit primitive to be honest. Old-fashioned. The texts were his idea of a compliment, all about how I'd shown the gang they couldn't hurt me, not really. It was only the last text that was nasty. And the fact that he knew about my scars.' She sat up straight. 'So, yes. It was frustrating to see Ollie getting close to him, but there wasn't anything for Huell to obsess over with Ollie, and if he'd tried to get personal? I knew Ollie would sort it out.'

She thought Ollie was a normal teenage boy. Angry, headed off the rails maybe, but not damaged. Not a victim. She didn't know about Carole's cage. Or that she and Ollie shared a secret of the kind which Huell had obsessed over two years ago. A secret of survival.

'Is there anything else you can tell us?' Marnie said. 'Anything that might help us find Huell.'

'Only that he'd wanted to be a paramedic since he was a kid, but he'd had to retake the exam after he failed it the first time.' She frowned in concentration. 'He talked a lot about his training that night we went for a drink. I suppose it was his way of leading up to my attack.'

'Where did he study, did he say?'

Zoe shook her head. 'Sorry.'

'He didn't mention any addresses?'

'Only mine. He knew I grew up in Hillingdon. I suppose he got that from my medical records.'

'He went to a lot of trouble,' Marnie said, 'to find out details about your personal life. But he dropped the obsession after a single warning?'

'I didn't believe it either,' Zoe said. 'I was expecting more texts, or worse. An escalation. But he stopped and I thought he must've realised he couldn't get what he wanted from me and moved on. If you'd been there that night we went for a drink . . .' She wrinkled her nose. 'He was just this . . . weird little man with wonky teeth. Like a kid, really. Old-fashioned, not frightening. I didn't give it a lot of thought, not until now.'

'What *did* he want from you, do you think?'

'Attention?' She shook her head. 'Gratitude, maybe.'

'Gratitude?'

'That he cared so much. That he'd gone to the trouble

313

to praise me for being a survivor.' She moved her hands, pressing their palms together. 'He wanted me to know that someone out there understood what I'd been through and wasn't just ignoring it. Too often victims are ignored, or forgotten. It's worse if there's a conviction because then we're supposed to believe it's been put right. Punishment's been meted out, justice has been served, but it's never equal to the crime.' She bit her lips together. 'I think he believes . . . That kind of justice, the kind handed down by the courts, is impersonal. Clean, somehow. We call it civilised but it's not enough, not for what they did. It's not personal enough. So . . . I was meant to be impressed by how much he cared about my injuries, about the injustice of the sentence they received. He kept asking whether they'd been punished properly. The men who attacked me. Whether I thought they'd been punished properly.' She looked at Marnie. 'You think he killed Kyle Stratton? That he's some sort of vigilante?'

'Do you think that's possible?' Noah asked. 'From what you saw of him?'

'Oh God . . . He was *obsessed* with justice. If he found someone else to impress? Someone he thought was a survivor?' She put her hands in her hair. 'What I don't understand is why he got Ollie involved in this crusade, if that's what it is.'

'Perhaps he wanted a sidekick. Or a lookout. You said Ollie was after a place to fit in. And Huell is plausible. He might've persuaded Ollie that this was a job worth doing. Vigilantism.'

'Ollie isn't a social justice warrior,' Zoe said angrily. 'Those lists he made weren't— They were a *game*. He's just a kid cut off from his dad.'

Ollie was much more, but Noah didn't enlighten her.

'Perhaps Huell took advantage of that. Played the father figure, flattered Ollie's need to be useful, to fit in.'

'He's delusional.' She pushed her hair from her forehead. 'Why didn't I report the texts? If I'd done that two years ago . . .'

'You'd have done it,' Harry said, 'if you'd been seriously concerned. You have a good radar for trouble.' He looked at Marnie. 'It sounds to me like Bevan hadn't hit his stride back then. It's taken two years for him to reach this stage.'

'I should've told the police about him,' Zoe said with bitterness. 'Then I wouldn't be sitting here wondering whether my *bravery* has put Ollie in danger.'

She didn't know about Finn. All her self-reproach and worry was centred on Ollie. But Huell had kidnapped a ten-year-old boy, to wage war—

On Stephen Keele? On Aidan Duffy? On Marnie Rome.

'If he found someone else to impress? Someone he thought was a survivor?'

Their killer had found Marnie.

A knock on the door made Zoe turn her head, tears shining in her eyes.

'CCTV came through, boss.' Debbie Tanner, her eyes catching on Harry before finding Marnie and Noah. 'We've got the Astra.'

51

'We're going.' Brady. 'Get up.'

Finn hadn't seen him in days, that's how it felt. Days and days. He'd forgotten how to be scared of Brady. Ollie was scary. The bath, being buried down here in the cold, was scary, the plughole chewing his eyelashes when he blinked. But Brady was just a voice, not even that, a noise. Finn ignored it. Concentrated on staying where Ollie had said Dad could see him. He didn't care about the cold as long as Dad knew where to find him. He tucked his taped hands between his knees and shut his eyes. Dad was coming. As long as he stayed right here . . . Dad was coming to get him.

'Get up. We're going.'

They'd go to the funfair, to the pier. Dad would win him another cat and Finn wouldn't ever leave it behind no matter how old he got. He'd keep that cat forever. The two of them would fish from the end of the pier with the stinky bait sold out of buckets. The beach would rub between his toes and he'd wake to a bed full of sand and Dad's white grin—

Booming in his head like a bomb going off, made his teeth shake.

'Get up!' Brady, kicking the side of the bath.

Hands reached in and got him by the armpits, lifting him up, setting him down.

Ollie, saying, 'I'll do it. I'll bring him,' the press of his fingers warning Finn to keep quiet.

Brady swung away. Gone.

The bathroom blazed black even though Finn knew the tiles were white because he'd washed them enough times. Everything in here was white, except Ollie's eyes. Purple. He'd squatted down, his hands in Finn's armpits, holding him upright. He was staring into Finn's face, saying something, saying, 'You need to do as he says. He's pissed off, he's scared—'

That couldn't be true. Finn was hearing it wrong. Brady wasn't scared. It was *Finn* who was meant to be scared. He tried straightening his legs, locking his knees so they'd keep him upright, but nothing was working. Tar inside his head, a mouse in his mouth, dead fly buzzing in his ear. Ollie had a stone. He was going to tie it round Finn's neck and throw him in the river. He hiccupped and his whole body shook like when someone's walking on your bed. No, not your bed, that wasn't it. Walking on your *grave*. Like that. A full body shiver.

Ollie pressed the stone to Finn's lips. 'Quick . . .'

Wet and grey and tasting good. *Water*. It was a cup of water. Finn sucked at it greedily, until Ollie said, 'You'll be sick,' and took it away.

Finn whined like Regan's dog, swaying forward for another drink. Ollie pushed him back, straightening until he was standing, so tall it hurt Finn's neck to look up at him. Miles and miles away, all the long way up there by the ceiling.

'You've got to do as he says. Go along with it, all of it. Okay?'

With what? With Brady? 'No . . .'

'Listen to me. He's got us, right? He's got you and me and a mallet, he's got a fucking mallet. That's worse than a baseball bat and a bat'll kill you.'

'No.' Finn's teeth were chattering. 'F-fucking Brady, fucking *no*—'

'His name's not Brady, it's Bevan. He's a nutter, and he'll kill you unless you do as you're told. D'you understand, cos I didn't. Not until it was too late.'

'I've got to wait here, you said. For Dad . . .'

'Change of plan,' Ollie told him. 'We're taking you to your dad. Come on. You want to see him, yeah? You want to see your dad. That's where we're going.'

'C-can't walk.'

'Yeah you can.'

But Finn couldn't. His hands were tied and he kept falling to the side whenever Ollie let go of him. So Ollie sat on the side of the bath while he unwound the tape from Finn's wrists and it took ages and all the while Finn was shaking from cold and wanting to puke but he was afraid to puke on Ollie's trainers which looked new and expensive and nicked and he couldn't stop shaking, he couldn't, not until Ollie gave him his hoodie.

Finn felt stupid with it flapping round his knees, but it was warm.

The hoodie was warm and it smelt of Ollie which was yellow cigarettes and Finn liked that even though he didn't and then Ollie was putting something hard into his hand and saying it was going to be okay and Finn thought *good*, it's going to be okay—

Right up until it wasn't.

52

Marnie buried her hands in the pockets of her coat, shivering. All the way up the street, ice shone like scar tissue from houses where every window was an empty grey eye.

The stolen Astra was parked outside a house with a yellow door, but it was the house opposite which had their attention, and that of the Armed Response Unit. Ferguson had summoned the ARU in spite of everything Marnie had said at the station; this was incendiary enough without firearms in the mix. They'd put the CCTV images into chronological order and in the last one, captured less than two hours ago, Bevan's face was immobilised by fear.

'He knows we're closing in,' Marnie had told Ferguson. 'We can talk him down. Let Toby Graves talk him down. Guns will only make him panic, and make it worse.'

'And Ollie? These two have done enough damage. They've an arsenal of weapons, we know that much. We shouldn't be surprised if one or both has his hands on a gun.' Ferguson had reapplied her lipstick in the ARV, after strapping on the Met vest. 'I learnt the hard way to be prepared.'

According to council records, the house which they

were watching had been empty for months. The Specialist Firearms Officers stamped their feet, keen to get moving. The cold was making everyone edgy and over-alert, too many fingers twitching on semi-automatics. The guns were loaded with hollow-point rounds designed to do the least amount of collateral damage, but the least amount might still be too much.

'Let me try and talk to Bevan,' Marnie tried again. 'Please. Before we storm in.'

Ferguson consulted her watch as if this was running to her schedule and not Bevan's. 'No one is storming anywhere.'

'And the press?' Noah asked.

At arm's length, no more than that, after they'd caught the scent of blood from Twitter.

'You learn to live with them,' Ferguson said. 'They can be useful, handled in the right way.'

'Bevan doesn't want a battle—' Marnie began.

A sharp scuffle of boots on tarmac cut her short; firearms officers bristling to attention.

The house was open, its door wide. Coming out—

Finn Duffy in an oversized hoodie that hung to his knees. Eyes like his father's but huge, drugged with terror. A hand on the nape of his neck, another on his shoulder—

Huell Bevan, his pale eyes pointing at them.

Then a new shadow in the doorway, filling it.

Shoulders like a squaddie, sniper's eyes on the street. In a T-shirt and jeans. Not yet sixteen, but passing for twenty. Ollie Tomlinson.

The SFOs tightened responsively.

A slam of sound: 'Get on the ground!'

Bevan raising a hand in surrender: 'I'm coming out!'

Hiding behind Finn, using him as a shield.

Finn staggering, out of focus, bare feet stumbling on

frozen tarmac. Marnie tried to catch his stare but it blinked on and off, broken.

'I've got him!' Bevan grinned with every one of his bad teeth. 'He's safe! I've got him,' as if Finn was a prize, *his* prize. Eyes sweeping the street but not for guns, or danger. Looking for cameras, someone filming this. That grin – he wanted it. The attention, everyone's attention fixed on him. His knuckles white at Finn's shoulder, holding hard.

Finn's face kept blanking then coming back then blanking again.

When it blanked, Marnie saw Stephen on the stairs, sitting on the stairs, wearing their blood like gloves.

'Get on the ground!'

Ollie checked over his shoulder for Bevan but they weren't moving in synch, not a team. *Two kids, one big, one small.* It wasn't like that; there wasn't any teamwork here. Just Ollie seeing Bevan's knuckles on Finn's shoulder. It was *his* hoodie – Finn was wearing Ollie's hoodie.

'Wait . . .' Marnie tried.

Finn's hands were hidden by long sleeves and he was—

Turning. Not quickly but steadily, the way a spiral spring must turn when it's been fully wound.

They all heard it—

The soft sound of the knife going in.

Wet suck of it coming back out.

Then the scream and Finn skidding sideways as Bevan clutched at nothing, at cold air, at himself, hands turning red, body folding forwards.

Finn had a knife, hidden inside the sleeve of Ollie's hoodie. He'd stabbed Bevan with it.

'Drop it, drop it! Get on the ground!'

Ollie was in the way. Going for Finn because Bevan was his friend, his partner? Wanting his knife back? Scared

Finn would go for *him* next? In that split second, it could've been any or all of those things. But Marnie didn't see fear, and she didn't see teamwork. She saw—

Ollie getting between Finn and Bevan, and it was *his* knife. He'd given his knife to Finn. A ten-year-old doesn't take a knife off someone built like a squaddie and moving like one, so *fast*—

One shot was all it took.

One SFO. One bullet, its hollow-point blooming like a flower in Ollie's chest. He grabbed at Bevan as he fell, tearing him from Finn, the pair of them thumping the pavement.

Shouting. Warnings. Threats.

Bevan on the ground, holding himself, screaming.

Ollie on the ground, spreading red, silent.

Finn with his hands at his side, the right one *drip-drip-dripping*.

Two SFOs powered past him to Ollie and Bevan, making sure neither was getting back up.

'DI Rome!'

Marnie walked away from Ferguson, towards Finn.

'DI Rome!'

'Finn.' Catching his stare and holding it. 'I'm Detective Inspector Rome. I made a promise to your dad.'

An SFO circled behind her, training his weapon on Aidan's son.

Grey eyes blazed in the boy's face, his right hand leaking blood from the blade.

She had to get him to drop it. The knife. It looked welded to his palm. He was scared, and he was on the brink of something bigger, worse. With the knife hot in his hand, stuck to his fingers by blood, feeling like the only solid thing he had. No wonder he held onto it so hard. What had it taken to bring him to this brink? What happened in that house to put a grown man's eyes in a small boy's face, ruined by terror and a strange reckless courage?

The street kept sliding away from Finn, she saw it in his eyes.

The street was sliding and Ollie was jumping under the SFO's fist, feet kicking at the pavement. Bevan was face down, sobbing and swearing, a slop of noise.

'Finn.' Marnie held him steady with her stare, refusing to let him look at the chaos to either side of them. 'I made a promise to your dad. I promised I'd find you and see you safe.'

His lips moved, and his eyes. Not hearing her, not quite. His fist clenched at his side—

The *knife* made him safe. He didn't need anything else.

'Please give me the knife.'

She held out her hand, empty.

She was close enough for him to stab her. He could put her on the ground, the way he'd put Bevan down. He had that power – she saw it bubbling on his lips. Spit, and power. One bubble building, bigger than the rest. Bevan's blood on him, stinking, and the bubble of spit building and building until it burst in a small star-shaped spatter at the edge of his mouth.

All around them the street was solid with shut doors, blind windows.

No one to bear witness to what had unravelled in the house. No one to speak about why Aidan's son went in as a child and came out like this, with blood on his breath and death in his eyes.

'I made a promise,' she said. 'Help me to keep it.'

53

It was getting dark by the time Marnie was dismantling the evidence boards, unpinning photographs, smoothing their edges. When she reached the pictures of Carole, she stopped.

Noah saw her studying the dead woman's face. 'What is it?'

'Does all of this feel too . . . easy to you? In conclusion, I mean. Not the case itself, but this.' She touched a hand to the board, slim fingers splayed between the spaces.

'It's neat,' Noah said. 'DCS Ferguson's happy.'

A press conference live from the street where the ice was black with blood.

'*Too* neat, don't you think?' Marnie was worn out, they both were. But her voice was full of worry. She hadn't let go of the case yet.

Noah moved to stand at her shoulder. 'Tell me what you're thinking.'

'If you were Huell Bevan.' She kept her hand on the board. 'Smart enough to pass under our radar for ten weeks. Arrogant enough to manipulate inmates, and to get a gang of kids to break into a house, and steal to order. Dangerous. You killed two people. You did it without leaving any DNA, at least until the bat was found in Ollie's flat. You did all this and then you stopped. Why?'

She took her hand away. 'And how was it so easy to catch you in the final instance? You walked out of that house into our arms.'

'Perhaps . . . I'd finished what I'd set out to do.'

Huell was hooked up to a post-surgical drip in a Haringey hospital. They'd have to wait for his full statement, but he'd been quick to confess. At the scene and later, in the ambulance. He'd told firearms officers, paramedics, anyone who'd listen, that he was their vigilante.

'You're Huell, and you'd killed Kyle.' A stitch of concentration marked Marnie's face as if it was the only thing holding her together. 'And Carole.'

'Kyle was an accident. I didn't want him dead. I didn't want any of them dead. They were meant to live with the shame and guilt of what they'd done, and what was done to them.'

'And Carole?'

'Colin had a theory about the lock-up. Her clock and the other antiques . . .' Noah looked at the empty squares on the board. 'They were camouflage for the scrapbook.'

'Go on,' Marnie prompted.

'The other attacks—' He stepped closer to the board. 'What if it was all smoke? To distract us from the victim that really mattered.' He put his hand on Carole's picture. 'What if I was *hiding her* in the glut of attacks? The chronology— That threw us. If this'd started or ended with Carole we'd have known it was all about her. Right from the start she was different. She stood out.'

'So why was Rawling the first victim?' Marnie asked. 'If you're Huell and you're after Carole, why attack the others? And why start with Stuart?'

'I had to work up to attacking a woman. I didn't make a move on Zoe when we went for that drink. She said I was old-fashioned. I'm not a monster; I don't think of myself that way. I go after people who haven't been punished properly. In my head, I'm Batman. Attacking a woman wasn't easy but I had to start somewhere. I didn't want to make a mess of Carole, not in that way. I wanted to take my time. I've never been impulsive.'

Marnie didn't agree, or disagree.

'Carole was different to the others,' Noah repeated. 'I left her face alone.'

'Why did you do that?'

'I don't know. So that Ollie would recognise her?'

Neither of them spoke for a moment, thinking about Ollie.

'Ferguson got it wrong,' Noah said at length. 'Armed Response when there was no evidence Bevan or Ollie had a firearm? She got it wrong.'

'It was my case,' Marnie said. 'My call.'

'You *told* her it was a bad call. You wanted hostage negotiation, but she had to go in all guns blazing for the cameras and her own ego. You were overruled.'

'I'd lost control of the relationship,' Marnie said quietly. 'She didn't trust me to get it right. If I'd kept her onside, Ollie would be alive.'

Noah might've guessed she wouldn't let anyone else take the blame, even when it rested so squarely on Ferguson's shoulders.

He sorted through the photos for Ollie's face and Huell's, putting them side by side. 'The pair of us – Ollie's big for his age, I'm skinny and short – we could pass for kids.

What if I attacked Carole alone that first time, but then I wanted Ollie to get *his* revenge? I found out about the cage, the abuse. I needed an accomplice because it justified what I was doing and because all this,' nodding at the dismantled evidence, 'was easier with two people.'

Huell's confession at the scene, repeated in the ambulance, had named Ollie as his accomplice. Noah wasn't extrapolating far beyond that, but something nagged at him. From the crime scene outside the house. Something didn't fit.

'Why didn't you kill Carole during that first attack?' Marnie asked. 'If this was about her.'

'I nearly did. I thought I did. But she was alive. Then after Kyle died, the rules changed. Or . . . Ollie wanted to finish her. Maybe he had to work up his courage, like me.'

Marnie sat on the edge of Ron's desk. 'Let's say this was about Carole from the start. How did you choose your other victims?'

'That's easy. I was the paramedic dealing with the fallout. I was there when Val Rawling came in with torn earlobes. I was in the eye of the storm, had my pick of victims to avenge. And I'd made friends with Ollie at the sports centre. He'd told me about Carole. I was looking for a survivor, someone who was owed justice, and I needed a fellow crusader. I was sick of seeing people hurt and not being able to do anything about it. Sick of being made to help people like Stuart Rawling, who didn't deserve it . . .' Noah was faltering.

It didn't feel right. This version of Bevan was a caricature, exaggerated. It wasn't the man he'd seen coming out of that house. The man Finn had stabbed.

'Aidan Duffy wasn't so easy,' Marnie was saying. 'He wouldn't do what you wanted, even when you threatened his son.'

'No, he wouldn't . . .'

Typically, when he and Marnie worked together like this to get at the truth about a crime and its motive, Noah felt the pieces slotting together. But nothing fitted here, not neatly. As if he was solving a jigsaw by forcing its pieces into the wrong places.

'Did you intend to hurt Finn?' Marnie asked.

'I didn't care. He was a weapon in my war. I used him as I needed to.'

'That doesn't sound like Batman.'

'Okay, but you saw that list of rules and consequences from the house where I kept him. Like the rules Carole used to train Ollie, except Finn was a lot older. He wouldn't fit in a cage, so I had to handle him differently—'

Noah turned, shaking his head. 'This isn't . . . You're right. It's *too* neat. I'm not making any sense. Huell, I mean. Something's missing. We've missed something.'

Marnie didn't argue. She'd reached the same conclusion ahead of him.

It was why she was here dismantling the evidence board instead of celebrating with the rest of the team. Drinks on DCS Ferguson, basking in the press briefing's afterglow. Never mind that Finn was in hospital suffering from dehydration and PTSD. Or that Ollie was dead. As far as Ferguson was concerned, it was a result. Case closed.

'Say you were Huell.' Marnie touched her neck. 'Focused on Carole, and Finn. All the other assaults – even the accident of Kyle's death – just smoke for us.'

'That feels right. It's the rest of it that doesn't. Huell's connection to Carole . . . I don't buy it. It's tenuous, at best. Feels fake.'

'Something else doesn't fit,' Marnie said.

He heard the clench of pain in her voice. 'What?'

'When I spoke with Huell in the ambulance, he had

no interest in me. It was a relief, if I'm honest. Except that we're supposed to believe he ordered the break-in at Lancaster Road and blackmailed Aidan into attacking Stephen . . . When I showed him my badge, he didn't know who I was. Not really. Not obsessively.'

'You think there's someone else,' Noah said. 'Someone we've missed.'

They looked at the almost-empty evidence board. It felt as if they'd scaled an ice-cap only to find, lurking under thick cloud, a hidden summit still ahead.

'Go back to the role-play.' Marnie straightened. 'How did you know to go into hiding when you did? Before we had a warrant out, even before we knew your name. You'd disappeared.'

'Perhaps I *did* see Sol at your place. He's sure he kept out of sight, but he could be wrong.'

'From what I saw of Sol, he knows how to stay hidden.' She shook her head. 'I think someone warned you. You knew *exactly* when to go into hiding. And when to come out, with your hands up.'

'Well, I wanted to be arrested. If this was about attention, recognition . . . My face is going to be in the news for a long time.'

'What if it's the wrong face?' Marnie searched the photos for the one from Carole's scrapbook, of the child taken before Ollie. 'This isn't you. It isn't Huell Bevan.'

'No,' Noah agreed. 'It's not.'

'Colin dated the print. It was taken twenty-two years ago. That's nearer your age than mine. Huell's thirty-five, too old. This child?' She touched her finger to the face. 'Is twenty-six now.'

'So . . . the photo was taken ten years before Ollie was caged by Carole. Whoever this is, they were fourteen when Ollie was taken. That's old enough to have helped in the kidnap, if Carole was controlling them. Assuming they weren't rescued the way Ollie was. But we couldn't find any other missing kids that matched the timeline.'

'Fran fast-tracked the autopsy,' Marnie said. 'Carole gave birth to a child. Not recently. Nothing in the police records, or from the trial. Perhaps she gave the child up for adoption. Or perhaps this,' nodding at the board, 'is her child.'

Noah fell silent, hypnotised by the lost look on the small face. Carole's child. Not one she'd stolen. A child she gave birth to, fourteen years before she took Ollie. No obvious resemblance, unless it was the blankness worn like bruises on both faces. No records from the trial might mean anything. It might mean the child died, that the cage became a coffin.

'One more thing.' Marnie's lips were colourless. 'When I spoke with Finn in the ambulance, he said Ollie had been in the house with him for days.'

'Not days,' Noah said without thinking. 'He was at Carole's when he sent me down those steps—' He stopped. 'Oh, shit. It *wasn't* Ollie?' His head throbbed. 'I got it wrong.'

Marnie shook her head. 'I'm not saying that. It's more likely Finn got it wrong. He's dehydrated, traumatised. It'll be days before he's ready for a proper interview—'

'No. It's me. *I* got it wrong.' Remorse made Noah's teeth ache. 'When I saw Ollie come out of that house, the way he moved? I *knew* it wasn't the same kid. I'd expected to recognise him, but I didn't. I didn't.' He turned away from the board, gripping the back of his neck. 'Shit . . .'

'You were concussed. We were looking for Ollie. You were at Carole's flat because of her connection to him.

We'd found a baseball bat *in his flat.* Everything pointed to it being Ollie.'

'So I saw what I wanted to see—'

'You didn't *want* to see anything,' Marnie said in her steady way. 'You didn't want to be concussed and knocked down those steps.'

'If it wasn't Ollie, who was it? Bevan?'

That didn't fit with the memory in his head. He tried to force the memory to fit but it wouldn't, another piece of the puzzle in the wrong place.

Marnie was saying, 'We don't know that it wasn't Ollie. Not for sure.'

But Noah was sure. He'd been uneasy ever since he'd seen Ollie shivering in a T-shirt because he'd given his hoodie to Finn. 'If Ollie didn't attack me, how do we know he was responsible for any of it? We've only got Bevan's word that he was an accomplice.'

The tabloids would destroy what was left of Ollie's story. Noah could see the headlines now: Thug Life; Violent Teen was Caged as a Kid. He'd played a part in that, naming Ollie as his attacker when he hadn't been sure, not a hundred per cent, because of the concussion. He should have kept his mouth shut, erred on the side of reasonable doubt.

'I need to get this out of my head.' Marnie's voice was very low. 'And I need you to debunk it. If that's what it deserves.'

A fresh jolt of adrenalin—

Noah turned on his heel.

She was standing so still and looking so serious that it unnerved him.

'The missing child.'

'You know who it is,' he realised. 'You've got a theory.'

331

He looked at the child's face on the evidence board then back at Marnie.

'You know who this is.'

54

'She was in the room with me when you called to say that Sol had seen Bevan. She could have heard me talking, and warned Huell to clear out.'

'Who?'

Marnie circled her wrist with her fingers. 'Everything we had on Ollie at the outset? The lists he kept, the knife he was carrying, Lisa's tiger instinct to protect him no matter what – she gave us all of it. The stolen golf clubs, and the stolen baseball bat. Not to mention the story of Huell's obsession with justice. It all came from her.'

'*Zoe*—?' Noah blinked. 'Zoe Marshall?'

'I want to talk it through. I need it out of my head.' She met Noah's eyes, the shadow of an apology in her stare. 'Cynical, I know. Cruel, even. So tell me why I'm wrong. You talked with her more than I did. I trust your judgement. Tell me about Zoe.'

'She's . . . tough. She doesn't look it or sound it, but it's there.' He fought his first instinct to defend Zoe because he liked her. 'She hated talking about the knife, you saw that. Said she didn't believe Ollie had it in him to murder anyone, and she didn't sugarcoat it. No evangelising, she kept it on the level.' He frowned. 'Say she lied about the lists Ollie kept. There's no easy way we can confirm that unless Mr Singh saw something back when he and Ollie were friends. Or unless we find the lists. But the knife was real. Ollie's prints were on it, under Finn's.'

Noah had watched Ollie bleeding out under the frantic hands of the firearms officer who'd shot him. Trigger-happy, the press had said, but Noah had seen the misery on the man's face as he tried to save Ollie's life. Meanwhile Huell was howling for help, both hands clutching his groin. Finn was on the ground, his head on Marnie's shoulder, her arms around him. He'd given up the knife when she'd pleaded for it. She'd brought him back from the brink. A result, Ferguson was calling it. Now Marnie was saying it wasn't over. That Zoe Marshall might be—

'The other child.' Noah blinked at the board. 'You think she's the other child.'

Pale eyes, strawberry hair. He looked more closely, trying to see past the blank mask which captivity and God knows what other cruelty had pinned to the child's face. The small nose and ears could be Zoe's. The curve of the jaw, maybe. Or was he seeing what he wanted to see, again?

'She told us she grew up in Hillingdon,' Marnie was saying. 'That's half an hour from Harrow. And she told me she had a nephew in Kent. At the trial, Carole's brother gave a statement in her defence. His address is in Orpington. He has two sons.'

'She's Zoe Marshall, not Linton. Did she change her name?'

'Carole wasn't married to this child's father. Perhaps he's Marshall. I tried to find out the names of Zoe's parents, but I hit a dead end. Missing paperwork.' She raised her eyebrows, but only for a second. 'It might mean nothing.'

'The assault she told us about, the scars . . .'

'They're real. She was stabbed and it was every bit as nasty as she said it was. She was treated at the Royal Free in Camden, where it's possible Bevan accessed her medical records.'

'She brought us the break in the case,' Noah said. 'Gave us a motive for Huell. You think all that was misdirection? Smoke.'

Marnie waited, not speaking.

'She's small,' Noah said reluctantly. 'Like Carole. Stuart said two kids, one big, one small. The eyewitness from Page Street said the same. We've been assuming Bevan was the small one, because Ollie's so much bigger. But Zoe could pass as a kid.'

Coming down those steps—

Bulked up by layers and layers of clothing.

A balaclava, a baseball bat.

Was that her? Was it Zoe?

'We should slow down,' Marnie warned. 'We need evidence.'

Noah nodded. 'What else do you have?'

'That's it. Not nearly enough to take to DCS Ferguson.' Her mouth crooked. 'Especially not mid-celebration. Huell confessed to killing Kyle, and to conspiring with Ollie to kill Carole. He confessed to Stuart's assault, gave no indication that anyone else was involved. We've charged him. It's doubtful he'll get bail. He'll be in prison as soon as he's out of hospital.'

'Let's say his confession's a fantasy. He met Zoe, but not the way she told it. She seduced him, he's in her thrall. That's speculation on our part . . . We know he was at your place. Forensics have linked him to the other envelopes. No additional DNA at any of the scenes, nothing to say a third person was involved. And if he's prepared to take the blame . . .'

'Well, exactly.'

A phone rang at Debbie's desk. Voicemail caught it.

'Finn,' Noah said. 'I know he's not well enough yet, but might he give us more? If there *is* anything, I mean.'

'He said something, outside the house.' Marnie straightened. 'When they were trying to save Ollie's life. "Ollie did it for her." I asked him what he meant but he didn't know. Only that Ollie had said it back in the house. He wouldn't be able to go home like Finn when it was over because he'd killed someone and he did it "for her". Finn was close to collapse; it won't stand unless he repeats it when he's stronger. And possibly not then.'

'Ollie could've meant Carole. Or his mum. We still don't know where Lisa is, do we?'

'You're right. It's too thin to take to Ferguson. But there are two things I can't get out of my head. The first is the way Tobias deferred to Zoe throughout the interview about the shoebox, as if he was taking cues from her. He didn't say a word which she didn't prompt out of him. Maybe it was trust but the way she used her voice, this rhythm to it . . . She'd made a point of befriending the Crasmere Boys, and Ollie. Of course that's her job. We can hardly accuse her of doing her job.'

'What's the other thing? You said two things you can't get out of your head.'

'This one's even less Ferguson-proof. Just . . . a bad feeling. An itch. When Harry Kennedy talked about her at Lancaster Road, the night before the pair of them came to the station . . .'

Marnie's eyes burned. 'He said she was young and smart, and that she took no prisoners.'

Noah looked at the child's face on the board.
If Marnie was right, if this was Zoe—
Young, smart, takes no prisoners.
But she had. She'd taken Finn.

55

The hospital smelt squeaky, not clean. Light crawled in under the door and between the slats of the blinds. When Finn shut his eyes it pressed at his lids like thumbs.

The bed creaked when he moved. He wasn't supposed to move because of the tube in the back of his hand and the fat bag of fluids to fix all the puking and fever that'd dehydrated him. His head was banging, but not as bad as it had in the house. He didn't care about the banging or the burning in the back of his hand, or even about the nurses who'd stripped him and washed him with sponges. None of it was as bad as what'd happened to Ollie.

He squeezed his eyes shut, but that was no good because the pictures were on the inside. So he stared into the bar of light coming from under the door in a straight line like a yellow ruler. It was good because it was so straight, like someone drew a line under the mess even though they didn't, even though it was just a lie left by the light. He could pretend for a bit that everything was ended.

'Fucking Brady,' he whispered at the yellow line. 'He's finished.'

Bevan, not Brady. But he'd always be Brady, for Finn.

His hand still itched with Brady's blood, the mess that came out of him when he'd shoved Ollie's knife into Brady's balls, hearing Dad's voice cheering in his head.

The way Brady'd rolled around on the floor crying like when Ollie'd kicked a kid who called him a freak. Brady made the exact same sound as that kid and maybe it wasn't Dad cheering in Finn's head, maybe it was Ollie. Who'd given Finn his hoodie and pressed a hard thing into Finn's hand which he hadn't known was a knife not until they were outside and the police were shouting and the whole street was shaking. Up and down, angry with ice that ate up Finn's fever enough for him to see straight, once he knew it was a knife in his hand and that Brady was hiding behind him, like Finn was huge and Brady was tiny.

Then—

'Get on the ground!'

Not actual gameplay footage.

That's what's going through Finn's head.

Not actual gameplay footage.

Puck-puck from the gun and Ollie goes down.

They all do.

'Get on the ground!'

They're all down. Brady with his balls in both hands, crying. Ollie with his T-shirt in red ribbons, like guts.

Not actual gameplay footage.

Finn's got his head on her shoulder. Detective Inspector Marnie Rome. She got him to drop the knife even when it was stuck to his hand with blood and it was like trying to drop his own fingers.

Everything was shaking, but she wasn't. She was a straight line like that yellow ruler under the door. She had her arms round him and he knew he stank of Brady

339

and pissy jeans and whatever bits of Ollie got sprayed on him, but she didn't care about any of that. She kept hold of him the whole time they were making sure Ollie was dead, and Brady wasn't.

Trying to save Ollie's life – Finn knew that's what they were doing. But it'd looked like they were trying to kill him, to keep him down and dead. Even now, when he squeezed his eyes shut, that's what Finn saw. Two of them pushing at Ollie's chest until he stopped moving.

The hospital hissed and rattled. If he made the effort to hear past the banging in his head, he heard trolleys being wheeled and doors swinging shut and shoes on the shiny floors that weren't clean, not really, just shiny. So shiny they scared him. Weird, the stuff he was scared of now. It wouldn't last, they said.

Stress and trauma, all that shit.

He'd stop being scared soon. Of shiny floors and light squeezing through the slits in the blinds, fat bags of fluids and nurses coming out of nowhere, his own blood bumping in his body.

Finn was sick of being scared.

At least in the house there'd been a good reason for it. He'd been snatched, held prisoner, made to follow orders. In the street there'd been Brady and guns and Ollie dying right in front of him; only an idiot wouldn't've been scared. But in *here*—

He was shitting himself at his own shadow, at all those little bits of him squirming in the steel pole that held up the fluids, and in the handles on the drawers.

Everywhere, he was everywhere. He couldn't get away from him. What would Dad say if he saw Finn now? Or if he'd seen the way he'd cried snot all over DI Rome, rubbing his head on her shoulder, not letting go even when the paramedics wanted to check him over, sobbing when they tried to take Ollie's hoodie off him because it was all he had left and it stank of cigarettes – of *Ollie* – and if they took it off there'd be nothing underneath, no skin or bones or blood. No Finn.

So, *yeah*.

He tried to imagine Dad hearing about that and not being disgusted, ashamed of his own son. In prison where he was probably a thousand times tougher than he'd been at home, where you had to be tough to survive, and then someone says, 'Heard your son pissed himself three times in one day,' and okay maybe Dad could say, 'Yeah, but he made a ball-kebab of Brady,' but it wasn't any good. It wasn't ever going to be any good.

Finn was crying again. He cried at anything now, his face opening like a leaky jar. Snot and tears and shaking like a little kid, wanting his blue cat to cuddle, wanting his dad, even his mum— No, not his mum because she hated him. Finn wanted *her*—

'Detective Inspector Marnie Rome.'

He liked the round sound of the words, like pebbles, like those from the beach where his dad carried him down to the sea. He whispered the pebbles to the room, 'Detective Inspector Marnie Rome,' and stared at the light under the door until the yellow line came back.

When it opened—

When the door opened, he heard its hinges at the back of his head because that's where he'd sorted all the sounds, into order, with the oldest ones – *puck-puck* of the gun, red bubbles bursting on Ollie's lips – on top. He had to reach underneath all of that for the sound of the hinges telling him the door was coming open.

'Finn?'

He knew the voice. He'd heard it before.

Not a nurse, or a doctor, but he knew it.

'Finn?' Like singing, like she was singing his name.

He squeezed his eyes shut. The yellow line was breaking up, cold air coming with her into the room, wiping it away. He squeezed his eyes so hard they leaked, balling his fists in the bed until the needle in the back of his hand burned blue as a match.

'Go away go away go away—'

'Ssh. Finn. It's okay. It is.'

Rocking him with her voice.

'It's going to be okay.'

56

Harry Kennedy was warming his long hands around a cup of coffee when Noah reached the café.

Behind the bar, Kim's face flickered when he saw Noah was alone. Marnie had headed to the hospital in the hope of finding either Huell or Finn well enough to be questioned.

'Thanks for coming,' Harry said. 'Not that you need an incentive when the coffee's this good.'

'True.' Noah slid into the seat opposite, returning the smile. 'And in any case I should be the one saying thanks. If you've got what I think you have.'

Names for the gang Sol was trying to escape, the people who'd threatened Dan.

Harry nodded. 'Your brother's smart to be getting out.'

Or stupid, to have ever been part of it in the first place. They waited for Noah's coffee to arrive. If Harry thought less of him because of his brother's connections, he didn't let it show as he laid out the facts. Names, places, charge sheets.

The gang was armed and organised. No flossing, or

strutting. These people were deadly serious. Knives. Guns. Noah's scalp bristled as he listened to the list.

'You know what I'm going to say.' Harry drank a mouthful of coffee. 'We could really use Sol's help. Inside information, anything he's got, would be invaluable.'

'It's why he didn't want to come home. He knew I'd tell him the best way out was to come in.' To Trident, he meant. But Sol had made it clear that he would starve on the streets before he turned police informant. 'I wish it was that simple.'

'He's scared, I get it. This isn't some blinged-up crowd dealing drugs out of their back pockets.' Harry scratched his cheek. 'The top boys are wearing Moschino and driving Mercs, holding down city jobs.'

'And they're running guns.'

'Yes. We've had eyes on them for months but they don't put a foot wrong. No recruitment going on, or none that we can see. Usually that's our way in, when the fresh blood starts spilling. Kids cock up and if we're lucky they help us move it up the ranks. But this lot have it all locked down.'

Noah tried to imagine Sol as part of the gang that Harry was describing. Good suits, expensive cars, city jobs. Smart enough to outwit Trident's best team. Sol had too much money sometimes, but he spent it in Superdry, not on Bond Street. Whenever Noah and Dan took him clubbing, Sol drank beer and danced like a goofball before falling asleep, face-first, on their sofa.

'You're sure about this?' He shook his head at Harry. 'I'm not in denial. I do know Sol's up to his neck in something. I just can't believe it's guns, or even knives.'

'I'm sure,' Harry said. 'And I'm sorry.' He looked it.

'Are you going to arrest him?'

'Not until we've something solid enough to take to the CPS.'

'So you're sure, but you're not certain? Okay, scratch that. I hear what you're saying, and I get it. I do get it.'

Dan, he thought, *I need to warn Dan.*

Harry was giving him a heads-up, from professional courtesy perhaps, but Noah needed to warn Dan that there might be a knock on the door, armed police calling for his little brother.

'How close are you to making an arrest? Or can't you tell me?'

'Not so close that I'm asking you to choose between your brother and your job.' Harry sat back, looking apologetic. 'You asked me to find out who might've sent those threatening texts. I've no evidence worthy of the CPS, but I've enough to know that we could use Sol's help in nailing a gang who're bringing illegal weapons into London and selling to the highest bidder. I don't know what he was doing for them, but I'm assuming it was important enough to make them edgy about his exit strategy. Unless it's a control thing, wanting to keep the rank and file in line. But if he's someone they count on to charm palms . . . I don't mean the deals, just smoothing things along. These people like a good party, and from what I've heard Sol's a one-man charm offensive.'

True. Dad always said Sol's smile could skin a cat while convincing the cat it was being stroked.

Noah looked past Harry to the front of the café. His eyes ached in their sockets. Kim was polishing glasses at the bar. How was Marnie getting on at the hospital? Better than this, he hoped.

'I'll talk to him.' He met Harry's gaze. 'See if I can persuade him to talk to you. But honestly? Your best bet is finding evidence to arrest him.'

The words stuck in his teeth. He wanted to take them

back. This was his *brother*. He saw the look on his mum's face, and his dad's. *Your brother.*

'If there was an easy way to get him out,' he said, 'I'd have managed it myself by now.'

Sol bounced like rubber from wherever life kicked him. Five, six smartphones but there'd be a seventh and eighth. Sitting on Marnie's sofa looking burnt-out. Then tucking into a bacon sandwich at the station, grinning at Debbie Tanner. Nothing stopped Sol for long.

'This's on me.' Harry took a fiver from his wallet. 'How's DI Rome? You must've been celebrating late last night.'

'Not as late as you'd think. One in the morgue, two in the hospital.'

'I saw DCS Ferguson on the news. She looked very . . . glossy.'

'Well, she likes to keep herself camera-ready.'

Harry shot him a look of sympathy. 'The rest of you are sweeping up, I take it. Give DI Rome my best. Tell her I was sorry to hear about Ollie. Zoe's cut up, too.'

'She would be,' Noah agreed. 'She liked him.' He checked his pockets for his phone. 'I hope she's not blaming herself for what went down with Bevan . . .'

He kept it light, inconsequential, not wanting to spook the other man.

They stood. Harry put the cash on the table, saying, 'I think she probably is. You're right, she liked Ollie. She likes all the kids.'

'They like her. Tobias and the others. They trust her.'

Harry nodded, following Noah out of the café. 'She amazes me. You know Tobias's cousin was one of the gang that attacked her?'

'No, I didn't. His cousin?'

'I didn't know either, not at the time of the interview,

but yes. Iziah Midori. He's on remand.' Harry turned up the collar on his coat, eyeing the black ice on the pavement. 'Looks like the weather's finally caught up with the people round here . . .'

'Cold as ice?'

'And twice as hard.'

Children's Services was a woman with a helmet of grey hair and a smile made gruesome by capped teeth. 'Heather Yardley. And you are?'

'Detective Inspector Rome. How's Finn?'

'Not doing too badly all things considered. A disturbed night, but the doctor's pleased with the way he's responding to fluids. His temperature's down and he's more lucid.' A portcullis smile. 'Which isn't to say he's ready for questions of the kind I expect you'd like to ask him.'

'My questions can wait,' Marnie said. 'What happened to disturb him in the night?'

'Terrors, from the sound of it. Shouting about someone in his room, working himself up into a state. They calmed him down, eventually.'

'*Was* someone in his room?'

'Oh no. I shouldn't think so. But after what he's been through it'd be stranger if he *wasn't* seeing things, don't you think?' She persisted with the smile. 'When they go quiet, that's when I worry. Always better to get these things out if you can.'

They stood back to allow an orderly to wheel an empty trolley up the corridor. The trolley had a dented pillow and twisted blanket, its stained paper sheets destined for the incinerator.

'What's the situation with Finn's family?' Marnie asked. 'Has his mother been to see him?'

'We're keeping her away while we work out whether

or not to move forward with charges of neglect. It's . . .
complicated. She's in counselling for anxiety, swears blind
her brother-in-law was looking after the boy and that she
trusted him to do a good job. Dad's in prison. So with
Mum out of the picture too, we'll need a foster home for
when all this is over.'

'There isn't anyone else? No grandparents?'

'Over in Ireland, but that's not terribly helpful. None
on Mum's side. Of course I expect you'll be charging him
with GBH or whatever. In which case, accommodation
won't be an issue for a little while, will it?'

If Finn was in a secure unit, she meant.

'I've sorted out tougher ones than this,' Heather
soothed, 'don't you worry. The important thing is to get
Finian fighting fit.'

It was *Finn*, not Finian. Marnie wanted to see him. She
could feel his hard head against her shoulder, black hair
roughing her cheek, the heat of fever from his skin. That
blurred handful of words, 'He did it for her,' fingers
twitching with distress at what he'd seen. Ollie's hoodie
swamping him, smelling of cigarettes—

'DI Rome?'

She turned her head to find herself looking into Zoe
Marshall's green eyes.

'Have you seen him?' Zoe asked anxiously. 'Finn? Is
he okay?' She was wearing her parka and the red mittens
with the matching hat pulled over her curls. Her nose
was pink with cold.

'I'm hoping to see him.' Marnie made herself smile.
'Have you been waiting for news?'

Night terrors. Finn thinking someone was in his room.

'I've just got here.' Zoe pulled off a mitten and rubbed
at her nose. 'I tried to get hold of Lisa last night to tell
her how sorry I was about Ollie.' Her face was fierce with

expression, nothing like the caged child's. 'I don't suppose you have a number for her?'

'I'm afraid not.'

'I'm sorry.' Her voice dipped with empathy. 'I know this was the last outcome you wanted. Ollie was— I know how you must be feeling.' She pulled off her hat. Chestnut curls sprang into a halo, snaked with static. She tucked her hands into her armpits. 'At least Finn's safe.'

'Did you know him?' Marnie used her lightest voice. 'He was friends with Ollie, of course.'

'I've been trying to figure that out. I *must've* seen him with Ollie because they were mates, but Finn wasn't on the Crasmere Boys' radar or I'd have heard about it. On the periphery, perhaps. Poor kid. But he's okay?'

'As you say, he's safe now.' Marnie looked away, up the corridor. 'We just need to keep him that way . . .'

It was easier to watch Zoe from the edge of her eye. Some people only came into focus when you stopped looking directly at them. Was she right about Zoe? Or wrong, as she'd been about DCS Ferguson? She'd let Ferguson take this case from under her like a magician's stunt with a tablecloth, all the plates and glasses still standing, save one. Ollie.

Marnie had smelt his sweat on the hoodie he'd given to Finn. He'd given Finn the knife, too. And now, because of what he'd done with that knife, Finn might be going to a secure unit. From where, unless fate was uncharacteristically kind, he'd emerge as brittle and broken as Ollie, the knife passed like a baton between the two of them. If only Finn had refused to use it. But he'd been scared and angry, pumped full of fever and adrenalin, after what he'd been through in that house – the game being played between Bevan and Aidan and whoever was behind the scenes, pulling the strings to make the lot of them dance, Marnie included.

'I hate hospitals,' Zoe said, 'don't you?'

Marnie kept her eyes on the corridor, studying the woman who stood a foot away from her as alert as a meerkat. Had she really just arrived, or had she gone out into the cold long enough to make that alibi believable? Her nose was the same colour as the caged child's hair, strawberry blond. A colour that often turned to chestnut.

Marnie needed to get her hands on a photo of Zoe as a child, even a school photo might be enough. But if she was the mastermind behind this twisted game, she'd chosen to leave the scrapbook in the lock-up. She'd *wanted* them to see the photograph of the child who wasn't Ollie.

Marnie's phone was ringing—

'DI Rome.'

'It's Himmat Singh.'

Lisa and Ollie's neighbour.

His voice was soft and urgent. 'Can you come?'

57

Himmat wasn't alone in his flat. A blonde woman, so washed out she was nearly a negative, sat on his sofa with the cat at her feet. Bleached jeans and brown boots, a cheap black fleece zipped to her neck. Her face was cracked across by pain.

'Lisa.' Marnie held out a hand. 'I'm so sorry.'

Ollie's mother smelt of glue and rubber. 'I've been working. Away.' Her voice was raw, as if she hadn't used it in a long time. 'Shifts, all the ones I could get. In a carpet factory.'

Himmat brought a big cup of sweet-smelling tea and put it into her hands. He'd explained how Lisa had seen the news and come home in the early hours. He'd found her standing like a ghost on his doorstep, brought her in and made her warm, tried to get her to eat and sleep but she wouldn't. It had taken him all this time to persuade her to speak with the police.

The cat followed Himmat to the chair on the other side of the room. Noah was next to him.

'You'll want to see Ollie.' Marnie sat beside Lisa on the sofa. 'I can take you to see him.'

'Can you *make* me do that?' She looked terrorised. 'I don't want to. I can't.'

Marnie waited, not speaking.

'I had to leave.' Lisa gripped the cup hard in her hands. 'I just couldn't stand it. I knew where it was headed, could *see* where it was headed. He was going to get killed, or he was going to kill someone. I didn't want to be around to watch. It's not . . . I'm not a bad mother. They'll say that, like they did before, but I'm not. I'm not *any* kind of mother. It's used me up, all this, there's nothing left.' She looked at her hands and then at her knees, as if she couldn't make sense of what she was seeing. 'I'd had enough, that's what they'll say. I'd had enough so I left, but it wasn't like that. There wasn't enough of *me*, that's the honest truth. No one ever tells the truth about being a mum. They say it's tough, that you have to take charge or you have to keep giving, as if it's about tactics, strategy, when it's not. It's about you, and them. If they won't meet you halfway, if you can't reach them? It's not about *trying*. Rules don't help, nothing does. You can cry your eyes out. Beg, be strict, set rules. None of it matters. All of it just— Makes you *less*.'

She pressed the cup to her lips but didn't drink. 'They'll say I was careless, that I let him slip through my fingers again, but I didn't. What they never tell you – the secret everyone keeps – is that being a parent sometimes means you have to care *less*. Sometimes . . . That's the only way you'll survive.'

She shut her eyes, calmer now she'd said her piece.

Himmat stroked the head of the cat softly.

Marnie thought of the boy in the morgue with a hole drilled in his chest. 'I have to ask you some questions. About Ollie.'

'I know.' Sipping her tea.

'You say that you could see where this was headed. That Ollie would be killed, or kill someone. What made you think that?'

'His mates. The gang. He wouldn't stop running. And hating.' Her voice didn't change. 'He hated everyone. Strangers, people off the telly, even his friends.' She looked across at Himmat. 'Anyone who tried to help him, anyone who got in his way. *Me*. He hated me.'

Marnie wanted to tell her how her son had helped Finn. How he'd given his hoodie to keep Finn warm, fought for him in those last desperate seconds. But a different version of events was already leaking to the press: Ollie had wanted his knife found on Finn in order to mitigate the charges against himself; he'd thought it all through. Her son had been a dangerous killer brought down by a conscientious firearms officer, that was the official version of Ollie.

'He hated me,' Lisa repeated. 'But I could live with that. It's when he started on about *her*— That was when I knew it was over.'

'Her?'

'Carole.' No new emotion in her voice. 'He wanted to know all about her. What she'd done and why I'd never talked to him about it. As if I should've been doing that all these years – making her part of our lives.'

'When did he start asking questions about Carole?'

'Three months ago. Half-term. I knew something had happened. Someone at school who'd heard the story. It crops up whenever another child goes missing, it's *her* face in the papers. And his. Not when it's murder, not then. But if it's cruelty, or slavery . . . They're not supposed to use Ollie's picture, but sometimes they do. I thought that's what'd happened. He wouldn't say how he'd heard. Just that he wanted the full story, from me.'

'What did you tell him?'

'I told him to go and look it up.' A dry sound, not quite a sob. 'I didn't want to talk about it any more. The first time he asked, I told him I blamed myself even though the police said I shouldn't. Mostly I talked about how happy I'd been when he was found, how close I kept him afterwards. We were always together. And *happy*. Even after his dad left. We had fun, went on holidays together. I kept photo albums; he *knows* it's true. But he said it was all lies, that he was never happy, always felt wrong inside, like a piece was missing. That's not true, I was *there*. I saw him grow up and he was happy, he was my happy boy . . .'

She stopped to drink tea, looking parched.

'Every day he came back with a worse question. Did she abuse him? Did she have a boyfriend and did *he* abuse him? Did they take turns to— *No*. I told him *nothing* like that happened. The police had all the evidence from the doctors, and the house. From the cage.' Her teeth locked on the word. 'But he didn't want to hear that. It was as if someone was whipping him into a fury. To start with I could calm him down, but it got so I couldn't. No matter what I said, he believed worse. As if it wasn't bad enough. Or as if he needed more reasons to hate her.'

Three months ago, half-term. That's when Zoe said she'd seen Bevan with Ollie at the sports centre. Was Bevan the one whipping Ollie into a fury? If so, was he acting on Zoe's instructions?

'He didn't tell you why he was suddenly so interested in Carole?'

'Interested? He wasn't *interested*. He was obsessed. He even called her *Mum*. Just once, but it was enough. As if she explained what was happening with him, all the rage and rule-breaking. He needed a reason, and she made sense. She explained what he didn't understand about himself. And she *excused* it, the way only a mum can. "*She*'d understand," that's what he kept saying to me.'

Lisa's face creased with fresh pain. 'I told everyone that he didn't remember what happened all those years ago. The car, the cage. I thanked God he didn't remember. But I was so *stupid*. Of course he remembered. It was in his head, a part of him. It *was* him. And when she came back . . . No one should have to face that, especially not a child. No one should have to face their torturer coming back into their lives.'

The way Stephen had, or said he had. Could Marnie believe it? That her parents had done something so reckless, so abhorrent? Ollie had been a good kid, once. Before Carole came back into his life. Had it been the same with Stephen?

'I'd have done anything to keep her away from him,' Lisa was saying, '*anything*. What parent wouldn't?'

Who were they, really? Marnie's parents. She'd fought with them when she was Stephen's age, and not just because she was spiky. Sometimes *they*'d started the fights. Stephen held all the answers, that's what she'd told herself, but she'd known they weren't easy people to live with. And if they'd taken an eight-year-old boy from his abusive mother only to threaten six years later to bring her back into his life—

'Ollie became obsessed with Carole,' she said. 'Did he want to find her? Get in touch?'

Lisa shut her eyes. 'Of course he did.'

'How was he going to make that happen, did he say?'

'A project he'd heard about, to do with forgiveness.' Her laugh sounded like a cough. 'He said that was his way in, that he wanted to forgive her. I tried to make a joke, asked when he was ever going to forgive *me*, but it wasn't funny. Nothing was ever funny back then. It's stupid, but that got to me more than anything. That we couldn't laugh to make it better, or just to try and stay sane. Nothing was allowed to be funny.' Her face changed, grief shouldering its way back in. 'When he was tiny he'd spend hours making me laugh. Pulling faces or mucking about, putting on my hats, doing funny walks. He was my funny little man. I missed my funny little man.'

Marnie waited a moment before asking, 'When were you last in your flat?'

'Next door?' Lisa dragged a hand through her lank hair. 'Days ago. A week, maybe? I've been sleeping in the factory. Why?'

'There was a bin bag in the kitchen, next to the pedal bin. Did you leave it there?'

'A bin bag? Full, you mean? Was I . . . putting the bins out?' She looked towards Himmat.

'Wrong day of the week,' he said softly. 'Collection is Thursday.'

'Oh God . . .' Lisa's eyes returned to Marnie. 'You found something. What did you find?'

'You don't remember leaving anything inside a bin liner in your kitchen?'

'In the bin, yes, but not in a liner. I'd let it all go. It was a pit, I know that. I had to stop caring so much because I was going mad.'

'Did Ollie have his own key to the flat?'

No key had been found on him. Not in his jeans, not in the hoodie.

'Yes, of course. And Himmat has a spare. Ollie was always losing his.'

Noah said, 'Did anyone else have a key?'

Lisa shook her head. 'No one.'

'No one you trusted, or Ollie trusted, to be inside the flat when you weren't there?'

'Only Himmat. Ollie had friends round sometimes, but less and less since he started on about Carole. None of his friends liked to hear about her. I warned him not to lose friends by pushing them away. Zoe warned him too. It's easy to fall out when you're that age and he hadn't many friends to start with . . .'

'Zoe warned him?' Marnie didn't look at Noah, she didn't need to.

He wasn't missing a beat of this.

'Zoe Marshall, you must know her. She's one of the few round here who actually *helps*— Not that there was any helping Ollie lately, but she tried. And she was getting somewhere for a while. He got tired of it, though, tired of anything positive. The *energy* he put into being negative . . . you wouldn't believe.'

'But Zoe tried to help. When was the last time you and Ollie saw her?'

'Back at half-term? She'd never have given up on him. They had a connection, right from when they first met. But that was over a year ago and he's changed so much.' She gripped the lip of the cup. 'Had, I mean. He'd changed so much. Even so she stuck around. One of those rare ones who's in it for the long haul.'

Lisa looked across the room, blindly. 'I thought *I* was one of those rare ones. Until I wasn't. Less and less of me every day and I *had* to leave. It wasn't just breaking my heart, it was breaking all of me. I wasn't *there*.'

She stopped, blinking. 'I'm still not.'

Blinking. 'I suppose I won't ever be, now.'

Noah followed Marnie across the frozen tundra between the blocks of flats where the kids were smoking. 'So much for tiger mum. That was a lie to put us on the back foot. Lisa thinks Zoe's a hero, one of the few who stays the course.'

'Another layer of Zoe's alibi, should she need it.' Marnie took out her phone, checking for messages. 'Colin's at the hospital watching out for Finn.'

'You picked him because he's the least likely to fall for her little-girl-lost act?'

'If it *is* an act.' She pocketed the phone. 'The evidence is hardly stacking up on all sides.'

'When you saw Zoe at the hospital earlier . . . How was she?'

'Upset about Ollie, worried about Finn. And sorry for me, given yesterday's outcome.' Marnie enunciated clearly, as if she was reading from a cue card: 'She knew that it wasn't what I'd wanted.'

'Was it what *she* wanted?' Noah said. 'I can't make sense of her motive, not entirely.'

Fourteen feet away, the kids turned their backs, huddling closer together.

'I think she told us,' Marnie said, 'when she was explaining Huell, or pretending to explain him. That speech about victims too often being ignored or forgotten, punishments never being equal to their crimes. And what was it she said about justice handed down by the courts? Too clean, too civilised, never personal enough. Well, she got personal.'

'Huell wanted more than attention.' Noah narrowed his shoulders against the cold. 'That's what she said. He was after gratitude. Is gratitude what *she* wants?'

'It's what she expects,' Marnie said. 'I imagine it made her angry when Mazi didn't thank her for killing Kyle. And she got no thanks from Valerie Rawling, who saw fit to warn her abusive husband about the vigilante.'

'It explains the press clippings,' Noah agreed.

He hesitated, watching her weigh the car keys in her hand.

Marnie nodded. 'You can say it.'

'She expects you to be *grateful* for what she's doing at Cloverton? Blackmailing Aidan Duffy into hurting Stephen—?'

Not just hurting. Killing him. Zoe had wanted Stephen hanging in his cell.

'It's why she took Finn.' Marnie unlocked the car. 'To get to Stephen. She wanted to punish him and, yes, I'm supposed to be grateful for that. Just as Mazi was meant to be grateful for Kyle.'

Was she blaming herself for what had happened to Finn? Or simply angry at the woman who'd eluded justice because she'd manipulated Huell Bevan into taking the blame, the way she'd manipulated everyone around her—

Ollie, and Tobias Midori, even Harry Kennedy.

'You're sure it's her, aren't you?' Noah studied the clean cut of Marnie's profile against the rinsed-white sky. 'You weren't, first thing this morning. But now you are.'

'Oh it's her,' Marnie said simply. 'But knowing it's one thing. Proving it's another.'

'So . . . let's prove it.'

'It's early in the day for optimism, but I appreciate the thought.' She got into the car. 'Be prepared for DCS Ferguson to take a more jaundiced view.'

'We need a photo.' He climbed in on the passenger side, reaching for the seat belt. 'Of Zoe as a child. If we put it alongside the ones from the scrapbook . . . Better still, we get her birth certificate and find out who her mum is. You think she's Carole's kid?'

Marnie put her hands on the wheel, letting the engine run. 'I think this is someone who's been working close to the criminal justice system for years. At least four years, but probably longer. And there won't be any photos. She'd never have let us find the scrapbook if it was that simple.'

'Then her connection to Bevan. We tell Ferguson we want to look into that, in the light of what's happened. As part of the clean-up job.'

'Zoe volunteered the information about Bevan.' Marnie turned the car towards the road. 'That doesn't make her look suspicious, the opposite in fact. She helped us short-cut the case. She's Ferguson's public ally number one.'

'Then the attacks,' Noah persisted. 'We were always looking for a victim and a vigilante. Bevan doesn't fit that profile. If we discount Zoe's misdirection, his motive's non-existent. But she was nearly killed, scarred for life. Her motive's château-bottled.'

'There's the link between Iziah and Tobias Midori,' Marnie conceded. 'That's as close as we'll get without digging. We need resources and,' Noah's phone was ringing, 'why do I get the feeling this is DCS Ferguson calling to tell us we've a new case that's going to take up all our time?'

Noah put it on speaker and they listened in silence to what Ferguson had to say.

'Spooky,' he said when the call ended. 'You, I mean.'

'Hardly. No shortage of bodies. This is London; I'm surprised we didn't trip over one coming back to the car.'

'She's told the press it's over.' Noah glanced out of the window. 'She should've waited. If she has to back down now it's going to ruin her complexion.'

Marnie looked a question.

'Egg on her face,' he elaborated.

'Oh I expect she has a contingency for that . . . She

doesn't look to me like a woman who's been caught in many backdraughts.'

Noah chewed on that thought, unhappily.

'Cheer up,' Marnie said. 'I'm not done yet.'

He watched the way she kept her eyes dead ahead. 'Damn.'

She flicked him a glance. 'What?'

'Just . . . damn. I wouldn't want to be Zoe right now. Or Ferguson, for that matter.'

'Right. I'm the dragon slayer.' She sketched a smile, shaking her head. 'I thought that story died a death years ago.'

'From where I'm sitting? It's alive and breathing fire.'

'Optimism *and* wishful thinking?' She clicked her tongue. 'Much too early in the day.'

'Tell me you don't have a plan.'

Marnie said nothing, tucking the car behind a taxi, checking the mirrors.

'You have a plan,' Noah said. 'I knew it.'

'My plan is to return to the station and reassure DCS Ferguson that we're aligned with whatever objectives she's set for the week. I might volunteer for some of the paperwork needed to tie off the Bevan case, given how stretched we all are. She'll consider that an appropriate penance.'

'It doesn't go with your suit,' Noah said. 'The hair shirt.'

'Let's see if DCS Ferguson agrees. I suspect she'll approve of my wardrobe choices.'

A bicycle courier came out of nowhere, cutting across them, a blur of black Lycra.

Marnie swerved so smoothly Noah hardly noticed her doing it. He knew for a fact that she was at least as exhausted as he was, but the tiredness no longer showed under the metallic finish of this fierce new focus. For the first time, he felt optimistic.

Zoe Marshall thought she could play Marnie Rome? Good luck with that.

58

'Good lad. You're doing much better.' The nurse wrote on the chart that hung from the foot of Finn's bed. 'Your temperature's coming right down.'

'That means I can leave, yeah?'

She just smiled at him.

Finn tried to hate her. He tried. But he was too scared. Everything was a fat wad of fear, like a hairball working its way up his throat. He wanted to be angry, to punch the wall or call the nurse a cow, kick the shit out of this stupid room. At least in Brady's house he'd had space. Here it was just one room and they didn't even lock the door to stop—

Her. Coming in here last night, and why wouldn't anyone believe him? He'd told them, why would he shout like that at nothing? But that's what he'd done, they said. Seen nothing, shouted at nothing, nearly pissed himself at *nothing.* This was his life now. Being scared of everything and even when it was real, when *anyone* would've shouted – being told he was seeing things. Fever, stress, whatever. That cow from Children's Services with her teeth as bad as Brady's, sneaking in when he was sleeping, waking him up with her rotten smile that was *exactly* like Brady's but he was only *seeing things*, yeah. That was it. No one here was a scary freak who told him to calm down when they said his mum couldn't come and of course his dad couldn't and anyway he'd have to answer a load of police questions when he was well enough— Yeah. Nothing to be scared of in any of *that*. He should just lie here and suck it up without making a fuss that made their jobs harder.

Stupid thick tears in his throat . . .

He'd thought he'd had it planned out. In Brady's house – he'd had it all planned out. Two plans. The first was to grow up and do good, make a difference in the world, make it a place where people never snatched kids from the street and kept them prisoner. The other plan came later, when he got sick. To grow up and teach those bastards a lesson. Get big and strong like Ollie, big enough to beat the shit out of people who thought they could mess with him, or with any little kid. But there were too many people he'd have to teach a lesson to – his mum, his mates, even his dad. Then there was that moment right in the middle of the worst of it when his head was banging and his legs were hollow and he was that whale, the one that went the wrong way and ended up stranded on the beach. First it's swimming with the shit in the sea – the plastic bottles and bags, all the crap everyone dumps there – then it's run aground, lunch for gulls, teeth as trophies.

Trollies banged in the corridor.

Cold sweat stuck his fringe to his forehead. He had to get out of here. And he had to do it by himself because no one else was going to help. Ollie wasn't going to walk in with a weapon and a hoodie he could hide in.

Finn balled his fists in the blankets. He wanted that hoodie back. He'd felt *safe*—

Shit, the door—

The door was opening. The nurse coming back, let it be her, *thenursethenursethenurse*—

'Just checking you're okay.' Glasses, good teeth, blue jumper and jeans. 'DC Pitcher. Colin. I said Hi earlier, but you were out of it.'

'Yeah . . .' A warm rush went through him, like a wave of relief, making him really sleepy.

'I'm right outside the door if you need me. Or even if you don't. DI Rome wanted me here, wanted you to know I'm here.'

'Yeah?' Finn blinked at him. 'Okay.'

Colin moved to close the door and he said, 'Don't—'

He felt stupid saying it, but it was okay because Colin didn't mind. He came into the room, pulling up a chair. 'Boring in the corridor, so thanks.'

'You've got a book, though.'

Colin held it up. Cool cover, the kind of thing Finn liked to read when he wasn't having the piss taken out of him for being a nerd.

'Read me a bit?' He didn't know why he said that, but Colin didn't care.

He read for a while. It was a good book. Finn listened with his eyes on the door because he didn't want to get too comfy and Colin was cool but he was skinny, didn't look like he could put up much of a fight if anything kicked off, the way it had last night.

'Is she coming back?' he said after a bit.

'DI Rome? Yes. She's on her way, wants to see how you're getting on.'

He shut his eyes because they were burning with being open. Any second now he'd be asleep. 'Okay, cos I want to make a statement about what happened with Brady.' He lifted a hand and rubbed at his eyes, so tired he was probably going to cry again. 'And *her*.'

'Her?' Colin echoed.

'She was here last night but no one believes me.'

A long pause then, 'Who is she? What's her name? Finn?'

'Ollie knew her . . .'

Pictures fizzing in his head, of a red snake with Ollie's purple eyes.

'Said he did it for her . . .'

'Finn?'

'Sleepy, sorry. Cool book, though . . .'

59

Aidan Duffy leaned forward, hands linked on the metal table, his eyes tracking Marnie intently as she crossed the visitors' room to where he was sitting. 'Well?'

'He's safe. In hospital, but safe.'

'Jesus and all the little children . . .' He put his hands in his hair. 'Can I kiss your hand, Marnie Jane, or will that get me re-arrested?'

'You can sit still,' she said, 'and hear me out.'

'How bad's he hurt?' He dropped his hands to the table, face flinching at her tone. 'That bastard didn't—'

'Finn's safe. He's been through a traumatic experience that could have been worse and still might be. He stabbed Huell Bevan with another boy's knife. That boy is dead.'

Aidan opened his mouth then shut it. His fingers fluttered until he linked them in a fist.

'Bevan's recovering after surgery. He'll live, but I wouldn't put it past him to press charges. That's if the CPS doesn't beat him to it.'

'You wouldn't put him in prison.' All the softness, the charm, had gone from his voice. It was as stark as the pain in his face. 'You wouldn't do that. He's ten years old.'

'The age of criminal responsibility.'

'The age of— Fuck you.' Tears burned in his eyes. 'Don't do that. Don't do that to him.'

'I'm not doing anything. I'm laying out the facts for you.'

'For what—? So I can cry myself to sleep over them?' He let the tears fall, not bothering to wipe them away. 'So I can think of my little fish in your fucking tank?'

'So that you can help me,' Marnie said.

Finn's father stared at her. She glanced away, keeping her expression neutral, hoping he'd take his cue from her. The last thing she needed was the guard at the door reporting a conspiracy.

Lorna Ferguson had allowed this visit to inform Aidan of his son's situation. 'Out of the frying pan, facing the fire,' was how she'd summed up Finn's predicament. 'Although there's every chance Aidan'll be proud of his son following in his footsteps.' Odd how little she understood of human nature given how high up the ladder she'd climbed, although Marnie was learning that much of the woman's flintiness was body armour worn, like her heels, to lend her inches.

Aidan dropped his stare from Marnie's face, relaxing his shoulders. Not a big show, just enough to take the strain from the picture they were presenting to the guard at the door. 'Tell me.'

'It involves Stephen.'

His cheekbones lengthened. 'You've changed your mind. All that bollocks about needing answers. You want to trade. Him for Finn. Is that it?'

'No, that's not it,' Marnie said crisply. 'But your talent for jumping to the wrong conclusion remains as impressive as ever. There's no deal to be done, no game to be played. I have Bevan, but he's not the one behind this. He was used, the same as the rest of us.'

Aidan creased his nose in a frown. 'He's not the one who took Finn?'

'Not the only one. And not the one who's at large.'

'Oh, Jesus.' He thumbed the socket of his eye. 'There's more?'

'One more. Finn's identified her, or he's tried to. But he's in shock, and can't give a clear description. Not enough for the CPS.'

'Her—?' Aidan paled, looking ill. 'A woman?'

Finn had told Colin about 'Brady', his dad's nickname for men who stole kids off the street. It followed that his nickname for women was one to strike fear into any parent's heart.

Marnie said, 'She wasn't in the house with him. Everything was done through Bevan, who's confessed. Taken all the blame, or the credit as he sees it. The case is closed.'

'By DCS Ferguson.' He tipped his head to the side. 'But not by you.'

'Maverick detectives don't exist outside of fiction, Mr Duffy. I'm already on a new case.'

'So – what? They're just ignoring my boy's evidence?'

'He's traumatised. He had a fever when he came out of the house. There's nothing to suggest anyone else was there. Just Finn and Bevan, and the boy whose knife Finn used to geld him.'

Aidan didn't say anything smart or vicious about Bevan's injuries. Contrary to Ferguson's expectations, he exhibited no pride in the vengeance his son had inflicted on his captor, knowing what its consequences might mean for Finn's future.

He kept his hands linked on the table, his eyes fixed on her face.

'What can I do?' he said seriously. 'Tell me.'

Outside the prison, Lorna Ferguson was waiting in her Range Rover Vogue, to escort Marnie back to the station. 'How's Mr Duffy?' She leaned to open the passenger door, revealing dark roots to her platinum hair, before straightening in the driver's seat. 'Grateful, I hope?'

'He's going to help.' Marnie fastened her seat belt. 'Or he's going to try.'

'Did you tell him your theory about this woman, Zoe Marshall?'

Marnie shook her head. 'Just that we need his help.'

'Well, he's around your little finger, thanks to Finn. That's a nice pet to have. Now you just need this theory of yours to play out, and who knows? We might be talking promotion.'

When Marnie didn't speak, Ferguson glanced her way. 'Is the theory giving you cold feet?'

'Not the theory. Just the practice.'

Proving it. Arresting Zoe, and making it stick.

'Thank you,' she said, 'for letting me run with this.'

'I messed up,' Ferguson shrugged. 'Now it's your turn.'

60

Noah dropped his keys into the bowl on the hall table, listening to the silence in the flat. 'Dan?'

'Bathroom,' Dan called back. His voice was thinned down.

In the bathroom, he was washing his elbow at the sink. 'Came off my bike.' Blood, and grit. A deep graze on his left temple. 'I'm okay.'

Noah took charge of the first aid, sitting Dan on the side of the bath, taking what he needed from the cabinet. 'How'd it happen?'

'Black ice. Being stupid. It'll teach me to make cracks about you and Eric Radford.'

Noah cleaned the cuts and smeared antiseptic cream over the damage, taping dressings in place. Dan's shoulders shook. He turned his head away from the light.

'Hey,' Noah said. 'Look at me?'

Dan looked. His pupils were blown by shock. 'The bike's a write-off. I'm sorry . . .'

The tap was dripping into the sink, an oddly dry sound.

Dan's hands curled at the lip of the bath, holding on, his bones too near the surface of his skin, the red smell of his blood under the pink of the cream.

Noah reached to close off the dripping tap.

He rested a hand on the wall and said, 'Tell me.'

'It was an accident,' Dan tried. 'I'm sure— It was an accident.'

Anger took a scoop out of Noah's stomach. 'A car?'

'A Merc. He—' Moving his hand, jerkily. 'Cut across me.'

These top boys are wearing Moschino and driving Mercs.

'Did he stop?'

'No, but when was the last time you saw anyone do that in London?' Dan searched Noah's face, looking desperate. 'It wasn't— I don't think it was deliberate.'

'But you're not sure.'

'Noah . . .'

'Yes?' He couldn't keep the anger out of his voice.

Dan shook his head. He didn't believe it was an accident, or he'd have argued longer.

'Where's Sol?' Noah asked him.

'Sleeping, on the sofa.'

'Right.' He moved, shoving shut the door of the cabinet.

'Where're you going—?' Dan straightened, sounding scared.

Noah smiled at him. 'To make you a cup of tea.'

In the kitchen, he filled the kettle and clicked it on.

While it was heating, he looked in on Sol.

He was sleeping on the sofa, just as Dan had said. Expensive trainers on the floor, cheap watch on the table. A new smartphone. His head was half-buried under the blanket that Dan had brought out of storage for him. He wasn't snoring, he never snored. His sleep was the sleep of the dead or the new-born, deep and contented and undisturbed.

Your brother. He's your brother.

Noah saw his father's face, and his mother's, distant with censure. Shutting him out. Some things cannot be forgiven, he'd grown up hearing that. Some things put you out in the cold and kept you there, with no way back. Be careful what you walk away from, and what you walk towards. A bad family's better than an empty sty. If a finger stinks, you don't cut it off.

He could hear the kettle boiling. Sirens in the street. Dan, getting dressed.

Sol slept on, curled under the blanket.

Some things can't be forgiven.

Noah walked to the kitchen and poured the tea.

Then he took out his phone, and made the call.

61

Harry Kennedy took a seat by the window with its dizzyingly tall view of London; one of the newer high-rise restaurants spreading like a rash over the smarter parts of town.

Zoe had been here a while, long enough to have lost the look of cold that haunted the faces of those like Harry more recently arrived. She'd kept her parka on; the air conditioning was a tribute act to the weather outside. 'Thanks for saving the table.' She tucked her fist under her chin and smiled at Harry. 'It's a nice spot. Just a good job we have a head for heights.'

'Have you ordered?' Harry shed his coat, but didn't sit. 'I'm going to the bar. I could get us some food?'

'I've got a ginger beer coming, thanks.'

'Great. I'll be right back.'

At the bar, Harry kept his eyes on the staff, away from the CCTV camera fixed high on the wall to his left. He ordered a second ginger beer and a bowl of rice crackers before returning to where Zoe was sitting with her head turned to the view.

The sun still touched the city here and there, that low

winter sun which was slow to rise but lingered, reluctant to set. Plate glass dazzled in all directions. In half an hour, the city would be punchy with neon.

'Lovely evening,' Harry said.

She turned to face him, her eyes flooded by the city's reflection, filled with tiny shards and the slow slink of the Thames below them. 'Long day, though.'

'We got through it.'

'Yes . . .'

'Hey.' He reached for her wrist. 'We did.'

'Ollie didn't.'

Harry waited before he said, 'Ollie was lost years ago.'

'He shouldn't have been,' she gave back fiercely. 'People shouldn't just lose kids.'

This was going to be tougher than Harry had anticipated.

'At least Finn's safe . . .' He knuckled the bridge of his nose. 'You know he's saying there was someone at the hospital last night. A woman.'

Zoe reached for her drink, not speaking.

'DI Rome's about the only person who believes him. Everyone else, doctors, psychiatrists, they're all saying PTSD. One has a theory about abandonment – Finn's conjuring his mum because God knows where else she's been in his life just lately. He's in a bad way, poor kid.'

'This job . . .' She ran her thumb around the lip of her glass. 'I hate it.' She drank a mouthful and set the glass down with a snap. 'And now he'll get juvenile detention because of the knife.'

It wasn't a question, not quite, but it was close enough.

'That's what I thought,' Harry said. 'But DI Rome has other plans.'

'I'm glad.' She put her glass at arm's length. 'I hope she gets him proper help. Children's Services, what a joke—' She dialled it down. 'Sorry, I'm spoiling the vibe. It *is* a lovely evening.'

Harry helped himself to a rice cracker. 'I'll do better next time.'

'Better?'

'Ginger beer and stale crackers. Not much of a thank you.'

'You didn't need to thank me.' Friction in her neck and fingers.

She looked little, light, but she was made of muscle. If Harry were to stand, even if he did it quickly and with his height advantage— If he picked her up and threw her at the expensive view, she'd fight back. Reinforced, just like the windows; the higher they climbed, the tougher the glass.

'I wanted to thank you,' Harry said, 'for Tobias. And the rest of the Crasmere Boys. We'd never have reached them without your help.'

'Great.' Her voice dulled. 'More kids in trouble because of me.'

'Not in trouble. Out of it. You know where gangs lead, what that life means.'

She jerked the neck of her jumper, a flash of white puckering the base of her throat as if someone had tugged a loose thread under the smooth skin. 'Sorry . . .' She pressed the jumper back into place. 'It's been a long day.' Forcing a smile. 'I should just've said no.'

'To what?'

'This.' She touched the back of his hand, awkwardly. 'I'm not in the mood.'

'For drinks after work?' He lifted his glass to his lips.

Her eyes flickered into focus. 'Oh God.' She took her hand away. 'Am I making an arse of myself? I'm making an arse of myself. I thought—'

'My fault,' Harry said. 'Should've just sent you a text.'

They smiled at one another. A boat went by on the water, trailing light and noise. The air changed: a helicopter churning the sky.

Marnie couldn't see the helicopter. It was out of range of the CCTV camera above the bar, the transmission from which was playing live on the monitor in the manager's office where she was seated, several floors below the restaurant. Harry's phone picked up the chop of the helicopter's blades, just as it picked up the smaller sounds of his and Zoe's conversation. Between that and the CCTV, Marnie was able to observe everything which was unfolding at the table by the window.

'I like stale crackers,' Zoe was saying.

'In that case,' Harry handed her the bowl, 'please.'

When Marnie had told him what was going through her head, he'd listened. She'd seen him thinking, 'You're wrong, you must be wrong,' because he'd worked with Zoe for over a year and he liked her. But he'd kept his mouth shut and his mind open, and thank God he did, because Marnie could not have done this without him. She'd given him all the evidence she had, told him what was missing because paperwork had been lost, or stolen. Plenty was missing. She'd admitted how much of it was gut feeling, which Harry didn't seem to mind, since their work relied on it.

'She trusts you,' Marnie had said, thinking, '*I* trust you.' It'd shaken her how much that mattered.

A waiter blocked her view of the scene, collecting empty glasses from the table. Harry ordered another round and the man moved away, letting Marnie see them again.

Harry, and Zoe.

Behind them, the sun was sinking fast now, draining

the gold from the office blocks, making way for the night's neon. The helicopter had moved east, taking its sound with it.

'DI Rome's got other plans for Finn?' Zoe said. 'I don't suppose you can tell me. I could use the good news.'

'I shouldn't.' He rubbed a hand over his head, as if rinsing off the last of the day's cold. 'It's good news, though. For Finn. She's got a reputation as a dragon slayer.'

'She's a survivor.' Zoe picked a loose thread from her sleeve. 'Gotta love a survivor.'

'Easy to see why Bevan fixed on her,' Harry agreed, 'though I'm wondering how it's going to hit her now that—'

'Ginger beers?' The waiter had fresh glasses stacked with ice cubes so huge they'd have intimidated the *Titanic*. He took the lids from the bottles, pouring a measure for each glass.

'How what's going to hit her?' Zoe asked, when the waiter was gone.

'What?'

'You were saying you wondered how it was going to hit her *now that* . . . ?'

'Sorry, not my story to tell.' He scratched his cheek. 'You're sure you don't want some food?'

Zoe took up a fork, using it to fish the ice from her glass. 'I heard about her foster brother, from the news. What is it with tabloids and dead bodies?' Contempt in her voice, and that special empathy one professional gives to another when each is trying to sidestep sentiment. 'It's not enough they have Ollie for their headlines, they had to go digging up her parents. *Shit*—'

An ice cube skated into her lap. If it was deliberate – to edit his impression of her interest in Marnie – it was expertly done. She fished the cube up and dropped it onto her napkin. All the ice was out of her glass.

'You wouldn't like to do mine?'

Harry was joking, but she took his glass and began scooping out the ice.

Marnie watched her small fingers, round wrists, the neat way she judged the angle of the fork.

Harry was watching, too. 'Her foster brother's dead. He was found a couple of hours ago.'

The fork rang a note from the glass.

Zoe lifted her big eyes to his face.

'I shouldn't have told you.' He shook his head, warningly. 'But it'll be on the news soon enough. You're right, the tabloids love a dead body.'

'God.' She gave back his glass, pushing her hands into the pockets of her parka. 'That's . . . I don't know what that is. Good, or bad? How does she feel about it?'

'I don't know. I heard it from DS Jake. She's had to go out there, of course, to Cloverton.'

'When did it happen?' The city stained her face with its neon. 'And how?'

'They're not sure. Suicide, or murder. He was hanging in his cell.'

She shut her eyes and shuddered. For a second, there was revulsion on Harry's face, but he'd wiped the expression before she'd reopened her eyes.

In the manager's office, Marnie held her breath, waiting for Zoe to excuse herself. To stand and head for the unisex loos with their hammered zinc doors. But she stayed seated, hands in the pockets of her parka and—

We got it wrong, Marnie thought, her throat squeezing shut. This plan of hers and Harry's was smoke on the wind, with an incoming Arctic blast of disciplinary procedure.

Go and make your phone call. You need to be sure, you always need to be sure. It's why you couldn't stop. It's why Kyle died, and Carole. You need to be sure. So make a phone call—

Finn's father had a handset taken from his friend, Jacob Collins, who'd been persuaded that it was safest in Aidan's keeping. Two of the calls received by the phone had been traced to a handset belonging to Huell who was still in hospital recovering from his amateur vasectomy. Which meant Zoe knew how to contact her man inside Cloverton, to confirm Stephen's death. Except—

Zoe wasn't moving from her seat by the window.

'Makes you realise how lucky we are.' She put her hands on the table. 'Having families that haven't imploded. At least— Yours are all good, yes?'

Back to the empathy, an eyebrow raised at Harry, not quite a smile.

Marnie's skin crawled. The moment, if it'd ever been there, was passed. Gone. There was only Harry, hung out to dry by this insane plan of hers—

Buzzing, from her coat pocket.

She reached for it, pushing back the chair and standing for a second with one hand propped on the desk where the CCTV was still playing on the monitor.

So many flights up to the restaurant from the manager's office, Marnie lost count.

Disorientating, to see the widescreen version of the scene she'd been viewing on the monitor downstairs. Worth it nonetheless, to find herself reflected in the woman's wild eyes.

Harry turned in his seat to see what was making Zoe stare.

'DS Kennedy. Ms Marshall. Hello.' Marnie had the sharp scent of traffic on her clothes. And a smartphone in her hand. 'I'm afraid Mr Collins isn't taking calls this evening.' She held the phone where Zoe could see it. 'Or texts.'

Movement across the table, but Zoe was too slow.

Harry clamped her wrist before her fingers could reach the fork.

'Pocket of her parka,' he told Marnie. 'She must've texted that blind.'

'Just one of her many talents . . .'

Zoe hadn't taken her eyes from Marnie's face.

Green eyes, full of the sun that was at the foothills of the city, a tight bright line breaking to black above the river, the last of its light burning back from the curved surface of her stare.

62

At street level the restaurant was poorly lit, its lobby a concrete box, uncarpeted. The Arrest Support Team shook their heads at Marnie. 'Car won't start. Cold battery, we reckon.' They shivered in their uniforms. 'We've called it in, but the traffic's a joke. We'll have to hang around here for a bit.'

A couple in smart suits swung through the main entrance and crossed the lobby to the lifts, trailing a shockwave of cold air. Marnie set her teeth. They couldn't wait here. It wasn't secure, for one thing. Her own car was back at the station. She'd taken the tube after looking at the traffic news. The ASTs were right, it was a joke. 'Should we cuff her?' one of them asked.

Zoe stood at Harry's side, her eyes as vacant as a child's. The plate glass walls made a fish tank of the lobby, putting them on show for passing crowds and cars. A headline waiting to happen: Met Police arrest promising young campaigner for children's rights. The adverse publicity concerned Marnie less than the prospect of a prejudiced jury, or a mistrial.

'How long's this wait likely to last?'

'Could be ten minutes, or fifty.'

London's streets were locked with cars and lorries, the winter grinding everything to a halt. At least Noah had made it to the hospital, staying with Finn until this was over. Marnie checked her watch, and her phone. Fifty minutes for a squad car then a slow crawl to the station. It felt as if the city was conspiring with the weather, against her.

'One of you wait down here for the car,' she told the ASTs, 'the other come with us.'

She nodded at Harry. 'Let's find a room.'

Harry put a hand around Zoe's upper arm, steering her towards the lift. Its glass doors gave back their faces. Of the four of them, only Zoe looked calm. She'd surrendered her phone, emptied her pockets, emptied her eyes too. Next to Harry, she was very small. For the first time she looked like the child in Carole's scrapbook.

On the ninth floor, the restaurant manager was persuaded to give up his office again. He eyed Zoe with sympathy, because of her size and her face. It would be the same in a courtroom. Even DCS Ferguson, who was surely the poster girl for pugnacity, had questioned Marnie's case against Zoe, only allowing her to pursue it because Ollie had died.

'I messed up,' she'd shrugged. 'Now it's your turn.'

The office at least was secure. Wide, its windows looking out towards the water. Two doors, the second one alarmed – emergency access only, to the roof.

Harry walked Zoe towards a chair, instructing her to sit. If she saw the CCTV monitor and registered its role in her arrest, she didn't acknowledge it. Harry stayed by the side of her chair.

'I'll call the station,' Marnie told him. 'And Noah.'

She wanted Finn to know that he wouldn't be getting any more midnight visits from Zoe.

In the corridor, the AST officer was placating the manager who needed to know that no sirens would be wailing outside his establishment, putting his guests off their expensive meals.

Marnie rang Noah, giving him her news. 'How's Finn?'

'We're playing cards, for gum. He's clearing me out.'

'Tell him I'll visit later . . .'

Laughter from the restaurant above them, the chink of glasses, oblivious. Marnie had a flash of Ollie's body on the ground, the red ruin of his chest. She had to shut her eyes for a second.

A slam of sound from inside the office made her turn.

The door was shut, but—

Her scalp was too tight, clenched with foreboding.

Two steps took her back to the door.

Inside the office—

Zoe was gone, her chair upturned on the floor. So much for the alarmed exit; she'd pushed the bar on the door and it had let her through without making a sound.

Harry was standing with one arm outstretched, palm pressed to the wall. 'Sorry,' the word slipped out of him thinly.

Sorry—?

He'd let her get away. He wasn't even in pursuit. He was—

Bleeding.

She smelt it before she saw it, a hot, ripe tang. Then Harry's pupils expanding, pushing the blue from his eyes. One hand over the wound, blood pressing blackly through the clench of his fingers.

Zoe had stabbed him, in the stomach.

'We need an ambulance!' Marnie shouted for the AST, reaching for Harry's elbow. 'Now!'

He gripped her wrist hard. 'I'm okay. Just—'

The slap of feet on the stairs, going up, not down.

Zoe, getting away.

Harry's legs folded and he sat. They'd searched her, but she'd been hiding a knife. The wound was deep, dangerous, blood pumping through his fingers. 'Go,' he said.

Marnie crouched, keeping her hand on his arm, shouting again for the AST. A shudder gripped the whole of Harry's body. 'Go,' he repeated. 'Don't let her—'

The office door banged open.

'Stay with him,' Marnie snapped at the officer, 'call it in. Get an ambulance. And get me back-up.' She hesitated, eyes snagging on his blood-soaked shirt.

Harry shook his head. 'Marnie . . .'

It was the first time he'd used her name.

'Don't die,' she told him.

An order. A plea.

She straightened, stepping back as the AST took over.

Three paces to cross the room, shoving with her fist at the fire door.

Going after Zoe, up the stairs.

63

Up the stairs, not stopping, breath burning in her lungs. Keep going. How many flights to the roof? Ten, twelve? Zoe was moving so fast it was hard to assess.

Keep going.

Another voice, in the back of her head: 'Let her go. Let it go.'

All that rage, violence, moving away from her, leaving her behind. If she caught up with it, what would she do? Put it back inside, where she'd been keeping it all these years. A swarm of red—

Too much blood beating in her body, fingers tacky where they'd touched Harry.

He might die. He might be dying right now. Zoe might've killed him.

Keep going. Keep—

The door to the roof opened with a slam when she shoved it.

Wind hit her so fiercely she almost fell.

Buffeting, full of ice, spiteful.

Nineteen floors up, over the river. Two floors above the restaurant. Steam from its kitchens punched out through roof vents, the red smell of meat frying in onions before the wind snatched it away. Layers of noise – from the water and roads, boats and cars, and the strange, tight sound of ice taking the city back into its fist for the night.

Where is she—?

There, by the smoke shaft's extractor fan. Biker boots planted on the shallow gravel. Chestnut curls snaking round her small face. She could have run down the stairs, taken her chances with the AST officer in the lobby, gone to ground. Instead she'd climbed up here, waiting to be followed.

Marnie called out, 'Come back inside the building,' but the wind took her words away.

Zoe lifted a hand and freed a strand of hair from her mouth, tucking it behind her ear, staying in the shelter of the smoke shaft. Looking small and quiet, but she wasn't—

She'd walked her violence into the world, letting it off the leash, again and again. Whatever abuse, whatever suffering had shaped her early years, the pain of it had turned her inside out; she was all spikes and blood-red rage. Marnie had no doubt she'd wielded the weapon that killed Kyle Stratton, before planting it in Ollie's flat, and swinging a second bat at Noah's head. But Zoe didn't need a weapon to be dangerous. With her tight fists and hard head, she shone with violence.

The wind dropped a fraction and Marnie called out, 'Talk to me.' Her phone buzzed in her pocket but she ignored it, keeping her eyes on Zoe. Harry might be dying or dead, but right now she had to give this woman all of her attention. 'Tell me what this was about.'

Attention, and gratitude. That's what she wanted. It was why she'd come up here, waiting for Marnie to join her. 'Tell me. I need to know.'

'You already know,' Zoe called back. 'But come here. We'll talk, if it's what you want.'

'Inside. It's too cold out here.'

And too high up. Too many ways for it to end badly.

Zoe moved backwards and sat, cross-legged on the gravel, propped against the metal ducting around the smoke shaft. 'I remember the cage,' she called out.

The wind took the rest of her speech, tattering it into stray words.

Attention, and gratitude. Under Marnie's feet, the building rocked to the restaurant's rhythm. Happy Londoners, enjoying their downtime. She should wait for back-up. She should go inside the building and close the door between her and Zoe. Wait for it to be over. It wouldn't take long, she knew that.

Instead, she walked across to where the woman was sitting, stopping four feet away. Out of reach, just.

'Go on. You remember the cage.'

'The smell of it, the tray sticking to my skin. Powdered milk and puddles, the ones I jumped in when she took me out. Feet first, making a mess of us. Sometimes she didn't mind. Sometimes she did.' She recited the words as if she was reading from a statement she'd prepared. 'Always, though, when we were home, I went back into the cage. I never minded, it was my safe place. Like a playpen, just a lot smaller than the ones they sell in most shops to most mothers. She wasn't most mothers. She was mine. She'd feed me through the bars like a bird, "You're my little bird," crumbs of cake. She baked a cake every week, and fed it to me like that.' Pinching her thumb and finger together. 'Carrot cake was my favourite. It made a mess coming through the bars, but I'd lick them clean. She liked the cage to be clean.'

Carole's child, driven to this by her mother's cruelty. And *empty*—

So empty inside, just like Stephen. The pair of them seeing something in Marnie which filled that void. She wished it didn't, but it was what'd brought them here. To this.

'You never told anyone.'

'It was none of their business.' Zoe's face blanked. 'She was my mother.'

'And now she's dead. Who killed her?' The wind moved around them, between them, so cold Marnie was almost afraid to breathe. 'Who killed Carole?'

'I knew Ollie.' Zoe pushed her curls from her face. 'When he was with us. Not for long, she didn't keep him for long. But I knew him.'

'You were fourteen. Old enough to have gone to the police and said what was happening—'

'Ollie was okay. He didn't mind being in the cage. At that age you get used to things. Kids are sponges, that's what she said. You can teach a child to do anything. Men, too. Look at Huell.'

It was no use as a confession, no use as an interview. But they were running out of time, Marnie knew that. Zoe wasn't going to sit here much longer, not like this. There was another reason she'd come up here, to the roof. 'What did you teach Huell?'

'To sit up and beg, make me happy. It's what men want. Instructions.' Her eyes moved around the roof, as if the question bored her. She'd shed all semblance of her earlier pretence, as if it was a dirty dress, stepping sideways into this new role. Unapologetic, unrepentant.

Emptying herself out, because it was over. She knew it was over.

'When did you see Carole again? You weren't living

with her in London, or in Harrow. The police and Children's Services had no record of her having a daughter.'

'I was with my dad.' Zoe shrugged. 'I visited her when I felt like it. I was fourteen, no one stopped me. *She* didn't.'

'What you did to Finn . . . After everything you went through, after the cage. It can't have been easy to target a child. To hurt Finn the way you were hurt—'

'I knew it would work,' she said simply. 'And he wasn't in a cage. He had a house. He was on the streets when we found him. He had a whole house.'

'He was a prisoner. You scared him, and hurt him. You risked his life. For what?'

'We should talk about Stephen. That's why you're really here, isn't it?' Zoe leaned towards her. 'Forgiveness, reconciliation, all that stuff they preach at you. It's a lie. Revenge is a dirty word, but it's *recovery*. You won't get better without it. You won't ever be free from the pain and the fear. Up here.' She pressed her fingers to the side of her head. 'You won't ever stop being a victim until you've found a proper place for pain like that.'

'Is that what you told Ollie? When you talked him into helping you kill Kyle?'

Zoe kept her fingers pressed to her head.

'You told him that he could stop being a victim by making someone else into one . . . But Ollie is dead, and Mazi loved Kyle. Did you know that? Of course you didn't. Because you're not interested in anyone's feelings but your own. Anyone's pain but your own.'

'I'm interested in yours,' Zoe said. 'Because you lie about it so much. All the time, to everyone, including yourself.'

'It's called projection, this particular symptom. Not that I'm trying to narrow it down. But go on. You're interested

390

in my pain. That's why you wanted Aidan Duffy to hurt Stephen Keele.'

Attention, and gratitude.

'You hate him,' Zoe said. 'Stephen. You must hate him, want him dead. All the rest of it's just dancing. Pretending for the cameras and psychologists and whoever else is getting in the way of you doing what you really want to do.' She was using the sing-song voice she'd used to comfort Tobias during the boy's interview. 'I was showing you how much better it feels.'

'Revenge.'

'*Yes.*'

'But it wouldn't be revenge, would it, if you'd been the cause of it. It would have nothing to do with me. Just as this,' measuring the distance between their bodies with a movement of her hand, 'is nothing to do with me. It's about you.'

'Us,' Zoe corrected. Her lips thinned with anger. 'None of them understood what I'd done. Mazi, Valerie Rawling . . . What I'd done for them. *You*— You understand.'

'I understand you want an ally,' Marnie said. 'Someone to validate your rage, who appreciates all this damage you've done. You wanted someone else who couldn't move on, who had to wallow in vengeance in order to get clean. But you don't look very clean, Zoe. You don't look happy or at peace, or pain-free. The opposite, in fact. So what's it all been for, really? Not for me. Not for anyone except you.'

Zoe heard her out, sitting with her shoulders rounded, her small face blank. Then she said, 'Do you have bad dreams? About Stephen, about being trapped with Stephen. I know you do. We all do. Everyone who's living like us, with the past on our backs. I've seen it again and again. In gangs, in their mums and dads. Even little kids

. . . Well, I don't have dreams, not any more. Because I put it down. All that pain, that weight? That *past*. I put it down.'

She didn't look like a victim. That much was true.

From below them came the bray of a boat party, amplified by the water.

'The knife attack,' Marnie said. 'Four years ago. Tell me about that.'

'That was nothing.' She laughed. 'Kids. I didn't care about that. I cared about Carole, and Ollie. And *you*. I saw you on the Garrett Estate last year, when you found that girl's body. I knew Abi Gull and her friends, all the gangs there. I saw you with Abi. That's when I knew.'

'When you knew what?'

'How hard you're trying to hold it together. How it's breaking you into pieces.'

Marnie let that go. 'And Huell? What did you see in him?'

'He's meant to help people with their pain. That's his job. He was helping me with mine.'

'Who killed Carole?' Marnie asked again.

'Who do you think?'

'I think it was you. You went to her flat and warned her that Ollie was coming back to finish what Huell had started. You said you'd take her somewhere safe and then you panicked her into climbing into the boot of her own car, telling her to keep quiet, saying she'd be safe. You hit her, because you wanted her blood on the bat and because you didn't want her calling for help. You locked her in the boot of her car. Then you took her handbag and car keys back to her flat and you left them, just like you left the evidence in Ollie's flat for us to find.'

'For *you* to find,' Zoe corrected. 'It was all for you.'

The wail of a siren somewhere, but not close.

Not coming their way.

'And DS Jake. When you beat him with the baseball bat. Who was that for?'

'That was for me.' Smiling. 'And Carole. I didn't want him in her flat. It was too soon.'

There was no reaching her, no prospect for remorse or redemption. She was armour-plated, unrepentant.

'All this . . . frenzy.' Marnie spread her hands, cold curling around her fingers. 'Three people dead, another three scarred for life. Because you couldn't deal with your own anger.'

'That's *how* I dealt with it. It's how you should deal with yours.'

'So I can be facing a long prison sentence, like you?'

'So you can be free.'

Sirens wailed, closer now.

Zoe slid upright, using the stack for support.

Marnie stayed at a safe distance, but she said, 'Don't. Don't do this.'

She'd known what Zoe meant to do as soon as she'd stepped onto the roof to be thumped by the wind. This wasn't a convenient confession, or an interview. She was here as Zoe's witness.

'Don't do this. Ollie is dead. You need to live with that, with what you did.'

'The way you're living? No thanks.'

Zoe turned her face away then looked back, her eyes lit by the sudden sweep of a police helicopter's beam. 'But I'll let *you* do it. Take your revenge. For Ollie, for whatever you want.'

She started walking backwards, towards the shallow barrier at the lip of the roof.

Marnie moved with her, keeping the same distance between them as tautly as if they were tied.

'What do you think? Are we high enough for the water to break my back?' Zoe stopped, right on the edge. 'Push me. I'll let you do that. It's what you need.'

'What I *need* is for you to stop pretending that this isn't real. That pain isn't real. That fear isn't real. And anger, and regret. Remorse—'

'The judge will like me.' Zoe cut her off. 'And the jury. They'll see the scars, and the good work I did with kids like Finn. You want justice for him, don't you? I won't get a serious sentence. I'll be out in eight years, and I'll have learnt new tricks in prison. Just like Stephen. What are you going to do when he's out? Are you going to tell him to stop pretending? Lecture him about remorse?'

The helicopter's blades whipped her hair about her face.

She had to shout to be heard: 'I'm giving it to you. Take it. Revenge.'

Marnie reached her hand to make it stop.

Not revenge.

Rescue.

She reached her hand to rescue Zoe.

'No.' Cold green eyes fixed on her for a second. 'Not that. You don't get to save me.'

A step back, and the city swallowed her whole.

64

For a ten-year-old with a recent history of trauma, Finn Duffy played a mean game of cards.

'Twenty-one.' He fanned his hand face-up on the bed: two kings and an ace.

'You're scary, you know that?' Noah slid another strip of gum across the table. 'Just as well we're not playing for cash. You'd be bankrupting me.'

And there it was at last – a grin. A normal ten-year-old grin, reconfiguring the cautious lines of his face. He was wearing new sweatpants and an oversized hoodie that Marnie had bought in an all-night supermarket, cutting off the tags before giving the clothes to Noah to bring here. Finn's face had lit up when he'd seen the hoodie, as if Noah was handing him body armour.

'By the way, a couple of your mates from school say Hi.'

'Yeah?' Finn wrinkled his nose. 'Say Hi back, I guess.'

'You were smart,' Noah told him, 'to stay wide of the Crasmere Boys.'

'Not really.' Finn studied his fresh hand of cards. 'If I'd been running with them I'd have been harder to snatch. Then people wouldn't be dead.'

He knew about Kyle and Carole, but it was Ollie's death that haunted him. Noah could see its ghost in the boy's big eyes. 'DI Rome's been to see your dad.'

Finn kept his stare down, but his shoulders were rigid. 'Is he okay?'

'He misses you. Sends his love.'

'Does he know what happened?'

'He knows you were in that house, and that you're out of it now. He knows how brave you've been.'

Finn flinched on the word *brave*, and didn't speak.

Noah tried to remember the tactics he'd used to talk to Sol when he was Finn's age. But whatever they were, he doubted the same words would work with Finn. And the thought of Sol, what he'd done to Sol, was still too raw.

'Couple of things you need to know,' he told Finn. 'We've arrested Zoe Marshall. She's not coming back here.'

Finn didn't need to know that Zoe was dead. There was enough death in his head already. Noah thanked God that Harry Kennedy was going to be okay. Post-surgery, but the prognosis was good.

Finn took another card from the pile, adding it to the ones in his hand. 'Okay.'

'And no one's going to be charging you with what happened to Huell.'

'Why not?' Taking a card. 'I stabbed him, didn't I?'

'There shouldn't have been all those guns . . . Our boss's in trouble over that.'

Finn looked up. 'DI Rome's in trouble?'

'No. *Our* boss. Hers and mine. DCS Ferguson.'

'From the telly.' Finn was studying Noah. 'That one.'

'That one,' he agreed.

Except now Ferguson was dodging the cameras, and

the awkward questions about why she'd put an Armed Response Unit in the mix. Overkill wasn't a joke so much as an epitaph. Marnie had made peace with the woman, and told Noah to do the same. They were moving on.

Finn threw the cards down and shifted backwards on the bed, crossing his legs under him, hiding his hands up the new hoodie's sleeves. 'Is she coming? DI Rome?'

'She's coming,' Noah said.

Finn was eating supper by the time Marnie got to the hospital. She'd brought a bag of books. 'From Colin. He says he thinks you'll like them.'

Finn wiped his mouth on his sleeve. 'Thanks.'

Noah got to his feet, stretching his legs. Marnie watched him, with concern. It was there in his face, well hidden from Finn but she saw it: Sol's arrest. He'd called to tell her what he'd done, sounding dazed and unhappy: 'It was me. I made the arrest.'

'I'm here,' Marnie told him now. 'If you need me.'

Noah nodded. He rubbed at the shadow on his cheek then crouched to collect a playing card from the floor, handing it to Finn. 'Dan's home. I'll be okay.'

She nodded. 'Get some proper rest.'

'What about the paperwork?' From Zoe, he meant. He searched Marnie's face.

'I've got it.' She was tired but the case was gone from her, that worry she'd been wearing for the last week. She smiled. 'At least there's good news about Harry.'

'Yes.' Noah reached for his coat. 'See you, Finn. Don't chew your winnings all at once.'

Finn nodded, but his eyes were on Marnie. He ate the rest of his food quickly, pushing the table away from the bed when he was done.

Marnie sat in the chair vacated by Noah. 'How are you?'

'Okay. Chart's there.' He jerked his head at it, fingers fidgeting with the playing card that Noah had rescued from the floor. 'You saw my dad.'

'I did. He sent his love.'

A photo, not a playing card. Creased across one corner, dulled by time and fingers. Two faces, both smiling. White teeth and black curls, a beach in the background. Aidan and Finn.

'What did he do?' Finn's face was pinched. 'No one'll tell me what he did. Ollie said they made him hurt people. That's what I was for – so he'd hurt people.'

'He didn't do what they wanted,' Marnie said.

'That's—' He stared at her with those grey eyes so like his father's. 'You're lying. My dad loves me. He'd do whatever they said. He *loves* me.'

'Yes, he loves you. That's why he didn't do anything stupid. Because then he'd be in prison a lot longer when what he wants is to get home to you.'

'Is that what he wants?' Finn's eyes jittered. 'Is it?'

'Yes. He told me, and I believe him.'

'And he didn't hurt anyone?' The photo was curled between his hands.

Holding hard to his fear, reluctant to let it go.

'They wanted him to.' Marnie ached with fellow feeling. Fear had been her insulation for years. 'But no. He didn't.'

'He's done it before.' Finn let go of the photo to grip his bare toes. 'Hurt people.'

'I know, but that's finished. He wants to get home to you. That's what matters now.'

She'd lost count of the apologies Aidan had made when he was thanking her for the good news that his son wouldn't be charged with assault. It had reminded her that she owed apologies of her own, to Alan and Louise Kettridge. They were here, in this hospital. When it was visiting hours, she'd walk to the wards and see them. And Harry too. She wanted to see Harry.

Finn said, 'I was *stupid*. I got sick because I was scared. I let them grab me and then I couldn't get out and Ollie came and I had the knife and Brady was *right there—*'

'You did what you had to do. They took away all the other options. And it's okay to be scared. Being scared's a big part of being brave.'

Finn stared at her, strawberry jelly at the corner of his mouth. *'You're* not.'

'Scared? Yes, I am. Every day. But that's okay. Scared's good. It keeps you alive, and it stops you from making too many mistakes. Besides,' she picked the paper towel from his tray and wiped the jelly from his mouth, 'it's okay to be scared when you're as brave as you are.'

The car park was patchy with ice but its grip was loosening, the cold less tight around her shoulders. She found a bench close to the entrance and sat with the hospital's noise muted at her back. She rang Ed first, to say she'd be home late, and to tell him that Finn was safe. And Harry, but she didn't tell Ed that. Ed didn't know Harry, didn't know about him. The cold crept closer and she buried her hands in the pockets of her coat, finding the hard edge of the paper wallet pushed there.

Across a frosted rank of cars, London thumped, beating time. Waiting for her.

She put her hand over the wallet of photographs, keeping it closed.

In a minute, she'd open it and look through the pictures taken by her father on the old camera which he'd loved too much to replace with a digital model.

Twenty-four prints, developed in an hour for a premium price. She'd walked to fill the time, looking in shop windows, seeing the slow shove of traffic as the city crawled home.

Noah was on his way home, but not happily. Blaming himself for Sol's arrest and whatever had forced him to make it. Marnie knew he wouldn't have taken that decision lightly. She wanted to tell him to let it go, the blame and the hurt. But it was too soon.

Harry was in a hospital bed, sleeping or not. She'd visit him, tomorrow. And Finn too, wanting to be sure that he was safe. She would put her hand on those heavy hospital doors, one after another, and walk down those long corridors to stand by their beds, because it was all that she could do.

The car park was freezing, one windscreen at a time.

Her breath was wet, her eyes watering with the cold.

In a minute, she would open the envelope and find out whether Stephen was telling the truth or just a new lie. Whatever she found, she'd take it home with her.

His truth, or his lie.

She would take it home and let it go, and sleep.

Author's Note

Quieter than Killing is a work of fiction, but I found the following to be particularly relevant and/or inspirational when I was writing and later editing the book:

The Forgiveness Project by Marina Cantacuzino, published by JKP, 2015
HM Prison Service – A Survival Guide by Aidan Cattermole, published by Ditto Press
Happy Like Murderers by Gordon Burn, published by Faber & Faber, 1998

Acknowledgements

This book would not be in your hands but for the support and enthusiasm, the kindness and cleverness, and the gin and the tonic of the following people—

Jane Gregory, Vicki Mellor, Mick Herron, Alison Graham, Alyson Shipley, Isabelle Gray, Susan Pola, Serena Mackesy, Jane Casey and the Killer Women, Julia Crouch, Anne Cater, Liz Barnsley, Tracy Fenton and The Book Clubbers, Pita and Becca, Lydia and Anna.

All of my family, but most especially my mother.

Thank you to Alex and Simon-Peter for the chems. And to Jacob Collins who won the *Get in Character* auction in support of the CLIC Sargent charity for children with cancer. I hope you approve of your role in the story.